I0763504

BELOVED

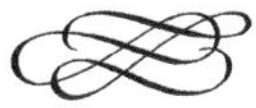

KENDRA THOMAS

❀ Created with Vellum

To Vick

And all the nights spent in our mapping room

Isles of Arradale
Trojan Waters
The Main
Land
Monsoon Current
N
W
E
S
Tetheria
South Territory

ONE

I gazed out at the trees; a sea of viridescent green. The oaks and pines hugged the mountainside, and I imagined that if they could speak, they would sigh in the warmth of the sun's apricot glow. It touched everything here.

I closed my eyes for a moment and allowed myself just to breathe.

This rock had become my oasis. Every day I would fly up the summit atop Diablo and land on this grey slab that jutted out from the sloped mountain face surrounded with trees. No one could see me up here. It was a good hiding place.

I sat astride Diablo, limply holding a chunk of his thick black mane in my hands. I could feel his torso expand with every breath he took. Strong and Steady. It seemed as though he was meditating with me. I think he enjoyed being up this high as much as I did.

I opened my eyes again, and the sun was disappearing. With

indifference, I observed how quickly time passed. *I wish I could make the world stand still,* I thought to myself, *just for a moment.*

I particularly despised when night came. Sleep evaded me these days. The darkness reminded me of how lost I felt. Only up on these mountains, so far away from everything, did I begin to feel slightly normal again; but it never lasted long. The night always came, and the reminder of everything that happened resurfaced in my dreams and the shadowed corners of my room. Those shadows seemed to take shape, as monsters that mocked me, and whispered that I might never be the same again.

Three months ago, I returned to Knadiel. I had come home after spending several months in the Sethen Courts as a prisoner and accompanying Shar on a rescue mission to save Embrosine in Obscurum. We'd successfully tricked King Elysian, and his son Obsidian into giving Embrosine to us in exchange for the tokens that had merely been an illusion.

I had discovered the truth of my family ties. King Elysian was my mother's brother and Obsidian, my cousin. We returned with Wesoltince's hammer and mere clues on where to find the others. I also had two very complicated relationships I was trying to figure out, with two very different people, and a symbol on my arm representing the Envorydian I had become.

To say things were complicated would be a massive understatement.

But that wasn't the end of it. All of those complications that had occurred while in Obscurum were minuscule problems in comparison to what happened when I walked through the gates that day upon returning to Knadiel. The new kingdom of Aveladon and Ethydon.

I still remember it as clearly as if it had happened yesterday.

The gates had finally opened after what felt like an eternity of waiting to enter, and a friendly voice washed over our caravan group.

"Well, aren't we glad to see you? Welcome to Knadiel."

I was overtaken with emotion, knowing the voice all too well. I pushed through the small crowd to the very front and found my guardian standing on the other side of the twisted silver gate. His blond curls were slicked back from his face, his green eyes just as bright as I recalled. He stood tall and regal. He looked every bit the leader that he was as Sentry Captain of Aveladon. I couldn't hold back the sob that ripped through my body. I launched myself into his arms and the strength of them wrapping around me made me feel like a child again.

"Oli," I cried, burying my head into his neck and inhaling the familiar smell of his red cloak. Ferns and the faint lingering trace of bergamot. He hugged me tightly, but only for a brief second before I was pulled away from him.

Roughly two guards grasped my upper arms and ripped me from his embrace. My eyes widened as I was suddenly held captive by two sentries. A mix of brown and red-cloaked soldiers, who seemed to think me a sudden threat, surrounded Oli, putting a barricade between the two of us.

"Let go of me!" I demanded.

"Rayon, Leo, release her. That is Princess Sabeara you are detaining. I promise there is no danger." The two guards let go of me with some hesitation, and I stumbled away, shooting them a glare. Oli gave the guards a nod, and they instantly retreated, returning to their stations to stand behind Oli protectively.

Oli reached out to me again, his hands now on either side of my face. His calloused palms were warm and familiar.

"Oh, Little Bear, how I've missed you." He seemed to be taking me in; his eyes flickered to the glow in my chest and then back up to my eyes that I knew were different from the eyes he'd once known.

Tears were leaking onto my cheeks and were now flowing freely.

"I'm so sorry," I instantly gushed, my voice hoarse. I wasn't able to fully express all my emotions for what had happened since we'd last seen each other.

"Shhh. . . no apologizing. You're here now." His words held no demand for recompense, not a sliver of animosity. I could tell he truly was just happy to have me home. Then he pulled me to his side, his hand intertwining with mine. He blinked back the tears in his eyes and addressed the caravan that was watching us with curiosity.

I could see Rouix, her mouth slightly agape like she hadn't been expecting any of that. Dusane and Rosen were beside her, both their expressions also slightly stunned.

Shar, who was standing with Mid and Embrosine, suddenly stepped forward and gave a curt nod towards Oli.

"Captain Olivine, it is good to see you."

Oli's gaze shifted from Shar to Mid beside him and then finally to Embrosine. I heard his sharp intake of breath at the sight of her.

"You found her. . . " he trailed off, and for several moments he just stared at Embrosine with wide green eyes.

"We rescued her from Obscurum," Shar explained.

"We must have a lot to discuss then," Oli whispered, obviously still shocked to see Embrosine standing there. Finally, after several long moments of awed silence, he shook his head and cleared his throat. "It's great to see you all. Now why don't you all come inside and we can get you settled."

It felt surreal walking side by side with Oli as we entered into this new place called Knadiel. The new kingdom was unlike anything I could've pictured in my head.

We passed through the gates into a meadow-like landscape that was too small to be considered a city. Settlements dotted the hillside and were surrounded by mountains that acted as walls, protecting everything. The grass was a plush carpet as we walked, and a couple of lone trees dotted the scenery. The houses resembled those I'd seen in Ethydon—dainty wood dwellings and straw roofs. I could see animals grazing in fenced pens and a dozen or so gardens and farms.

I wasn't the only one admiring the new kingdom in wonder. The entire caravan stared with wide eyes at the humble establishment they'd created. And as we made our way past the homes, I could see several people outside working, turn and bow as we passed. I vaguely recalled who I was at that moment, nearly forgetting my true identity as princess of Aveladon. My brow furrowed, wondering how they would have recognized me, then I remembered Mid was a couple of paces behind me, also a prince that would be deemed high enough to constitute a bow from other civilians.

I felt Oli squeeze my hand as if he could sense that I was trying to take everything in. I looked up at him and smiled, hoping to convey to him that I was not overwhelmed but rather pleased with what he'd created. It was not a large population, and it broke my heart to think about how many people we'd lost in the war. But those who had survived hadn't given up, and that was all that mattered.

We passed through the center of the little town, where a market and a couple of shops had been established, and then we came upon another gate.

Oli nodded to the guards, and they let us pass through. It

wasn't a castle by any means, not really. But it was a large stone mansion with a couple of lone twisting spires as if trying to resemble one. We walked up the rock path they'd created, and on the front steps of the mansion, I noticed King Knadian and Queen Ruby waiting for us.

When Ruby caught sight of her daughter, her eyes widened, and her hand flew up over her mouth.

"Embrosine!" she cried. Ruby lifted the skirts of her gown and sprinted down the front path.

Embrosine pushed through the group and met the embrace of her mother. Their arms wrapped around each other fiercely, and more crying ensued.

I watched the familial display, a lump forming in my throat. I couldn't wait to do the same when I saw my family again.

King Knadian reached his wife and daughter and pulled them both to him. Mid went to join them too, and I watched him wipe tears from his eyes as he kissed his mother's cheek.

Oli gestured for us to follow him then, wanting to allow the family some privacy. With Oli's hand still in mine, we walked into the castle foyer, and my eyes searched for a familiar face. To my disappointment, only a young servant girl occupied the room. The foyer was cozy, with a stone fireplace and red cushioned sofas. A large fur rug covered the floor while lanterns lit the shadowy vaulted ceilings. The young servant girl was dusting the shelves when Oli called for her to come over to us.

"Mia, would you mind taking these soldiers to some empty guest quarters?" Oli asked, and the girl quickly nodded. Then, I watched as Dusane, Rouix, and Rosen were led in another direction.

That left Oli and I alone with his group of guards, and he gave them an exasperated sigh.

"You can return to your stations, men."

They all seemed to hesitate for a moment before finally dispersing.

Oli smiled and shook his head. "Sorry about that." He led me down another hall and together we started up a flight of stairs.

"Oli, Jasper and—" I started to say, but he spoke before I could finish the words.

"She's upstairs. I thought you two would like a more private place to talk," Oli said gently. I felt my chest tighten and my hands begin to sweat. I took in a shaky breath just as we reached the second floor. The last time Jasper and I had seen each other; she'd been angry with me. Things between us were never resolved, and I didn't know how our reunion would play out.

We made it to the end of the hall, and Oli opened the door.

I stepped into the pleasantly quaint room, decorated in shades of amber and deep-hued greens. A bed with a flowing comforter was pressed against the wall, and I immediately noticed who was sitting at the edge of it.

"Jasper," I whispered.

Her head turned, and her dark plum-colored eyes met mine, tears already coursing down her cheeks. My heart thrummed painfully in my chest, and I opened my mouth to speak, but a small whimper was all that came out. I didn't have to say anything more because she leaped off the bed and threw her arms around me. I clung to her, and a part of myself that had been lost finally resurfaced, taking a breath. I hadn't realized I had been drowning. For so long I had buried my memories of home, pushed them down in the dark corners of my soul so I could become someone else. I had wanted to remain focused, I had ignored the feelings of wanting to return because of what I felt I needed to do. Now that they were resurfacing, it was a hurricane of emotion.

"Sabeara, are you alright?" was the first question off her trembling lips.

I nodded into the crook of her neck where I'd already soaked the shoulder of her dress with tears.

"Yes, I'm fine, just fine," I said.. "I'm so sorry, Jasper, for everything." I lamented, but she rushed to shush me.

"Shhh, Bear, I am not angry. You're here now, and that's all that matters." I don't know how long we stayed in that position, hugging one another, but eventually we pulled apart and went to sit on the bed. I wiped the tears from my cheeks and she did the same.

"I've missed you so much," I said, still taking in the sight of her.

"I've missed you too," she said, reaching out to stroke a strand of my short black hair. "You're Stone-Hearted now," she said, smiling with watery eyes.

"Yes, I am," I said, sniffling.

"So much has changed since you left, hasn't it?" she whispered, and that's when I remembered.

Elysian.

"Jasper, King Elysian, did you know he was our uncle?" I suddenly asked, needing to know.

Jasper's eyes widened, and so did Oli's. "You remember?" Oli whispered, coming to sit beside us now. The comforter dipped with his added weight.

"It came back to me while I was in Obscurum. Why don't I remember him killing mother?"

Oli hesitated for a moment before explaining. "When that night happened, you sort of went into shock. And the next day, you couldn't remember what happened. The healers said they thought you might have had a traumatic episode," Oli said.

"He told us not to force you to remember. That you would face what happened when you were ready," Jasper said.

"So it was always there? I just wasn't ready to face it. . ." I considered what happened to me, losing my mother at such a young age. It was the hardest thing I went through as a child. It took me years to feel okay after her death. "Why did he do it?" I asked, thinking back to the look of pure vindictiveness in Elysian's eyes that I'd witnessed in the throne room only days before.

Oli sighed. "I don't know everything, but I do know they had a falling out after she married your father. King Elysian was upset that she left their lower caste family for a royal. I think part of his reasons for creating another kingdom was from jealousy, and those feelings spread into hate that eventually consumed him."

"Now he wants power, and he wants it so he can continue to destroy Aveladon," Jasper whispered sullenly.

A quietness spread throughout the room as we all seemed to contemplate this. I'd once been told that Elysian wanted to rule everything. That power was his motive. But now I knew there must've been more to the story, a story that only one person in the castle would probably be able to tell.

"Where's Father? I need to see him." I stood up from the bed and started for the door, desperate to see the other member of my family I had yet to greet.

"Wait, Sabeara. . ." Oli reached out a hand to me; then slowly, it fell back to his side. I stopped with my hand on the doorknob and couldn't help but notice the pained look that suddenly entered his eyes. His brow furrowed, and he ran a hand through his hair. Jasper looked down at the comforter, and I watched her hands fist the bedsheet.

"What's wrong? Why can't I see Father?" I asked, an edge of fear beginning to paint my tone.

"I thought Shar told you. . ." Oli whispered. His jaw clenched, and then he stood from the bed and came over to me. The closer he got, the more I could see the deep sorrow in his eyes. Fear prickled my nerves.

"Oli, tell me what's going on," I demanded. The look on Jasper's face was one I had seen before. I'd seen it when we'd been standing beside our mother's grave listening to the speeches that were given about her. I'd seen it during the weeks following my mother's passing when I saw Jasper curled up in her bed, her gaze fixed on the window, the blankness in them enough to sink a soul. I'd seen that look—the deep sorrow that had aged her and nearly consumed both her and me in those months following my mother's death.

"Shar didn't tell you. . ." It sounded like a question but not really. Oli reached out to lay a hand on my shoulder, steadying me for the impact of his words, but I knew what he was going to say before he even said it. "Sabeara, your father. He fought during the war in Ethydon, and he didn't make it. He's gone Sabeara . . . he's gone."

TWO

I was enjoying the last bits of twilight as I descended towards the stables on Diablo. Remembering the day I returned always made my chest ache. In the beginning, learning of my father's death had been excruciating. It was the kind of pain that could make a person feel frozen, unable to move because the agony clutches so tightly that it threatens never to let go.

But over the last couple of months, the pain had dulled. I'd become slightly numbed. And instead of crying and lashing out in anger, I was now content to curl up and wallow. I wanted to hide away under my bedsheets in the darkness. I wanted to disappear. I oftentimes waited to simply slip away, but I never did.

Diablo landed on the grass by the stables, and I dismounted to guide him to his stall. The smell of fresh hay and manure filled the air as I reached for a brush and began soothing his sweat-slicked fur. The rhythmic strokes and the sound of the bristles eased me as I continued to contemplate that day.

After learning that my father had died during the Ethydon war and that I had been lied to, my first instinct had been anger. I had wanted so badly to confront Shar, to fight him for not telling me. But the anger I felt about Shar's dishonesty had been swallowed up in the sorrow of my father's death and the betrayal of Oli and Jasper that soon had followed.

I clutched the brush in my hand tighter, my knuckles turning white as the memory from that day continued in my mind.

~

"Gone?" I whispered. Oli pulled me to his chest, but my arms stayed at my sides. I was too stunned to move.

"He was in the wrong place at the wrong time," Oli whispered. "It was a messy battle. With many casualties," he added.

I tried to grasp onto the news and failed. It wasn't sinking in. I stared numbly ahead until finally, Oli released me, and his eyes frantically searched my face.

"Bear, are you okay?"

I felt like I was being transported. I felt distant from my body. Jasper came over, and the sympathy in her eyes was almost too much to bear. "Sabeara, it's going to be alright," she said.

And for some reason, I was unable to fully process what they'd said.

"But what about the kingdom? Is King Knadian ruler of this place now? What does that mean if Father is gone. . . is Aveladon gone too?"

Oli and Jasper shared a glance, and it wasn't hard to miss the unspoken conversation that passed between the two of them.

"What, tell me," I said, very near the point of yelling.

"Aveladon is still intact." Oli started to say—his words slow as if not wanting to provoke me. "The two kingdoms were joined together when we came here. That's why the name is now Knadiel. It's a combination of both our family names, Aigoviel and Knadian." He paused, running a hand through his hair nervously. "And you see, when your father died, Jasper became Queen in his stead, and I. . ." Oli trailed off, and I watched the two of them share another glance.

That's when it hit me.

I remembered the way the guards had pulled me off Oli, afraid for his well-being—remembered when the people in the streets had bowed. And I started to wonder if maybe they weren't bowing to either Mid or me.

"You what?" I asked sharply, taking a step back from him.

"Sabeara—" Oli started to say, and I could hear the petition, the desperation in his voice that I not get upset. But it was too late.

"Tell me, Oli!" I screamed, and my eyes flitted to Jasper. She looked at me, her expression pained. I could see the guilt in her eyes.

"Jasper and I—" I watched him reach out and grasp her hand, and when their fingers intertwined, the memory shattered.

~

I took in a sharp lungful of air as I came back to the present. I was still clutching the curry brush in my hand, my knuckles ghostly white. I forced myself to relax my hold.

I stiffly patted Diablo's shoulder then locked the stall door. I started up the hill towards the mansion and felt nauseous as the memory I recalled slowly faded.

Jasper and Oli. The two of them had fallen in love and were now married. It had been the last thing I'd expected to return to. But, in my absence, they had found a love for each other I hadn't known could ever possibly exist. Oli was now King of Aveladon, working side by side with King Knadian to rule the new kingdom of Knadiel. And my entire world was turned upside down. It wasn't long before I had slipped into mourning my father and began to harbor resentment towards Oli and Jasper.

I had yet to untangle my emotions. And I didn't know why I felt the way I did. The fact the two fell in love shouldn't have bothered me so much, but for some reason, it only added to everything else that had changed.

And then I stopped talking to everyone. I'd crumbled. It had all been too much to bear. Three months and I'd barely said two words to anyone. I tried to feel bad about it. But I didn't have the willpower to feel anything but numbness.

I knew that conversations needed to be had, arguments needed to be settled. But I didn't want to scream and yell and work through my problems. I wasn't ready for that. So I just stopped talking and ignored everyone. It wasn't a great coping mechanism, but it was all I had.

I stepped into the cool air of the castle and headed towards my room, knowing that everyone was at dinner at this hour. I never joined them these days, so the halls were blissfully empty and free of any other residents. I made my way to my room and was grateful for the quietness that greeted me. I lit a candle, but my room was still extremely dark. I always left the curtains shut. The deep blue undertones of the room were nearly black when in the darkness, and the golden accents were rather eerie in the candlelight. I shuffled across the rug and stripped off my shirt and trousers, and traded them for some softer nightclothes. I had stuck with my usual Envorydian attire during the day because I was too accustomed to the freedom of pants to ever return to a dress.

I sat down at the vanity table for a moment and picked up my hairbrush. As I brushed through the tangles of my hair, I caught sight of the Envorydian symbol on my arm in the mirror and cringed. It was just another problem amongst my already weighing issues.

Three weeks after I had gone into isolation, Oli had tried to approach me. It was the only time I'd broken my silence, and I had quickly returned to not speaking to anyone afterward.

I tried not to think about it, but the disapproval in his expression was hard to forget.

~

"Sabeara, we need to talk," Oli folded his arms across his chest. He had dragged me into one of the sitting rooms, insistent on talking with me. He glared at me with eyes that looked older, somehow wiser. I felt torn inside. I wished for my old guardian, my best friend. Not this regal king I didn't even know.

"There is nothing to talk about," I said, starting for the door again.

He stretched his arm out, hindering my escape. "You can't just ignore me, Bear. It's been three weeks. Talk to me," he demanded. His green eyes burned with frustration.

"You are sleeping with my older sister. What else is there to talk about?" It was the first angry retort out of my mouth.

His eyes flared with impatience.

"I'd really appreciate it if you wouldn't use such garish terms to describe the relationship I have with my *wife*," he spat. The word *wife* sent a zing through my body that nearly knocked the air out of me.

"I'm sorry, Your Majesty," I dropped into a dramatic curtsy. "I cannot believe you willingly stuck your oh so royal. . ." I made an obscene gesture towards him.

"Stop it, right now," he growled angrily.

I wanted to scream at the top of my lungs at how stupid he'd been.

"Did you ever think about what this would do to me? Finding my best friend married to my sister and my father dead, with *you* on the throne in his place?" I shrieked. "Because I don't think you did."

"I couldn't exactly tell you what happened, Bear. You were across the realm, in prison!"

I opened my mouth to say something sarcastic, then closed it again. I was being unfair. I knew I was. But I was just so upset, so emotional over everything that had happened. It was hard to think of anything rational to say.

"Don't you dare blame this on me."

"I'm not!" he said, exasperated. "I'm asking you to listen to me and consider that maybe I didn't do this to hurt you. But because I sincerely love her and wanted to be with her."

I felt the tears well in my eyes then, unable to hold them

back. *"She's happy. . ."* Mid had said, but I had never expected this had been the thing. I turned away so Old wouldn't see the tears leaking onto my cheeks.

"Why are you so upset?" His voice softened, and he tried to turn me around to face him. I shook him off roughly.

"I don't know! Because it's a lot to take in, Oli. I'm emotionally spent, and dealing with this was not what I anticipated when I came home."

"Well, I think we've all had our fair share of things we didn't expect to deal with when you came home," he said. And I could hear the insinuation in his voice.

I spun back around, glaring at him again. "I *chose* to be an Envorydian, Oli. It was my decision," I seethed, knowing precisely what he was saying underneath his words. We had yet to speak about it, but for some reason, I had known this would be the way he reacted.

"Did you even think for a second what that meant? What *that* would do to *me,* Sabeara? You coming home an Envorydian, a. . ."

"A what, Oli?" I asked, raising an eyebrow at him, daring him to say the words.

"They are killers, Bear. Assassins. You are not. . ." he trailed off and ran a hand through his hair, letting out an exasperated sigh.

"No, don't do that," I said, hating the hint of disapproval in his tone. "You don't get to tell me what I should and shouldn't be. Not anymore." I stomped towards the door. I was done talking to him.

"Don't walk away from me, Bear," he demanded as my hand fell onto the door handle.

"Is that an order?" I asked, fusing my words with as much venom as I could.

It took him a moment to reply. "No, it's not an order," he finally relented, his words defeated.

"Don't follow me. I'm going out," I said and slammed the door shut behind me.

THREE

The memory faded, and I sighed, standing from the vanity table. I didn't know if Oli would ever come to terms with me being an Envorydian. But every time I thought about the symbol on my arm, I couldn't help but wonder if things would ever go back to normal. *Would he forgive me? Would I forgive him?*

I walked towards my bed and could see the corner of the black box beneath it. Inside was the red cloak that Oli had tried to drop off for me the first week I'd been here. I hadn't taken it out yet. I kicked the edge of the corner poking out, and sent it deeper into the shadows beneath the bed. For some reason putting on the cloak seemed like treason to the person I'd become.

When I blew out the candle and climbed into my sheets, I didn't hesitate to pull the comforter over my head. I relaxed into the darkness, and with my eyes open, waited.

I never really slept. I stared blankly into the darkness. Sometimes I'd drift to sleep, but usually, I just laid very still, waiting for the morning to come so I could get back on Diablo and fly away from everything again. I was content to slip into nothingness.

Then a knock sounded at my door.

It was unusual and so unexpected I actually lifted my head out from beneath the covers.

Everyone knows not to disturb me. I looked at the door, thinking maybe it had been a mistake, when suddenly the knock sounded again.

Because it was so out of the ordinary, I became curious and hesitantly stepped out of bed. I tiptoed across the rug, unable to resist opening the door and peeking out into the hallway.

A young sentry stood on the other side, a boy with dark brown curls and brown eyes. He wasn't Stone-Hearted yet and looked maybe fourteen.

"I'm so sorry to disturb you, Your Majesty. But there is someone in the foyer for you. And they say it is urgent." The boy was nervous. He twisted his hands in front of him, unable to fully meet my gaze.

I didn't reply, hoping that the boy would remain uncomfortable and walk away if I didn't say anything.

"I was instructed that you come immediately, Your Highness. Your visitor is very adamant." I don't know why I followed the boy, but after three months of the same thing, it seemed that my cursed curiosity got the best of me and unexpectedly burst through the fog of numbness. I nodded and opened the door wider to follow after him. He hurried down the hallway, every so often turning to look back to make sure I was following. I was still in my nightshirt and pants, but I didn't much care if someone saw me. I just kept my eyes on the boy and followed him down to the foyer.

I don't know who I expected to see standing there, but when I spotted the slight figure with the short black hair dressed in a blue day gown and brown cloak, I couldn't help but feel. . . relieved.

"Liony?" I heard myself whisper. She turned around. She had been speaking to Shar, who was standing beside her.

When her grey eyes landed on me, a bright smile spread across her face.

"Ehren!" She skipped over to me, a light grace to every step she took. When she pulled me into a hug, I couldn't help but hug her back.

"Liony, what are you doing here?" I whispered, a lump forming in my throat.

"I'm back from another rescue assignment." She pulled away from me, and her bright smile was enough to lift my spirits just a little. "It's so good to see you safe. We were all so worried about you."

I didn't think anyone would be able to lift the constant melancholy that consumed me, but I'd been wrong. I wondered if she was working her powers on me, but then I realized I didn't really care if she was. It was nice to feel something, even for just a moment.

"Did you find anyone?" I asked, and she nodded enthusiastically.

"We found four more stragglers on the very edge of the Ethydon border," she explained happily.

Rescue missions had been in effect since the war had transpired. After the battle, some who had survived had gone into hiding. Search parties had been established to rescue those who had fled, and it was an effort to salvage as many people as possible. I hadn't seen Liony since being home because she was always participating in these rescue efforts.

"That's good news," I said.

Speaking felt sort of awkward. I'd barely said more than a couple of words over the last several months. But Liony merely smiled, not seeming to notice that anything was out of the ordinary.

Shar beside her looked at me with those familiar sharp green eyes, an unreadable expression on his face. I realized standing there, that I missed him. . . but then I quickly reminded myself that he lied to me, and all evidence of missing him promptly vanished.

"Well, why don't we have tea on the porch, and you can tell me all about what happened to you," Liony said, giving Shar a dismissive glance. He seemed to understand what his sister was trying to convey and turned reluctantly to call a servant to help us set up tea.

"Sure, I'd like that," I said, surprised that I genuinely did want to talk with her.

We ended up outside on the south tea porch, overlooking the thick forest and mountains that surrounded the mansion like giant walls. I thought once again how safe I felt being tucked away here.

Two cups of tea with sugar and milk were laid out for us, but instead of drinking the tea, I watched the wisp of steam coming off the top of the copper-colored liquid.

"So start from the beginning. Why didn't you return to Ethydon after taking Sunn to the docs? And where did you end up?" Liony lifted her cup, took a dainty sip of her tea, then looked expectantly at me to begin. Liony had never been one to beat around the bush.

"Well, I burned down the Spirit Tree," I said. If I'd shocked her with my confession, it didn't show.

"And what made you think to do that?" she asked simply. And I realized I liked the nonchalance. It made it easier to talk about the complex parts. So I played along and continued to relay my story with the same amount of insouciance I'd begun with.

"My mother came to me in spirit and told me to do it. I ended up in the Sethen Courts because of my crime, but Shar happened to be there and got me out. Oh, and I miraculously became Stone-Hearted as well."

"And then?"

"Shar tried to contact my family to come and retrieve me, but the letter took quite some time to find its way to this hidden place," I gestured to the mountains around us. "I then convinced Shar to let me train to be an Envorydian, and I fought in the Regal and earned my freedom. Just as the fight was happening, Mid showed up, and then we went to save Embrosine."

"Ah yes, Shar was telling me about your guys' little rescue mission." Liony leaned back in her chair, and I wondered how much she knew about the Envoy. For some reason, I doubted she was in the dark.

"We almost got caught. Mid saved the day with his illusions, and then we came back home," I finished, knowing that it was the simplest explanation of a much more complicated story.

She didn't know the tiny details that had changed me, the difficulty of my training, the feelings I'd developed for Dusane, losing Conland, and figuring out that Elysian was my mother's brother.

"Well, I just have to ask one thing, and please don't be mad."

I hesitantly nodded.

"What were you thinking?" Her eyes flitted to the symbol on my arm and then back up to my face, where I could now see the tiniest bit of unease.

"Honestly, I'm still wondering that myself," I mumbled, finally reaching for my tea and forcing myself to take a sip. It was lukewarm as it hit my tongue, and I tried my best not to look disgusted as I placed the teacup back down on the saucer.

I must've not succeeded because Liony smiled, reached her hand out, and tiny blue sparks came out of her fingers, hitting the porcelain cup. Steam rose from the top again, and I raised an eyebrow at her.

She ignored my look and continued to interrogate me. "Shar told me you haven't talked to anyone in months," she said.

I averted my gaze, not answering her.

"Ehren, you can talk to me," she urged.

I sighed, daring to look up at her again. "I haven't talked to anyone because when I came home, I found out Shar had lied to me about my father being dead, and Oli and Jasper got married," I deadpanned.

"Spirits! Why would he do something like that," she suddenly cursed, obviously not knowing about her brother's lack of honesty.

I tipped my tea towards her in agreement and smirked.

"Well, everyone knows that my brother is an imbecile. It's something you have to get used to dealing with the longer you know him." Liony rolled her eyes as if recalling all the times she'd dealt with him. "But as for your father, I am sorry about what happened. It really is such a tragedy." She sobered and reached out across the table to grab my hand.

I looked down at our clasped fingers, feeling the weight of my father's absence wash over me again.

"We weren't close by any means," I whispered.

"But you still loved him, Ehren, I can see that," she said gently.

We stayed in that position for a while until she squeezed my hand and released me. She sipped her tea again.

"But that's not all. Jasper and Oli got married," Liony pressed, and I avoided her gaze again. She was broaching all the painful questions. "Why are you upset?"

"I don't know," I said, and I heard her sigh softly.

"Ehren, I understand the mourning of your father. But Oli and Jasper aren't gone. You don't need to mourn them too." Her words stung a little only because I knew she was right. It was stupid of me to be mad at them like this.

"I suppose you're going to tell me to talk to Shar too then?" I asked, not bothering to hide the cynicism behind my tone.

"No, you can ignore him all you want. He deserves it," she said indifferently. "But keep in mind that Shar does a lot of things because he thinks he's protecting people. It's one of his greatest flaws. . . so you may want to consider asking him why he did it in the first place."

I was just about to reply when suddenly the door to the porch opened, and someone interrupted us.

Rosen's tousled brown hair and topaz eyes greeted us, and I was surprised to see him.

"Rosen?" I asked, and it felt like stretching tired muscles talking again.

He smirked as if seeing he was interrupting something important and strode over to us.

"Shar sent an order to have me retrieve you and your friend.

Your presence has been requested at our planning meeting." His eyes shifted to Liony, who was eyeing him suspiciously. I wondered if she could see what I saw—the cocky posture of his shoulders, the sharp, handsome cheekbones, and full lips—the sneaky glint in his eye. He was nothing but trouble.

"Ehren, who is this?" Liony asked, ignoring his inquiry. Before I could answer, Rosen reached out to grasp Liony's hand and kissed her knuckles dramatically.

"I am Rosen Damaris, and who might you be?" he purred.

Liony raised an eyebrow at him but answered easily.

"I'm Liony, Liony Vell." For a moment, the two just looked at each other, and I cleared my throat, slightly uncomfortable.

"Well Rosen, tell Shar I'm not coming I . . ."

"Ehren, you've come to none of the meetings," Rosen began to argue.

"We will be there," Liony suddenly interjected.

I glared at her from across the tea table.

Rosen's lips slowly spread into a satisfied grin. "Wonderful, I look forward to seeing you there," Rosen winked at her, then turned and slipped out the door.

"What in Spirits' name was that?" I hissed just as the door clicked shut behind him. Liony simply shrugged her shoulders, but I could see she was suppressing a smile.

"I just think we should go to the meeting," she said innocently.

"Not that. The way you just acted in front of Rosen! Liony, he's not. . . good company," I finished lamely.

"Something makes me think he would be very, *very* good company," Liony giggled.

My mouth fell open. "I should've stayed in my room," I decided, shaking my head in disbelief.

"Oh stop, I'm only kidding."

But I didn't think she was kidding in the slightest. But before I could press her more on the detriments of getting caught up in someone like Rosen, she grabbed my hand and began leading me back inside. "Now, let's go to the meeting. Everyone is probably waiting for us."

And just like every other instance with Liony, I couldn't help but follow.

FOUR

The planning room was a small den on the third floor of the mansion. It was more of an attic than a room. It was barely large enough to hold a table, and the walls were covered in maps and papers. A small window shed some light into the place, but it wasn't much.

Everyone was already seated when we entered, and I could see and feel the waves of shocked surprise. Eyes widened, mouths fell agape, and someone even gasped softly. My arrival was as unexpected as my own lack of resistance to join them. I was as surprised as they were.

I averted my gaze quickly, knowing that if I met eyes with anyone in the room, I'd be unable to stay as composed as I was.

Liony, to my dismay, took a seat beside Rosen. I had no choice but to take the empty seat beside her and ended up with Shar on my left. I quickly looked down at the tiny rivulets in the wooden tabletop, trying to occupy my eyes.

Someone stood from their chair and cleared their throat.

"Thank you all for coming. We have a lot to discuss this morning on the groupings for our operations. Shar, would you like to begin?" I recognized King Knadian's voice. Then I heard Shar clear his throat beside me.

"I'll be going to the coast to find our transportation across the seas so we can search for the compass. Unfortunately, the boat Mid used originally is no longer available."

"What happened to it?" I heard Jasper ask.

"It was raided. But no need to worry, Embrosine will be able to request another ship be sent to us from the Isles. She's already sent word. So she'll be coming with me to retrieve it, and then we will safely dock the ship till we are ready to depart. But I'd like to take at least one more trained fighter with me on the journey for precaution," Shar said, and I heard several murmurs of approval.

"I'll go with you," I heard Rouix say. And the sound of her twinkling voice sent a chill down my spine. I almost looked up at her, longing to see my friend's face but forced myself to stay looking down.

"Good, that's settled then," I heard Oli say. "On another note, Severesi has allied with Obscurum now, so anyone who leaves Knadiel is going to have to make sure they are discreet. Some rescue groups have had encounters with the white cloaks on the Ethydon border, and I don't want things getting messy." Another wave of murmurs was heard across the table.

I'd discovered through gossiping staff that Severesi had allied officially with Obscurum, and it wasn't good news. An alliance with Severesi would bring Obscurum more power and make it harder for us to defeat them.

"We must also decide who will be going back to Obscurum."

My head snapped up, unable to stay down then.

But looking up was a huge mistake.

My eyes immediately met with emerald-scarlet eyes across the table, and I couldn't speak for a moment. Something in my chest tightened—a longing, a desperate craving for comfort, for consolation. But I couldn't very well run across the room and throw myself into his arms.

I tore my eyes away from him, forcing myself to look over at Oli.

"Why are we returning to Obscurum?" I suddenly interjected. Everyone at the table went silent. I'd been absent from their planning meetings for a while now. It had been naive to think I wouldn't have questions. My curiosity was bound to get the best of me.

Oli seemed startled that I had spoken, but he quickly recovered and explained. "We have decided it would be best to figure out what King Elysian's powers are. We are uncertain of his abilities, and it would give us the advantage to figure them out. We also think that a token may be there,"

"The dagger?" Memories of the glowing purple dagger and the way it had burned Embrosine's skin immediately flooded my mind. I began to feel nauseous.

"Not the dagger. Something else," Dusane's husky voice carried over to me, and I dared to turn and meet his gaze. His cerulean eyes met mine, and another ache formed in my chest.

I'd been avoiding them both. I'd been nearly swallowed in my agony, and I'd not reached out to them once. And they hadn't reached out to me because I had ordered no one to speak to me. I knew I would break apart the minute I sought either one of them. *And how did I seek comfort from one without hurting the other?* It was too complicated, and isolation had been the only option. *But now. . .* I forced my feelings down, stomping them deep into the darkest parts of me.

"I felt a great sense of power that day in the throne room. I must have used your abilities with the amulet. It was powerful. . ." I trailed off lamely, not knowing exactly what I was trying to explain. I had used some of Dusane's Reminant abilities while in the throne room back in Obscurum. And I remembered feeling a massive wave of power coming off the dagger. I'd never experienced anything like it before.

"I felt it too. Which is why I know the dagger isn't the token," Dusane explained.

"How do you know that exactly?"

"Because I granted the person who made it. I recognized the power coming off the dagger that day in the throne room. The person who forged it is a blacksmith. Last time I heard, she was living in Severesi."

"And we are going to send a group to Severesi to meet with her," Oli said.

"Why are we going to the blacksmith?" I asked, surprised by my desire to be involved with the conversation.

"We are planning to ask the blacksmith to help us create a weapon like she created that dagger," Mid suddenly jumped in again.

"Do you think creating a weapon like that will help us defeat Obsidian?" I asked.

"Not a weapon, a device," Dusane clarified. "We think we might be able to ask her to help us create something that can subdue Obsidian's power. We have been discussing it, and we think that if we are ever going to defeat Obscurum, then we have to get around Obsidian's power."

"Obsidian's power is dangerous, I agree. But is it our biggest problem?" I asked.

"He's basically the king's puppet. And every time Obsidian gets near, he hurts someone, and his power is unpredictable. So I think he's one of our greatest obstacles," Rouix chimed in, and memories of Conland came back to my mind, his lifeless body on the jungle floor. I clenched my teeth together, trying to swallow back the memory.

"Okay, so some of us will go search for the blacksmith. And the rest will go to Obscurum to see if we can find another token and figure out Elysian's power? How are we going to do that?" My mind was spinning.

"We are going to send someone in secretly, pretending to be a Severesi Ambassador. They'll infiltrate the castle and get the information on Elysian's power and at the same time see if there might be a token in his possession they can retrieve," Oli explained.

They'd done more planning than I expected while I'd been away.

"Who is going to be the one to pretend to be the Ambassador?" I asked, starting to think maybe this plan was too elaborate.

"From what I've gathered, they've been arguing for some time about that very question. But everyone knows I will be the best candidate, which is why Oli asked me to be here today. I can persuade anyone to think I am the Ambassador," Liony smiled, sitting up a little taller in her chair.

"Over my dead body," Shar snapped, shooting a glare at Oli from across the table. I must've missed most of the drama up to that point.

"Shar, it's okay. We've been over this." I heard Embrosine

speak for the first time, and I watched her lay a hand on Shar's arm to calm him.

"Oh, don't be ridiculous, Brother. I'm the best one for the job and you know it. Why else would I be in this meeting?" Liony said, rolling her eyes.

"You'll get yourself killed. You can't do that," Shar insisted.

"I'm also one of the only people that wasn't there with you during the raid at the Obscurum castle. So he won't even recognize who I am."

Everyone went quiet, contemplating this.

"I'm also very versed in my political vocabulary, It won't even be that hard, plus I'll take guards with me," she added for good measure.

Shar glowered, obviously not liking the plan, but he didn't say anything more as if he couldn't find any more reason to argue.

"What about the blacksmith? Who's going to meet with her?" I asked.

"Me. I'm the only one that will probably be able to find her," Dusane said.

"I'll go with you," I volunteered, realizing that I wanted to be a part of this.

"Now, Sabeara, let's not get ahead of ourselves," Oli cautioned.

I turned to narrow my eyes at him. "Oli, I'm a trained Envorydian."

"Olivine. . ." Jasper warned, and his jaw clenched.

He'd only ever known me as Princess Sabeara, the girl he had to protect. But I wasn't defenseless anymore. *Would he be able to let me be a part of this? Or would he continue to shelter me here?* The reason I became an Envorydian was to be able to go on missions like this one. I wasn't about to let him sideline me.

"Fine, go with Dusane," Oli relented. "You'll probably go anyway, even if I tell you not to." He let out a frustrated sigh.

"I'm coming too then," Mid suddenly cut in, and I realized too late what I'd done. I'd landed myself with Mid and Dusane on a mission.

"I guess that leaves me to go with the pretty lady," Rosen teased, turning to Liony at his side.

"Wait a second, hold on. Rosen, you're not going with Liony," Shar said firmly. "Mid will go, or I will."

"Elysian knows Mid. He'll be too noticeable. The last time I checked, he knew him by name. And are you really going to allow Embrosine to go by herself to get the boat? Plus, the king didn't even glance at me during the battle, and I'll wear a disguise," Rosen argued.

"Mid can put on an illusion, pretend to be someone else," Shar persisted.

"I'm not leaving Ehren, and I can't hold an illusion that long anyway. I could slip up, and if someone saw me, I'd risk giving the entire operation away. It will be better if Rosen goes, pretending to be a close guard," Mid argued.

"Can I trust you?" Shar suddenly asked Rosen, his eyes darkened with an almost vicious intensity.

"Yes, Shar, I promise nothing will happen to her," Rosen said seriously. I couldn't help but notice Liony fighting back a smile, and I inwardly groaned.

"What about you, Oli? Are you coming with us to find the blacksmith?" I asked, hoping he'd say yes despite how angry I currently was with him.

I didn't want to go alone with Mid and Dusane, knowing that would probably not end well.

"I'm staying here with Jasper. Someone has to help King and Queen Knadian run everything while everyone is away, but we will send guards with you, just to be safe," His words did little to relax me.

But it seemed that the groups were settled, and there wasn't much I could do to change them.

I asked the next question that was sure to follow. "So when do we leave?"

FIVE

Three days.

It wasn't long to prepare, but it would be enough. Everyone was eager to get on the move. The longer we waited, the more time wasted defeating the curse.

I packed my things, still avoiding everyone the best I could. But I'd agreed to go on the journey to meet the blacksmith, and I knew I wouldn't be able to avoid speaking with Dusane and Mid forever. And soon, I was going to be in close proximity with them.

Before leaving, I rode Diablo up onto the mountains, mentally preparing myself for what was to come. It helped a little, but no amount of mental preparation was going to erase the awkwardness that surely awaited me on this mission.

When I returned to the stables around dinner time, I was surprised to find someone waiting for me. My heart rate sped up, not expecting anyone, and then I saw the blonde curls and realized it was just Oli.

"What do you want?" I asked dismissively. Refusing to meet his gaze as I led Diablo to his stall.

"I wanted to talk to you," Oli said simply. I didn't respond, and I could hear the exasperation in his sigh. "Bear, I don't want to go on like this. I hate that you're angry with me."

I shut the stall door and turned around to face him, crossing my arms over my chest.

"I don't know how else to feel," I said, then I brushed past him. He followed, and I crossed the field towards the mansion. We passed through a small section of trees, and in the shade of the oaks, he called out to me again.

"Please, can we talk?"

I slowed because I could hear the desperation in his voice. And I was tired of fighting too. But I wasn't ready to admit that yet.

I turned around, and he gestured towards a small section of shade beneath one of the trees. I settled into the grass, not relaxing my indignant posture.

He sat beside me and sighed heavily again.

"Why are you upset about Jasper and me?"

"I don't know, Oli," I said exasperated. "Maybe because you two were never supposed to—" I threw my hands up. "Ugh. . . You're my guardian, and it's weird!" I trailed off, and a look of realization filled Oli's eyes.

"You know I'll always be your guardian, right? This doesn't change that." He gently reached out to clasp my hand in his.

I looked down at where our fingers were intertwined.

"I know. . ."

"But that's not all, is it?" Oli urged.

"I guess it's just so typical. You've never seen me that way, and then, of course, Jasper would appeal to you." The words were out before I could stop them.

I watched his brow furrow, and I blushed furiously.

"What—" Then he stopped mid-sentence, and his eyes widened. "Do you. . . have feelings for me?" he asked slowly.

"No! Definitely not!" I said, panicked. "I mean. . . uh. . . once maybe, but. . ." I averted my gaze, trying and failing not to stutter.

"Wait, what?" His tone was perplexed.

"A long time ago . . . as a kid. But you never really saw me that way." I stumbled more, digging the hole even deeper.

His eyes remained wide. Obviously, he was shocked. I rushed to explain myself.

"I guess it's just my younger self. I don't know, being jealous?" I questioned aloud, unsure what I was really even feeling and untangling it slowly and awkwardly in front of him. "It's stupid, really. I'm just irrationally seeing once again that Jasper will always be better than me,"

"You had feelings for me?" He mumbled under his breath, still stuck on that.

"Oli, I was like ten. Honestly, it's stupid for me to be feeling this way. Look, I'm over it. No hard feelings. Can we just stop talking about this?"

"I mean, it is kinda sweet," he suddenly said.

"Sweet?" I paused, stunned by his reply. His green eyes brightened with obvious amusement, and he chuckled.

That's when I realized that he was laughing at me.

"You had a crush on me. How cute is that?" Oli reached over to pull me in for a hug, and I grumbled aloud.

"Great, glad I amuse you," I rolled my eyes and shoved him off me.

"I mean, I honestly had no idea," he said, still laughing.

"Ugh, of course you'd make fun of me." I stood from the ground and started to walk away, beginning to feel angry again. He quickly stood and followed after me.

"I'm sorry, Bear, I shouldn't laugh. It's just, I really didn't know. And as for Jasper, you know she isn't better than you." He paused, then added. "I mean, it looks like you have your hands full with other suitors right now anyway."

I stopped mid-stride. "What did you just say?" I whipped around, my eyes narrowing.

"Those boys have been asking me about you for three months now."

"Dusane and Mid have been asking about me?" I asked.

Oli nodded, pursing his lips as if trying to hold in another laugh.

I groaned and buried my head in my hands. I was severely dreading talking to them.

"Hey, it's going to be okay." Oli pulled me into a hug, and this time I didn't reject it.

"What am I going to do?" My reply was muffled in the shoulder of his red cloak.

"That's up to you."

I pulled back and looked up into his peridot eyes. "Why couldn't we have fallen in love with each other?" I was only partly joking.

"Because you would've annoyed me to death." He winked and ruffled my hair while continuing up the path towards the mansion.

"You know I hate you sometimes," I said as we fell into stride beside one another.

"I know, but you also love me." He smirked, and for a small

moment, it felt like it did before everything happened—before Jasper's Granting, before the curse.

"Yes, I do."

We walked in silence for a moment, and it wasn't until we were almost to the castle that I spoke again.

"Oli?"

He looked over at me expectantly.

"About me being an Envorydian. . ."

"I'm not upset," Oli said abruptly, but I saw his jaw clench for the slightest second.

"Are you sure? Because if you can't accept who I am now. . ." I trailed off, worried that the answer might be that he wouldn't be able to.

He stopped again and turned to look at me seriously. "You'll always be my Little Bear." He reached out and turned my hand over so he could see the tattoo on my forearm. "Just a tad bit more dangerous now."

~

Talking to Jasper was the second item on my list of relationships to mend. I headed to my room to change my clothes. I planned to go to her chambers and apologize for everything. During the process of changing my trousers, I remembered the black box beneath my bed.

Curiously I reached down and pulled it from beneath its resting place. I undid the lid and found the vibrant crimson fabric folded neatly inside.

Maybe this would show Jasper that I was ready. I knew it would mean a lot to her if I wore it, it represented our kingdom, and by not putting it on, I had sort of been rejecting my heritage.

The cloak enveloped me as I put it on, like a warm embrace, and I sighed aloud. For so long, I had wanted to be Stone-Hearted. It had been *all* I'd ever wanted at one point. It surprised me that such devotion to that ideal could have changed. I had gotten everything I'd wanted. Yet still, things weren't perfect in my life. I had been wrong in assuming that all my problems would disappear once I became Stone-Hearted.

I snorted aloud on my way to the door, realizing that my life had only gotten more complicated, if anything.

~

Jasper wasn't in her chambers, and I ended up finding her in the music room. She sat on a beautiful black piano bench, playing a soothing melody across the alabaster keys. I watched silently in the doorway, not wanting to disturb her. It wasn't until she finished her song that I knocked, announcing my presence.

She turned around, her expression one of surprise at seeing me. "Bear?"

"Can we talk?" I asked. I was nervous for some reason, fiddling with the amulet beneath my cloak. *Did I think she was going to reject me?*

"Of course," she gestured for me to take a seat on the bench beside her.

"I wanted to apologize," I began.

"You don't need to apologize. Father's death wasn't easy news, and neither was finding out about Elysian and my relationship with Oli. I don't blame you. It was a lot to take in." She reached across the space between us and clasped my hand. Of course, she would be perfectly understanding and forgiving. It almost hurt worse that she wasn't even the slightest bit upset with my behavior.

"I still shouldn't have gotten angry about your relationship." I swallowed thickly. "I'm glad you're happy." I spit the words out, hoping she missed the reluctance in them.

"Thank you, Bear, that means a lot," she smiled, her bright plum eyes glistening.

"And about Midennen. . . I should have told you—"

Jasper shook her head and stopped me before I could continue. "He told me everything, Bear. And there are no hard feelings," she insisted.

My brow furrowed. "But I thought you were falling for him."

"I was *pretending* to fall for him," she corrected and smiled wanly. "I wasn't too keen on the idea of marrying him either. I was putting on a show for everyone just as much as he was," she admitted.

This news shocked me, and my mouth fell open a little.

"I appreciate you trying to protect me, but you don't need to worry about that anymore." A flicker of gold glinted off the windows from where she fiddled with her coin between her fingertips.

"You're my sister. I had to try and do right by you," I mumbled, still trying to process that everything in my life seemed to be a lie.

"I always knew that I loved Oli. It was just never possible to be together until father died," Jasper explained.

I shuddered unwillingly, unable to hold back my reaction. "Sorry, I'm still trying to get used to it," I said sheepishly.

Jasper chuckled and then warmly embraced me. "I love you, Bear,"

"I love you too," I said, taking in a deep breath of her clean lavender scent.

When she pulled away, she gestured to the cloak around my shoulders. "You're wearing it."

I nodded, blushing a little. "Sorry it took me so long to put it on,"

"It looks great on you." Her eyes flickered to the small sliver of gold light shining up from the collar of my cloak. "Shar informed us of your healing power. It sounds pretty incredible."

I shrugged. "I'm still trying to master it," I admitted.

She nodded in understanding. "It can take some time to master a power. But I'm sure you'll get the hang of it."

I nodded, not sure why I was so embarrassed.

"Well, I better go. I need to pack my things for tomorrow."

"Of course," she stood and walked me to the door. I paused in the hallway just before leaving.

"See you in the morning?" I asked, my voice almost a whisper.

"I'll see you in the morning," she assured me, then gently shut the door behind me.

SIX

I said goodbye to the mansion the following day, then packed my things and retrieved Diablo from the stables. I met the others outside the front gates, and the caravans were already established.

Shar, Embrosine, and Rouix would be headed to find a boat for transportation across the seas. Liony and Rosen would penetrate the Obscurum castle to discover Elysian's power and possibly find a token. Then Mid, Dusane, and I would be going to the blacksmith. A group of Ethydon and Aveladon guards would follow each group for safety, but it felt like I was going into this alone despite having guards with us.

I walked over to Liony, not quite ready to join my team.

"Are you ready for this, Ehren?" Liony asked brightly. Her black hair was curled around her face that morning, her storm grey eyes wide with excitement.

"I think so," I said, but I knew the honest answer. *No, I was definitely not ready.*

"Looks like we will be traveling together halfway," she commented.

"What do you mean?" A surge of hope filled me.

"Once you head for the blacksmith, we will have to part, but at least most of the journey we will be together."

I smiled, relieved to hear that not all of my journey would be spent alone with Mid and Dusane. The two of them were watching me, and I could feel the heat of their gazes on my face, but I refused to look at them. I would avoid confrontation as long as possible.

At that moment, Oli came walking from the mansion's front doors, Jasper at his side, and I was saved for several minutes.

"Thank you all for arriving on time this morning," Oli spoke to everyone gathered. "It's sad to see you all go, but I'm sure we will all be together again soon."

It was quiet then as Oli and Jasper walked down the steps over to me.

"Be safe, will you?" Jasper asked, pulling me into a hug.

"Don't worry about me," I told her, realizing she only knew me as her little sister and not the skilled Envorydian I'd become.

When she pulled away, Oli reached out to pull me into a hug too.

"Take care of yourself," was all he said.

"I'm going to be fine, Oli." I was a little embarrassed by all the love, not used to having people fret over me in a while.

"Are you sure you won't stay?" he asked as he pulled back to look at me.

"Oli, I can't help if I stay. Please, you've got to trust that I can do this."

He nodded as if forcing himself to accept it. Nothing more was said then, and the two walked over to a couple of

Aveladon guards to discuss something with them, and I was left alone.

I glanced across the clearing and spotted Shar. He had Wesoltinece's hammer attached at the hip. He'd become its caretaker since retrieving it in Obscurum. He looked up then as if feeling my gaze on him, and his gaze burned into mine, and I felt my breath hitch. I wanted to turn away, show him that I wasn't going to acknowledge his existence, but then I felt something inside of me tug painfully at my consciousness, and I inwardly groaned.

"I'll be right back," I told Liony.

I walked in Shar's direction and gestured with a nod of my head for him to follow me.

He left Embrosine and Rouix and followed me over to a quieter spot in the shade of some brambles and pine trees.

"Would you care if I apologized?" Shar asked bluntly.

"It would be nice," I fired back quickly.

"I'm sorry," he said, his face impassive.

"Why did you do it?"

"You know why," he said, and instead of my anger flaring, it surprisingly eased.

He was right. I think I did know why.

"I thought you didn't have a heart," I accused.

"I don't usually. But you had already been through so much."

I thought back to that time when I'd woken in a strange prison, a new person. I remembered Shar had told me all that had happened, and maybe it would have been too much if he'd told me the truth about my father's death.

"You still should have told me." My voice remained surprisingly steady.

"I know," was all he said.

For a moment, nothing was said between us. Then I watched his eyes flicker back over to his caravan. I followed his gaze and knew he was looking at Embrosine. She was watching us.

"When are you going to tell Mid about you two?" I asked.

"When the time is right."

"It may never be the right time," I reminded him.

"Don't do anything stupid," he suddenly said, ignoring my last comment as he turned back around to face me. It was his twisted way of saying he cared for me.

I gave up trying to convince him to do the right thing. Shar was too stubborn to listen to me. He'd tell Mid about his past with Embrosine on his terms. "You know I will."

I walked away from him then and headed for my group. Liony's caravan had merged with ours, and they all stood together now. Every step increased the suspense that had been growing inside of me. I forced myself to take a deep breath and used all my Envoy training to focus my mind and remain calm.

Dusane sat stride Elesame, his straight black hair longer than usual—falling unkempt into his cerulean eyes. He wore his envoy attire, all black, looking dangerous and even lethal.

Then my eyes shifted to Mid. He was atop Ghost, his bow and arrow slung across his back. His brown cloak wrapped around his shoulders. He looked regal and noble. His hair remained in a short style I'd yet to become accustomed to, and his emerald-scarlet eyes burned brightly in the noonday sun.

I inwardly groaned as I mounted Diablo, thinking once again about the predicament I'd gotten myself into.

This is going to be a long journey.

SEVEN

The trek to Severesi started off well enough. Neither of the boys confronted me. For which I was grateful. I rode near Liony, and the two of us chatted aimlessly. Every once in a while, I'd catch one of the two boys staring, but they would quickly glance away when I noticed one of them. That was the worst of it.

It would be a four-day journey to Severesi. On day three, we would split. The terrain was quite beautiful the first day, with rolling green hills and pleasant level weather. The following day was when the weather became less favorable. At first, there was a slight chill in the air, then as the day wore on, it grew colder. Soon snow flurries began to fall. Quickly, the light snow compounded until Diablo was treading through a foot of snow.

I was grateful for my cloak as the weather got colder. I shivered into the soft crimson fabric, dreading an entire journey with this sort of weather. I almost wished to be back in the Sethen Courts. Never did I think I'd miss the hot, humid jungle.

We didn't encounter any trouble on our way, which was pure luck. As we set up camp the second night, a big fire was lit, and I was too cold to hide away in the tent. So I stayed out with the others, enjoying as much of the warmth from the thick flames as I could.

"Tomorrow, we will split off," Liony said beside me. She was munching on an apple, her storm grey eyes nearly black in the firelight.

"Guess it will just be you and me," Rosen commented while taking a seat beside Liony. I could've sworn I saw him wink.

I glared at him.

"Not quite alone, need I remind you," Liony interjected, her lip twitched with a demure smile.

"Do you have what you need for disguise?" I asked her, hoping to avert their attention from each other.

"We have what we need. Which reminds me, I also had cloaks made for the three of you." Liony stood and went to her saddlebag to retrieve the cloaks. I took the soft alabaster material from her outstretched hand. She handed the other two to Mid and Dusane.

"Will this be enough to disguise us?" I asked, and Liony nodded.

"It should do the trick."

We lulled into a comfortable silence then, and I glanced across the fire, meeting Mid's gaze.

I couldn't look away for a moment.

I didn't know where to begin. Part of me wanted to talk to him and Dusane. But for some reason, I was reluctant to jump back into it all. We had promised each other we would have a conversation when we returned home, but that conversation never happened. I knew more needed to be said and that he wished to learn more about what happened to me in Obscurum. I felt guilty then, knowing I'd pushed both of them away for so long.

I averted my gaze, forcing my eyes back onto the fire.

That night I went to bed, guilt heavy in my gut.

Tomorrow. I promised myself. Tomorrow I'd break the silence.

~

The following day we rode on to the point in our journey where we would split. I didn't know how Liony and the other guards knew where they were going. Only snow and trees surrounded us. But at some point in the day, one of the Ethydon guards halted his steed and made the announcement that we had reached the end where we'd have to break off.

"This is where we change course," he ordered. Those in Liony's caravan began down a different path through another expanse of trees.

"I'll see you soon?" Liony asked, just as light and chipper as any other day. She reached for me still on her horse, and we gave each other a quick embrace.

"Be safe out there," I told her, the weight of her leaving crashed down on me suddenly.

"Don't worry, she'll be protected. She has me." Rosen rode up to her side and flashed me a smirk. I nearly barred my teeth at him.

"Keep your hands to yourself," I threatened. Feeling suddenly protective over Liony because of my lack of trust in Rosen.

"No promises," Rosen smoldered, his topaz eyes glistening

with amusement. He turned to follow the others, and I looked at Liony, my face still distorted with disgust.

"Don't worry about me. I can handle him," she reassured me, smiling a little. "I've spent my entire life around rambunctious boys."

Her response did little to relax me, but I nodded.

Liony turned her horse then and headed off into the trees. Leaving me alone with four Ethydon guards, Mid, and Dusane.

I turned Diablo to follow after Ghost, and we headed deeper into the trees.

~

A couple of hours later, we stopped to take a break, and I was emptying part of my boot that had gotten snow in it when I suddenly heard the crunch of footsteps. I looked up to find Mid standing in front of me. Surprise washed over me, and I jolted upright.

Mid didn't seem the least bit phased by my sudden jitters and handed me a small loaf of bread and some cheese.

"Here," he said gently, and I took the food from his hands. He smiled at me and then turned away, and I inwardly sighed.

Well, that wasn't so bad, I told myself. The first interaction was over with. It may have been small, but technically it was the first time we'd spoken again.

He was several feet away when something came over me, and I quickly called out to him.

"Mid."

He paused to turn back around. I didn't miss the hopeful expression on his face.

"Thank you," I said, hating how pathetic it sounded.

His smile faltered a little like he was hoping I would have said something more. But he quickly recovered and nodded politely, acknowledging my thank you, and as if to say, "Don't worry about it." Then he mounted Ghost again.

We rode on for several more hours, only stopping to take short breaks. Then the sky darkened, and we set up camp.

One of the guards lit a fire, and I settled in close to the flame.

"So, where does this blacksmith live exactly?" I asked.

"Somewhere in Severesi, but as for her exact location, that's still to be determined." Dusane took a seat beside me, resting his elbows on his knees. "But we aren't actually going to find the blacksmith first."

"What? Where are we going then?"

"We thought it might be best to visit Sydidel in Eslecaster before we journey to find the blacksmith," Mid said from across the fire.

"Sydidel?" I remembered the old man we visited so long ago. The faraway look in his aged eyes—the birds on his porch that he would cluck at as if speaking to them.

"He may be able to give us more information about the tokens," Mid explained.

"Wasn't he extremely unhelpful last time we saw him?" I questioned. I looked at Dusane for help, wondering what he thought of visiting some random ancient Stone-Hearted that spoke nonsense.

"Mid has informed me that Sydidel is a Reminant, a very old Reminant, and I am curious to see for myself what he may know. About Amberidium and. . ."

"Oh no, not this again," I groaned. "You don't really believe in a place called Pendilore, do you? And the seventh stone? Has

Rosen really got his hooks so deep into you?" My voice rose with slight aggravation.

"That's not all. Syd may have answers about your power," Mid interjected.

"I already know I'm a healer. I've pretty much figured out on my own what I can and can't do. So what else is there to even figure out?"

"We still don't know why you became Stone-Hearted after you burned down the tree," Dusane interjected.

"And Syd may know more about Elysian too," Mid added.

"Whatever, if you two want to go and talk to a crazy man and chase some crazy fairytale Rosen told you, fine! But I'm only giving up one day. Then we need to go to the blacksmith. It's more important that we figure out how to stop Obsidian."

"Don't worry, we will," Dusane insisted.

It was quiet then as I gazed into the fire and tried to remain calm due to the sudden change of plans I had not been informed of.

Eventually, my eyes began to droop, and I excused myself from the group. I barely slept that night, fitfully tossing and turning. So many questions were unanswered, so many mysteries we had yet to solve. It felt almost impossible to unravel all of them. At one point, I stared up at the tent ceiling, clutching the amulet in my hands. The familiar weight of the ruby was comforting in my palm. I fell asleep that way, holding the amulet and dreaming of the nonsense Syd's birds would sing to me when I woke up.

EIGHT

I slept only a couple of hours, sleep still not the solitude I wished it could be. I left the warmth of my tent and winced at the cold wind that immediately greeted me. The sky was barely beginning to lighten, and none of the others were awake yet. Diablo was resting beside the other animals. I walked over to him and gently patted his flank. A light snowfall had occurred during the night, and his black fur was dusted with snowflakes.

"Good morning," I whispered to him.

The entire forest was muted with the thick snow all around us. Every footfall was silenced, the thick blanket of snow covering everything. It felt like we were in another universe.

As I began packing up my things, the others gradually woke, and soon we were on the move again. We reached the lake a couple of hours later.

It was just as I remembered it, steam rolling on the top of the glassy surface, the black cliffs surrounding it on all sides.

I dismounted Diablo and reached into my pack to grab the white cloak Liony had given me. I removed the red cloak from my shoulders and put on the white one in its place. Dusane and Mid did the same, and then Mid walked up to the shore, nearly disappearing into the mist until he reappeared again, dragging the fishing boat behind him. Mid stepped inside, taking one of the paddles, and then Dusane followed after him, turning around to offer me his hand.

I looked down at Dusane outstretched palm, unable to stop the image of Mid's hand that had once reached out similarly. It seemed like so long ago when Mid had taken me here. I had been so unaware and still had yet to learn of the curse. The impact of the memories that accompanied the lake washed over me, and something in my chest tightened.

"You coming, Ehren?" I was pulled from my thoughts. Dusane's blue eyes searched my face, and I knew he was probably wondering why I was hesitating.

"What about the other guards?" I gestured towards the four Ethydon guards in the trees' safety—Diablo, Ghost, and Elesame with them.

"They are going to stay here and set up camp while keeping watch over the animals," Dusane assured me.

I nodded and then finally took his outstretched hand and stepped into the little fishing boat.

It was similar to when I'd first floated across the lagoon. I couldn't see anything ahead until suddenly, the two statues of the pegasus came into view, towering over us. We slipped into the dark tunnel moments later, and I was surprised to see I was still fearful of close, dark spaces, even more so with my Stone-Hearted senses. Everything was extra humid, the intensity of the darkness almost weighted. I tried very hard to breathe steadily until finally we reached the other side and entered the city.

Everything was just as I remembered it. Waterfalls cascading down the giant black cliffs and the architecture weaving through the foliage. Bridges and canals made the highways that interconnected everything. It was hot, and mist sprinkled against my face as we floated past white water pouring into the riverway.

Alabaster cloaked civilians dotted the landscape, not the least bit knowledgeable of our existence. We floated into the midst of it all and pulled up to one of the docks. I stepped out, and the boys tied up the boat securely before we started down the streets.

It was silent as we walked. We all seemed to be taking in the scene. New sights and smells tantalized my senses, and I was a little overwhelmed trying to take it all in again. Everything was bustling with life here. So much different from the quaint and quiet of Knadiel.

Mid turned around a street corner, and soon the buzz of the busy markets and hum of the waterways began to fade. We came upon the alleyway I vividly remembered with the aged door and pulley crate.

Mid reached for the handle and shoved open the reluctant door. It squeaked and whined but eventually caved beneath his weight and revealed on the other side was the pulley system that would take us up to Syd's house.

"Who goes first?" I asked, and Mid jumped into the rickety contraption with ease as if he'd done it a thousand times.

"Well, two can fit, so I don't see why we wouldn't go together," Mid smiled invitingly and gestured for me to come in after him.

I looked at Dusane, and he was looking at Mid with what I

assumed was an incredulous look. But Dusane was so good at hiding his emotions I honestly couldn't tell.

"I'll just go up by myself," I said, quickly averting the situation. Whoever I decided to ride with might get the wrong impression which was the last thing I wanted.

"Well then, Dusane, my friend, would you like to join me?" Mid gave Dusane a teasing smile. "Time is of the essence," he reminded us.

I was slightly shocked by Mid's bold invitation. But also knew I shouldn't expect less. He was known for his sarcastic wiles.

Dusane simply sighed and joined Mid in the crate.

"Just take us up," Dusane said. And that was the last thing said before they both disappeared into the shaft.

I stood in the cramped alleyway waiting for the crate to be returned down to me, the whole time nervous butterflies in my stomach over the fact they'd ridden together. It was unnerving to see the two of them interacting. I tried to imagine what conversation they might be having, but that was just too unsettling to think about.

Soon the crate landed with a thud, empty and waiting for me again.

I jumped inside, hating the tight, restricted space that the shaft offered. Taking a deep breath and forcing myself to ignore the overwhelming darkness, I grabbed the wheel I'd seen Mid use once before and began turning it. The crate slowly began to move up the shaft. It required quite a bit of strength to get the thing moving, but eventually, I made it to the top. The boys were waiting for me, and I quickly leaped out of the crate onto the safety of the stone bridge beside them. I shuddered, looking back at the crate.

"I really hate that thing," I commented.

But neither of them answered me. They had begun walking over to the dainty cottage that rested in the safety of the black rock face. The tiny house sat on a bridge outlook that gave a view to the entire city of Eslecaster.

Mid knocked on the door, and the birds on the porch that rested in their cages fluttered their wings nervously at the noise. A couple of seconds later, the door swung open, revealing Sydidel's round bald head on the other side.

Syd's wide green eyes landed on Mid, and the first words out of his mouth were not wholly unexpected.

"Curses and Spirits, Mid, what are you doing here?"

NINE

Despite Syd's irritable greeting, Mid eventually got him to invite us in. Once inside his home, he ambled about the clutter of plants, making way for us to allow us a seat at his table. Soon we were all drinking herbal tea that tasted of bitter yarrow flower and dandelion.

"I see you must have taken my advice," Syd said, pointing to the amulet around my neck. "You've found a token."

"I'll admit your advice wasn't much help at first. But eventually, I think I understood," Mid smiled sheepishly at his old friend.

"So why are you here again, Mid? Something to do with the curse, I presume?" The old man wasn't wearing the white cloak he wore last time, and I could see beneath his shirt this time a silver light like Mid's.

"Well, sort of," Mid said, and he appeared to hesitate before asking his next question. "Do you know anything about a stone called Amberidium?"

Syd's forehead scrunched, making his spectacles off-kilter, and he began to mumble to himself. "Amberidium, Amberidium. . ."

"A friend informed us it might be the seventh stone," Dusane added.

"If you seek for the seventh light, you must be prepared to wield its power," Sydidel suddenly said.

We all looked at each other.

"So it is the seventh stone?" Mid asked eagerly.

"I cannot tell you if there are more stones. I only know that there is light within everything. A light that has been subdued and minimized." A frenetic expression began to brighten Syd's eyes, and he shuffled over to me. "This light has always been within us." As he spoke more about light, he reached out and touched my heart. "And it will save us all."

I held my breath, trying to understand what the old Remnant was even saying. The last time we'd come, he'd spoken about angry spirits and the consequences of the tokens getting into the wrong hands. He even mentioned the moon turning to blood and many lives being lost. All of those things had happened in one way or another. The fires during the Ethydon war had caused the moon to turn red, and many people had perished during the burning of Aveladon. And the spirits had indeed gotten angry because the curse was happening.

"We also came to ask you about Ehren's powers. Somehow she received her healing ability without being Granted by a Reminant," Mid rushed to ask. As if he didn't get the words out, Syd might disappear.

"A Reminant is not the one who holds the power to grant," Syd whispered. "It has always been in the hands of him who is light and spirit."

I looked over at Dusane and gave him an exasperated expression as if to say *I told you so*. Syd was speaking nonsense. I didn't understand any of it.

"What about Pendilore? Is there such a place?" Dusane's jaw clenched as if determined to get some sort of coherent answer from the man.

"Pendilore? You are asking for things not yet ready to be revealed!" Syd turned on Dusane angrily. "You mustn't speak of things that may disrupt destiny! You must understand that a savior will not come until he is ready to save!"

Mid stood and reached out to Syd, putting a steadying hand on his shoulder. "Alright, Syd, I think we have asked enough questions. We thank you for what you've told us. But maybe we should be done now."

Syd grumbled some more and shoved Mid's hand off his shoulder.

"You push too hard Mid, you have always pushed too hard," he scolded, and Mid merely nodded as he helped the old man to his room.

~

Syd allowed us to stay the night, despite the incessant questions that had flustered him. Mid spoke to him for a while alone, and the old man seemed to calm down.

Mid returned from helping Syd to his room and handed us blankets and pillows to set up our makeshift beds for the night. I was slightly discouraged, realizing that the detour to talk to Syd had been rather unhelpful. But then I reminded myself that Syd's words had some truth to them the last time we'd come. So maybe the nonsense he spoke tonight would end up being like the previous. Maybe one day, it would just fall into place and make sense.

I sighed, realizing I was so impatient that it was hard for me to wait for the unfolding of things related to the curse. I just wished everything could make sense right when I needed them to.

It wasn't a surprise when I couldn't sleep that night. I maybe got an hour of shut-eye before I ended up staring at the ceiling. It was a futile attempt to try and sleep. Insomnia plagued me whether I was in Knadiel or in Eslecaster. It was a testament that no matter how hard I tried to run from something, it would end up just following me.

I crawled out of bed and headed for the door, seeking the refuge of midnight's serenity and starlit sky. When I stepped out into the night, it was warm, and the humid air fell across my skin like a comforting friend.

The fresh air was just what I needed. Bringing me a perspective that somehow lacked when in the sunlight.

I meandered over to the balcony and admired the city, the light of the moon casting blue shadows across the marble bridges below and making the water that gushed from the cliffs nearly black.

I tried to conjure the deep hatred I felt for the curse staring at the beautiful scenery, but I found it impossible. At that moment, I couldn't help but think that maybe I would never have had the chance to see Eslecaster or the Sethen Courts without it. I would've never met my friends from the Envoy. My mind wandered back to Theon. Then that thought inevitably made me think of Conland, and the ache in my chest returned. No, without the curse, I would never have the memories of that short time I had with either of them.

I had to face the idea that maybe I'd rather have had those brief memories than not have them at all.

I began thinking of my father and my mother. Why fate was such a cruel author in my story, I had no way of knowing. But I knew one thing for sure, and that was I couldn't give up because otherwise, all of their deaths would be in vain. All the friendships I had to leave, all the heartache I had to experience, it would have been futile. And that was just too unbearable. So I had to press on. And despite the frustration of Sydidel's words earlier that morning, I had to remain hopeful that one day the mysteries of this entire curse would somehow make sense.

"Is it as beautiful as you remember?" The voice startled me from my pensive thinking. I turned to see Mid walking towards me.

"More beautiful, I think," I said, trying to control the sudden nervousness in my stomach at the sight of him.

His cloak was off his shoulders, and he wore a simple grey shirt and black pants. The silver in his chest pulsed beneath the cotton fabric, and I focused on the light, trying to avoid looking at his eyes.

"It makes me envy those who were smart enough to run away here," he said, leaning casually up against the railing beside me.

Unsure what he meant, I looked into his eyes, searching his face for the meaning of his words.

"Runaway?"

"Eslecaster is mainly an immigrant city. That's why it has so many different people."

"So that's why Syd is here," I said, and Mid nodded.

"I think I told you once that he was my tutor as a child. He was also the Reminant that served our family. He was always a little eccentric, talking about leaving and escaping to a place of freedom. I guess it was only a matter of time until he actually did it."

"Hmmm. . . how did you know this was where he went?" I asked.

"He left me a letter, telling me if I ever needed him, this was where I could find him."

I thought back to our first time in this city.

"And you obviously went looking," I commented.

"Yes, you were there," he smiled, and my heart stuttered. I thought back to that time so long ago when I'd only known him as the stranger who had saved me. I couldn't help but think how much easier it was when I hadn't known him as the prince.

"I'm sorry if the second time around wasn't what you wanted either," I said quietly.

"I haven't given up hope yet. Syd appears to speak nonsense, but I've found that eventually, his words start to make sense. I'm just waiting for that moment to happen."

My mind immediately jumped back to a memory I had of black smoke rising from the ashes of where Aveladon used to be. *Yes,* I thought. *Maybe eventually, his words would be fulfilled again.*

"You know, I'm breaking all the rules talking to you right now," Mid suddenly said, fighting a smile.

I looked at him, my brow scrunching in confusion.

"What do you mean breaking the rules?"

"Dusane and I promised we wouldn't talk to you alone until you approached one of us first," he explained.

It took me a moment, but after I'd processed what he'd said, my mouth fell open slightly.

"You two made rules? Not to talk to me?"

"We both thought it best to let you mourn without any

distractions," he said seriously. I was still stunned, and for a moment, I just contemplated the two of them even speaking to each other and felt a weird feeling inside.

"Hey, don't take it the wrong way. We just didn't want to hurt you." His voice held a pain of its own as he said those words, and for the first time, I considered what it must have been like for them in those three months I'd been so distant and silent.

"I'm sorry, Mid," I whispered suddenly. He took a step towards me and looked about to touch me but then stopped himself.

"You have nothing to be sorry for. Oli told us about Obsidian and Elysian being related to you. I can only imagine how hard it would be to discover that your family is fighting against you."

"I didn't know how to reach out to either one of you," I explained. And it was the truth. I'd had times when all I wanted was to confess the truth about my family and feel Mid's arms around me, to have him sing a lullaby to me, or help me escape into a blissful sleep that would be painless. But then I also imagined Dusane holding me, his presence comforting me, his strength a tangible lifeline. And that was confusing, wanting the both of them, and too painful to consider hurting either of them. I just accepted that it was impossible to seek either of their comforts.

"I understand. I'm just glad you're doing better now," he said, the forgiveness in his voice was apparent, and I realized I didn't deserve it.

"Well, no more rules okay, I don't want you two to avoid talking to me."

"Maybe I'll hold off on telling Dusane that," he teased, and I reached out to shove his arm.

"Mid. . ." I warned, and he held up his hands in mock surrender.

"Consider him informed," he amended, chuckling. I rolled my eyes. "I've missed you," he suddenly whispered, the conversation taking a sudden somber turn. I bit my lip, feeling the butterflies return to my stomach in full force.

"I missed you too, Mid," I said, and it was the unavoidable truth. "And I'm sorry we never got to really talk after I came home. I know we haven't been able to catch up with everything that happened while I was away, and I know you're probably wondering about me becoming an Envorydian an—"

"Ehren," he breathed, his voice so full of emotion I stopped mid-sentence taken aback. "We will have plenty of time to catch up. I'm just glad you're okay."

"Why have you stayed?" I asked quietly. "Things have gotten so complicated. Don't you ever think I'm not worth all the trouble?"

He seemed to honestly consider the question.

"When the Ethydon battle ended and I found out you were missing, a lot of things became very clear to me. I remember weeks of wondering if you were dead. . ." He paused, and the pain in his voice was tangible. "Sa. . .Ehren, I have felt no greater pain in this world than thinking I'd lost you. The moment we said goodbye at the wedding, I knew that at least I could love you from afar, that even though I was being forced to marry someone else, I could still live in a universe where you existed."

I thought back to that moment when we'd said goodbye. I remember the kiss we'd shared, and I remember running away as if running would fix all the problems that had been created. How naive I'd been.

I saw his fist clench against the railing. "But the possibility that you would never exist at all. That was unbearable. And I vowed that I would never stop searching for you. Because I couldn't—" he paused "—no, wouldn't live in a world without you in it. Even if I spent the rest of my life looking for you, I would. Because the alternative was so much worse."

I lost my breath, feeling the sincerity in every word he spoke. I hadn't realized how much my disappearance must have affected him. And I felt guilty that I'd spent almost an entire year trying to push him from my mind in order to accept a greater responsibility—to cope with the reality I'd been faced with in the Sethen Courts. But I knew that if I had allowed myself to feel the total weight of losing him, I would've experienced a similar hopelessness. Still, I'd never allowed it to take hold of me in fear of the pain he was describing now.

"So when I found out you were alive, I knew that I could never stop fighting for you. And if I ever got the chance to see you again, I would do everything I could to prove that love to you." His eyes bore into mine, causing my cheeks to flush. I'd forgotten how much his gaze affected me.

"I'm not the same girl anymore," I whispered.

"I know," he said.

"And Dusane. . ."

"I know," he said, cutting me off. I guess it didn't need to be said. I still had my reservations. But he didn't seem to care about them.

I sighed. "And yet you still want me?" I asked, feeling somewhat defeated.

"Ehren, answer me one thing," He asked, and I could see the pleading in his eyes. "Do you still love me?"

I felt my heart skip a beat and my breath catch in my throat.

His emerald-scarlet eyes earnestly sought my face searching for the answer.

"You already know the answer to that," I whispered, averting my gaze. Of course, I still loved Mid. That was part of what was making this so hard.

"I want to hear you say it," he whispered gently. It wasn't a command. It was a plea.

"I love you, Mid," I said, so quietly I wondered if he'd even heard it. I felt tears prick the corners of my eyes. It was the absolute truth. *So why was everything still so difficult?*

"Then there's the answer. It isn't over. As long as you still love me, I'll be here. Fighting for you."

I blinked rapidly, trying to push back the tears and regain my composure.

"And what happens when one of us gets hurt in the end? What will have been the point of it all?"

Mid smiled gently as he reached out to wipe away one of the tears that had managed to leak onto my cheek.

"We will have learned to love." He put his hand back down to his side, and I was about to respond, but he gave me a small smile and started back towards the cottage. I was alone on the balcony then, and I was left to contemplate everything he'd said.

*We will have learned to love. . .*I sighed. I could only hope that it would be enough.

TEN

Diablo's whinny was the first thing to greet us when we returned to our camp. I stroked his neck and kissed his nose, feeling guilty for leaving him.

"I missed you too," I whispered.

Mid talked with the Ethydon guards informing them of our travels, and then it was decided we would pack up and get on the move towards Severesi.

It was the longest I'd ever been traveling, and I was already beginning to feel the weariness in my body. I forced myself to push aside thoughts of a warm bed back home and focused on the task at hand. I mounted Diablo, and soon we were in the deep of the alabaster trees.

I shivered into the white cloak around my shoulders, burying my gloved hands in Diablo's mane for extra warmth.

It was hours on horseback before we reached a stopping point.

"Let's take a break," one of the guards ordered. It was nearly dark at this point, and begrudgingly, we set up yet another temporary camp.

As I fiddled with the flaps on my tent, I heard boots crunching in the snow and knew someone was approaching.

"Need some help?" Dusane asked.

I hesitated, about to deny his assistance, but then I reminded myself I wasn't hiding away anymore.

"Sure."

He helped me tie the canvas to the tent poles, and then when we finished, we stood beside one another, an awkward silence stretching between us. Mid and the guards were sitting around the fire they had built and were talking amongst one another. This was probably the closest we would get to a private conversation.

I tried desperately to find the right words to say.

"Mid told me you're doing better," Dusane started.

My eyes widened. "He did?" I wasn't expecting that.

"Oddly enough, over the last three months, we have sort of come to an . . . understanding."

"You're friends?" I asked, my tone tinged with disbelief.

Dusane chuckled, the husky tone reminding me just how much I'd missed him. "I wouldn't go that far," his eyes were light with amusement.

I was glad to see he didn't seem to be mad at me, which made it easier for me to speak the words I'd meant to say for some time.

"I'm sorry, Dusane. I know deciding to stay was hard for you, and then I ignored both of you for three months and. . ."

"Ehren, you have nothing to be sorry for," His cerulean eyes were serious as he said this.

"You're not going to scold me, tell me I should've had better control of my emotions or something like that," I was only partly teasing. It was a big training point in the way of the Envoy. Having control over our minds, emotions, and actions. Without control, everything else would fall apart.

"Normally, I would say something like that if I was acting as your Captain right now, but I'm not."

"What are you then?" The question held more weight than I'd intended it to.

He reached out slowly to gently brush back a strand of hair from my face and tucked it behind my ear. Over the past three months, my hair had grown nearly to the length it was before it had been cut. As a result, it had been harder to tame, and I was seriously considering cutting it again.

"I'm someone who cares about you." His response sent my stomach into little flips. It wasn't as if he'd said he loved me or anything, but for Dusane, it was more than he usually displayed.

I thought about how only the night before Mid had told me he loved me, and I had said it back. Dusane and I had never said those words to each other. *So why was I so conflicted?* Shouldn't it be simple? Go with the person you love. But unfortunately, it wasn't simple at all. Even though we hadn't said we loved each other, I could hear it in the way he told me he cared for me.

Maybe it was difficult because he made me feel things that I was pretty sure meant I loved him. But it was so different from what I felt with Mid, so it was enough to make things very complicated.

"Thank you."

"Get some sleep, Envorydian," he said in his authoritative voice. But the playfulness in his eyes was unmistakable.

"Yes, Captain," I responded, fighting a smile.

~

The following day we rode on and discussed our plans for when we arrived in the main hub of Severesi.

"Iradence is much different from Eslecaster. We will have to change our strategy if we are going to roam the capitol undetected," Dusane said.

"What do you mean different?" I asked, trying to imagine what he could mean.

"The people in Iradence dress differently. They pride themselves on dressing. . . unusually," Dusane explained.

"The Mistings, yes I've heard of them," Mid commented.

My brow furrowed. "How do you both know so much about Severesi?"

"I have to know everything about the other kingdoms for political reasons," Mid explained.

"The Envorydains in Obscurum are very interconnected with those in Severesi. So I spent a lot of time there," Dusane replied.

My eyes widened. I forget Dusane was an Envoydian for the Obscurum kingdom. It was hard to imagine him once protecting the enemy we were fighting against now.

"Okay, so we have to dress differently. What's a Misting?"

"You'll see once we get into the city. We will all have to be Misted in order to blend in with the other civilians," Dusane said.

I tried not to panic about being "Misted," but it made me nervous for some reason. I remained on edge the whole rest of the way to Iradence. When we were a mile or two from the city's border, we halted our animals and dismounted.

"The guards will watch the camp and animals while we go inside. Once we are Misted, I will contact the man I know, who may or may not know the location of the blacksmith. Then we will go in search of her," Dusane said.

"What happens if we can't find her?" I asked, and Mid and Dusane exchanged a glance.

"Then we will return to the guards and head back to Knadiel," Dusane said, and then as if remembering something, he turned to the Ethydon guards traveling with us. "If we don't return after three weeks, send word to the kingdom that we have been killed or captured," Dusane instructed the guards. They nodded, and I felt my insides twist with worry.

"Are you sure they can't come with us?" I asked.

Dusane immediately shook his head. "We don't want to draw attention to ourselves. Us three in the city will be risky enough."

"How long should this take?" I asked. I couldn't completely hide the nervousness in my voice.

"If we're lucky, two days. If we're unlucky a week. If we're very unlucky. . . well, we won't return," Dusane said, not even bothering to deliver the news lightly.

"We will be fine, Ehren," Mid said, reaching out to touch my arm. But unfortunately, his reassuring words did little to relax me.

"Okay, let's just get this over with."

ELEVEN

Iradence was surrounded by colossal city walls. The front gates reminded me of what the city Asmede used to be like, only they were white like snow. They stood tall, towering into the clouds while a line of civilians superseded the entrance.

We pulled up the rear, and at first, I didn't notice anything different about those we stood in line with. Most of the people around us wore white cloaks, the hems muddied and soaked from the snow. But as I started to examine more closely, I noticed these people were even more disgruntled. Their expressions were downtrodden, and they all had circles beneath their eyes. Even their movements were slow, as if they were fatigued. I took an even closer inspection and noticed that every person we stood in line with had a red or green heart.

"Are these people Misted? I don't see a difference?" I whispered to Dusane beside me.

"No, Mistings are for the richer society," he whispered back, his eyes remaining straight ahead.

"So why are we being Misted? Can't we just blend in with these citizens?"

Dusane gestured towards my heart and then to Mid's.

"You'd stand out in a group of lowly Stone-Hearted with a heart like that."

"Right," I said, realizing once again how little I really knew about the whole system. In Aveladon, I'd never noticed that those who served me had different colored hearts and that their status depended on that. Dusane had explained to me that the color heart you had in some kingdoms could mean life or death. That red and green were considered low in power, blue and purple a slightly greater power, and silver and gold were considered the most powerful. I felt something unsettling watching the scene before me.

"Where are they all coming from?"

"I assume they are coming from the mines. Some travel ten miles on foot every day to the mines and back to the city to feed their families."

My eyes widened, and my heart sank nearly into my stomach. Aveladon, when it existed, didn't have a mine. Aveladon made a lot of trade with the other kingdom's and I wondered then if it was with Severesi.

"Why don't they leave or work somewhere else?"

Dusane's jaw clenched, and I could tell I'd said something that bothered him.

"There are only so many jobs you are allowed to have with a red or green heart. And you can't travel to another kingdom if you have no money. Also, in some circumstances, the kingdom won't let you leave. Not to mention finding a job somewhere else when all the jobs are occupied, it's a complicated process," Dusane said. We were nearing the front now, and I wanted to ask more questions but forced myself to stay quiet.

We were close enough that I could hear the guards that protected the entrance. Each person was asked for their city papers, and I felt a bolt of dread shoot through me. In Eslecaster, no one had stopped to ask us for documents.

We had no evidence of being Severesi citizens. I was about to tell Dusane to stop, but then we were up next, and I clenched my jaw shut, forcing myself to remain calm.

"Papers, please," one of the guards ordered.

I wondered if Dusane had papers we didn't know about, but then he turned his head, moving the hair from behind his ear, flashing the Envorydian symbol. The guard nodded and then looked at me. Quickly I lifted the sleeve of my cloak flashing the mark on my arm. Dusane motioned towards Mid before they could ask him for his identification.

"He's with us," was all Dusane said. The guard nodded then let us pass through.

I didn't understand why being Envorydians let us through, but I didn't have time to ask because we entered the city, and all my attention was focused on what I was seeing.

The city of living spirits. I'd heard the term. It was one of the things I'd actually paid attention to during my tutoring lessons. And now I knew exactly what that meant.

Buildings tall and crammed close together covered the streets, and they all looked to be made of ice. But this thick glasslike material wasn't see-through. Instead, it gave a distorted view of the interiors of the buildings. Blurred shadows were the only visible activity behind the walls and windows.

How they were built and how the architecture was maintained, I couldn't possibly understand. It appeared to be layer upon layer of clear, crystal glass. What made it all so magnificent was when someone walked past the buildings, the faint glow of someone's heart would reflect off the architecture and cause a shimmer of color to illuminate the ice-like walls of the buildings. It was the palest of reflections, but there were so many Stone-Hearted the colors bounced off the buildings frequently.

Then there were the people. Suddenly the term Misted made complete sense. Those roaming the streets appeared as if they had frost covering their hair and eyebrows, lips, and eyelids. The colors of their hair ranged from pale pinks to purples to light blues to pale greens. I didn't see any colors that weren't pastel. It was light, airy, angelic. They indeed looked like they were living spirits. It was the most unique fashion statement I'd ever witnessed.

We walked through the crowded streets, following Dusane. Some weren't Misted, but as I'd observed, they were civilians with lower-level hearts. The white cloaks didn't do very well at hiding the lights in our chests, and I worried someone might notice us. I followed close behind Dusane, trying not to gawk at our surroundings.

We were deep in the city at this point, and I wondered where Dusane was going when I heard the trumpets. The horns caused everyone in the streets to pause what they were doing. I looked at Dusane, fear tingling my nerves.

"It's okay, just keep your head down," Dusane seemed to know what was going on, and he urged us to follow where a crowd was forming along the street. We huddled between a group of civilians, and I could barely see over the heads of those around us.

The horns blared a happy, celebratory tune, and soon a

group of beautiful white Gracelings came trotting down the street, pulling a beautiful sleigh. I'd only ever seen the white, horned horses before guarding the gates to the Spirit Tree.

Severesi guards surrounded the entourage, and inside the carriage were two individuals. One was a man, his heart a bright gold. He was misted, all white appearing rather ghostly. He had a long white beard, and his skin was nearly translucent. His eyes were as white as the snow on the ground, and he stared at those around him with a rattling intensity. The woman next to him was Misted too, her hair long and white like the man's beard beside her. They blended so perfectly with the snow, their lips and eyebrows painted the same frost white as their hair. Beautiful white crowns graced both their heads, looking like they were made of icicles.

"Who are they?" I whispered to Mid beside me.

"That's the king and queen of Severesi. King Saerus, and Queen Livia."

I realized then that I'd seen the woman before. It was the same woman who had almost made an alliance with Obsidian.

"That's the same woman," I whispered to Mid, and his jaw clenched.

"I remember her," Mid replied.

We kept our heads down as best we could amongst the other civilians until the sleigh passed. The people in the streets waved white flags and cheered loudly for them. I shivered, realizing just how dangerous this was all of a sudden.

"I would really like to get off these streets, Dusane. Are we close?" I didn't know precisely where Dusane was headed. All I knew was we needed to be Misted, and then we would search for his friend who knew the blacksmith. I hoped he had a plan.

"We are almost there," Dusane said, and when the crowd

dispersed, we continued on through the streets until we turned down a lone road which was much quieter. The buildings weren't as tall as in the central part of the city, and I had a feeling we were getting further from the main hub.

Dusane stopped us at one building with a sign that read MISTINGS.

He grabbed the clear glassy handle and pushed open the door, ushering us inside.

It was surprisingly warm inside. The foyer we stood in had white marble, and a glassy chandelier hung from the ceiling. But it wasn't all white. There were green plants in some corners and a bright green couch on one wall. It was sleek, pristine, and smelled very fresh like lemons and soap.

"Welcome. How can we help you today?" A woman came from around the corner, her voice bright and unnervingly happy. She had dark skin that contrasted beautifully with her pale pink hair and light periwinkle eyebrows. Her dress was even the same periwinkle as her eyebrows, and her violet heart finished off the entire ensemble.

"I need these two to be Misted." Dusane gestured to Mid and me, and the woman clapped her hands together happily.

"Perfect, please come this way."

We followed after the woman down a long hallway, and as we walked, I took the opportunity to question Dusane.

"Why aren't you being Misted," I asked him.

"Because those I'm meeting with might not be able to recognize me if I was."

"Speaking of people recognizing us. Why did the gate guard let us in because we are Envorydians?"

"It's a universal law that Envorydians are allowed to cross borders to do their jobs."

"So basically, border guards turn a blind eye to any Envorydians?"

"Something like that," Dusane said. Which confirmed it was exactly like that.

I wanted to ask more questions, but I lost my train of thought when we suddenly entered a new room. It had rows of chairs, all seated in front of beautiful floor-to-ceiling mirrors. Four other people occupied seats, their hair and makeup being done, and I felt a nervous flutter at the thought of being Misted. I hated being pampered.

"Take a seat here, please." The woman gestured for me to take a seat in one of the chairs, and once I was seated, she proceeded to take Mid away. He winked at me before he was led across the room to another row of mirrors.

Dusane stayed by me, sitting on a velvet settee next to the mirror so he could face me.

Another woman appeared, and she greeted us politely.

"Hello, my name is Kalea. I'll be taking care of you today." She was Misted in pale green and orange colors. She began setting up her supplies on the vanity.

"I can't believe I'm doing this," I hissed at Dusane.

He laid back against the comfortable cushion of the seat, settling in as if readying himself for a long chat. He seemed so nonchalant, content even.

"It won't last long, a week or two maybe," he explained.

My eyes widened. "You mean I'll be Misted for two weeks?"

"It's a temporary look. I promise it will fade." It was weird to hear him speak like this, as if from experience.

Before I could respond, another woman came over to us with cups of Lush Fire and a bowl of beautiful white fruit. I had never seen anything like it, but she handed the fruit to me, and I realized suddenly how hungry I was. I took a chunk and popped it into my mouth, surprised by the sudden burst of sweet flavor that flooded my tastebuds. My eyes widened.

"Whoa," I said, and Dusane flashed me a knowing smile before popping two into his mouth when the woman offered the fruit to him.

Kalea came up behind me then and started to brush my hair.

"Does it hurt?" I asked her.

Kalea laughed. "Oh no, dear, it won't hurt a lick."

I stayed quiet then and let Kalea work. The first thing she had me do was change out of my cloak and black fighting suit into a plain white shift dress behind the mirror, which was actually a dressing room. I did as she instructed but kept my amulet on to be safe. Then she began washing my face, neck, and arms. She even washed my feet, scrubbing mercilessly between my toes. Soon all the dirt and grime from our journey was gone, and I felt clean for the first time since we left Knadiel. It was an awkward sensation being so clean, and I felt somehow naked.

Next, she prepped my hair and plucked my eyebrows, which was a little painful but not unendurable. Then she buffed my nails and started to paint a clear coating across my lips and eyes. Then she squirted some clear stuff onto her hand and applied it to my hair. It smelled awful, and I coughed a couple times at the stench.

I couldn't help but glare at Dusane as I watched the slight twitch of his mouth at my discomfort.

"Don't look at me like that," I growled at him.

In the mirror's reflection, I saw Kalea smile to herself as she massaged my scalp.

"It's just amusing how much you hate being pampered.

Shouldn't you be used to this?" Dusane asked. I guessed he was referring to my princess lifestyle of expense and leisure.

My eyes narrowed even further. "Surprisingly, no, I've always hated it. I think it's ridiculous."

"Hmm. . ." he mused, and I realized I was probably a mystery to him. A princess that despised being pampered. I wondered if he thought less of me for not appreciating the exemplary lifestyle I was blessed with. *How do I explain to someone who isn't royal what it is like to be royal?*

After Kalea coated my hair with the gross smelling liquid, she reached for another bottle and began mixing something together on a palette.

Then, she turned me around, not allowing me to look into the mirror, and began painting more stuff into my hair. This went on for hours. She moved from my hair to my eyebrows, then my lips, and then my eyelids. Then she painted my nails and my toes. I was getting extremely antsy by the time Kalea finally stopped fiddling with me.

"Are we done now?" I asked, exasperated.

"Almost," she said, "We have to dress you now." She helped me down from the chair and ordered me not to look in the mirror as I walked towards the dressing room. She closed the door behind me, and I turned to see the light blue dress on the hook. I pulled it on, and the smooth, silky fabric felt heavenly against my clean skin.

I had to admit that it was a stunning piece of clothing. I hadn't been in something so fancy since the night of my sister's almost wedding. It was a sheer baby blue fabric with a straight neckline and decorative bodice. The tulle skirt fell to the floor and billowed around my feet. I slipped into some pale blue lace-up boots that they'd left out for me and then dared go outside and take a look in the mirror.

Dusane looked up at me from his seat when I stepped out, and I watched his eyes widen. I went to stand in front of the mirror where Kalea was nearly jumping up and down.

"You look beautiful, darling," she said excitedly.

The person looking back at me was definitely not me.

My hair was a very pale light blue and curled in ringlets around my shoulders. My eyebrows were the same soft pastel blue as my hair, along with the makeup covering my lips and lids. My skin had been dusted with light blue sparkles making my skin glitter when I moved. I looked angelic and entirely unrecognizable. My intense sapphire eyes and bright golden heart were a stunning contrast to the light blue covering nearly every square inch of me.

"Kalea, you did an amazing job," I whispered, unable to ignore the magnificence of her work.

"It's my pleasure," she assured me, then she seemed to remember something. "I almost forgot, your jewelry!" She took off down another hallway leaving Dusane and me alone for a moment.

"You look beautiful," he said, walking over to where I was standing. He looked me up and down and then stopped on my eyes.

"This better be worth it," I warned. "I can't fight in this dress."

"Well, the goal is not to have to fight at all."

"If you're trying to keep me from fighting. . ."

"I'm not. Trust me. This disguise is just necessary for the job," Dusane assured me. "It would be suspicious for someone of your colored status not to be dressed like this here." He reached out to touch one of the light blue locks of my hair that once used to be stark black.

"What is it?" I asked, watching him admire the strand of hair far longer than was normal.

"Your hair grew out again," he observed thoughtfully.

I nodded, pursing my lips. "One time, you told Rouix not to cut it. Why was that?" The memory came back to me as if it had happened yesterday.

His face remained serious as he looked up from the piece of hair between his fingers, and he stared into my eyes. He reached out then, allowing his fingers to comb through my hair gently, so he could bury his fist deep within the blue curls.

"Because if you cut it too short, I couldn't do this." He tightened his fingers ever so slightly and gently tugged my head back, so I was now looking up at him, our mouths suddenly very close.

A warm, fluttering sensation exploded inside my stomach, and I lost my breath.

Time seemed to stop, and I was unable to move as his gaze held me captive.

"Midennen finished several minutes ago. He's outside waiting for us." His fingers abruptly left my hair. And just like that, the spell was broken.

I looked around the room, and sure enough, Mid was nowhere to be seen.

Just then, Kalea reappeared, holding a set of jewels in her hands. "This should do the trick." She secured a beautiful bracelet to my wrist and diamond earrings to my ears. After putting on the jewelry, Dusane handed Kalea a pouch of coins. She thanked him, then led us up to the front.

Mid was waiting there for us, and I didn't recognize him at first.

They'd Misted him in colors of silver to match his heart. His silvery hair and eyebrows made his tan skin pop, and he was even dressed in a fitted silver tunic and pants. He looked very handsome, Misted. When he saw me, he had a similar reaction as Dusane. His emerald-scarlet eyes widened, and he appraised my dress and hair.

"You're stunning," he breathed, not even bothering that Dusane was standing right next to us. I blushed and hurried to avert the attention away from me.

"We should get going. We need to find a place to stay for the night," I said.

Both men nodded, averting their gazes.

Dusane pushed open the door, revealing the dark street we'd come in from now blanketed in darkness. We thanked the women at the Misting shop and then headed out into the night.

TWELVE

It was significantly darker now, and the glass buildings weren't reflecting much of any light at all now that the sun was down. Dusane seemed less insistent on sticking to the shadows now that Mid and I were misted. We followed him down many streets until we came upon a busy road filled with tent vendors. Small fires were spread out between them, many people surrounding their flames trying to get warm. Dusane stopped at one tent selling meat and vegetables and passed him several coins.

"We'll take two bags of produce. . ." As Dusane traded with the vendor, I turned my eyes to a young woman and her child. They were curled up in the shadows, wrapped in a series of blankets that looked to be doing little to help keep out the cold. It was freezing here. I could see my breath every time I let out a shivering breath, and I couldn't imagine how this woman and child felt. Something in my heart ached at the sight of them, and before I knew what I was doing, I was walking over to them. Bending down, I came face to face with the young woman.

She looked at me with wide blue eyes as if not expecting me to approach her. She hugged her infant child closer to her chest, appraising me with hesitancy.

Without a word, I reached for the bracelet on my wrist and passed the sparkling jewels to her.

"I can't take this," she immediately said, shaking her head.

"Please," I begged, and after another small moment of hesitation, she tucked the bracelet away into her cloak. I gave her a weak smile before straightening and returning to Dusane and Mid.

They were holding several bags of food, both watching me.

"What?" I asked, immediately defensive. Neither of them said anything. "Look, she needed it more than me. I'm sure that bracelet wasn't doing anything to fool anyone anyway. This dress is enough." I wondered if they disapproved of me giving away part of my disguise.

Dusane shook his head and passed me a small bag filled with what looked to be potatoes.

"I'm not upset," was all he said before he started down the street again. I looked at Mid in puzzlement before he gave me a small smile and reached out with his free hand to squeeze my shoulder.

"You know what I think," he said, and I narrowed my eyes at him, not knowing where this was headed. "I think your heart was made of gold long before you became Stone-Hearted."

My expression went blank. That wasn't what I was expecting. I blushed and started after Dusane, uncomfortable with the sudden praise. I hadn't done it for praise. I had done it because that woman and child were obviously suffering, and it was because of the twisted color system that existed in our world.

I hugged the sack of potatoes tighter to my gold chest as we wove through the shivering groups of Severesi civilians and tent vendors into a deeper part of the city. Eventually, we pulled up to a rundown brick building with a sign on the window that read *Vacancy.*

I figured the glass buildings we'd seen were an expensive production, reserved for the beautiful heart of the city. Away from the center of Iradence, on the outskirts, people were not nearly as opulent.

Dusane led us into the rundown building, and inside was a roaring fire and a small desk. A woman sat behind it, reading a book. When she looked up at the sound of our entrance, her face turned into a scowl.

"How can I help you?" she asked, obviously only asking us out of obligation.

"We need a couple of rooms," Dusane requested.

The woman gestured with her hand to the ceiling overhead. "We only have one available."

Dusane sighed, then nodded, passing the woman some money. "We will take it," he said. The woman didn't reply. She simply gave Dusane a single key from a hook on the wall behind her and gestured towards the stairs on her left.

"Your room is on the second floor, two doors down." She opened her book again, clearly dismissing us.

Silently we climbed the stairs, and when we found the door, Dusane fiddled with the lock for a moment before pushing it open with a rough shove of his shoulder. The hinges squeaked, and on the other side was revealed an incredibly quaint room. It was equipped with two small beds, a dainty round dining table with two rickety chairs, and a very small sofa.

"You guys get settled in. I'll be back in a couple hours," Dusane set the key on the table and started for the door.

"Wait," I said. "Where are you going?"

Dusane turned, his eyes expectant. "I'm going to meet with a friend of mine. He may know where the blacksmith is. I won't be long." He stepped into the hallway.

"Let us come with you," I argued.

"Trust me, it's better if you stay here. He doesn't particularly like. . . unexpected visitors. Especially ones he doesn't know." He gave me a rare smile and reached out to squeeze my hand softly. "Don't worry about me. I'll be back soon."

The door closed with an ungraceful squeak, and I could immediately feel the atmosphere change as it was suddenly only Mid and me inside the flat.

THIRTEEN

"Are you hungry?" Mid asked unexpectedly as he rifled through the bags of food we'd purchased. He began sorting out the items onto the little table.

"Very," I admitted. I tentatively sat in one of the old chairs across from him and watched as he pulled a small knife from his belt and began to chop up some vegetables. "How do they even grow that stuff here?" I asked, looking at the fresh produce with puzzlement.

"I assume with Stone-Hearted power," Mid said, his focus remained on the tomato he was slicing.

"Where did you learn to cook?" I asked, eyeing skeptically the way he was using the knife so expertly.

He peeked up from beneath his lashes, his emerald-scarlet eyes met mine, and a handsome half-smile tugged on the side of his mouth.

"Liony taught me."

"Hmm. . . why am I not surprised?" I pursed my lips. I was

making small talk. Trying not to worry about Dusane out in that strange city, possibly putting himself in danger. I forced myself to calm down. *He'll be fine, I* told myself. *It's Dusane. He can take care of himself.*

"Something about making me a more well-rounded person or something like that," he chuckled, and I couldn't help but smile.

"I wish cooking was something someone had taught me, instead of all the other useless political knowledge I was forced to obtain."

"What, you didn't find Introduction to Imperial Correspondence interesting?" A teasing smirk grew on his lips.

"Far from it. I was so bored listening to my tutor once that I literally jumped out the window." I couldn't help it. The memory made me giggle.

"Jumped out the window?" He looked up, his eyes wide with curious amusement.

"I was only on the second level, and the shrubbery caught my fall, but yes, I did."

His head tilted back slightly as he let out a hearty laugh.

"I commend your escape. You are much more dedicated than I ever was. The only thing I can say I ever did in that class was sleep."

"Oli was so angry with me. I think he actually said he was going to kill me." I bit my lip, trying to contain another laugh.

"Oh, you think a verbal scolding is bad? Shar made me run." Mid shook his head.

"Run?"

"Around the entire castle. If he was really angry, he'd make me do it twice."

"Why does that not surprise me either?" I rolled my eyes, thinking about Shar's personality.

"Liony was the only one that could ever get him to back off of me, still is the only one that can talk him down."

"So she's like a sister to you then?" I asked, reaching across to grab a small potato chunk to pop it into my mouth. "Liony?"

"Yeah, she's family. Sometimes I feel I have a better relationship with her than even my own sister," he said, and I raised my eyebrow in surprise.

"You and Embrosine don't have a good relationship?" I realized I was prying after the words left my mouth, and I shook my head. "Sorry, you don't have to answer that."

"No, I don't mind. Embrosine is a wonderful sister, but she's a lot older than me, and we don't have much in common."

"How much older?" I asked. I assumed Mid was around Jasper's age, but I'd never really asked him. It didn't really matter that much, considering our kind didn't age for such a long time, but I was still curious.

"She's about ten years older, and if you're asking how old I am, I've only been Stone-Hearted for three years," he smiled, and I blushed, seeing he'd caught my meaning. So he was twenty-one, and I'd been right. He was right near Jasper's age.

"Worried I was a hundred?" he pressed, grinning. I rolled my eyes at him.

"Maybe if you were, you'd have learned some manners by now and be less obnoxious," I teased, and he chuckled.

"No amount of aging is going to tame me, I'm afraid," he winked.

"A girl can dream," I said.

He teasingly chucked a small carrot at me, and I caught it easily.

"So why was she so busy?" I asked. All teasing vanished as I reinitiated the conversation about his sister.

"When I was a kid, she was always traveling back and forth to the Isles. I didn't see her that often and when I did, she was always wrapped up in some meetings. I spent more time with Shar, which ended up resulting in spending more time with Liony."

"And your parents? What were they like growing up?"

"I was always closer to my mother. I didn't much like the ocean, and my father was a very adamant sailor. He took me hunting whenever his schedule permitted because he knew I didn't like the water like my sister, but I could tell he would have rather been on the sea. My mother spent most of her time with me."

"You don't like the ocean?"

"I'm sort of scared of it. . ." He was suddenly very focused on the vegetables in front of him.

"You're scared of the ocean?" I asked, not believing Mid could be scared of anything.

"I fell in once, and it was quite traumatizing. I'll have you know." He narrowed his eyes at me.

"I'm not making fun of you, just surprised," I tried to assure him, holding my hands up in mock surrender.

"Yeah, well, Embrosine loves the sea, so she spent a lot of time out on the water with my father. Especially because of her travels to the Isles so often, I think she had to learn to love it."

"What is Embrosine's title anyway?"

"She's princess of the Isles. She and her husband are heirs to the Isles of Arradale. Once Ashelor's parents die, they will rule that land."

"Embrosine seemed to think the Isles were safer for Sunn." I tried to imagine an island being any safer than Knadiel.

Mid nodded his head.

"Obscurum doesn't have an extensive fleet. They'd need lots of ships to defeat the Isles, and I don't think it is King Elysian's main target because it's so far, and they keep to themselves. He's pretty much stayed away from them. She's much safer there for sure."

"And so when your parents die. . ." I trailed off.

"I'll be king of Ethydon," he said, suddenly very focused again on the food in front of him. "That's assuming Ethydon ever gets rebuilt."

"Hmm. . . sounds like a lot of pressure," I said. Jumping down from the stool, I took the cooking pot he'd finished filling with meat and vegetables and carried it over to the hearth. We started a fire and placed the stew carefully over the flames to begin cooking.

I sat on the sofa, settling into the cushions, and tucked my feet beneath me.

"Can I ask you something?" Mid suddenly asked. He took a seat on the other end and propped his arm on the back of the couch.

"Sure."

"Why did you choose to become an Envorydian? Why didn't you just wait for someone to come and rescue you?"

I pursed my lips, not expecting things to take this turn but knowing it was bound to come up at some point.

"I guess I just realized I didn't want to be useless anymore."

He stayed quiet, so I assumed he wanted me to keep going.

"I didn't know if anyone was going to come for me. And that scared me, but what scared me most was that I would return home, and I'd continue to be locked away in a castle. And I knew that if I became an Envorydian, I just might be able to help."

Mid looked at me intently, his eyes searching my face. "I was never more surprised than to see you in that arena."

"Trust me, I was surprised too," I said, remembering the moment we'd locked eyes during the fight.

"I thought the worst when I saw you facing off against those other Stone-Hearted. I assumed you weren't in there by your own free will. . ."

"You helped me," I said, remembering back to my contender who had fallen with the illusion of pain. "Which was against the rules, I might add." I gave him a teasing smile.

"I honestly thought you needed me." He shook his head, laughing to himself. "But I quickly realized you didn't need me at all. You were more than capable of handling yourself in there."

His words were like a healing balm against the many wounds of faithlessness I'd inflicted upon myself.

"I knew you had something in you when I met you. Something fiery. . ." He trailed off. "I didn't think I could fall more in love with you, but I was wrong."

I blushed and looked down to tug on the hem of my shirt. "Well, you're the first person to see my new title as a good thing,"

"Oli is just protective," Mid said, realizing quickly who I was referring to.

"Yes, he is," I said while standing from the couch to check the stew. It wasn't done, so I returned to my seat. It was weird to simply sit and be together. It was oddly normal, and felt. . . nice. "So you know what I was doing while I was away. What about you?" I asked, gazing into the hearth. I used to enjoy watching fire. I found it hypnotic and soothing. Now it reminded me of the Spirit Tree, and it wasn't a comfortable memory.

"The first couple weeks, we searched for you and Sunn. Then we all set off to find the new location for Ethydon and Aveladon, and eventually, we laid the groundwork for building. Then I went off to find the compass."

"What was it like?" I asked, not really knowing what in particular I was asking about.

"It was. . . an interesting time," he admitted, not saying anything else.

"Is that all I'm going to get?" I asked, trying not to show how curious I was and failing. He chuckled and leaned back into the couch cushions a little further. His hair had grown out, and the soft curls were barely beginning to touch across his forehead. He gazed at the fire, getting that faraway look in his eye again.

"I already told you, it was hard not knowing what happened to you." His jaw clenched, and I felt suddenly guilty. "And I used illusions to cope." He seemed embarrassed he'd said it aloud.

"What do you mean?" I asked, but he quickly shook his head.

"Nothing, it's stupid." He laughed nervously and ran a hand through his hair.

"Mid, tell me," I said.

He sighed in defeat. An emotion in his eyes I couldn't quite read. "At one point, I thought that the only way I would be able to see you was if I imagined you." He said it so quietly I had to lean closer to hear.

"Did it help?" I asked but then mentally berated myself for asking such a stupid question.

"Well, the thing with illusions is I can control what they do and say. The illusion you is definitely more agreeable." He smiled, and I laughed nervously, trying to imagine it. "But it did help for a time." He slowly reached across the space between us, taking my hand in his. He caressed my palm slowly, his gaze fixed on the delicate lines of my skin. "I could hold your hand." He laced his fingers with mine. "Feel the heat of your skin." His eyes lifted from where he gazed at our entwined fingers, and suddenly, he was looking deeply into my eyes again. I had stopped breathing a moment ago. I could only stare back, transfixed by him. "It was enough for a time until the reality set in that none of it was real."

His fingers left mine abruptly, and he leaned back into the cushions again as if he hadn't just caressed my hand in the most intimate way anyone had ever done.

"Well, I'm sorry the real me is disappointing." Without his hand in mine, I felt suddenly empty.

"I'm not disappointed," he said thoughtfully. "I'd take the real you any day."

I blushed, and in an attempt to hide the red in my cheeks, I changed the subject. "The stew is probably done now." I took the escape to go and grab some bowls and spoons from the table. Once I filled both our bowls, I handed Mid his portion, and then we ate in silence. The only sound for many minutes was the soft clinking of spoons against ceramic. When we both finished, Mid cleaned out our dishes and stuffed them back into his pack before he came back to sit beside me on the sofa again.

"You and Shar seemed to have become friends while you were away," Mid suddenly said.

"I guess you could say that." I was suddenly reminded of the secrets Shar had kept from me. I know we'd sort of made up, but I was not entirely convinced I'd forgiven him yet.

"I've known Shar for a long time, and he's definitely not the easiest person to get along with," Mid said, and it was nice to talk to someone who knew more about Shar's character.

"It took me a long while to get his approval." I thought back on how hard the first moments of our relationship had been in the Courts.

"Once he warms up to you, he's not so bad," Mid said, still smiling. "You may not believe this, but Shar wasn't always so cold."

"You're right. I don't believe you," I said, laughing. It was pretty hilarious to even imagine Shar without his grumpiness. It was such a far reach of an idea it was funny.

"Over the years, something has happened to him. He's gotten harder. I guess time will do that. But if you get him to relax, he's actually pleasant to be around."

I thought back to the night in the Drego when we all went to the Galloway fight and then to dinner afterward. It was a rare moment, but I had seen Shar relax a tad, and he *had* been more pleasant.

Then I thought about the secret I knew about Shar that Mid didn't and knew there was a deeper problem than just being able to relax that contributed to Shar's cold demeanor. I wished that I could tell Mid, knew I probably should. I hated when Shar had withheld the truth about my father, and now I was doing the exact same thing to Mid. I felt a surge of guilt and told myself that if Shar didn't tell him about Embrosine soon, I would.

"You should probably get some rest," Mid said abruptly.

I was startled from my thoughts, realizing I'd dazed off.

"I would but, I won't be able to sleep knowing Dusane is out there," I admitted.

"Let me help you sleep," Mid immediately offered, and I blushed. For some reason, when Mid got inside my mind, it felt somehow intimate. . . and when things got intimate with Mid, I felt like I was cheating on Dusane. It was a tricky balance, trying to understand my feelings for the two of them, and at the same time, not getting too close.

"It's okay really. . ." I started to say.

"I know you haven't been sleeping well," he said gently.

"Who told you that," I snapped, cutting him off. For some reason, I didn't want Mid to know about my sleeping problem. Maybe it was because it was a weakness of mine. I didn't know the exact reason, but it bothered me.

"Does it matter?" he asked softly, standing from the sofa.

"I don't need anyone's help Mid, I can—"

"Ehren—" he interrupted, sitting on the edge of one of the beds and gesturing to the spot beside him, "—come here."

A chill went down my spine.

He never said my name like that.

It wasn't teasing or mocking, but a warm caress. I took in a sharp breath, trying to find a comeback and coming up blank. *Why wasn't I protesting?*

When I couldn't think of any words to retort, I slowly stood from the sofa and walked over to the bed. I sat down next to him, and we stared at each other for a moment before he pulled back the sheets gesturing for me to climb in.

I shyly moved beneath the covers and laid my head on the pillow. When I was settled, he proceeded to move them up and over me. He had to lean in closer to do this, and I got a whiff of his pine scent. It was rather intoxicating. He smelled so wonderful.

"Is it just me, or did that feel good?" he suddenly whispered.

"What?" I asked, blushing as if he could see right through me and somehow read my thoughts.

"Talking," he explained.

Immediate relief flooded me. "Yeah, it did. . ."

He stood and reached out to brush a strand of hair behind my ear. I was about to say something when suddenly, the golden light from his hand fell against my face, and I could feel myself being pulled away into one of his illusions.

"Sweet dreams, Ehren."

I considered fighting his power but selfishly wished for sleep after so long of not having it that I willingly allowed myself to drift away, falling quickly into the sea of dreams that awaited me.

FOURTEEN

"What do you mean she's gone," I nearly shrieked.

"Exactly what it means, she's gone," Dusane nearly growled. "She disappeared a couple years back, and now he's unsure of her location." He looked defeated, tired. The circles under his eyes were evident. I felt guilty knowing he'd had a rough night, and I, on the other hand, had slept like a baby after Mid had helped me sleep. I'd dreamed of wildflower fields and white sand beaches all night.

Dusane had just returned from meeting with his friend early that morning, and it had been a dead end. Whoever he'd met with didn't know where the blacksmith was, and we were right back where we started.

"Well, what do we do now?" Mid asked. His face was set into a serious scowl. He rubbed his forehead as if attempting to rub away a headache.

"I have another plan, but it's dangerous," Dusane said.

"How dangerous," I pressed.

"Moderately dangerous," Dusane gave an exasperated smile, and I groaned.

"Okay, what is it," Mid asked, impatient.

"I know a couple of Envorydians in this area that might know where the blacksmith is. I didn't want to have to visit with them, but it seems we have no choice."

"Why would meeting with other Envorydians be dangerous?" I asked.

"Envorydians outside the courts are different from those you met at the academy. They're more lethal, they kill for a living, and they don't follow the mantra of peace."

"Well, if they're the only ones that may know where to find the blacksmith, I don't see another way," Mid interjected.

"I had a falling out with them before I was sent to the Courts, so they may not want to help me," Dusane said. I could hear a hesitancy in his tone and knew that this was serious just by that slip of emotion alone.

"What do we have to do?" I asked.

"The only way I see this working is if I pretend to work for you," he said, looking pointedly at me. "We go to them with you alongside me and tell them that you want information on the blacksmith. You give them money, and then hopefully, they will tell us where the blacksmith is."

"Why do I have to give them the money?" I asked.

"Because Envorydians always work for someone. Also, they know I've been banished to the Courts. It would raise too much suspicion if I suddenly showed up and went searching for the blacksmith on my own. It's better if you pose as my proprietor or "client," as they like to call it. That way, they think you're interested in the blacksmith and that you're only using me to get to her. If they think I'm working alone, things could get ugly."

My brow furrowed in confusion. Then, as if seeing I was still not fully comprehending, Dusane explained further.

"Let's just say none of them have a reason to trust me, and they will take the first chance they get to come after me if they think I'm a threat."

"Alright, what is my part in all of this then?" Mid asked.

"You'll stay outside while we work out the negotiation. Keep an eye out for anything suspicious. Can you do that?"

Mid nodded reluctantly and sighed. "Yes, I can do that."

A wave of newfound anxiety came over me. I didn't like the way Dusane said these Envorydians had a "falling out" with him. I tried to subdue the worry I was starting to feel, but it was loud and hard to ignore.

What if they didn't listen?

~

Dusane could only guess where his 'old friends' would be that night, and apparently, the most probable location required us to travel back into the main streets of Iradence. The building came into view and illuminating yellow candlelight from inside the glass walls and windows. Misted Stone-Hearted traveled in and out the front doors, laughing and stumbling into one another as if they were intoxicated. It was then that I realized it was a pub.

"Are you sure this is the place?" I whispered. We had taken refuge around the corner of another building. One street lamp a couple feet away gave us some light, but we were mostly hidden in the shadows as we prepared to head inside.

"This is a common pub for them to meet. It's our best bet," Dusane assured me.

"There's a decent spot across the street for me to keep watch," Mid said.

"If you see something suspicious, knock on the south window four times. We'll escape out the back if necessary," Dusane instructed Mid.

"Be safe," I told Mid as he stood to leave.

Mid nodded, then disappeared into the darkness, leaving Dusane and me in the dim light of the alley.

"Ehren," Dusane whispered earnestly to me. Even in the shadows, I could see the worry creasing his brow.

"What's wrong?" I didn't like the tone of his voice. Dusane didn't usually waver in his confidence. And the slightest sliver of doubt shouted loudly that something was wrong.

"I need you to do something for me," he said. His blue eyes were intense as he held my gaze.

"Anything," I agreed immediately, not realizing that such an answer could have serious consequences.

"Do you remember when I told you that the types of Envorydians here aren't like the ones in the Courts?"

I nodded.

"The person you're about to see me become is not the person you know. Promise me you'll remember that." The plea in his voice made my skin prickle.

"I promise," I agreed, more anxiousness forming a rock in my gut.

The Envorydians in the court were the minority, and the Envorydians in the kingdoms didn't follow the ancient customs that the small group lived by in the Courts. Dusane said that he hadn't known there was another way until he met those in the Sethen Courts. I thought about the surprise and fear that flashed across the faces of those I'd loved when I'd told them I was an Envorydian. I knew the Envorydians as a peaceful, loyal guild. But it seemed that the rest of the realm didn't see them that way. I shivered thinking about what Dusane could've been without the mantra of peace that was ingrained in him now, and I suddenly worried what side of him I might see tonight. . .

"Thank you. Now remember, less talking the better," he reminded me.

I nodded. My hands began to sweat, and I quickly wiped them on the skirt of my dress.

Dusane tugged us from the shadows, and all uncertainty left his features, and his expression hardened with determination.

I couldn't help but peek at the shadowy corners in search of Mid as we walked, wondering if he was watching us at that very moment as we neared the door to the pub. I hoped he wouldn't have to return to Ethydon and deliver bad news. I could only pray this meeting went well.

I forced myself to walk swiftly and with an air of confidence. Reminding myself of the facade Dusane needed me to create. I was his client. I needed to appear businesslike. Inside I felt anything but confident, but I forced myself to keep my shoulders back, and my head held high as we came face to face with the man outside the pub's front entrance.

"Name please," the man asked. He was nearly two feet taller than Dusane. He was misted with colors of silver, matching his silver heart. His muscles bulged beneath the shirt he wore, and I noticed a weapons sheath and an impressive sword hilt sticking out from his waist. He raised one silvery eyebrow as Dusane took a couple seconds to respond.

"Phantom," Dusane said.

I was confused but did well to hide my facial expressions. I had never heard the name but assumed it must be a code to help us get inside.

The guard's jaw clenched, and he cleared his throat.

"One moment." The guard slipped inside, and I turned to give Dusane a questioning look.

His eyes remained fixed on the door, he didn't turn to me, and I assumed he was trying to focus on staying in character.

When the door opened again, the guard didn't look as confident. Wariness creased his brow.

"I've heard of you before. Your name isn't a pleasant one around here." The man was trying to be stern, but I didn't miss the quiver in his voice.

"I mean no trouble," Dusane quickly combated—calm and collected as ever.

"Do the other Envorydians know you?" the guard asked, his eyes flitting towards the door. They must be inside then.

"I assure you, they know me very well," Dusane insinuated.

The guard pursed his lips then nodded. "I'll be keeping an eye on you," he warned, but it wasn't compelling. I was immediately confused about why someone so much larger in size and someone entirely unknown to Dusane would be afraid to let him into the pub. The fear of seeing this *other* side of Dusane returned.

The guard reluctantly opened the door, and then we stepped inside.

All eyes turned to us as we entered.

The room had a musty air, smoke floated throughout the air, and I felt myself getting dizzy from the fumes as I breathed in. It was sickly sweet, like candy. The pale pastels of the individuals in the room looked as if they were floating amongst the clouds of smoke in the room, and I had an odd idea that I was in some sort of twisted afterlife. Glazed eyes looked at us, and I could see they were wide and filled with fear.

I was more than a little confused as we passed the tables and heard small gasps as we walked by. I began to feel self-conscious of the attire the Mister had put me in. But I realized after several moments of seeing the shocked faces and hearing audible gasps from the dozens of pale lips it wasn't me they were looking at. It was Dusane.

A thousand questions raced through my mind, and I wanted so badly to understand. But I continued to play along, confident that I would soon find out the reason for the tangible tension that was as thick as the smoke in the room.

There were only three dark dressed individuals in the entire pub. They sat together at a table—demons among angels. They wore dark, thick clothes, a familiar sight that I was used to. The black leather material and weapons belts made them stand out amongst the angelic figures filling the pub.

Dusane swiftly strode over to an empty chair at the table and sat down. There were no extra chairs I could see nearby, so I stood off to the side, trying to remain statuesque in an attempt to be confident and quiet as we'd rehearsed.

"What a surprise." One Envorydian broke the tension. He wasn't misted like the others. His hair was a dark brown, his eyes nearly black. His heart was pulsing a soft green color, and he smiled at Dusane, his dark red lips spreading across a striking set of white teeth. He was rather eerie.

The three Envorydian's glanced at me briefly, but they were quick to pretend I wasn't there. And I was content to remain invisible unless Dusane needed me.

"Jade, it's good to see you again," Dusane said while flashing a self-satisfied smirk in his direction.

"You've got some serious guts showing up here," the other Envorydian added. This man was seated next to Jade, his hair misted a light purple color. And what I was now realizing seemed to be the fashion. His eyes were a similar purple shade along with his heart.

"Oh come on, Deadshiv, don't be like that," Dusane chided. The tone of voice didn't even sound like him.

"I'm curious, how did you escape?" The last Envorydian queried. His light red hair and red heart were bright against his pale complexion. His crimson eyes reminded me of a rabid creature, a rat maybe. The tattoos on his skin weren't typical dark ink. They matched his skin, more like a branding than a tattoo. He was a scarred canvas of symbols—his entire body and face covered in them. I couldn't stop the shiver that ran up my spine.

It wasn't hard to see that these Envorydians were different.

"You were never one for reunions, Bloodstreak." Dusane shook his head, still grinning playfully. But it wasn't an innocent grin. Something dark lurked behind his smile. And it scared me to see the quiet confidence that usually surrounded him be turned into an outward mocking that was obviously sinister and calculating.

"Phantom? Is it really you?" Abruptly a shrill voice jumped into the conversation. All eyes turned to see a waitress coming to the table, a tray of Lush Fire in her hands.

She was stunning. Misted light pink, her frosty pink hair cascading in beautiful ringlets down her back. She wore a scandalous dress with a swooping neckline showing off her red heart and large breasts. Her eyes were a beautiful pink color, matching the hue of her lips and cheeks. She set the drinks on the table and abruptly sat in Dusane's lap. Wrapping her arms around his neck, she leaned in and planted a deep kiss on his lips.

I was so shocked my jaw almost dropped. But I somehow managed to stay composed, allowing only my fist to clench at my side.

Dusane didn't fight the kiss, and something twisted angrily in my chest when I watched his hand reach up and tangle into her long pink locks. His other hand reached out to grip her bare thigh, no doubt leaving finger indentations on her pale skin. A deep throaty growl came from Dusane's throat, and when he broke the kiss, he leaned in to playfully nip the girl's throat.

"Rosie, what a pleasant surprise," he purred. I felt nauseated watching the scene, and at the same time, I felt my heart wrench, like someone had grabbed it and was squeezing it too tightly. I tried to think back on the promise I'd made Dusane in the alleyway. But everything he'd told me to promise was instantly gone watching the display before me.

"It's been so long, I honestly thought I'd never see you again," she pouted, running her pointer finger along his lips and chin. Her voice was a high-pitched whine as she said the words with a sultry longing.

"So little faith," Dusane teased, his cerulean eyes burning with playful desire. I didn't think I'd be able to unsee the way he was staring at her—hungry and ravenous.

"You were telling us how you escaped?" Jade urged, rolling his eyes. Obviously, I wasn't the only one disturbed by what was happening before me.

"How I escaped is unimportant. Why don't we talk about why I came here." Dusane said, not making any moves to push Rosie from his lap. He gently caressed her leg as he spoke, lazily drawing circles on her thigh. Rosie sighed, leaning into his touch.

"Enlighten us," Jade said, and I couldn't help but notice the way he was now clutching the hilt of his dagger.

"I need to find Steel Tooth," Dusane said easily.

Bloodstreak threw his head back, laughing aloud.

"You want us to tell you where Steel Tooth is?" Deadshiv deadpanned as Bloodstreak continued to laugh, a deep throaty laugh that caused his entire body to shake.

I glanced around the pub and could see that the conversation had resumed throughout the room somewhat, but most people were still sneaking wide-eyed glances at our table. We were far enough away in the shadowed corner that the conversation was mostly muted.

I ached for the conversation to end quickly but forced myself to remain calm and patiently wait for Dusane to do his work.

"Why would we give you information about the most powerful blacksmith in the realm? Do you think I'm stupid, Phantom?" Jade asked, his eyes narrowing.

"Yeah, and since when do you need our help?" Deadshiv asked steelily.

"The contact I had with her is now a dead-end, and I need to find her to finish a job."

"Well, you know how this works, Phantom." Bloodstreak quieted his chuckles to speak. "No money, no answers."

"I didn't come empty-handed," Dusane said. And that's when they all turned to me again.

"Who's this? Can she be trusted?" Deadshive asked, still the most skeptical of the situation.

I watched Rosie suddenly acknowledge my existence, and her pink eyes narrowed at me from her view over Dusane's shoulder.

"Bring a friend, did you?" she asked, and it wasn't a welcoming tone.

Dusane looked at me, and it was as if he was just barely remembering my existence. With an unimpressed expression on his face, he nodded and turned back to the others.

"This is my client. She's the one that will be paying for your efforts."

"How much?" Jade instantly asked. His eyes ran up and down my body, and I felt very exposed under his sudden scrutiny.

Dusane, still looking at Rosie, answered, "Remember Grashien Court?"

All three of them, including Rosie, looked at him in disbelief.

"You're playing us," Deadshiv accused, nearly spitting the words.

"No, I'm not," Dusane said easily. I assumed It was a job from the past they were all very familiar with and that the price for the job had been surmountable to receive such a reaction from all of them.

"Oh Phantom, you never disappoint," Rosie giggled, and she kissed him again. They locked lips for several minutes as the group tried to regain their composure. The same gut-wrenching, nauseated feeling overcame me, and I was surprised at the violent feelings I felt towards the woman.

"That's a lot of money, all for information on the blacksmith?" Bloodstreak asked. He had a small smile on his lips now, almost as if he was amused by the absolute absurdity of the situation.

"And detailed information on how to get there. Don't think I'm naive enough to believe she's not hiding somewhere difficult to reach," Dusane added.

The three of them looked at each other, and finally, Jade nodded.

"Fine, payment, then answers."

"Half, give me answers, then you'll receive the rest once you tell me."

"Deal."

Dusane looked expectantly over at me, and I tried my best to not shake as I passed them the bag of money. Jade examined the pouch before speaking again, and that was when I noticed the Envorydian symbol on his hand. The other tattoos on his body were symbols and designs I didn't recognize, but I knew this one. Only it wasn't exactly like the one Dusane and I had. The only difference was that the half-circle had two little lines dashed through it. I made a mental note to ask Dusane about it later.

"She's living in the Eroded Caves on top of the Naifell Mountains."

"How do we get to the caves," Dusane pressed.

"There is a hidden trail that starts at the base of the town of Eastholde. It's the town directly below the mountain. If you can get one of the townspeople to tell you where the trail starts, you follow it up until you reach the caves. It's that simple."

Dusane smiled wickedly, then gestured for me to give him the second pouch of money. When the coins landed with a resounding thud on the table, Jade counted the money and pocketed the second pouch.

"You should leave. If word gets out that the Phantom has returned, I can't say people won't go looking for you. There's no doubt a large bounty on your head," Jade warned.

"No one even knows I've returned," Dusane said.

"They do now."

Dusane's smile didn't falter. He remained cool and collected as he lifted Rosie off his lap and stood from the table.

"It's been well doing business with you,"

"Do you have to leave so soon?" Rosie pouted, her hands pawing at Dusane's chest as she shamelessly pressed her body against his.

"Sorry Rosie, I can't stay. But if I do return, I'll definitely come back to say hello." He promised, leaning in to press a kiss to her lips one last time.

Every eye was on us as we left the pub. I could feel my heart racing erratically in my chest, my skin slick with sweat. When we finally stepped outside into the cool air, I was never more grateful to be rid of a situation.

The door to the pub closed behind us, and the wary guard watched us intently as we disappeared down the street.

FIFTEEN

"How did it go?" Mid asked.

Neither of us answered.

"Did they give you the information?" he pressed.

"It went fine, and we got the answers we needed," I said, not slowing my pace as I headed back in the direction of our flat.

"Ehren," Dusane said, and I could hear the apology in his voice, the twinge of regret behind his tone. But the tears were already coming. And I couldn't stop them.

"What's going on?" Mid asked, seeming to catch on to the fact that something wasn't quite right between us.

"Nothing," Dusane muttered.

"Is she alright?" Mid nearly growled.

My shoes crunched against the snow, and the path ahead blurred as the angry, resentful tears came.

"Ehren, please stop." Dusane tried to catch up to me, gently tugging on my arm, but I pushed him away.

"Don't touch me!" I hissed, and he recoiled away instantly. I wanted to yell, but I didn't want to risk anyone hearing us.

Mid was at my side almost instantly, putting himself between Dusane and me.

"What did you do to her?" Mid demanded. Right as I turned around, I watched Mid shove Dusane's chest.

"Nothing, she's just angry about the encounter with the other Envorydians," Dusane said, not making any moves to fight back.

"I'm fine!" They both turned to look at me. "Just take me back. Please," I pleaded, hoping that the darkness was shrouding the tears that had leaked onto my cheeks. Dusane looked at me, and I had to look away from the ashamed look in his eyes.

I knew it was an act. That the entire thing that had just happened in the pub was a show. He'd even made me promise I would remember he wasn't the person I'd just witnessed. But the way he'd kissed Rosie was replaying over and over in my head, and it was more and more painful every time I relived it.

Mid was obviously upset, but I didn't have time to explain and didn't need him standing up for me right then.

"Alright, let's just go," Mid finally agreed. But I could see that the conversation was far from over.

It was silent as we all returned to the Inn. Mid double-checked to make sure we weren't being followed before we made our way to the room.

I immediately went to sit on one of the beds and hugged my knees to my chest, trying to shake the images of Dusane's wicked smile, his amused laugh, and the way he'd kissed the skin of Rosie's throat.

"I'm going to do another quick check to make sure no one followed us," Mid said, passing me another worried glance before reluctantly leaving Dusane and me alone.

I knew this was not the way to be acting. It was unnecessary, pathetic, and most of all, not what an Envorydian was trained to do. I tried to reign in my emotions with no success. He had made me promise. And it was humiliating that I was reacting in such a way. But the nausea wouldn't leave, the jealousy flooding my veins still burning like a fire.

Dusane slowly walked over to me as if approaching a wild animal that might bite him. I looked at him, finding my Dusane standing there and feeling conflicted because of the Dusane I'd just witnessed. He'd been a completely different person.

"Who are you?" I whispered.

He came to sit on the bed beside me, the mattress sinking in with his weight.

"I told you before that I was a different man before I entered the Courts."

I stayed silent.

"Phantom is the name I was given because of my reputation as an Envorydian."

"I gathered that," I deadpanned.

Dusane sighed and looked down at his hands.

"I was raised in the Obscurum castle. My father was a valued Envorydian to the king, and my mother was a maidservant. My father's heart was blue, and my mother's was green. For such Stone-Hearted, they lived good lives. Most in their caste would never have been given the opportunity for such positions. So I was raised in the castle knowing that I would most likely become an Envorydian too. I was granted and became even more valued because of my Reminant abilities."

He looked to struggle with his next words.

"I did many things, Ehren, that I'm not proud of. And the name Phantom soon became what people knew me by because I never left any evidence of the jobs I'd done. I was like a ghost, a Phantom. Spying, killing, and wreaking havoc for the kingdom of Obscurum. But you have to believe me when I say I only did it for a means of survival."

"Why didn't you leave?" I whispered.

"Obscurum doesn't let you leave. And if you do, they hunt you down. So many times, I spoke with my father, and he wished he could run away with my mother and me. But it was too late. We were slaves to him."

I knew he was talking about Elysian.

"My grandfather had gone to Obscurum originally hoping for a better life. King Elysian promised a free kingdom, and he didn't deliver. Instead, he imprisoned those that followed him, giving them something good for a time before making them slaves to his tyranny." His jaw clenched.

"Ehren, I told myself if I was always the most terrifying person in the room, no one could hurt me. But that was no way to live. So I eventually ended up in the courts, and I met Rouix and the others." I watched the look on his face as if he were remembering that time in his life. "They changed me."

"How long ago did you get sent to the courts?"

"Five years ago."

I thought back to the way I'd seen Rouix look at Dusane. It made sense then why she might have feelings for him. The courts changed him, and she had been part of that. And that must have changed her too.

"I learned the truth about the Envorydians, what they actually stood for, and I became a different person. Ehren, I'm sorry you had to see all of that. Please believe me when I say it was all an act." He laid a hand on my arm, and his eyes pleaded for me to understand.

"I know that wasn't you. It was just hard to watch."

"I know. . ." he looked down again, jaw muscles clenching.

"Your family, do they know what happened to you?" I asked.

"About a year into the Courts, I learned they had escaped Obscurum. But I've never heard from them since."

My eyes widened. "That's terrible," I said, my heart breaking at the thought of him being lost to his family.

"It helps if I think they are safe and happy."

"Is there no way to contact them?"

"They left without the intention of being found. I'd rather they stay hidden than risk giving them away by searching for them."

It was logical to want to keep them safe. But I don't know how I'd ever give up hope of seeing my family again if it was me.

"The king, he didn't recognize you when we invaded the castle."

"I suspect he thought I was dead or still in the Sethen Courts. I don't think he remembered me after all those years."

I contemplated all he told me for a minute. It left me feeling sad and frustrated at the unfairness of it all.

"I'm so sorry," I finally said.

"It's okay." He pulled me to him, embracing me.

It was unexpected and not something we'd ever really done before. We just held one another for several long minutes. My head was pressed into the crook of his neck, and I breathed in his musky scent. I hadn't realized how much I needed to hold him like this until now.

Then I remembered something I needed to ask him.

"The symbol on Jade's arm. Why didn't it look like ours?"

"It's the rebel Envoy symbol," he explained. He released me and stood from the bed. After a brief moment of what looked to be hesitation, he turned around he pushed aside the fabric of his cloak, and lifted up the back of his shirt. Right on the lower part of his back was another Envoy symbol, the one with the two slashes through the half-circle.

I reached out tentatively and touched my fingers to the design.

"I'm sorry I overreacted tonight. I let my emotions get away from me," I said softly as I admired the stark black ink against his warm skin.

"Mastering emotions is the hardest thing for an Envorydian."

I pulled my fingers away, and he let his shirt fall back into place.

"Thanks for the reminder, Captain," I said sarcastically.

"Anytime, Envorydian." He gave me a small smile, then gestured toward the pillow on the bed. "Now, get some sleep. We have a long journey ahead of us."

SIXTEEN

The following day we left the flat and started for the Niafell Mountain. I discarded the clothes the Mister had given me, leaving the beautiful dress behind, and changed back into my winter gear.

According to the directions that Jade gave us, there was a small town called Eastholde at its base, and it was there we would find the trail that would lead us to the Eroded Caves.

"Should we go back and tell the guards we are going to be longer," I asked, unable to hide the worry in my voice.

"No, as long as we get back in time for the two-week mark, we should be fine," Mid said.

I bit my lip worried that maybe we wouldn't return in time and they would leave thinking we had been killed.

"How are we going to climb the mountain once we get there?" I asked. We had been walking through the busy streets for about an hour now. The tall buildings were beginning to fade, and the houses were becoming more sparse. The whiteness all around was unsettling.

"We'll have to get gear in the next town and hope they sell Worm Torches," Dusane said.

"Worm torches?" I asked, never having heard of such a thing.

Dusane didn't answer, just continued to walk on, and I assumed it was another thing I'd just have to see for myself. Mid glanced at me, winked, and I couldn't help but feel reassured. If he wasn't worried, I shouldn't be either.

The towns became less frequent the further we traveled, and eventually, we became submerged in the forest again. For a time, it was just white trees until the sun began to set. I began to feel the fatigue settle in from all the walking, and just when I was about to say we should rest, we emerged from the tree-line to find a giant mountain and village lights glimmering in the distance.

It was a massive peak, with parcels of black rock jutting out beneath the white blanket of snow covering it. The town was minuscule in comparison to the giant mountain protruding behind it. It was a magnificent sight.

"We're here," Dusane said, and I sighed in relief.

Small wooden cabins were grouped together while farm animals roamed in open white fields. As we approached the homes, a woman on a mage pony came riding up to us.

"Stop there, who are you?" she asked, and I noticed she wasn't Misted. I guessed that the capitol was the only place in Severesi such fashion statements were being made. The woman wore a white cloak and a furry winter hat. She had long white hair that must have been from age because she seemed to be an older Stone-Hearted. Her dark ebony skin had faint sight of wrinkles, further affirming her age.

"We've come to find the trail to the Eroded Caves," Dusane said.

"Do you have a death wish?" The woman asked, staring us down boldly with her bright green eyes.

"We require equipment for our travels. If you could guide us to a store, we would be very grateful," Dusane added, and very subtly, he pushed the hair behind his ear, revealing the Envorydian symbol.

The woman did not miss his gesture, and her eyes widened a little.

"There is a shop in town that can help you." She gestured for us to follow her then, and together we ventured into the little village.

Curious eyes examined us as we walked through the torch-lit street that was just a dirt-treaded pathway on the verge of turning to ice.

She gestured us into one of the log cabins, and inside was another woman. A fire was blazing in one corner, and it was significantly warmer. It smelled like wool, leather, and fur. We found all sorts of winter clothing, climbing gear, provisions, and other camping items.

"You won't be able to take much with you. You'll fatigue quicker with a heavy load," the woman guiding us said.

"We'll take one tent then, and some rope, and then Worm Torches if you have them."

Another woman who looked to own the shop began helping Dusane find the supplies he needed. The shop owner handed him something that looked like an icicle, but it glowed a beautiful shade of green and blue. I realized then it was the Worm Torch he was speaking about. He bought three and stuffed them into his pack.

Dusane also purchased larger bags from the shop owner and put the tent, ropes, food, and other items into. Dusane handed me one bag with the lighter items, then the other to Mid.

"Thank you, now if you could lead us to the entrance to the trail," Dusane said as he finished packing away the rest of the things we needed. The white-haired woman who had first greeted us took us from the shop and back out into the cold. It was dark now, and the stars were beginning to twinkle in the night sky. We walked away from the little village across a long white field with various animals until we were deep in a forest again. The woman had a Worm Torch and the faint green and blue light cast an unusual fluorescent glow onto the trees around us.

Eventually, a sizeable glassy arch came into view. It was a magnificent structure and looked to be the entrance to a trail freshly dusted with snow. The glow of the Worm Torch cast beautiful light onto the glass-ice arch, and I gazed up at the structure as it towered over us.

"This is as far as I can take you," the woman said.

Dusane nodded and handed her a bag of coins. "Thank you," he said, and she nodded, disappearing back into the trees where we'd come. Soon we were alone, and Dusane proceeded to pull out the Worm Torches from his pack. He handed one to me and then Mid.

"Don't lose those," Dusane ordered.

I held tightly to the torch, gazing in wonderment at the beautiful green and blue lights within it.

"I want to wait until morning, but there isn't time. So we should get at least an hour or two of climbing in," Dusane said.

"Let's go then," I said, affirming without saying that I was fine to keep going. My feet ached, but that was the least of our worries right now. We had to climb a mountain, reach the top, convince a blacksmith to make us a weapon to stop Obsidian, and then return in time for the guards not to think we had been kidnapped or killed. *Easy.* I thought sarcastically.

"You sure, Ehren? If you're tired, we can rest," Mid said, reaching out to touch my arm. His emerald-scarlet eyes searched my face, and he looked majestic with his silvery hair glowing in the light of the Worm Torch.

"I'm sure," I affirmed. The boys looked at each other, and then both nodded.

Dusane took the lead, and I followed after him with Mid trailing behind me.

~

The path was steep, and the trail wasn't definitive. A lot of the time, we had to step over huge rocks and boulders in the way of the small trail and what didn't help was the snow, making everything slippery and hard to grasp. I fell multiple times and grumbled angrily to myself when I tried to clear a rock and ended up flat on my butt again. And I wasn't the only one struggling, Dusane nearly fell off a ledge at one point, and Mid's gloves were soaked from falling one too many times. No amount of skill was helping us against the black ice and steep slopes.

"This is hopeless. How are we ever going to make it up there in time?" I growled.

I glared up to the top of the mountain, barely illuminated in the light of the moon. Dusane said the caves were presumably at the top. When both the boys turned to look at me, I pointed to the top of the peak and gave them an incredulous expression.

"We'll make it," Dusane said, giving me what I thought was his attempt at a sympathetic expression, then turned around and started up the mountain again.

Mid walked down the trail a couple of paces to me and gave me a small smirk while holding out his hand.

"Do you trust me?" he asked, and I rolled my eyes at him while taking his hand to help to get over the rock that had defeated me only moments before.

"I thought we established you weren't going to keep asking me that," I accused.

"The trail levels out up ahead," Dusane called, somehow already twenty paces in front of us.

We hurried after him, Mid helping me over the obstacles I couldn't manage to clear. Then finally, we reached a part of the trail that wasn't so steep. My calves sighed with relief when we began treading a more level section of the mountainside.

"Let's set up camp here," Dusane said, coming to a halt.

"Thank the Spirits," I mumbled, unhooking my pack and letting it fall to the snow with a muted thump.

It was a quick setup. We only had one tent, and it was agreed that I would sleep along with Mid while Dusane took first watch. Dusane made a fire only because if we didn't, we'd have frozen to death. I reached my hands out to the fire, nearly sighing in relief as my numb fingertips began to dethaw.

"I'll switch you in a couple of hours," Mid said to Dusane.

"I can help keep watch," I said but right as I said it, a yawn escaped me. Both of the boys looked at me with unconvinced expressions.

"Sleep, Ehren, we got this," Dusane ordered, his tone slipping into his trainer voice. Not wanting to argue and actually really desiring sleep, I left the warmth of the fire and climbed into the small tent. Mid came in after me, laying down on the opposite side of the tent.

No words were said, only a quiet rustling as we both became situated. And I didn't have time to dwell on the awkwardness of sleeping so close to him because the minute I closed my eyes, I instantly fell asleep.

SEVENTEEN

When I woke the next day, the tent was empty. I sat up groggily, running a hand through my tangled hair that had unraveled from its braid in the night. It was so cold, and as I left the warmth of the blankets I'd been cocooned within, I groaned aloud.

"Well, good morning to you too," Mid said as I stepped tiredly out of the tent into the sunlight. I squinted against the brightness and found the two boys resting by an open fire. Dusane sat sharpening his knife, and Mid was munching on some bread. They sat on a pine log they must have rummaged from somewhere in the trees.

"I have to say, the morning light really becomes you," Mid added with a chuckle, and I shot him a menacing glare.

A stifled laugh came from Dusane, but he kept his eyes on his knife. *Smart man.*

"I'm glad my disheveled appearance amuses you two," I said sarcastically.

Mid stood from his seat, dusting off the crums on his pants. "Easy now, I'm only teasing," he assured me.

I ignored him and proceeded to try and detangle my hair with my fingers. After about ten minutes, I realized that the knots were too tenacious, and I was just making it worse. I growled aloud, dropping my hands to my side in defeat.

A pair of hands touched the back of my hair, and I was startled.

"What are you doing?" I panicked.

"Trying to help you," Mid said behind me. His fingers started gently working through the tangled strands of my hair, and I could but stand with rigid hesitancy while he worked.

"I appreciate your concern, but I assure you it's impossible," I insisted.

"You're just impatient," he said, and after several minutes his hands left my hair.

I turned around to face him. He had a satisfied smile on his face.

I reached up curiously to touch my hair and found to my surprise, the knots I'd previously wrestled with wholly unraveled.

"Thank you," I muttered. I tied it back into a braid, avoiding his gaze.

"We need to head up further on the mountain. I'm hoping to complete the journey today," Dusane said while beginning to disassemble the tent.

"You think we can make it all the way up there?" I asked, looking at the high snowy peak of the mountain. In the light, it appeared even taller. I could feel the memory of my burning calves and inwardly groaned.

"It shouldn't be too hard," Dusane said.

Once we cleaned up camp and started on our way again, I found to my surprise, that Dusane was right, the terrain was less rocky the further we journeyed, and we had completed another third of the mountain by noon.

I also decided during our hike that I held a deep hatred for the snow. I would have much rather been stuck in a hot, humid jungle than be faced with slippery ice traps and numb limbs. I couldn't feel my nose, and every time I breathed, a dry burn scorched my throat and lungs. I swallowed, wincing at the ache that elicited.

I was so focused on the discomfort I was feeling I barely noticed when Dusane came to a sudden stop, and I nearly ran into the back of him.

"What is it?" I asked, my eyes darting around the icy mountainscape.

"We are being followed," Dusane said, his voice lowering to a whisper.

Mid came up beside me and pointed to the rocks about fifty paces ahead of us. The jutting black rocks made for a great place to ambush.

Mid nodded grimly at Dusane, a silent conversation passing between them. I felt my heart speed up in my chest. *Who was following us? And how long had we had company?*

"Stay very quiet," Dusane ordered, his voice so low I barely heard him. I gritted my teeth and reached to my side, where my dagger hung at my hip. It was the most comfortable weapon for me, like greeting an old friend when I gripped it between my fingertips.

"I'll push them out," Mid whispered, leaving my side and climbing up the slope to my right.

"Tell me what to do, Captain," I whispered as Mid disappeared.

Dusane's eyes remained steadfast on the black rocks where our company was hiding, the only indication that he'd heard me being the slight tick of his jaw when it clenched.

"Once they come into view, I'll take the right. You take the left," Dusane said, and I could feel the tension in his body beside me as he prepared for a fight.

I looked down at my amulet out of habit, but I must have been getting better at controlling when I siphoned other people's powers by accident because it was still just a ruby. I would have no extra power in this fight. I was on my own.

"And if there are too many?" I questioned. I positioned myself into a battle stance, feeling my body also tensing and my senses sharpening. It was the feeling I got every time I was about to become the fighter, the Envorydian.

"Now, what have I told you about theoreticals?" Dusane asked, turning just a little to meet my gaze and raise an eyebrow.

It had been a while since I'd had a real fight, and accompanying the rush of adrenaline was something I'd never experienced before—a craving, an excitement for what was about to happen.

"Something about them being inconsequential and empty worries with no substance if I recall correctly."

"Exactly. Also, just out of curiosity, have I ever told you that you talk too much?" Dusane fired back.

"Frequently." I grinned, and just then, three individuals came out from behind the rocks, Mid in the midst of them. He had successfully driven them from their hiding place.

Conversation forgotten, both Dusane and I started into a

run. Out of the three, I started after the one on my right. He met my attack with full force, and I nearly stumbled across the icy landscape when his knife met my dagger. The hood covered most of his face, but I could see a small streak of dark brown hair beneath his white hood. I gritted my teeth and gave it my all.

Each movement loosened me up, and I felt alive each time his weapon met with mine. Despite the slippery terrain, I somehow managed to keep up the fight. I was using muscles that had slept for a while, and the struggle was what I craved. I started breathing heavily, but the burning in my chest every time I breathed was welcomed. I think after so long of feeling nothing, it was invigorating to feel something so intense.

The man grunted when I landed a clean cut across his left forearm, and blood began to seep through his white cloak. He backed away for a moment, gripping the wound. A gust of wind swept over the mountain ruffling my hair and causing a chill to pierce my bones. This sent the hood back from my contender's face, and I gaped. I knew him. He was from the pub.

Jade.

"You," I said, glaring at him.

Despite the pain he seemed to be in, he grinned.

"Well, hello again."

I looked around at the others and realized then that I knew all of them. These were the men from the pub. Dusane was fighting Deadshiv, and Mid was facing off to Bloodstreak.

I lunged for Jade once more, my mind reeling. Dusane had been right to be wary of them. *What reason did they have to attack us? Was it because they didn't want us to reach the blacksmith?*

Mid managed to quickly take down Deadshiv and went to help Dusane with Bloodstreak. The man was lethal, and I was distracted for a minute when I heard Dusane grunt in pain. I turned for a mere moment, and amid my distraction, Jade landed his knife into my side. I yelped, and with the knife still embedded into me, he shoved me against the black rocks of the mountainside. The cold stone dug into my spine, and I lost my breath. He sunk the blade a little deeper into my side. Pain bloomed throughout my body like lightning, hot and fast—my knees buckled.

"I can see he trained you. You have the same weaknesses as him. He should've been more careful," Jade said darkly before he ripped the knife from my side. I pitched to the snowy earth clutching the wound gushing crimson blood, spattering the innocent snow. Jade started for Dusane and Mid, and I could but kneel in agony, waiting for my body to recover.

It took a little longer than I'd liked, but eventually, my side stopped throbbing, and the wound closed. When I could breathe again, I wiped my bloodied palm across my pant leg and stood.

Something inside me stirred, like storm clouds forming in the night sky. My resolve thickened, and I cracked, a thunderous boost of adrenaline quaking through me. I headed up the slope to my right, onto the rocks that Jade had just rammed me into. Using the jutting black stones like a ladder, I climbed. When I reached the top, I didn't hesitate before starting into a run.

I jumped from the highest point of the rocks—adrenaline flooding my veins as I leaped through the air onto Jade's back, landing my dagger straight into his shoulder. He crashed heavily to the earth with the weight of me atop him and let out an agonizing yell. I grunted as I fell with him, absorbing some of the fall. I pulled out the dagger from his shoulder and, once I gathered my bearings, managed to stand. Jade laid on the ground, clutching the wound. I wiped my blade on the snow, cleaning it of the blood.

Mid and Dusane had defeated both Bloodstreak and Deadshiv. They both laid motionless a couple feet away. I wondered if Mid had put them to sleep or if they were both dead.

The boys were breathing heavily as Dusane came over to me, putting a hand on my shoulder.

"Ehren, calm down," he said. I hadn't realized I was shaking until he touched me. Something was happening to me. I hadn't fought like that since the throne room with king Elysian. And all I could think was I wanted to fight someone else—almost *needed* to.

"Envorydian," Dusane said sharply, turning me to face him. His expression was grim. "It's over."

I nodded, pushing his hand off me. I took in a couple of strangled breaths forcing my heartbeat to calm. *What was happening to me?*

"I'm fine," I said, sheathing my dagger. I knelt beside Jade again, who was still writhing in the snow.

"What are you doing here?"

He moaned, not answering me.

"I said, why are you here?" I reached down and dug my fingers into his wound.

He yelped, flinching away from me. "They paid me, they paid me!"

"Who?" I demanded.

"He knows," Jade turned his gaze on Dusane. I stood and looked at Dusane with a puzzled expression.

"What is he talking about," I asked.

"Before I was banished to the courts, I had made a lot of

enemies. If those enemies learned I was still alive, it is very likely they would come searching for me." His jaw clenched.

"King Elysian?"

"No, other enemies." He sighed. "They must have paid them to come after me,"

"Great, now we have a bounty on your head we have to worry about?" Mid said, exasperated.

Dusane's jaw clenched. "We need to get out of Severesi as soon as we can."

Jade let out another agonizing moan.

"Leave him. We need to keep going," Dusane ordered, starting up the trail again.

"What if he goes back?" I asked.

"Let him. I don't think he'll make it that far."

I took one last glance at Jade, not as queasy as I should have been when looking at the other bodies beside him.

"They are killers bear." Oli's voice echoed in my head, and I felt suddenly ice cold and not just because of the winter chill. It was the first time I feared Oli may be right.

EIGHTEEN

The next several hours were filled with thick silence. We all seemed to be thinking. Someone knew Dusane was out of the courts and obviously wanted him dead. *How long could we survive in Severesi with Dusane's bygone enemies vying for his life?* The mission was now more time-sensitive than ever, and we could all feel it.

On top of that, I was still trying to understand what happened to me during the fight. The excitement and adrenaline that had fueled me during that fight had been a sort of frenzy. I was fearful I was losing control of something, and I didn't even really know what that something was.

"Up ahead. It looks to be the entrance to the caves," Dusane said, pulling me from my thoughts.

Sure enough, a gaping entrance into the mountain appeared on the trail before us. It was a massive stone cavity, the mouth leading into pitch-black darkness. I didn't want to know what lived in the depths of this cave, but it was our only way to the blacksmith. Dusane pulled his worm torch from his pack. Mid and I did the same.

"We don't even know what's in there," I said nervously. I could feel the eeriness radiating from the darkness. Dusane stepped over the cave threshold, leaving the snowy path.

"Well, we will just have to find out," he said.

I took one glance behind me and could barely see down the mountain. We were up so high now the clouds blanketed everything from view. I could see the very faint flickering of Iradence in the distance, but it was a minuscule speck now.

The only comfort I had was that I could see the stars and the moon much more clearly up this high. Still, that comfort immediately left me knowing that once I stepped into the caves, I would no longer be able to see those beautiful constellations, and that unnerved me.

"I'm right behind you," Mid said, giving me a small smile.

I gazed into his emerald-scarlet eyes for a moment, selfishly drawing strength from their familiarity before I nodded, accepting what had to be done.

I took a deep breath, and as Dusane disappeared into the inky blackness, I couldn't do anything but follow.

~

The dark cave stretched on endlessly, it seemed. I didn't do well with close dark spaces and found my chest tightening, making breathing harder. I assumed it was mind over matter when it came to my fear of intimate spaces. So I forced myself to breathe and push out the fear that was threatening to close in on me.

It was hard to relax, knowing that we didn't have any idea where we were going other than the rumors Dusane had heard about this place. We could get lost, never make our way out, and die in these dark caves with no one ever knowing what happened to us. I cursed myself for being so negative and tried not to think about the possible outcomes of our demise.

"I see something up ahead," Dusane called, his voice echoing eerily off the cave walls.

I felt my spirits lift a little, hoping he'd found an exit. But then, we came to an abrupt halt, and instead of an exit, we were met with an unexpected dead end.

"Great, a dead end," I deadpanned.

"Not exactly." Dusane smiled victoriously as he reached out into the darkness and grasped onto something. He brought it into the vicinity of his Worm Torch, and in the greenish light, I could see he'd found a rope.

My eyes widened and I looked upwards to find a dark abyss.

"Don't tell me we have to climb up that," I said, feeling suddenly nauseated at the thought.

"It seems to be the only way." Dusane wasn't put off by the challenge and began to situate his gear to start the climb. I watched nervously as Dusane grasped the rope and jumped, pulling himself upwards into the darkness.

I looked back at Mid, who gestured for me to go next. I let out a breath and hesitantly walked up to the rope. I reached out to clasp it in my hands and found it was so thick I couldn't grasp it very firmly.

Despite my flimsy hold, I closed my eyes, took a deep breath, and when I opened them again, jumped. My arm muscles strained as I started to try and climb. But it was only a matter of seconds before I realized it was impossible.

My small hands slid back down the rope almost instantly, a stinging sensation erupting across my palms.

"Spirits," I cursed, landing on my feet again. I shook my hands as if that would somehow stop the burning.

"Are you okay?" Mid took my hands in his and examined the damage, but they were already healing. I glared at the rope, then to the abyss above.

"I can't wrap my hands around the rope. It's too big." I felt my cheeks burn with embarrassment.

"What's wrong?" Dusane called from somewhere up in the darkness.

"She can't climb the rope. Her hands are too small," Mid called back.

"Can you carry her?" Dusane asked.

"Yes, I can." Mid took my things and started strapping them to his back.

"Mid, you can't carry me all the way up this. You don't even know how far it is," I said nervously.

"You have so little faith in me." He smirked, but I was in no mood for joking.

"There has to be another way," I continued to press.

"There isn't, so come here and wrap her arms around my neck," he said. He finished strapping everything to himself that needed securing and gestured for me to come to him.

Feeling embarrassed and slightly nervous all at the same time, I walked over and wrapped my arms around his neck. His hands fell onto my waist, and he lifted me with ease so I could wrap my legs around his waist. He used some extra rope from his pack to securely strap me to him, and I tried unsuccessfully to avoid his gaze during the process.

I knew I shouldn't be worried. He'd been the one to save me

from an Obscurum camp and rescue me from a rushing river. He'd fought off many enemies in my presence, and not to mention Shar, an Envorydian, had probably been the one to train him throughout his life. I knew I could trust him. But it still scared me to be at the complete mercy of someone else climbing up a rope into a dark space that we didn't know the destination of.

"Don't worry, I got you," he assured me. I relaxed a little then and closed my eyes, not wanting to watch.

I waited for us to start up the rope. . . but we didn't move.

I felt something soft and warm touch my neck, and my eyes flew open in surprise.

"Mid, what are you doing?!" I squeaked. The soft, warm feeling on my neck were his lips.

"Hmmm. . . you were just too tempting," he murmured.

I couldn't do anything. I was trapped with the way he'd secured me to him. But even if I hadn't been trapped, I wouldn't have had the power to tell him to stop. I was breathless, my heart speeding up in response to his kiss. My head fell to the side on its own accord, allowing him more access.

"Mid. . ." I tried to say, but it came out as more of a gasp. My mind was fuzzy, everything was burning now, and it felt good. Too good.

His head rose from the crook of my neck, and I came back down to reality slowly. Our eyes met, and a small satisfied smile rose to his lips.

"I've missed the taste of you," he said, and before I could manage to come to my senses, he leaned in again, only this time he kissed my lips. It was a short kiss, but it still caused my cheeks to flush and the world to spin a little.

When he pulled away, he didn't even give me a chance to say

anything before he jumped and began climbing. All thoughts of the kiss left me when the swaying of the rope sent my stomach sinking. I cursed under my breath. In the dim, greenish fluorescent light of the worm torch, I found I couldn't shut my eyes as I'd planned to. I stared wide-eyed at the darkness below, fear stealing my breath away as I imagined us falling back into the sea of darkness.

Mid's jaw was clenched, and his eyes intently focused on the rope as he rhythmically clasped one hand over the other. His arm muscles bulged beneath his shirt as he carried the two of us up the rope, and I was cognizant of my staring at him far longer than I should've.

Before I knew it, Mid stopped, and he was moving us carefully off the rope onto flat ground again. Dusane was waiting for us, another long tunnel stretching behind him.

Mid was breathing heavily, but he seemed exhilarated. With flat ground beneath my feet now and the fear from our climb gone, the memory of the kiss came rushing back to me. I hurriedly untangled myself from the mess of ropes Mid had strapped me to him with.

Mid smiled at me as I stumbled, releasing myself from the entanglement, and I glared at him when I finally broke free.

"Aren't you going to thank me?" Mid asked, his smile widening into a smirk. Something resembling a growl came out of me when I responded.

"In your dreams," I muttered. I didn't want to make a scene with Dusane right next to us, but I badly wanted to confront him about the kiss he just stole. *Who did he think he was?* Oh right, he was a cocky, self-assured flirt with a devilish streak in him that I should've known would make a reappearance.

My heart hadn't stopped beating erratically, and I couldn't shake the warm buzz that was still faintly tingling the nerves inside my body. This was why I had told him not to kiss me, for this very reason. I was disoriented. My emotions were now all over the place. I was out of control. He was a rushing river, and if I got too close, I risked falling in and never resurfacing.

Dusane raised his eyebrow at the two of us, but I ignored the look on his face and simply hefted my pack onto my back and started down the tunnel.

Dusane caught up to me, though, falling into stride beside me while Mid hung back.

"You alright?" Dusane asked me.

"Fine," I said bluntly.

"You sure?" He asked, his tone full of skepticism.

Just then, the crackling of falling rocks echoed from the darkness ahead, and we all slowed to a stop. The conversation was suddenly forgotten. I felt the hairs on my arms rise.

"What was that?" I asked, peering ahead into the darkness. I could see nothing. The worm torches only gave us a couple feet of light. Other than that, everything was black.

"Probably just some loose rocks," Dusane said. He stepped forward and kneeled down to pick up a handful of gravel that must have shaken loose from the cave ceiling.

"Why do I have such a bad feeling then," I said, my voice reducing to a whisper.

Another trickle of loose rocks fell down from the ceiling, this time sprinkling us in a small shower of stones.

"Okay, something is definitely not right," Mid said, coming up beside me.

The ground beneath us began to shake. Not expecting the

sudden abrupt quavering of the floor, I reached out to steady myself. I grabbed Mid's arm on my right and Duane's on my left. We all hung on tightly to one another, trying to keep steady. The shaking lasted what felt like an eternity. But it was really only about ten seconds, and then the floor suddenly went still again.

My heart was beating so loudly I could hear it in my ears. We all waited to see if another quake would come. But it never did, and then all that could be heard was a faint sliding sound like someone was dragging or scraping something across the tunnel floor. It started out so quiet I could barely make out the noise. But soon, the scraping got louder, and it started to sound like slithering.

I reached for the dagger at my side, and the boys did the same with their weapons.

A light at the end of the tunnel appeared within the thick darkness. The light was pale blue and slowly began to get closer and closer to us. I squinted in confusion at the sapphire light as it appeared to be floating towards us.

"Are you two seeing this?" I asked, and they both nodded their heads, eyes transfixed on the light.

Soon a smell filled the cave, and I caught the scent of rotten eggs. It was sulfuric, and I nearly gagged, forcing myself to breathe through my mouth.

My focus was taken from the blue light when a head bigger than me came into the faint glow of our worm torches. It was stark white, with silver scales armoring its head and body. Its mouth was open, black tongue slithering towards us. It had long white fangs and two silvery fins shooting out from its neck like decorative fans. Its eyes were a milky white, and the opaque orbs stared at us hungrily.

"Snake," I whispered, too terrified to even scream.

It didn't take long for the creature to strike.

Its head swung towards us, majestic yet deadly, and we all jumped away, veering in different directions to avoid the snake's epic strike.

"Spirits!" Dusane cursed as he lunged away.

I slammed myself into the tunnel wall to my left so hard I groaned. My eyes frantically searched the darkness for the snake. I could see the flickering of scales in the viridian light of my torch covering the snake's body that was the size of a redwood trunk. My heart was threatening to jump out of my chest, and I forced myself to focus and gain control of my fear.

"What do we do?" I yelled out. The snake's scales grated across the floor, making a slithering noise like fingernails across ice. It lashed around in response to our scatter, trying to decide which one of us to attack.

I could see the blue light again, pulsing somewhere in the darkness with the snake, and I realized it must be inside of the creature. The blue light had to be its heart.

"We have to either outrun it or kill it," Dusane called out from somewhere further down the tunnel. "But I'm betting we won't be able to outrun it," he added.

Relax, I tried to tell myself, *control.*

I kept breathing through my mouth, the smell of sulfur even more pungent now.

Then I heard the sickly sound of blade meeting scales—fingernails scraping across ice—and an angry hiss resonated throughout the cave.

"I got a hit on him!" Dusane said from somewhere farther down the tunnel. The angry slithering rattle of the snake's tongue brought me back to my senses. It sounded like an instrument, the melody of a deadly song.

"I'm going to try and distract it," I heard Mid say.

Just then, Mid's hands were illuminated by a familiar yellow light, and a horse appeared. I knew it was an illusion, but the realness of the animal was uncanny. The illusion horse whinnied, and the snake's head whipped around to face the animal.

We all stayed very still, trying to make out the snake's reaction to the illusion in the blackness. The snake slithered towards the horse slowly, and Mid, with his power, kept it at a safe distance, leading it along to follow after the stallion like bait.

Just when I thought we might get lucky, and the snake would follow the horse until we could safely run from it, his head whipped to the side again. It had forgotten the steed like an abandoned toy that it was no longer interested in playing with and landed its gaze on Mid.

"It knows it's not real," Mid said, almost in awe. "How does it kno. . .'

The snake gave a loud hiss, striking towards Mid.

Mid scrambled for his weapon, and just before the snake could snag him with its sharp fangs, he managed to string his bow and shoot one of its fins, slicing through the webby skin at its neck.

The snake tossed its head with another angry hiss, and Mid quickly, while the creature was distracted, scrambled away. He darted into the darkness, disappearing again.

"We have to do something!" Mid yelled.

The snake didn't take long to recover, and it started to search the darkness again for one of us to satiate its hunger.

I raised my dagger, trying to find a patch of glittering scales on its body that I could strike. Once a good section of its tree trunk body was in the green light of my torch, I took a deep breath and rammed the point of my dagger into whatever part of the snake I had found. It was hard to penetrate the scales, they were thick like armor, and I had to use all of my strength to pull the blade out again. Black liquid squirted everywhere and dripped down my dagger onto my hand. I resisted the urge to vomit.

Another furious hiss left the snake. The creature whipped around, its white eyes and large silvery head coming into the small ring of light my worm torch provided.

Before I could freeze up and allow its white eyes to paralyze me, I heard a battle cry beside me, and Dusane tried once again to attack the creature. He stabbed his dagger into the snake's pearlescent eye, and the animal tossed and writhed. Dusane didn't retreat fast enough, letting go of the blade too late and allowing the snake time to prick his shoulder with one of its fangs. The strike sent Dusane flying halfway across the tunnel. He groaned when he hit the floor, his back slamming against the cold stone.

"Dusane!"

I ran to him unthinkingly, my knees banging against the cave floor as I fell at his side.

The snake gave another loud hiss, and I looked up, only to meet the creature's single white eye. The other was bleeding black from where Dusane had punctured it. The monstrous creature reached for me with its open mouth, tongue outstretched, fangs dripping with what I could now see was glittering white liquid.

Venom.

But the snake didn't touch me. Instead, I heard another screech of a blade against thick scales, and I watched the reptile's single pale eye droop closed. Its head fell to the floor with a heavy thud, shaking the entire cave.

Mid came into the light of my torch and in his hand dripping in black blood was a stone. A heart. The blue light fading slowly from it.

NINETEEN

"Careful, don't touch the venom," Mid cautioned.

I was sitting next to Dusane, assessing the puncture wound on his shoulder that the snake's canine had inflicted. A gooey white liquid trickled down from the open cut, and I didn't know what it was capable of. And despite my ability to heal, I was careful not to touch it in case it could hurt me too.

The snake's carcass laid beside us, stinking of sulfur. I had to avoid looking at it, worried I wouldn't be able to keep it together.

Mid held the snake's heart in his palm still, the clear glass stone empty now of color. He was cleaning off the black blood from the heart as I assessed Dusane's wound.

"If I can't touch him, how am I supposed to heal him?" I asked in frustration. Dusane's head was leaned back against the cave wall, sweat beading down his forehead. He didn't look good. The pain was evident in the way he clenched his jaw and the guttural groans that would escape him every couple of minutes.

"You may not have to touch him to heal him." Mid stuffed the heart into his pack and knelt beside me. My fingers were shaking, the aftereffects of the snake attack starting to get to me as the adrenaline began to fade from my blood.

Mid reached out to grasp my hand, forcing my shaking to cease.

"It's an instinct for us as Stone-Hearted to want to use our hands when utilizing our powers, but it's not necessary. I, for instance, can produce illusions without touching someone."

"Okay, I'll give it a try." I closed my eyes, searching frantically for the power inside of my body. I felt for the heat that usually surfaced inside my chest and focused intently on trying to heal Dusane's wound.

It took me some time, and each painful intake of breath I heard from Dusane distracted me, and I had to refocus. But eventually, I managed to close the wound. Once he was healed, we carefully cleaned away the poison with a tattered cloth from my pack and tossed it as quickly as we could.

Dusane took off his cloak and used some water from his pack to clean off the remaining poison from his skin.

"Let's keep going. We need to find a place to set up camp and build a fire," Mid said.

I looked at Dusane. He was putting on his pack. I reached out to gently touch his shoulder.

"You alright?" I asked.

I don't know what I would've done had I not been able to heal him. The thought was too horrible to consider. But it was hard not to worry about the curse depleting my abilities and what might happen in the future if someone got hurt and I became too weak to heal them.

"I'm fine, don't worry about me," he said, his cerulean eyes locking with mine. "And thank you."

I nodded sullenly, wishing he wouldn't have had to thank me at all.

We started down the tunnel again, and to my dismay, had to climb over the body of the snake because its carcass was blocking our path. The boys helped me over its twisted body each time it hindered our course, and I tried my best to avoid touching it whenever I could.

It was tedious. The snake was longer than I could've imagined. It took us an hour, but we finally cleared the snake and were back to the quiet darkness of the tunnel. I was more alert, strung tightly, waiting for another snake to come slithering into our midst. I couldn't help but think the worst. *What if the snake had babies? What if it had a mate that was about to come kill us for killing the love of its life?*

I was so alert that when I saw a tiny pinprick of yellow light in the distance, my mind instantly thought it was the heart of another snake. I gasped and nearly stumbled backward.

Mid put an arm around me, stopping me from falling. "Easy, it's just a lantern," he said gently.

With hesitancy, I walked a dozen more steps, and sure enough, he was right. It wasn't a snake heart, it was simply a lantern, and as we got closer, I could see a wooden door illuminated in the soft light it was emitting.

"Maybe we won't have to camp in the tunnels after all," Dusane said. He then walked up to the door, reached for the black iron knocker, and tapped it a couple of times. The noise echoed off the cave walls, and I shivered.

It took a moment, but soon the doorknob twisted, and the door cracked open an inch.

"Who is it?" The voice belonged to a woman. She had a raspy voice, and she didn't sound happy about having visitors.

I could see a dark brown eye through the crack, and it scrutinized us suspiciously.

"Don't you recognize me?" Dusane asked, stepping under the lantern light so his face could be seen better.

"Dusane?" The woman's voice reduced to a shocked whisper, and then the door was swinging open.

A flurry of blonde hair and white cloak came through the door as the woman threw her arms around Dusane. He held her close, and Mid and I watched uncomfortably as she clung to him.

"I thought I'd never see you again," she whispered. When she pulled back, she gazed up at his face looking as if she was seeing someone come back from the dead.

"Nixie, it's good to see you again," Dusane said, and a genuine smile broke out across his face.

My eyes narrowed. Now it was my turn to be suspicious. *Was this really Steel Tooth? And why was she so affectionate towards Dusane?*

"It's so good to see you too, Dusane." She suddenly took notice they weren't alone and turned to address Mid and me. "Who are your friends?" She asked.

"This is Ehren and Midennen. They have come with me to ask you for help," Dusane explained.

"Help?" Nixie's eyes narrowed on the black bloodstains on my cloak, then she looked at Dusane. "I see you ran into the Massauka," Nixie said. "Why am I not surprised you made it past her?" Nixie raised an eyebrow.

"Clever, putting a Massauka as a bodyguard, but did you really think I wouldn't find you someday?" Dusane gestured for

Mid to give him his pack, and when he did, Dusane reached inside to pull out the stone heart Mid had cut from the snake's chest.

"I had to protect myself somehow." Nixie smiled, glancing at the trophy in his hand. "She was a wicked thing, but I can't say I'm not happy to see her go. It was getting exhausting leaving for supplies."

I looked to Mid, who seemed just as confused as I was over the encounter. Dusane had told me he knew this blacksmith. But I didn't think she would be such a friendly acquaintance. Once again, I was reminded of the things I didn't know about Dusane and the life he lived before I knew him.

Nixie gestured back to her door. "Well, why don't you come in? I'm sure we have a lot to talk about."

TWENTY

We entered Nixie's home, and I braced myself for more dark tunnels and more terrifying reptile creatures. But as we walked through the door, darkness didn't greet us. Instead, we walked into a vast, brightly lit cave.

Brassy chandeliers hung from the tall rock ceilings in curling complexities, and the floor was covered in luxurious fur rugs. The cave was illuminated with candelabras and what looked to be glow worms. Like our worm torches, the walls were peppered in the turquoise lights the worms created. Long couches were laid out in front of an elegant fireplace, and laying next to the hearth laid a creature. As we got closer, I could see that it was a fox. It was white with leopard spots, and it assessed us carefully with sleek black eyes.

"So, what brings you to my humble abode?" Nixie asked, taking a seat on the fluffy cushions and leaning one arm casually along the back of the sofa.

As we joined her, I sat rigidly, trying not to touch anything with fear that I might get something dirty.

"We came to ask you a favor, actually," Dusane said. He also seemed taken aback by the cave's extravagance, and I could see him looking around at the decor.

Everything was either decorated or framed by twisting metal designs and trims, and I guessed she must have forged it all herself. Just as I realized this, my eyes caught sight of several swords mounted above the fireplace. They were utterly magnificent. The blades were sleek and shiny, the handles designed with so much detail. Some glittered with stones; others had metallic patterns and ridges. She was an artist.

"And here I thought you just missed me," she said flirtatiously.

"I know about the dagger you made for King Elysian," Dusane suddenly blurted.

Nixie didn't react. She simply stood from the couch and walked calmly over to the beautiful fox lying by the fire. She reached down to scratch one of its pointed ears, and the creature leaned into her touch.

"I didn't know what I had created at the time," she said, her voice suddenly almost a whisper.

I leaned forward in an attempt to hear her.

"I was experimenting with. . . new materials. And then, by accident, the dagger was created. I realized too late what I had done, and I vowed never to do it again." Nixie looked away from the fire, her eyes locking with Dusane's. "You have to believe me. I didn't give it to him by choice."

"Then how did he get it?" Mid asked. He was eyeing the blacksmith suspiciously.

"He took it from me. I tried to destroy it before anyone could find out. But security was tight. And word spread," Nixie said.

"Nixie used to work for the Obscurum kingdom as a blacksmith," Dusane explained.

"Once I'd created the dagger he wanted me to create more, I refused. I had no choice but to disappear then. So I went to the only place he'd least likely find me." She gestured to the cave around us.

"Those in the Mantle knew where you were. They told me how to find you then followed me up the mountain. We killed Deashiv and Bloodstreak. Jade is wounded but alive."

"Spirits," Nixie cursed. She began pacing the fur rug.

"What's the Mantle?" I asked, speaking up for the first time.

"It's the name of a rogue Envorydian group that exists between Obscurum and Severesi. The men we just fought were some of its members, but it has many more. They are spread out across Obscurum and Severesi." Dusane explained. I thought back to what he'd told me back at the flat in Severesi. About his past and what he used to be.

"This is the rogue group you were telling me about before? The one you were once a part of?" I pressed, my eyes narrowing on Dusane.

"Yes," was all Dusane said, avoiding my gaze.

"So you found out about the dagger. Why do I have a feeling this has something to do with the favor you're about to ask me?" Nixie asked.

"We need you to create a weapon. Or a device. Something that can stop a Stone-Hearted from using their powers."

"No way," Nixie immediately said.

"Why not?" Dusane asked.

"I vowed never to create anything like the dagger again," Nixie said, her arms crossing over her chest.

"Please, Nixie. We need it to help defeat the curse," Dusane pleaded.

"It's not you I don't trust. There is just no guarantee that if I create something like that for you, it won't end up in the wrong hands." Nixie shrugged apologetically.

"Nixie, I wouldn't have come to you if I wasn't desperate. Obsidian's power, as you know, is lethal. We are bound to have another encounter with him. Eliminating him as a threat would help us immensely."

Silence emanated throughout the cave. I could hear my heart beating in my chest.

"I never pegged you as someone who helped defeat curses." Nixie eyed him, her lip turning up slightly with a smile.

"What's that supposed to mean?" Dusane growled.

"Since when are you in it for the greater cause, Dusane?" Nixie's eyes shifted to me, then back to Dusane. Something looked to click in her mind. "Ohhhh. . . I see. It has something to do with this beautiful girl right here, am I right?" Nixie pointed towards me.

"Don't," Dusane warned.

"What happened to you in that prison, Dusane?" Nixie asked, eyes bright with amusement.

"I changed." Dusane was glaring blatantly at the blacksmith now.

"You joined them, didn't you?" she asked, and when she put her hand over her mouth in pure disbelief, that's when I saw the symbol on her wrist. The Envoy symbol, with the two slashes in the half-circle.

"I don't believe my eyes. Dusane Nevrair, tamed by the Peace

Tribe." She laughed some more, and Dusane, angrier than I'd seen him in a long time, stood from the couch and walked over to Nixie. He reached out to grasp her by the front of her cloak, pulling her roughly towards him. Her laughter died away. "I may have joined them, but that doesn't mean I'm not still willing to do whatever it takes to get what I want. Now, will you make the device or not?"

My heart quickened watching Dusane grab Nixie, and the same feeling I'd felt while attacking those rouge Envorydians on the mountain came rushing back to me. An excitement, a craving for a fight to erupt. I clenched my fist at my side, trying to subdue the sudden violent desire.

"Okay, easy." Mid stood from the couch. Putting himself between Dusane and Nixie. "It's not worth it, Dusane."

Dusane shrugged Mid's hand from his shoulder but made no move to attack Nixie. I felt the tension ebb a little, and I sighed as the feeling in my body eased too. I took in a couple shallow breaths, trying to calm my racing heart.

"Fine, I'll do it," Nixie suddenly said. We all looked at her in disbelief.

"You will?" Mid asked.

"Under one condition," Nixie said, now smiling to herself. "When this is all said and done. The dagger and the device get returned to me."

"I don't know if that's going to be possible," Dusane said.

"I'm sure you'll find a way," Nixie said easily. "Now tell me what you need me to do." she walked over to sit on the edge of the couch again. The boys returned to their seats on the sofa—the static that could have erupted into a storm, settling.

"I was thinking a cuff or a band of some sort that would inhibit powers when placed on the individual," Dusane said.

Nixie nodded, slowly contemplating his request. "I'll see what I can do,"

"And one more thing," Dusane said. He reached into Mid's pack again and pulled out the crystal heart. "Can you explain this to me?"

"That is the heart of the Massauka," Nixie said innocently.

"That's not the part I need explaining. The heart was Stone-Hearted, which is impossible because animals can't be Stone-Hearted," Dusane said.

Nixie pursed her lips and sighed after a moment. "You're correct. The creature was Stone-Hearted."

"How?" Dusane pressed.

"I don't know. But I do know this." Nixie's gaze flitted back to the fire, her gaze wistful. "Everything in this world only gets stranger the farther you run from it."

My brow furrowed. It hadn't even crossed my mind in the fit of panic I'd been in back in the cave that the creature shouldn't have been Stone-Hearted. *Why was it Stone-Hearted?* Only humans could be Stone-Hearted.

A chill went down my spine.

Dusane's jaw clenched, then he put the crystal heart back into Mid's pack.

"Fine, don't tell me. Let's just get this device made. We need to get back before any other Envorydians from the Mantle try to kill me," Dusane said, standing from the sofa impatiently.

"We'll start in the morning. You all need rest. And quite frankly, I do too. So let me show you to your rooms." Nixie led us through her cave, down more glowing tunnels that led to several empty rooms.

They were in small carved-out dens in the rock—the floors cloaked in furs and the beds piled with fancy cushions. All the luxurious fabrics somehow managed to make the rocky atmosphere seem less. . . cold.

She found each of us some spare clothing to change into, all just as extravagant as the rest of her cave mansion. I felt odd slipping into the silk pajamas after being in my dirty winter gear for so long. She also brought us some food and water. The water was so clear and tasted so pure I nearly groaned when drinking the contents of the glass.

I don't know what I had expected to find when meeting Nixie, but it definitely hadn't been this. I'd pictured a dark cave with smoke and smithy tools—everything covered in soot and us roughing it in the dark caverns for another several days, cold and hungry. Instead, the luxury I was experiencing was making me feel guilty.

When I laid down to sleep that night, I was still dirty and covered in sweat from the journey, but Nixie had assured us we'd be able to bathe in the morning. So I endured the grime a little longer as I snuggled into the feather-stuffed pillows and fell asleep.

TWENTY-ONE

I woke before the others and found Nixie in the living room, drinking tea.

"Good morning. How did you sleep?" Nixie asked, sipping delicately at the honey-colored liquid in her cup. The leopard fox slept at her heels, a fluffy ball of grey and white.

"Fine, thank you," I said, still wary of her light-hearted nature. I took a seat on the couch, eyeing the woman suspiciously. This blacksmith was odd. Her deep brown eyes shone with mystery, and she seemed far too clever for her own good.

"You're an early riser like myself, I see." She smiled, and I awkwardly smiled back. I had never been good at making small talk.

"Do you mind if I ask where you. . . make things. . .?"

"My workshop is in another part of the caves. I'll be going there after breakfast to start on the device." When I didn't reply, she set down her tea, her smile proving she was unfettered by my social awkwardness. "Well, now I'm sure you're dying to get clean. The springs are prepared for you when you're ready to take a bath." She gestured towards another worm-lit hallway opposite the room.

"Thank you," I said and hurried to my feet. I shuffled out of the living room, grateful not to have to make small talk with the blacksmith anymore. I walked down the tunnel, the glowing walls guiding me until the space opened up again.

Steam filled the air, and the room immediately felt warm and humid. The bathing room was a large open cavern, the ceilings covered in long dripping stalagmites. Small craters of water were the source of the hot vapor. I walked around the pools, admiring the bubbles. The turquoise light from the walls cast a shimmering emerald gleam onto the water, giving the pools an ethereal glow.

I found a stack of towels at one of the pool's edges and some sweet-smelling soaps. I took a quick look around before I undressed and then slipped into the water. It was hot, so hot it sort of hurt. But it felt too good not to endure it.

I scrubbed my scalp and my skin nearly raw, rinsing out the suds covering my head until I felt I was spotless. Then I swam around for a minute, just enjoying the water, when I heard footsteps echo off the caves' high ceilings.

I stopped swimming and floated to the edge, quietly peeking over the side to see who had entered.

Mid came through the doorway, towel in hand. He stopped at the closest crater pool and dropped his towel to the stone floor. I was several pools over. He probably couldn't see me amidst the steam. I was about to say something when suddenly he began undressing.

He removed his shirt, letting it drop in a heap next to his towel. My breath caught in my throat as I got a full view of his bare chest. I was transfixed. Unable to look away. I was already warm from the hot spring I was in, but somehow I felt even warmer watching the scene before me.

He stopped after taking off his shirt, placing his hands on his hips, and looking up at the fluorescent cave ceiling, admiring the long stalagmites and their tapered points. His brief moment of distraction caused me to ogle further, and I noticed a V in his hips that met with the hem of his pants, and I gulped.

"Before you take off any more layers, you should know I'm in here," I called to him, somehow finding my voice. *Did I sound out of breath?* I hoped he couldn't tell.

His head turned in my direction, and when he finally spotted me among the mist, he smiled.

"Enjoying the show?" he asked.

I rolled my eyes at him. "You think if I was enjoying it, I'd have asked you to stop?" I asked. "Maybe I was actually repulsed and would have been permanently scarred if you had gone on any further." I was surprised at my sarcastic remark. But for some reason, he brought out the worst in me.

"Or maybe you're just timid because you've never seen a man naked before," Mid smirked.

My eyes widened, and my cheeks reddened.

"I'll have you know, I've seen plenty of . . . naked men. . ." I trailed off. I had indeed *not* seen a naked man with my own eyes. And him knowing that for some reason made me embarrassed. *How did this conversation turn so quickly to talk of naked men?* I became suddenly very aware that I was naked and pressed myself even closer to the pool's edge. Even though he was across the cave and the mist was definitely shrouding me, and I was beneath the water, I felt the need to make sure I was out of sight.

"Really? Well then, if that's the case, I don't see why it should bother you that I continue on with my bath." One of his fingers slipped beneath the hem of his pants, and I panicked.

"At least let me turn around first before you do that," I squeaked.

His hand paused, and his smirk was suddenly replaced with a smoldering expression.

"As you wish," Mid said, his eyes piercing as his gaze locked with mine.

"Thank you," I said snappily as I turned around to face the other way. As I waited, I heard the rustling of fabric, then what I assumed were his pants meeting the floor. A soft splash echoed, and I knew he'd entered the water. I turned back around slowly to see him swimming peacefully, his silvery curls slicked back away from his face. The misting was beginning to wear off, and bits of his dark brown roots were starting to show.

"I know you don't find me unattractive," he said casually.

"That's a very bold statement," I said, relieved that he was in the water, a couple pools away, and his naked body was hidden from my direct line of sight.

"Well, considering the way you reacted to me when I kissed you on that rope, I wouldn't say it's very bold, just the truth," Mid said cockily.

"That reminds me. I'm angry with you," I said while starting to swim around in the water again, making small circles in the pool.

"Angry?" Mid asked, his tone amused.

"Yes, I told you I didn't want to be kissed until I figured things out, and you kissed me anyway."

"If I say I'm sorry, will you forgive me?"

"Probably not," I said stubbornly.

"Well, then what do you want me to say?"

"Why would I forgive you for something you aren't sorry for?"

"I'm sorry! Truly!" he assured me.

"No, you're not," I scoffed.

"You're right. I'm not."

"You're impossible," I growled, gliding to the side of the pool again. He did the same, resting his chin on his arms that he propped up onto the edge. I mirrored him. Our eyes met.

"I'm only human," he said innocently.

"No, you're not. You're literally not even human anymore," I reminded him.

"Okay, fair point. But I'm still a man. A man that is weakened by your beauty and kissable lips."

"My kissable lips?" I gave him a droll stare. I could not believe he'd just said that.

"Look, I'm sorry I kissed you. But need I remind you that you didn't exactly protest while it was happening?"

I remembered the way I'd allowed him more access to my neck. The utter pleasure that had pulsated throughout my body as his warm lips had kissed me there. I blushed, thinking back on the memory.

"Nixie is going to start on the device. She asked me to come get you two so she could show us all her plans."

The voice penetrated the air like a knife. I froze, a sick feeling roiling through my stomach. I turned and met a pair of deep cerulean eyes. Dusane.

He stood in the doorway, his arms crossed over his chest. He had obviously been listening to our conversations from the look on his face.

"We will be right there," Mid responded.

Dusane left through the archway, disappearing into the tunneled hallway.

I cursed aloud and rushed to get out of the hot spring, careful to use my towel to shield my departure. I grabbed my clothes in my wet hands, my chest burning with panic. Dusane had heard everything. *He must be so upset with me.*

"Ehren," Mid called, but I ignored him. My bare feet slapped wetly against the rocks as I started back toward the main cave. "Ehren, slow down."

Mid's hand was felt on my shoulder, and I turned around to see him clutching a towel around his waist.

"He heard everything, Mid. This is why I didn't want you to kiss me. Everything is just too complicated. Now please, let's just go see what Nixie wants."

He frowned, his eyes apologetic. But I ignored his pleading gaze and turned around again, hurrying back the way we'd come.

TWENTY-TWO

After I changed into new clothes and braided my hair, I met the others out in the main room. Nixie guided all of us down another hallway, and there seemed to be endless tunnels leading to different sections of the mountain. I wondered how Nixie kept everything straight.

Soon we entered another room where a colossal furnace existed, taking up almost the entire room. A hot orange light burned and smoldered in the hearth, and an assortment of tools was laid out on a work table.

Nixie gestured to the large furnace. "This is my shop and my smithy where I make all my weapons," she said proudly.

Dusane seemed to be inspecting the place, carefully avoiding my gaze, it seemed while doing so. I felt horrible for what he'd heard and seen. But now wouldn't be the best time to bring it up. Mid was trying to catch my eye as well, but I wasn't in the mood for apologies. I decided to focus on the device and listened carefully to Nixie.

"I'll use titanium to fashion the cuff. It shouldn't take me longer than a couple days to make it," she said simply.

"You said before that you were experimenting with materials when you created the dagger. What will forge the device with magic properties?" Dusane asked.

We all looked at her expectantly, and Nixie bit her lip.

"Promise to keep it a secret if I tell you?" she asked, her voice hushed now. We all nodded, and I watched suspiciously as she opened the door to the furnace. I could see the heat waves and the hot red orbs coming off the wood burning inside. I had to squint against the brightness. I was surprised to see it wasn't coal in the furnace but wood. I stared, hypnotized by the beauty of the fire and the sparks. With the hatch open, the golden speckles bounced off the singed wood and floated to the ground. I was surprised to find that when the sparks hit the floor, they didn't die out. Instead, they remained glowing the same bright gold—the pile of golden ash continuing to grow.

"It's the wood I use. It's not just any tree," Nixie explained.

I could feel myself slipping away as Nixie talked. Then something took over my mind, and a memory resurfaced without my consent.

Burning tree limbs. The heavy delirium of the spirit tree. Gold sparks all around me. The light taking me into its warm embrace.

I gasped aloud, and all eyes turned to me.

"Ehren, are you alright?" Mid asked beside me. I stared wide-eyed at the open flame now, confident I knew what was burning inside. *But it couldn't be.* I thought

"Snap out of it, Envorydian," Dusane was by me then, shaking my shoulders.

I finally awoke from the spell I seemed to be under, and my

gaze shifted to look at Nixie. Ignoring Mid and Dusane's worried inquiries, I blurted out the words.

"It's the Spirit Tree."

Nixie's eyes widened.

"What is?" Dusane asked, sounding frustrated now.

"The wood. It's from the Spirit Tree," I said numbly.

Dusane's head whipped around to face the blacksmith, his eyes narrowing. "Nixie, what have you done?"

~

After suddenly realizing Nixie was burning wood from the Spirit Tree to fashion her magical weapons, some explanations were in order.

"How did you know that?" Nixie was in a state of shock; it seemed that I'd guessed her secret material.

"Because I burned down the tree," I stated.

"You? A small, insignificant girl?" Nixie asked, and it wasn't really a rude question. She seemed to genuinely be taken aback by my appearance and that I was connected to such an appalling transgression.

"That's beside the point right now. How did you get wood from the Spirit Tree if it's been burnt down for almost a year now?" Mid asked.

Nixie's gaze stayed fixed on me as she answered.

"I've had a stash for many years. Before the tree was burned, I had established an operation that allowed me access to the tree's roots. I would cut off small pieces and take them back with me to Severesi."

"How? Wouldn't you need special access to even get near the tree? What about the Nurturers?" Dusane pressed.

"There is a tunnel. An underground tunnel that only a select few individuals know about. It leads to the roots of the tree. The nurturers are on a schedule and when they change shifts. . ."

"You would steal the wood," Dusane finished for her. Nixie looked down sheepishly.

"So, how much do you have left?" Mid asked.

Nixie pointed to a small woodpile a couple feet away.

"That's all I have. I'll have to work fast to make the device," Nixie said, but she was still looking curiously at me. Obviously trying to figure something out. "How did you survive?"

I blushed a little, taken aback by her interest. "Somehow, when the tree burned down, I became Stone-Hearted, then I woke up with the ability to heal, so I'm assuming because of my powers I survived."

Nixie's eyes widened even more at my explanation. "You weren't granted by a Reminant?" She looked at Dusane. He shook his head.

"Like I said, I just woke up Stone-Hearted," I repeated.

"You realize what happened to you, don't you?" Nixie said, suddenly talking fast and excitedly.

"Not really . . ." I said, unsure what she was getting worked up about.

"You were forged by the tree," she said seriously.

"Forged?" Mid asked incredulously.

"Yes, forged. As in when the tree burned down around you, the power within it must have literally bathed you in its power, granting you. The same way I made the dagger. You see, somehow, when the Spirit Tree's wood is burned, it infuses whatever is forged in its fire with power. You should've died during the process alone, but because the power granted to you was healing, you survived the process." She stared at me like I was a living Spirit. "It's miraculous. . ." she murmured.

I laughed nervously, crossing my arms over my chest, embarrassed by how she was looking at me.

"How did you know it was Spirit Tree wood just by the way it burned?" Nixie suddenly asked, her brow furrowing.

"The sparks," I stated, pointing to the gold flakes that had gathered on the floor. "I saw those same sparks right before I lost consciousness in the roots of the tree," I said.

"These?" Nixie swept up a couple of the peppery gold ashes and gazed at them in wonderment. "I've tried for so long to figure out why when the wood is burned, it creates magic. Maybe it has something to do with this."

"Well, why don't you get started on the device, and we can worry about the source of the magic later," Mid suggested.

Nixie snapped from the trance she seemed to be in and nodded. "You're right. I'll get started and let you know when it's finished." She glanced at me with wide, curious eyes once more. "Thank you. Your story has brought me new things to study."

She got to work then, grabbing her tools and starting to fiddle with the things on her table.

We left her alone, leaving her to her workshop.

I was distracted walking back to my guest room, thinking about all the things she'd said. *Forged by the tree? Could it really be?* For some time, I thought maybe I'd never figure out what happened to me that day, but now the answers were beginning to unfurl, and they sounded so impossible. . .

When I crawled into bed, I found myself staring up at the turquoise dotted ceiling of the cave. I couldn't seem to close my eyes. I was wide awake, my mind a mess of thoughts about the Spirit Tree and my subsequent rebirth by its flames.

After an hour, I knew sleep was wishful thinking.

I threw back the fur covers and carefully tiptoed out of my room, not wanting to disturb anyone. I padded down the hallway through the living room and down one of the halls I had yet to explore.

It led to more caves and tunnels with dripping stalagmites. It was much cooler at night, and I crossed my arms over my chest in an attempt to keep warm, wishing I'd brought my cloak. But not wanting to turn back just yet, I did my best to ignore the chill and continued to admire the dripping stalagmites that made the cave glow a thousand shades of aquamarine. I had never witnessed anything so magical without magic being present.

I wandered, gazing in amazement at all the sickle-shaped protrusions illuminating the cave walls and ceiling. At some points, I'd have to duck my head and travel through a shorter tunnel only to end up in another section of the caves completely. Each emergence felt as if I was stepping into a new world. Sometimes I saw small pools of water shimmering with the blue-green light—little creatures scurrying around within the mystical water. I made sure to pay special attention to which caves I passed through because I was afraid I might get lost.

One of the tunnels I traveled through led me to a large spacious section of the caves. I was surprised to see that I was no longer encased by walls on all sides. An icy wind blew in from a large opening that gave a view to the steep mountainside the caves rested on top of. I stepped up to the edge, my stomach twisting with unease as I looked down to see the drop-off, which was absolutely deadly. Below I could see the jagged slate grey rocks and blanket of snow that dusted everything. Then down even further were puffy white clouds floating between the crevices of Iradence, sleeping beneath the light of the stars.

"Are you scared of anything?" I heard a voice echo behind me.

I turned around sharply, my heart jumping into my chest. My foot met the edge, and a loose rock slipped free, succumbing under my weight. I was almost sent falling thousands of feet down the rocky mountainside before I leaped frantically away from the crumbling edge, landing safely a couple feet away.

Dusane's arms were around me before I could fully right myself.

"Damn it, Ehren," he muttered, and I clutched his shirt in my hands, gasping for breath.

"You startled me," I scolded and pushed him off me after I could breathe again.

"I'm sorry, I didn't mean to," he amended.

I glared at him, trying to get my trembling hands to relax. "You shouldn't sneak up on people like that," I said, hating that I was so easily spooked.

"You should be more prepared," he said in his cool tone that I was starting to realize sounded awfully smug.

"Oh right, Envorydians should always be on guard. Well, sorry, sometimes I like to relax and not always feel like at any moment someones going to come around the corner and kill me," I said sarcastically.

The stalagmites were casting a greenish-blue hue onto his face and somehow made his blue eyes more electric in the darkness. He chuckled, a rare sound that made me suddenly very aware that we were alone.

"What are you doing here?" I asked, averting my gaze from his, trying to avoid looking anywhere but his eyes.

"I heard something, and I thought I'd check it out to make sure it wasn't a threat. But turns out it was just you," he explained, walking a little closer to the edge now. "What are you doing here?"

I looked up, watching him curiously as he gazed out over the city. I was unable to decipher the emotion in his voice.

"Nixie just told me I might have been forged by the Spirit Tree. It's still something I'm trying to process."

He nodded, pursing his lips. "Wouldn't it explain things, though?"

I nodded. "Yeah, I guess."

Silence emanated between us for some time.

"Are you worried?" I suddenly asked. "That Nixie won't be able to make the device?"

I heard him sigh, but he didn't turn to face me. "No, I trust Nixie. If anyone can figure out how to make a weapon to stop Obsidian, it's her."

More silence filled the cave, and I knew I had to say something about the conversation he'd overheard between Mid and me earlier that day.

"Dusane, about what happened with Mid. . ."

"It's okay," he said, suddenly turning around to face me again. Our gazes met, and I could see that nothing in his expression was sad or disappointed. Rather I could see a solid determination in his eyes, and that worried me more for some reason.

"I am scared of things, you know," I suddenly blurted.

"Oh yeah, like what?" He began walking back towards me and the muscles in my body tensed. I held my chin a little higher as if it would help me face him and could feel the tension between us increase as the distance between us decreased.

"Death, for starters," I began.

"Death is part of life. You shouldn't be scared of it," he said in his trainer voice. It was such a Dusane reply, but I knew better. That was the Envorydian talking.

"I'm scared that we won't defeat the curse," I added.

"That's more valid, but you still shouldn't linger on failure," he said simply, coming to a stop a couple feet away from me.

Determined for him not to dismiss all my fears. I added another I was sure he couldn't just banish.

"I'm scared I'm going to hurt one of you," I admitted, and for a moment, I thought he wasn't going to answer. He stood so still, his eyes studying my face so calmly. The suspense of his reply was almost too much.

"It's sort of insulting, how fragile you think we are," he said casually, his tone indicating I was overacting. My temper flared.

"Would you rather I not care about your feelings?" I proposed cynically.

"What makes you think I cared that he kissed you at all?" he asked, raising his eyebrows.

"I thought you would be angry. I mean, I. . .I thought you cared." I stumbled on my words, feeling suddenly flustered by his nonchalance.

"Not really," he said, passively, dismissively.

I couldn't help it. His words stung. "Glad to know how little you care," I spat. I couldn't stop it. Angry tears began to blur my vision. I was about to turn around and leave the cave at that point. But he spoke again, stopping me in my tracks.

"You know he isn't the only one capable of kissing you, Ehren." I turned around and could see him trying to hold back a smile which only made me angrier to know he was amused by all of this.

"What's that supposed to mean?" I growled, forcing myself to blink back the angry tears that had surfaced.

He started to walk towards me again, and I took several steps back in response, trying to distance myself from him only to realize that the cave wall was behind me.

He very, very slowly leaned in towards me, our faces coming very close when he spoke again.

"It means I know exactly how I make you feel. And I'm not worried about your feelings for him getting in the way." His warm breath washed over my face, and the musky scent that always accompanied him was enough to make me dizzy.

He didn't touch me though, he simply looked at me with that expression of intense determination in his blue eyes. He reached up, pressing his palm on the glowing wall beside my head. Having him this close after so long of being apart made me physically weak, and my knees trembled.

"And I know one day you'll give in, and I won't have to steal a kiss from you." He leaned in even closer, and I shivered when the slightest touch of his lips brushed my ear.

"Because you'll ask me—" he paused "—*beg* me to kiss you."

I heard myself gasp, my heart stumbling in my chest, hearing the certainty in his voice. I pressed my hands against the wall behind me for support, forcing myself to remain steady.

"So don't worry about me or my feelings," he breathed while slowly pulling away from me. "I'm a very, very patient man."

TWENTY-THREE

I laid awake in bed the next day, having not slept a wink. Everything Dusane had said to me the night before was replaying in my mind. Intermixed with the conflicts I had about Mid, it was a literal hurricane of confusing emotions. I hated myself for putting them through this. Trying to distance myself from them both while figuring out my feelings for them was hard and probably impossible. But everything was just so complicated. I needed more time to work through what I wanted. There was more I needed to learn about both of them before I made some permanent decision. *What was the decision? If I picked, would that mean I was going to marry one of them?*

The utter panic that seized me made my breath stop. *Okay, calm down.* I told myself. *No one is asking you to marry them.* But then again, I wasn't going through this to just have some sort of flirtatious fling. So I would end up choosing, and I wasn't going to be making that decision lightly. I wanted something that was going to last. . . forever.

I sighed and did my best to shove my incessant thoughts and erratic emotions somewhere deep down inside me as I got ready for the day. When I walked into the living room, it was empty, so I checked the workshop.

Dusane and Mid were there, Nixie showing them something in her hands. The forge wasn't burning as usual, and everything seemed pretty quiet that morning. When I came up beside them, I saw that Nixie had a small silver band in her palms.

"You finished it?" I asked. Both the boys looked up at the sound of my voice; they had been engrossed with the little silver band.

She'd finished the device, which hopefully meant that we could go home now.

"I finished it this morning. I was just showing the boys how it works." Nixie gestured to Mid, and he held out his hand. She clasped the tiny piece of metal around his wrist, and we all stared at Mid, waiting for something to happen.

"What does it feel like?" I asked.

Mid smiled wearily and nodded. "It feels weird. I can't use my powers. If I try, it's like I hit a wall. It's wild," Mid murmured. His brow furrowed as if he was trying to create an illusion of some sort but couldn't.

"What's keeping him from removing it?" I asked.

Nixie unloosed the band, and Mid shook his wrist for a moment where it had been clasped. Then Nixie held it out to me.

"I've made it so the band can sense who touches it. It will only open for you, Dusane, Mid, and me, of course."

"It's magic." I touched the silver on the device, and it shimmered slightly at my touch.

Nixie smiled, taking the band from me. She placed it into a small wooden box, then passed it to Dusane.

"Well, my work here is done. You should probably be on your way. The last thing I need is a group of Envorydians showing up at my door."

"Yes, we should get going," Dusane said, then he seemed to hesitate before saying, "Thank you, Nixie."

"No need to thank me. Just remember the promise you made. One day return the dagger and the bracelet to me, and we'll be even."

Dusane nodded, then together, we made our way back into the main cavern. We gathered our packs and filled them with fresh food and water. It was surreal to finally be leaving. When I tightened a new white cloak Nixie had given me around my neck, I found myself nearly giddy at the prospect of returning home.

"Take this door. You'll find it easier than the way you came in." Nixie guided us to a tall wooden door I hadn't noticed before. It was on the opposite side of where we'd originally entered.

We stepped out of the safety of her mansion into a new dark cave, and Dusane turned back one last time to face Nixie. Unexpectedly he hugged her.

"Be careful. They know where you are," he cautioned.

"Don't worry about me Dusane, I can take care of myself." As they pulled apart, she reached out to tentatively touch his violet heart—it was glowing faintly through the white of his cloak.

"Peace through the heart," she said gently.

Dusane's impassive expression was hard to decipher. But I thought he seemed sort of sad.

"Peace through the heart," he responded gently.

With a final wave, Nixie closed the door, shutting us inside the darkness of the caves again.

~

The descent down through the mountain was much smoother than when we'd come in. This new path didn't have any obstacles, and I wished we'd traveled it the first time. We didn't encounter snake creatures, and there were no ropes to climb. There were actually carved out stairs for us to walk down. Soon we could see the sun shining at the end of the tunnel, and as we emerged, I tilted my head back to let the bright rays hit my face. I'd never been so grateful to see the sun. It touched everything that morning, overcoming the winter clouds and leaving a crisp, clear view of Iradence below.

"We will camp halfway and then complete the journey tomorrow morning," Dusane said.

I was eager to be off the mountain, so I had energy in my step that had been non-existent on the hike up. My spirits were high, my heart beating with the anticipation of finishing the journey we started. It wasn't until a couple hours later that our easy journey back down to Iradence took an unexpected turn.

The beautiful sunlight that had the snow twinkling and my soul singing all afternoon had suddenly become shrouded. Unexpected dark clouds started to filter into the clear sky. It seemed that snow began to fall in an instant, and we all stopped in our tracks as white balls of fluff began to whisk around us.

"Where did this come from?" I asked in disappointment.

Dusane looked up at the sky. "It looks like a storm."

"It's coming on fast," Mid observed.

"We can keep going, right? It's just a little snow." Just as I said this, a heavy wind smacked into the side of me, causing my hair to whip around my face. I laughed weakly, not liking the severe expressions on Dusane and Mid's faces.

"We need to set up camp," Dusane said, his jaw clenching. He dropped his pack to the ground.

"Should we go back to the caves?" Mid asked as he watched Dusane work the tent from a set of leather straps.

"No time, we have to set up now, or we may not have time," Dusane said.

The wind continued to pick up, and I had to squint to see through the flurries of snow now. It became increasingly cold without the sun shining, and I shivered into my cloak.

The seriousness of the situation settled in on us, and I helped the boys with the tent. It usually didn't take us long to set up camp, but it was hard to see with the storm picking up, and it took some effort to keep the poles in place.

Eventually, we secured the tent, and we all hurried into the safety of the canvas. Despite our heavy winter gear, all of us were shivering. Snow that had latched onto my eyelashes began to freeze there, and I had to brush off the little shingles of ice so I could see better.

More wind blew against the tent, flapping the canvas so violently I feared it might tear in two.

"Are you sure we can't make it back to the caves?" I asked, hugging my knees to my chest. I could feel the cold beginning to seep into my bones deeper and deeper with each passing minute. My cloak was usually sufficient to keep away the chill, but the temperature was lowering to a level that penetrated even the thick layers I wore. I clenched my teeth together, forcing myself not to let them chatter.

"It's too dangerous. We wouldn't even be able to see where

we are going. We'll just have to wait it out," Dusane said. He seemed pretty calm. But I could see the way he was rubbing his gloved hands together every so often for warmth.

I turned to look at Mid. He was gazing through the nearly minuscule crack in the tent flap, examining the storm.

"If we weren't so high up, this wouldn't be so bad, but because of the elevation we are at, the temperature is significantly lower," Mid said.

"How long do you think it will last?" I couldn't stop the shiver that coursed through me.

"At least through the night," Mid said, his face grim as he continued to stare at the tiny slit in the door.

Another whistling wave of wind smacked into the tent, shaking the canvas again. It was loud, the snow sounding as if it had turned into sleet as it hit against the tent. I closed my eyes then, burying my head in my hands.

I hated the wind. It always had terrified me how it rattled windows and seemed to beat against things as if it was a physical fist shaking everything in its wake. And the cold . . . it only made it that much worse.

"We should try and get some sleep," Dusane said, and he began to lay down, pulling his blanket up over him.

I didn't think I'd be able to sleep much with the wind, but I tried anyway. I tucked the blanket up to my chin and closed my eyes again, trying to block out the storm.

Mid stayed up, watching the tent door for a bit longer before finally laying down too.

We stayed like this for a time. Mid on my left, and Dusane on my right. No one said anything.

For the first hour, I successfully endured the cold. I clenched my teeth, squeezed my eyes shut, and pretended I was somewhere else. Then the second hour hit, and I began to go numb. I tried to ignore it for some time, but it became nearly unbearable when the third hour rolled around.

I didn't even know I was shivering so intensely until Mid sat up and pulled his blanket over me.

"Ehren, are you okay?" He asked, the concern in his voice evident. I forced myself to open my eyes and could barely manage to unclench my jaw to speak.

"I-I-I'm f -f-fine," I said through chattering teeth.

"You're turning blue," he said, and he was shivering too. But not quite as bad as I was.

"I-I-If my t-t- toes f-f -fall off, I-I-I w-w-will h-heal"

"I'm sure you can, but I'm not about to stomach watching that," Mid said, and even though it was supposed to be sarcastic, the humor was lost in the seriousness of the moment.

I continued to shiver. It was too painful to talk, so I didn't respond. After a couple more minutes of fiercely shivering, I heard the rustling of Dusane on the other side of me.

"We're not going to make it through the night if we don't do something," Dusane said, a tremble in his voice.

I somehow found the willpower to open my eyes again and met Mid's emerald-scarlet gaze. He seemed to be seriously contemplating something. His expression was hard as he looked from me, then to the tent door, and finally to Dusane. Then he cursed under his breath and stood from his blankets.

"Help me take off her clothes," Mid ordered.

It took me a second to register what he'd said.

"Are you insane?" Dusane asked, but Mid had already made up his mind about whatever he was about to do.

He stood up the best he could in the small tent and began undressing. He did it as fast as possible, trying to avoid the cold,

I guessed. He threw down his cloak, then started working the ties of his tunic before he threw off his shirt, and all that was left was his bare chest.

"Undress and then help me get her down to her undergarments. She'll warm up faster if there aren't as many clothes in the way." Mid continued to make demands, and Dusane looked like he wanted to argue but then took another look at me and seemed to realize it was the only option.

He stood and began to remove his clothes.

I couldn't move, so I could merely watch as the two of them stripped down to near nothing but their underwear. Mid finished first, and he quickly knelt beside me, his body convulsing with shivers. All the muscles in his broad chest and shoulders were strung in an attempt to fight the tremors in his body, and I noticed he must have been training because I didn't remember him being so brawny.

He pulled the blanket back from me, and I immediately protested, moaning and tugging the fabric back over me.

"Sweetheart, please, you have to let me move these. I promise you'll only be cold for a second." I reluctantly allowed him to pull the blankets back. He then helped me out of my shirt and pants. Getting my shivering, shaking body out of my clothes was more complicated than I realized.

Dusane came over to help not long later. My eyes were drawn to his body too, only for a different reason. He was muscular, no doubt, but I noticed for the first time that he had a nipple piercing in his left nipple. I wondered how I'd missed it before then scolded myself for even focusing on such trivial things at the moment and went back to concentrating on trying not to freeze to death.

I knew I should've felt more exposed having both of them

undress me. But it seemed insignificant at the moment. And I trusted both of them enough to know they weren't doing it for any other reason than to keep all of us from freezing to death.

I was in the sparest of dress conditions I'd ever been in front of them before, but it was only for a second before Mid took all the blankets and draped them over all three of us. Then they turned their backs to me and pressed me as close as possible between them.

The skin of their backs was so hot against me it burned. But it felt so good I couldn't protest.

"Spirits, you're cold," Mid said, pressing into me a little more.

"I'm s-s-sorry" I shuttered, pressing my cheek against his back.

"You'll warm up soon," Dusane assured me. And sure enough, the shivering started to cease.

After an hour, the warmth from both their bodies dethawed my bones, and I could finally relax. It was like a furnace beneath the blankets, sandwiched between the two of them. I closed my eyes, relieved I could finally sleep.

But sleep never came. It was hard to concentrate on keeping my mind blank with two gorgeous, nearly naked men on either side of me. I mentally groaned at the irony and then looked to either side of me and found them both sleeping soundly. *Of course.* I thought.

Trying to think what to do, I impulsively turned over and shook Mid's shoulder, seeing if he'd wake.

He stirred and turned groggily over to face me.

"Why aren't you asleep?" he asked, his voice gruff.

"Because I can't sleep," I whispered. His eyes were drooped as he seemed to still be half asleep.

"Are you asking for help?" he asked, a small smile tugged at the corner of his lip.

"Don't make me regret it," I fired back.

"Any requests?" his eyes opened fully then, and I wasn't expecting the effect of his gaze. His eyes were bright in the darkness, and they bore into mine. It was then I realized our faces were extremely close, and I began to feel uncomfortable about the fact we were both practically naked. I blushed but then mentally berated myself for being so shy. I recalled one point in time when I had willingly jumped into a hot spring with him with the same amount of immodesty. *Why did it feel so much more intimate beneath a blanket?*

"No requests. Just someplace warm."

"Someplace warm, got it," he said easily, his eyes closing again. I thought he might have fallen asleep, but then I jumped a little when I felt his hand on my waist. I saw a faint gold light illuminate beneath the blankets, and I knew I would be asleep very soon.

"I thought you didn't have to touch people to make illusions," I slurred, already feeling myself slipping away into unconsciousness.

"I don't," he said, and that was the last thing I heard before slipping into the dream he'd created for me.

TWENTY-FOUR

The next morning when I awoke, I felt something heavy weighing on me. As my eyes fluttered open and adjusted to the morning light now brightening behind the tent canvas, I looked around to see what was constricting me.

Mid had his arm around my waist, holding me tightly against him while I'd somehow managed to get my legs tangled with Dusane's. Then my arm was asleep beneath Dusane's shoulder, and Mid's other arm was snug beneath my head, acting as my pillow. We were a tangle of limbs, and my eyes widened. Warmth spread across my cheeks like wildfire, and I was thankful they were both asleep, so they couldn't see my reaction to being tangled in both of their arms.

Spirits, help me, I thought.

Somehow I managed to untangle myself without waking them, but it wasn't without effort. I found my clothes amongst the blankets and hurried to pull them on. It was still freezing, but the storm looked to have completely passed, and the sun was starting to warm up the tent.

Once I was dressed again, I looked down to see the boys sprawled out amongst the blankets. They both looked so peaceful. Mid's hair was a disheveled mess, and he was snoring softly. Dusane looked to have remained relatively in the same position throughout the night. He let out a soft sigh, and I wondered what he might be dreaming.

Mid had stayed true to his word the night before. My dreams were warm and quite soothing. I was riding Diablo most of the time, flying over a beautiful beach. It had been a pleasant place to slip away to for a while.

Tugging on my boots, I stepped outside the tent flap into the winter sun. The freshly fallen snow from last night's storm blanketed everything, glistening like tiny diamonds. I treaded through the thick snowfall and found a fallen tree that had been pushed over by the storm's mighty winds and dusted it off the best I could. I took a seat there and began braiding my hair. As I plaited the blue strands, I noticed that the amulet around my neck was glowing silver.

"I can't seem to figure you out, can I?" I said to the amulet.

I touched the glowing stone with fascination. It must be Mid's power.

My attention was pulled away from the amulet when Dusane emerged from the tent, thankfully fully clothed again. He ran a hand through his hair, looking around at the expansive of white snow. When he spotted me, he gave me a simple nod in greeting.

Mid woke soon after. He yawned and stretched out his arms when he emerged from the tent flap, then he shot me a lopsided grin when he spotted me on the log.

"Sleep well?" he asked, and he was obviously hinting at the dreams he'd given me.

"Fine, thank you," I replied, avoiding his gaze.

"If we don't encounter any more storms, we should be able to get back to the others by tonight," Dusane said, as he was strapping things to his pack already.

I forced myself not to get my hopes up. After last night's detour, I was starting to think the Spirits somehow were conspiring against me and wanted me to suffer on this mountain with these two men for as long as possible.

~

The spirits had mercy on us because we made it down the mountain in one piece. No storms. No Envorydian attacks. We journeyed back through the small village of Eastholde and on through Iradence and its glass buildings, and by the time we left the city gates, it was nightfall.

I was moving at a sluggish pace at that point, my feet dragging through the snow.

I thought I might collapse with exhaustion when we spotted a flickering light of fire through the thick frosted trees.

The guards that had initially journeyed with us were all sitting around a fire, talking together. Ghost was a pile of white fur resting in a bed of snow. Elesame was up in one of the trees sprawled on a branch, tail flickering lazily, and Diablo was a stark contrast of black standing by the fire.

The guards jumped up as we emerged, all of their eyes wide as if they hadn't expected us to actually return.

"Thank the Spirits, you're alive," one of them said as he got to his feet.

My Pegasi whinnied at the sight of me and trotted over to my side. I gently pet him, nearly falling onto his neck as my knees wobbled with fatigue. I was too tired to even talk to the guards and retreated to one of the empty tents almost immediately.

Selfishly wanting a peaceful sleep, I clutched the amulet resting against my chest and used Mid's power to fall asleep. I drifted just as I heard Dusane and Mid start telling the guards of our journey.

We'd made it with a couple days to spare. I sighed as a pleasant dream filled with wildflower fields filled my head, grateful that for now, we were okay. We could finally go home.

TWENTY-FIVE

I awoke to a loud pounding and the sound of a door swinging open. Someone strode in, shoving back the curtains on the windows. Light streamed into the room, and I groaned in protest.

"Please let me sleep," I begged.

"Since when do you come home and not wake me? I've been worried sick." Oli's familiar reprimanding tone actually made me smile. I peered up at him from my sprawled position on my comforter, squinting against the sunlight.

We'd arrived back at the castle from Severesi earlier that morning. And I'd immediately headed to my chambers to get a couple more hours of shut-eye.

"Oli, so good to see you," I said in the most cordial tone I could offer.

"Don't patronize me."

"Sorry, Your Grace," I teased, and the giggle that escaped me was impossible to stifle.

I heard him let out a long, exaggerated sigh.

"I'm fine, Oli. We just didn't want to wake you when we arrived early this morning," I said, serious now. I sat up and proceeded to rub the sleep from my eyes.

"Well, next time. Wake me," he said stubbornly. He sat on the edge of my bed and looked at me with his soft peridot eyes. I reached out to hug him, and he didn't hesitate to embrace me back.

"I'm sorry I worried you," I whispered gently.

"What happened with the blacksmith?" he asked.

I pulled away, smiling. "Dusane was right about the blacksmith and her abilities. She made us a device that can hinder a Stone-Hearted's power."

Oli visibly relaxed upon hearing the news. "I'll admit I had my doubts. But that is so good to hear."

I debated on telling Oli about what Nixie had said to me about my powers. Her theory of how I'd been forged by the tree, but I decided against it. I thought of something more pressing I needed to ask.

"Have the others returned?" I remembered Liony and Rosen splitting off from us on their journey to Obscurum.

Oli's demeanor tensed again. "We haven't heard word yet."

I frowned. "I hope they're okay."

"I'm sure they're fine. The plan was solid. We just have to be patient."

"And Shar's group?"

"They returned a week ago, they managed to get a ship, and it's waiting for us to depart to find the compass."

"When do we leave?"

"I don't suppose you'd stay. . ."

"Oli, you already know the answer to that," I said, narrowing my eyes.

"Next week, we depart," he said, sighing.

That would give me a week to get my bearings before going on another journey. I was grateful to have some time to myself, if only for a few short days.

"Do you mind if I ask what happened to your hair?" Oli lifted a faded piece of blue hair from my shoulder. It was starting to turn black again, but small pieces of pale blue still clung to the ends.

"I had to be misted in Severesi," I explained.

"Sounds. . . exciting," he said, his brow furrowed looking at the strand of hair.

I chuckled. "You could say that."

"Well, your sister is eager to see you. She told me to tell you to meet her on the porch for breakfast."

I sighed, realizing going back to sleep wasn't going to be an option. "Alright, just give me a moment to change."

Oli left me alone then, and I groggily dressed for the day. I donned a pair of trousers and a shirt, tied the red cloak around my neck, and then laced up my combat boots.

When I opened the double doors onto the porch where Jasper had set out tea, I was greeted by sun and sweet mountain air. As it always was in Knadiel, the temperature was pleasant, the weather moderate.

Jasper came over to greet me, pulling me into a tight hug.

"Welcome back," she said.

"I'm giving up precious hours of sleep for this," I teased but hugged her back just as tightly.

"In case you were to be angry with me for waking you, I made your favorite." She smiled and gestured to the table where a spread of eggs, ham, and potatoes were laid out along with fresh glasses of orange juice. My stomach growled.

"You know me too well," I said as I sat down and began cutting myself a slice of ham.

"How was your journey?" she asked.

"Evntphool," I said with my mouth full. Jasper narrowed her eyes at me, obviously disapproving of my bad manners.

"Well, that's good to hear. You got the device, I presume?" she asked, holding her teacup most delicately, sipping like a dainty hummingbird from a flower.

I took pity on her and wiped my mouth with a napkin.

"Yes, we did. The blacksmith made us a cuff that can subdue Obsidian's power."

"Well, I'm glad everything went smoothly.".

"I wouldn't exactly say smoothly," I said, remembering the rogue Envorydians and the snake we'd encountered. A shiver passed up my spine just thinking about it.

"Well, I'm just glad you're safe." She frowned suddenly. "It's too bad you're leaving again so soon."

"I'm sure you'll be sick of me by the time next week rolls around," I teased, trying to give her an encouraging smile. I had to admit I'd missed being around her. I hadn't seen much of her after returning from the courts and being angry with her for so long, and it felt like we were in great need of making up time.

"So I've been thinking because you will be leaving next week. . ."

I stopped inches away from shoveling more potatoes into my mouth. *This couldn't be good.*

"I thought maybe we could throw a party." The nervous expression on her face proved she knew I wasn't going to be keen on this idea.

"A party?" I asked, my brow furrowing. "What reason would we have to throw a party?"

"There are lots of reasons! But if you really need one, how about the fact it's your birthday in three days. And we never celebrated your eighteenth birthday."

I paused, thinking back on my time in the courts and realizing I had indeed turned eighteen while there and had forgotten my birthday. Now a year had almost passed, and in three days, I'd be nineteen. With everything that had happened during my time in the Courts, the last thing I'd thought about was my birthday. And if Jasper hadn't brought it up, I'd probably have forgotten again this year.

"I thought after eighteen age was no longer kept track of," I tried to reason with her. After our kind came of age, birthdays no longer existed. Someone long ago made the comprehensive decision to eradicate them after turning eighteen. I was in debt to this individual. It would be exhausting to celebrate birthdays after several hundred years.

"Don't ruin this for me, Bear. Come on, please?" Jasper pleaded.

"Isn't it a little late to celebrate?"

"Not at all! Your eighteenth birthday should have been the most important birthday of all. It signifies adulthood and gaining your powers. You never got to experience that!"

I'd never had a real Granting, which was the main reason I'd wanted to turn eighteen in the first place. Now that I had my power, a party seemed futile.

"I don't know, Jasper. I really don't mind that I missed it. . . '

"Well, I mind!" she said stubbornly, and I was surprised by her fervor.

"Fine, we can celebrate. But nothing big." I caved, seeing how important this was to her. I figured I owed her this much after isolating myself for three months.

She jumped to her feet and ran over to me, hugging me tightly again. "Thank you, thank you," she said, and I could barely breathe; she was squeezing me so tightly.

"Can't. Breathe." I managed to say.

She released me, and the smile on her face was worth the pain I was about to put myself through.

"I promise, Bear, you won't regret this."

TWENTY-SIX

Leading up to the party, I spent most of my time in my sanctuary, up on the hillside with Diablo. When I trained, I felt in control. I could think through the problems I faced, and everything was put into perspective. After the journey I'd taken with Mid and Dusane, I needed to do some thinking.

But my feelings were all but impossible to untangle. I hadn't seen much of either of them over the last two days. I said hello to Mid in the dining hall one morning and passed Dusane in the library at one point. But that had been the extent of my contact with them since being back.

I wished so badly my heart could just know what to do. But I felt like I hadn't had enough time with either of them. It was hard to focus on my romantic relationships when defeating the curse was our main priority. Any free time to continue getting to know them was cut short by meetings, training, and missions. *Maybe the party will give you some clarity,* I reasoned with myself.

I sighed as I flew down to the stables. The view from up in the sky was so beautiful. I wished I could just fly away from everything.

I landed and took my time taking Diablo to his stall. I wasn't at all eager to get back. Jasper had ordered me to get a new dress for the event. I tried desperately to convince her to just let me go in a shirt and trousers. But she wasn't having it. She was going to make this every bit the extravagant gala her Granting party had been, and I was mentally trying to prepare myself for it.

I sighed as I stepped inside and made my way down the hallway toward the sitting room Jasper had instructed me to meet her at. When I opened the doors, the room was busting with unexpected chatter.

Embrosine, Ruby, and Jasper all stood together, talking amongst themselves as they admired a beautiful gown that was being fitted to Jasper. The gown had bright yellow flowers bursting from the skirt and the bodice. And a fresh smell of daisies filled the room. Willow, the castle dressmaker, stood working little tiny beads to the silky flowers. I was relieved to see her there. She had been one of the few that survived the castle attack that fateful day of Jasper's almost wedding.

"Sabeara, so glad you could join us!" Embrosine said, coming over to greet me. We embraced, and then Ruby also reached out to hug me.

"Good to see you, dear. You're looking well," Ruby said.

"Thank you." It had been some time since I'd been thrown into a social situation such as this. A lighthearted chat with women of more delicate manners meeting together. I think the last time such a moment presented itself to me was when we all had tea together before the castle was raided back in Aveladon. I was out of practice. Awkward. Choppy. I guessed living with a rugged fighting guild for nearly a year would do that.

"We were just finishing up Jasper's dress," Ruby explained as she reached out to touch the beautiful flowers on Jasper's bodice that Willow was embellishing.

"Ruby made me this, Bear. What do you think?" Jasper asked excitedly.

"You made this?" I asked Ruby in awe, touching the flowers and realizing they were indeed real. She must have used her ability somehow to fashion the flowers into the design. I'd never seen anything like it.

"Indeed I did," Ruby beamed proudly. "But Willow here is doing all the finishing touches."

The dressmaker blushed.

"And you're next," Embrosine said delightedly, pushing me over to a small stool where I could stand in front of a mirror.

"Is this really necessary?" I asked weakly, already knowing there would be protests.

"The party is flower-themed," Jasper said, "It is essential you match."

I gave Embrosine a sidelong glance. She laughed at my expression, then proceeded to help me undress.

"I've learned it's easier not to fight it," Embrosine said with a wink.

I sighed and allowed them to whisk around me.

I was put into a basic shift dress that would be the base for the design, then Ruby started working her masterpiece by bringing over a small potted plant that had a tiny little sprout inside. I couldn't recognize the species. Then Ruby began growing the flower. Slowly, vines began to wrap around my body, and flowers started to bloom in bunches. They were roses. Big, soft, red roses. I gaped as they attached to the shift dress and slowly enveloped me until an elegant gown took its place.

I gazed in the mirror at my reflection and touched the supple petals that now made up the skirt of the dress. Somehow the roses had no thorns, and the branches were actually not as uncomfortable as I'd imagined them to be. It was soft and felt heavenly against my skin. Not to mention the smell was delightful.

"Wow, Ruby, this is incredible," I said in awe.

"Stunning," Jasper agreed.

"Thank you," Ruby said as she cut the stem connecting the dress to the potted plant. She then directed Willow on where to sew in beading to make the flowers sparkle.

It didn't take as long as I had expected. And by the end of the hour, I found myself actually enjoying talking with them all.

"You got quite fit while you were away," Embrosine said at one point, gesturing to my arms. "I wouldn't want to be on your bad side," she joked. I blushed and looked down at my arms that were more toned and defined than they'd ever been.

"It's all the training," I said shyly.

"I'll say," she smiled knowingly.

"I think it's admirable the steps Sabeara has taken to become an Envorydian. Not every woman would be capable of such a feat," Ruby said, and I was surprised by her comment.

"You don't have to spare my feelings," I assured her.

"I'm sparing no feelings. I mean it. You should be proud of yourself," Ruby stated firmly, and for some reason, her comment hit my heart more heavily than normal. It's something I imagined my own mother would've said.

"Well, thank you, Ruby."

Ruby came over to fiddle with one of the petals that was slightly twisted on the skirt of my gown.

"It's always wonderful to see a beautiful young lady grow into who she's supposed to become." Suddenly emotion caught in Ruby's voice, and I was shocked to see a tear fall onto her cheek.

I met Jasper's gaze in the mirror, and she also seemed surprised by the queen's sudden emotion.

"Mother," Embrosine said gently, coming over to lay a hand on her mother's shoulder.

"Oh, I'm sorry. Forgive me. It's just, whenever someone comes of age, it makes me look back on fond memories of my own children." Ruby stepped away for a moment and walked over to the tall windows letting in the last bits of sunset into the sitting room.

"Well, I think it's time we wrap this up, don't you, mother? It's going to be a big day tomorrow," Embrosine whispered gently.

"Right, of course. Willow, why don't you help Sabeara out of that dress," Ruby said while lightly dabbing at the corners of her eyes.

"I'll help as well," Jasper offered.

I didn't know why Ruby was suddenly so emotional. But my heart ached to see her that way. Ruby was usually a very happy person, not at all the type to burst into tears. As the girls began helping me out of the gown, I made a mental note to ask Mid about it later.

TWENTY-SEVEN

The night of my birthday arrived, and my nervousness increased as the day went on. I realized I didn't like the attention on me and would've much rather have spent the day in peaceful solitude.

But I knew it would be futile to try and stop the inevitable. So I dressed for the party, allowing Willow to help me because putting on the rose gown was impossible to do by myself. Then I did my hair, allowing it to just fall around my shoulder in waves. I wasn't keen on doing much with my appearance that night. But I did brush some makeup on my eyes and lips just so Jasper would think I'd tried to at least look presentable for what was starting to feel more and more like her party.

I sighed as I stared in the mirror at my reflection.

"Are you okay, Your Majesty?" Willow asked.

I forced a smile. "Yes, I'm fine."

"Well, you look beautiful," she said, gently touching the curls on my shoulder.

I thanked her, and when she left me alone, I had to force myself to have the courage to go downstairs. I was a trained warrior, an Envorydian, and I was afraid to go down to my own party. *Coward,* I berated myself.

I reasoned then that Jasper would be angry with me if I showed up late and forced myself to start down to the main ballroom, where she'd instructed me to meet her.

I wiped my sweaty palms on the feathery petals of my gown before pushing open the doors.

My mouth dropped open.

There were flowers. Everywhere.

It took me several moments to take it all in. The entire room was covered in all types of flowers. Climbing the walls, the ceilings, and the long dining table in the center of the room. Candles illuminated the floral masterpiece and music played by a band of musicians. Luckily it seemed that the only people in attendance were those that lived in the mansion. I relaxed a little —grateful Jasper hadn't invited the entire town.

"Sabeara!" Jasper called my name, making her way over to me in her beautiful gown of daisies.

"Jasper, I thought we agreed to something small," I said through a forced smile, my eyes still wide, trying to take it all in.

"This is small," she frowned, and I sighed. Mine and Jasper's views on what was considered small were definitely different.

Just then, Embrosine joined us. Her gown was entirely made of Corydalis flowers. A light blue flower that was absolutely stunning with her dark red hair.

She hugged me. "Happy Birthday," she said.

I laughed nervously. "Thank you." I was embarrassed by the attention already.

Embrosine and Jasper grabbed my arms then and paraded

me around the room. They led me over to King and Queen Knadian first, who both gave me cordial birthday greetings. Then we found Oli, who kissed my cheek and told me I looked beautiful that evening. He wore a thin gold crown on his head, and it was weird to remind myself that he was Aveladon's king now.

Then I was led over to where Shar stood in a small group with Rouix and Dusane, each holding glasses of Lush Fire in their hands. They all looked a little uncomfortable. I wondered if they grouped together for comfort. The rugged Envorydians probably weren't used to such. . . elaborate celebrations.

"Well, if it isn't the birthday girl," Shar said, a smirk tugging at his lips. I glowered at him, which only made him more amused.

"Happy Birthday, E," Rouix said, smiling and causing her wing tattoo to crinkle. Rouix was wearing her fighting jumpsuit, and I was immediately envious she didn't have to wear a dress that night.

My eyes flitted to Dusane then. His face was completely neutral. No emotion. I searched for something, any reaction. But of course, I received none.

"Happy Birthday," he said cooley.

"Thank you," I said to them all.

"Shall we head over to the table now?" Jasper asked. I looked around then for the one person I hadn't seen. But he was nowhere to be found. A sinking feeling formed in my stomach. *Had he skipped the party?*

We all headed toward the big table, where alongside the beautiful floral centerpiece were delicious dishes of food and desserts. I stared at the spread, my mouth starting to water as the smells wafted toward me.

We all took our seats. Jasper was on my right, Embrosine on

my left. As we began to dig into the masterpiece of food, I couldn't help but glance toward the doors every so often to see if Mid would walk through the door. When another thirty minutes passed without him making an entrance, I stopped looking. I decided just to try and enjoy myself.

And I was surprised to find that it wasn't unbearable. The conversation was actually relatively easy. I could tell Ruby and Knadian were grateful to have everyone there. Well, not everyone, but most of us. Having Liony at the party would have made it so much better. And Rosen. . . well maybe I wouldn't have cared much for his presence that night.

"Time for the cake?" Ruby asked excitedly, interrupting my thoughts.

"I'll go grab it," Jasper said, leaving the room for a moment.

My eyes met Shar's across the table, and he winked at me.

I glared at him. *Why was he so amused? Did he like to see me suffer?*

Sadist, I thought.

Jasper returned moments later, a beautiful white cake in her hands. She set it down in front of me. It had beautiful frosted flowers covering every square inch of it. And acting as the center of each flower were. . . cherries.

I gulped and forced a smile. I hated cherries—like couldn't eat one without spitting it out, despised. But I knew I would have to eat it, not wanting to hurt Jasper's feelings, and I felt a pit of dread form in my stomach.

Everyone talked excitedly as the cake was cut and pieces were distributed about the table. As a slice was set in front of me, I could but stare at the bright red cherry on top, trying to maintain my disgust.

It's just a little cherry, I told myself.

"You weren't planning on eating all that by yourself, were you?" A voice said over my shoulder.

I watched a hand pluck the red monstrosity off my cake, and I looked up to see Mid standing behind my chair, chewing on the cherry he'd just snatched.

He looked insanely handsome. Long brown curls slightly disheveled, with hints of silver clinging to the tips. His emerald-scarlet eyes were bright with mischief. He looked as if he may have been outside. An excitement radiated from him, and I wondered what had him in such a good mood.

"Mid! Keep your hands to yourself!" Jasper scolded him. Little did she know he had just been my savior.

"Shall we dance?" he offered his hand, and I took it.

He pulled me away from the dreaded table with the cherry cake and into the middle of the empty dance floor and began to sway with me. His hands fell onto my waist, and his pine scent surrounded me. My heart fluttered, fire erupting across my skin where he touched me. The back of my dress stopped pretty low, and I could feel the very edges of his fingers against my bare back. I looked up at him, meeting his gaze.

"Thank you," I said.

"For what?" he asked, but the knowing smile on his lips told me he already knew.

"For saving me back there," I said.

"I recall you telling me about your distaste for cherries. But humor me, what would have happened had I not saved you?" he asked, raising a curious eyebrow.

"I probably would have spit it out," I said honestly.

He chuckled. "You really wouldn't have eaten it?"

"Maybe, but if I had, I definitely would've felt sick later." I shivered. Just thinking about the terrible texture and taste in my mouth caused me to almost be ill.

"So *dramatic*," he teased, brushing a stray hair from my face.

I blushed and avoided his eyes. It was hard for me to concentrate when he looked at me like that.

"I thought you weren't going to come," I said suddenly.

"You didn't think I'd miss your birthday party, did you?" he asked.

I shrugged. It had definitely crossed my mind.

"Well, I assure you I was not trying to get out of coming to your party. I was simply late because I was . . . finishing something."

"Why does that sound so secretive?" I asked, my brow furrowing.

"Because it is," he smiled, his gorgeous lopsided grin that sent my thoughts spinning.

"When will I get to find out what this secret thing is?"

"Soon enough," he said elusively.

My curiosity flared, wondering what in the world he had planned.

"May I cut in?" We both turned to see Shar standing besidc us.

"Always the fun killer," Mid growled, but his guardian simply smiled smugly at him.

Mid left the dance floor, leaving me with one last longing glance before returning to the food table.

Shar placed his hands on my waist, and I awkwardly put my hands around his neck.

"What are you doing?" I asked bluntly.

Shar's intense green eyes narrowed.

"Why do you always suspect ill-intention? Maybe I just wanted to dance with you,"

"Come on, Shar, what do you want?" I asked.

"What are you doing?" he finally asked.

"What do you mean?"

"With Dusane and Midennen."

I looked down at the floor, watching the edge of my dress twirl across the wood floor.

"I don't need you to lecture me, Shar," I said, guilt consuming me.

"Don't you? Because I think that's exactly what you need," he said simply.

"I'm figuring it out," I said quietly, feeling the weight of the decision weighing heavily on me.

"You know you'll have to break one of their hearts eventually."

"Can we not talk about this on my birthday?" I asked suddenly, looking up and meeting his eyes defiantly.

"Fine, what do you want to talk about?"

"How about finding the compass? Do you have a plan?"

"I do," he said.

I glared at him. Irritated with his lack of elaboration. "And?"

"King Knadian will be joining us. He can control the water, and he will be extremely helpful in obtaining the compass."

I was surprised by this. "Who else is coming?"

"Basically everyone except for Jasper and Oli who will stay here, along with Ruby."

I was surprised not to hear Embrosine's name. "What about Embrosine?"

"She insists on coming, but I'm trying to convince her to

stay." His jaw clenched, and I could see he was not particularly keen about this.

"I see."

"Mind if the King dances with the Birthday girl?" Oli interrupted us.

Everyone at the tables had come out onto the dance floor then. And it was suddenly quite crowded. Mid danced with his sister while King Knadian and Ruby swayed in a sweet embrace together. The only people who weren't dancing were Dusane and Rouix, who were standing off to the side still.

"It was a pleasure, Captain," I said to Shar as I took Oli's outstretched hand.

Shar nodded, his intense green eyes giving me one last penetrating glance before he headed toward the Lush Fire table.

~

I danced for quite some time that night. Passed between partners, only taking breaks to snack and take sips of Lush Fire. I began to get quite anxious after about an hour and a half of conversation and dancing. The bright atmosphere was a little too much—the night maturing into sensory overload. I needed a break, a quiet place to think.

I left the raucous of the party, slipping away as silently as I could so no one would notice me. It wasn't that I wasn't enjoying seeing everyone again. I was just . . . tired.

I found an empty, dark sitting room down one of the hallways. The curtains on the window were pulled, and I could see the beautiful view through the glass. The moon was shining, covering everything in its soft pale shine.

Being sociable after coming home from our mission to

Severesi wasn't so easy. I knew that our problems were far from over. We had a weapon to detain Obsidian, but that was if we could even manage to capture him long enough to put the cuff on. I was nervous for another journey, knowing that we'd be heading off to find the compass soon and that this normalcy, this pretending that everything was fine. I knew it was going to be short-lived. I wished I could take the night for what it was worth, allow myself to just let go completely. But I was too hardened now to believe that pretending the world wasn't crumbling stopped it from crumbling any faster. I knew that tomorrow the sun would rise, and the memory of tonight's party would only be a painful reminder of the things we'd lost.

"Leaving your own birthday party? Isn't that against the rules or something?" Dusane suddenly appeared—a dark silhouette in the doorway. He had been the only one that hadn't danced with me that night. I tried not to take it personally. He didn't seem like the dancing type. . . but sometimes, his calm, cool demeanor made it hard to know what he was feeling.

"You of all people should know I don't follow the rules," I said.

"Something is on your mind," he observed, coming to stand beside me. He looked out at the view I was admiring, and I wondered if he appreciated it as much as I did.

The mountains surrounding the mansion were a peaceful solitude. The night sky shining with millions of stars that were unveiled from the clouds. I doubted I'd ever see the stars so clearly again. Up here in these mountains, everything was more beautiful, and nothing seemed to be able to touch us.

"I'm thinking about how pessimistic I've become," I admitted, giving him a rueful smile.

"It's part of the job description," Dusane teased, his lips twitching with amusement.

"Oh yeah? Well, I don't want it. Can you take it back, please?" But in truth, I wasn't really joking. I wished I could go back to when I thought all my problems would disappear once I became Stone-Hearted. When all I ever had trouble with was the jealousy for my sister's Granting and trying to escape castle solitude and boredom.

"I have something for you," Dusane suddenly said, his controlled facial expressions not giving anything away.

"You didn't have to get me anything," I said, but I was unable to stop the excited flutter in my stomach.

My protest fell on deaf ears as he reached into his pocket and pulled out something thin and sparkly. He held it up in the light of the moon, and I could see it was a bracelet.

"It's a set of mediator stones. I cut them down and put them onto a bracelet," he said, looking at my face as if gauging my reaction.

I reached out to take the bracelet and pulled it closer to see that six dainty charms dripped from the thin gold chain. Each stone was carved into a near-perfect little circle and hung from a small pendant.

"You won't be able to use them, of course, but I thought they were still pretty and would hopefully remind you of me," he said softly. It was the first time I'd heard a hint of embarrassment in his voice.

"Dusane, I love it," I whispered.

I remembered Dusane telling me that mediator stones were simply a set of stones. Ruby, emerald, sapphire, amethyst, moonstone, and citrine. But to a Reminant they were so much more. They could be used to pull power from the tree. They would simply be beautiful stones on my wrist, but it was the fact that they reminded me of Dusane and who he was that made it so special.

"Thank you," I said, looking up at him and meeting his cerulean eyes. He simply nodded as if not really knowing how to accept the compliment.

"Want me to help you put it on?" he asked, and I nodded.

I held my wrist out, and he gently fastened the chain. I moved my hand back and forth, admiring the way the stones sparkled when they hit the light.

"I feel as if I should give you something now," I admitted, laughing nervously.

Dusane shook his head. "I don't need anything,"

My eyes fell on his lips for a moment, and I remembered what he'd said to me in the caves only a couple days before. "You'll *beg me to kiss you,"*

I wondered if he'd stick to his words. *Would I beg him?* I doubted I could stoop to such lengths for a kiss. . .

"How are you liking living in the mansion?" I asked, forcing thoughts of kissing him from my mind.

"It's. . . interesting," he said as if struggling to find the correct words. "I've never lived with so much. . . luxury."

"Hard to get used to?" I asked.

"You could say that," he laughed weakly. "I don't think I could live this way forever. I'm meant for a more. . . simple life."

"What do you mean?"

"I mean that after living in the courts for so long, I think I found that solitude suits me."

"Do you think you'll go back?" I asked, realizing as I said this that at one point, he almost did go back. *How could a prison be the place he wanted to be?*

"I don't think I'll return to the Courts. But I don't think I'll stick around here either," he admitted.

I felt a tiny flicker of panic pass through me, thinking about him leaving. What would that mean for us if Dusane left after the curse was defeated? I wouldn't force him to stay in a place he didn't want to be. *But if I decided to be with him in the end, would that mean leaving everything I knew behind?*

I didn't have time to consider it further because we were suddenly interrupted.

"Time for presents!" Jasper sang, appearing at the doorway. "Dusane. . ." She frowned. "Gifts were supposed to start at eight," she scolded, noticing the bracelet on my arm.

"My apologies, my queen," he said, trying to contain a smile.

We gave each other amused sidelong glances before following my sister back into the ballroom.

TWENTY-EIGHT

The presents part of the party was even more embarrassing. Jasper made me sit on a chair in front of everyone while they all watched me open gifts. I didn't remember Jasper having presents at her party. Then again, it hadn't been nearly as quaint as this, and it had been raided. . .

I sighed as I tore the paper away from another present.

I'd already opened King and Queen Knadian's present, which had been a set of beautiful gold hairpins. Jasper had given me a new pair of shoes. And as I currently opened Oli's gift, I unraveled the paper to find a sort of shield thingy.

"What is it?"

"It's protection that goes beneath your clothes." He gestured to his chest, where I guessed his own protection vest was hidden beneath.

"Subtle," I said, rolling my eyes good-naturedly.

"Hey, I got to keep you safe somehow," Oli argued.

"Thank you, Oli," I said in all seriousness, then proceeded to the next present from Rouix. She got me a letter opener shaped like a knife. I laughed aloud.

"Thanks, Rouix," I said. She nodded, giving me one of her rare smiles.

Embrosine passed me hers next, and it was a journal. "I thought you could write down all your adventures in it," she said. I gazed at the beautiful leather-bound book and was pleasantly surprised to find that I loved it.

"It's perfect," I assured her.

I thought I'd opened them all and was about to get up from my chair when suddenly I was passed one more long rectangular box.

"Who's this from?" I asked, looking at the plain brown paper.

"Me," Shar said quietly.

I looked skeptically at the box.

"Oh, just open it," Shar said impatiently.

I tugged on the paper and removed the lid. Inside was a dagger. It had an elegant red handle and a sleek golden blade. Etched into it were several symbols. I realized then that they were Envorydian symbols.

"Shar. . ." I whispered. I was in complete awe. Entranced by thc wcapon's beauty.

"I thought you could use a weapon of your own."

"Peace through the heart," I said, still speaking in an awed whisper. All the designs were the ones that made up the guild symbol on my arm.

"How can I thank you for this?" I asked genuinely, unsure how I could accept such a gift.

"Think of it as an apology," he said.

I looked up and met his gaze. And it was then I knew for sure. That after all this time, he really was my friend.

After the dagger, there were no more presents to open. Jasper helped me put all my gifts in a pile, and then the party resumed. There was more dancing and plenty more Lush Fire refills, and I tried to enjoy the rest of the evening, but I could feel Mid's eyes on me, and I knew he had been the only one yet to give me a present. I couldn't help but think about the vague conversation we'd had earlier. I had a feeling that he had something planned, but he still hadn't come over to me. It was actually giving me anxiety. The longer the suspense grew, the more curious I became.

When I started to think I had imagined the entire thing and was about to call it quits for the night, he finally came over to me. I had slipped away to the Lush Fire table and was just about to grab my last drink. Everyone was preoccupied with other conversations. It was the perfect moment to slip away. My heartbeat increased with anticipation as I felt him come up beside me.

"Come with me," he said quietly, gently grabbing my hand.

"Where are we going?" I whispered as he began tugging me toward the doors.

"I told you I'd show you something later, didn't I?" he said, smiling an infectious grin I couldn't resist.

And then the same feeling came over me again that always came with his company. A dangerous cliff edge feeling. And something told me that a fall from such heights wouldn't be something I'd recover from.

We slipped out of the ballroom, and soon, we were outside. My mind and body were instantly rejuvenated the moment I took in a couple lungfuls of the sweet mountain air.

We crossed the courtyards and ended up at the stables. I was at home when the scent of horses and fresh hay overtook my senses.

Mid went to one of the stalls and retrieved Ghost.

"Where are we going?" I asked again, eager and cautious at the same time. *Should I go somewhere alone with him?* I bit my lip, unsure if it was a good idea to follow him.

"Up the mountain," he said as he began to saddle the beast. I took a glance back at the party. The dread that filled me when I thought of returning was the answer to my hesitation.

"If we're going up the mountain, we can take Diablo," I offered.

Mid looked up from where he was tying the saddle on Ghost. As if not expecting this twist in his plans, his eyes widened.

"Or not. . ." I said, seeing the surprised look on his face.

"No, it's a good idea. We would definitely get there faster. It's just—" He paused.

"What?" I asked.

"Well . . . I've never ridden a Pegasi before," he said.

I couldn't help myself. I walked over to him and placed a hand on his shoulder. "Oh, Midennen. Don't you trust me?" I asked in a mocking tone.

Mid's eyes narrowed. "Now I see why you don't like that."

I laughed and went to retrieve Diablo from his stall while he let the big white beast return to his slumbering.

Diablo didn't require a bridle or saddle, so I hiked up the petals of my skirt to mount his back and gestured for Mid to join me. Mid hesitated only for a moment and then swung up easily behind me.

He carefully reached around to hold onto my waist.

"You'll have to guide me," I said as I urged Diablo into a gentle walk.

"Just head east. It's not far," he said.

I swear I heard a quiver in his voice, but that only made it that much more exciting. Maybe I could rattle the prince for a change.

When I made it to a good take-off point, I gathered a thick handful of black mane in my hand and kicked Diablo's side. Then we were taking off into the air.

It was always exhilarating, shooting into the sky and feeling the wind brush against my face. As Diablo leveled out and began to ride the wind, that's when things calmed down a little, and I could focus on the view. At these heights, the world below us was so much less complicated. It was exquisite. Nothing could touch me up here. I was courageous. Free.

I felt Mid's arms tighten even more around my waist and could hear his uneven breaths.

"Scared?" I yelled to him, speaking loudly to combat the wind.

"How do you do this every day?" he yelled back.

I laughed, the sound getting lost in the wind.

"It's not so scary once you get used to it!"

Mid didn't reply, and I glanced back to see him looking down, his emerald-scarlet eyes wide. The expression was so vulnerable. Unlike I'd ever seen him. Usually, he was so self-assured and confident.

"Should I land over there?" I asked, pointing to a patch of land on the mountain amongst a series of pine trees. It was actually not that far from where I usually perched every day to train.

"Yes, over there should be close enough."

I guided Diablo back down to the ground. It was a smooth landing. Diablo was used to these parts of the mountains, and he readily came to a standstill on the dirt carpet of the forest floor.

The wind stopped. Everything was suddenly quiet, and I felt refreshed as I dismounted.

"So, what do you think?" I asked Mid, my hands on my hips. I couldn't stop the wild smile from manifesting on my face.

"Terrifying," he said simply, shaking his head. His hair was ruffled from the wind, and he looked a little rattled.

"Good," I smirked. "Now, what was it you wanted to show me?" I asked.

He seemed to slowly recover from the flying escapade and motioned for me to follow him further into the trees.

"This way," he said. He became more and more like himself with every passing minute.

We roamed through the bushes and around the large trunks of trees, the moonlight our only escort as Mid led me to the secret he'd been keeping.

Soon we came upon another clearing of trees, and I could see a small light up ahead through the foliage. When we neared, I stopped in my tracks, unsure if I was seeing correctly.

Up in a large oak tree was a house. A small ladder climbed the trunk until it met with the wooden structure. It had a black roof and a wooden balcony. I could see glimmering lantern light glowing inside through the windows that were framed by delicate curtains. My breath caught in my throat, and my heart clenched as memories of my childhood came rushing back to me. A piece of my hardened soul chipped away, revealing Sabeara underneath. The girl that used to sneak away to her treehouse for a piece of solitude.

"Mid. . ."

"Do you like it?" he asked, uncertainty creasing his brow.

I didn't respond right away. I walked up to the ladder and touched one of the rungs reverently. *He did this for me?* I thought. I slowly turned around to face him and felt tears blur my vision.

"How?" was all I managed to say through the lump in my throat.

"I got to talking with Oli about what I should get you for your birthday. During the conversation, your old treehouse got brought up." He looked shyly down at the ground. "That's when I had the idea to recreate it. I had some sentries help me with the building. We've been working all day and night for several days now. That's why I was late to the party." He nervously ran a hand through his hair.

"It's incredible," I said, still in awe.

"Are those happy tears?" he asked hesitantly.

I looked over at him and nodded. "Definitely happy tears."

"Shall we go inside?" he asked, pointing up at the house.

"Please."

He went first and reached down to help me climb up in the confines of my dress. When I finally made it up, I was surprised to discover blankets laid out on the wooden floor with a bottle of Lush Fire waiting for us. A couple candles gave a dim light to the room, casting shadows of our movements onto the walls.

"What part of this is real?" I asked, smiling knowingly.

"That obvious, huh?" he asked, and then his hand flashed with golden light, and the candles and blankets disappeared. He was illusioning some of the masterpieces, but the treehouse and bottle of Lush Fire remained.

His hand flashed with light again, and the candles relit, and the blankets returned.

"I didn't have time to get real candles and blankets," he smiled sheepishly.

He sat on the blankets and popped the top off of the bottle.

He poured us both a drink into two crystal glasses as I settled into a voluminous pile of my rose petal skirt.

He passed me the sparkling orange liquid.

"You didn't have to do all this," I said to him as I looked around, admiring the treehouse.

"I wanted to," he said.

He set the bottle back down, and as he did, I noticed that he had some scrapes on his hand.

"You're hurt," I observed.

He reluctantly allowed me to examine his palm.

"It's nothing, just a little cut," he said nonchalantly. He must have gotten the scrapes from working on the treehouse. I conjured my power and quickly made the wounds heal.

"Thanks," he said.

A comfortable silence passed between us as we sipped our drinks. I was still trying to comprehend the gift he'd managed to give me when he broke the silence.

"I have one more thing for you," he said. Reaching into his pocket, he pulled out a small rolled piece of paper. He handed it to me, and I stared at it quizzically.

"Should I open it now?" I asked.

"Wait till you're alone to read it," he gave me a secretive smile, then his eyes flitted down to my wrist, his smile fading. "What's that you got there?" He gestured to the bracelet Dusane had given me. "I've never seen it before."

"Oh. . ." I blushed. "It's just a gift," I said lamely.

He raised an eyebrow, and I knew I'd given myself away. Desperate to find a way to change the subject, I brought up the dress fitting with his mother and sister.

"Your mother is very talented. She made me this dress," I said, gesturing to the petaled gown.

He seemed to notice my not-so-subtle subject change, but he smiled anyway. "She loves to cover things in flowers. If my father had allowed it, our entire castle back in Ethydon would have been overgrown with them," he joked. I chuckled, trying to imagine the Ethydon castle covered in nothing but flowers from top to bottom.

Then the conversation I'd had in the sitting room with his mother came to mind, and I was too curious not to bring it up. "When I was being fitted for the dress, I talked to your mother and sister."

"Oh really? That can't be good then," he said teasingly. "Did they say something about me?"

I chuckled. "No, she didn't say anything about you. But she did seem sad at one point."

Mid broke my gaze, letting out a sigh. "She gets . . . emotional on birthdays."

"Why?" I asked quietly.

Mid looked up again and seemed barely able to meet my eyes. "Because. . . they remind her of my sister."

My brow furrowed. "Embrosine?"

"No. . . my other sister."

My eyes widened, and Mid's emerald-scarlet eyes held a pain in them I'd never seen before.

"You have another sister?" I asked.

"Had," he corrected.

Silence emanated between us as I took this in, and I could feel something in my heart contort painfully as I realized what he was saying.

"What happened?" I whispered, unable to speak normally with the lump forming in my throat.

"She was my twin. Her name was Esemere. She died when we

were young in a drowning accident." Mid looked down at his hands again, and I could've sworn I saw a tear leak down his cheek.

I reached out to touch his arm. I remembered him telling me he feared the ocean. Something told me that fear probably had something to do with losing his sister.

"That's why my mother was emotional. Something happens to her when she sees other young women growing up and receiving their powers. I think it makes her think of what could've been."

"I'm so sorry. . ."

"You don't need to be sorry, Ehren. It's not your fault," he assured me, a pained expression in his eyes. "It's the reason I am the way I am, you know."

"What do you mean?"

"All sarcastic and self-assured," he said, letting out a bitter laugh. "I wasn't the same after she died. She was very close to me, and after losing her, I started acting out. Breaking things, expressing fits of rage. Basically, anything to get out my grieving frustration. It took many years for me to get over the incident and for Shar to help refine me in my teenage years. And even then, I don't think I ever really behaved the way my parents wanted me to. In place of the fights, and rage, and acting out, I sharpened my tongue. I became witty, cocky. . . sarcastic. It's my defense mechanism. When I'm worried or afraid, that's what manifests."

I gazed with wide eyes as he let out his confession. And it was like I was seeing him for the first time. The regal, confident, devilishly charming prince I'd always assumed him to be. . . that wasn't all of him. It was a shield. *Could it really just mean he was afraid?*

"What are you afraid of, Mid?" I whispered.

He looked up, his emerald-scarlet gaze meeting mine. "Losing you," he said.

His response hit me straight in the center of my chest. I couldn't breathe for a moment.

"I've never known someone like you. . ." he continued. "Somehow, you make things brighter—clearer." He gently reached for my hand and then laid it on his chest, right where his silver heart was pulsing. "I've wanted to be with you from the moment I kissed you on that roof in Ethydon."

"Mid—" Being around him felt like I was about to be swept into a giant whirlwind. It was intense, heightened, passionate. . . I knew the risks of allowing myself to feel too much for him. I might actually spontaneously combust of heat and emotions if I wasn't careful. "—sometimes, I feel that I'm on this ledge. And that if I go too far with you, I'll fall, and then everything will break into a million pieces when it hits the ground." I spoke in a mere whisper. I didn't know exactly how to explain it all to him. "I fear that if I give you my heart, I'll never recover."

He considered my confession for a moment. "I promise —*you* and *me*. We are not going to break." He moved my hand from his heart and intertwined our fingers together. "And, you forget. . ." I couldn't help but look into his eyes, the emotion in them a burning complexity. "Your heart. You already gave it to me, Ehren." He leaned in closer, and then I felt his lips brush against my cheek—my neck. "You already gave it to me," he repeated.

A quiver passed through me, tingles shooting across my skin, through my bones. It was a voracious thrill, and it dared to overwhelm me. I didn't know how to stop it. Didn't know how to command my faint heart not to tremble for him. I was defenseless when he got close to me like this.

I was a soldier without armor, and instead of finding something to shield myself with, I was contemplating surrender.

Cerulean eyes jumped into my mind, trying to break through the thoughts that were overtaking me. *It's not fair,* I thought, *to either of them. I have to make a choice. I have to jump.*

"Mid. . ."

He pulled away to look at me, his nose brushing softly against mine.

"Yes?"

I didn't know how to tell him how I was feeling. So instead of using words, I simply closed the gap between us and kissed him.

He didn't hesitate to kiss me back. And when he did, it was deep and unforgiving. My fingers wound into his hair, and I tugged him closer, tighter. It wasn't just attraction that heated the kiss between us to spectral heights. It was the connection we had that was still awake and alive since the moment we'd met one another. A groan escaped him as his hand found my waist, and he grasped a fistful of petals. He leaned me back against the blankets and pressed his body atop mine, fitting us together like a perfect puzzle piece.

When he broke the kiss, I looked up to find the roof was gone. In its place was a sea of stars against a midnight black sky. Confused, I glanced left then right and found we were no longer in the treehouse. But instead, we were on a roof overlooking a quaint town. Fireworks erupted into the sky, a rainbow of sparks flashing into magnificent shimmering speckles. We were on the roof in Ethydon.

"You're going to hurt yourself," I mumbled against his lips as he kissed me again. The illusion was so real I could smell the assortment of treat carts down in the village square and hear the musicians playing a delightful tune. I could feel the wind on my skin. It was like we were there again, where he had kissed me for the first time.

"I'm fine," he assured me, silencing me with more hungry, insatiable kisses.

And I didn't fight him. I let him illusion us on that roof for as long as he wanted. Because it was beautiful, and wistful, and reminiscent. I'd have done anything to go back to that time. Where things were simple and less complicated.

So I let go. And we ended up sharing kisses and soft caresses until the sun risked coming over the horizon. In his arms, I was in a state of bliss, and I never wanted it to end.

TWENTY-NINE

"We have to go," I said, sitting up from where I'd been laying on Mid's chest. He'd returned us to reality in the treehouse a while ago, and we'd been stalling leaving.

I worried if we enjoyed ourselves too much longer, someone might come searching for us.

He tugged me back down playfully. "But I haven't had enough time with you."

"Oli will come looking for us!" I said, giggling when he turned me over, pinning me to the blanket.

"Let him find us," he growled, brushing a series of rapid kisses across my face and neck.

"Mid! I'm serious. He'll have the entire royal guard out here soon if we don't return," I said through gasping breaths.

He released me and sat up. His hair was disheveled, his emerald-scarlet eyes wide with contentment. His expression mirrored the felicity I felt.

"Fine, I guess we'll go back." He groaned, then he stood up and grabbed the empty bottle of Lush Fire. He extinguished the illusion, and just like that, the treehouse was empty of candles and blankets.

I made sure to grab the little scroll of paper he'd given me before we hurried down the ladder to Diablo, who was waiting for us. We rode back to the stables, and I took my time, enjoying being up high with Mid's arms around me. Mid wasn't as shaken this time, and he seemed to enjoy the ride the second time around.

I was still trying to contemplate what had transpired exactly in the treehouse when we put Diablo in his stall and started walking toward the mansion. It had all happened so fast. It seemed that I'd decided that I'd pursue Mid, and I was still trying to process it. *Was I really doing this? Had I chosen Mid?*

I knew that there would be many things I'd need to work through when I got back, and the bracelet on my wrist felt suddenly heavy.

From a distance, I could see the mansion lights were dim, and I assumed the party was over. As we walked, Mid grabbed my hand, and I let him hold it.

We entered the front doors and stayed as quiet as possible, winding through the halls back to our rooms. I thought for sure no one would be awake at this hour. It was nearly midnight. So I was surprised when I heard voices as we turned down one of the halls.

People were arguing. The voices were distinct, and it only took me a moment to put a name to them.

Shar and Embrosine.

I halted, instinctively pushing Mid against the wall of the mansion's corridor.

"Wha. . ." Mid started to protest in confusion.

I slapped a hand over his mouth, pressing the both of us up against one of the walls in the corridor. His eyes widened, and I simply shook my head and motioned for him to be quiet.

"Shhh. . ." I ordered.

My heart thudded in my chest like the heavy beating of a drum. I could hear in my ears, feel it pulsing throughout my body. Hot fear seared my skin as the severity of the situation washed over me. It would be impossible to shield Mid from what he was about to hear. I could only pray nothing incriminating was said. I held my breath. But the spirits were against me.

"I'm done pretending, Shar," Embrosine said. "I spent too much time in that cell to keep living this lie."

"Sparks, you're still recovering from everything that happened, maybe we should talk about this another time. . ." Shar's tone was on the verge of begging. He was obviously distressed. Something was very wrong.

"The only thing I'm recovering from is the broken heart I've had for the last seventeen years. The heart that *you* broke," she accused angrily.

"That's not fair," Shar growled.

"It's not. You're right," Embrosine said. "Nothing about this is fair. And I'm not going to subject myself to any of it any longer."

I looked at Mid, my hand was still over his mouth, but I could see the mix of confusion in his eyes as he listened to their argument. I mentally cursed. I could only stand frozen with my hand over Mid's mouth, not sure if I should interrupt or let their fight continue.

"You're married. You love him. . ." Shar tried to argue, but Embrosine immediately interrupted him.

"I love you! I don't love him! And no matter how long I stay with him, I will never love him the way I love you." She screamed the sentence.

I felt Mid go stiff beneath my hand. Then, our eyes met, and I could see his emerald-scarlet eyes harden. And just like that, he knew.

Mid pushed my hand away from his mouth roughly, and he pushed past me toward them. I immediately chased after him.

"Mid, wait. . ." But I was stopped in my tracks when I saw Shar and Embrosine.

They were locked in a passionate kiss. Embrosine had Shar's shirt fisted in her hands, Shar's arms wrapped around her, holding her to him.

Mid had stopped in the hallway too and was staring at Shar and his sister with a look of complete shock on his face.

"What in Spirit's name is going on," Mid said.

Shar and Embrosine pulled apart abruptly. Both their expressions went from surprised to guilty in a matter of seconds.

"Mid, I can explain," Shar suddenly said, taking a step toward us.

"You two. . ." Mid looked between them, obviously still taking it all in.

"Mid—" Embrosine said as tears filled her eyes.

"How could you keep this from me?" Mid whispered. He was hurt, the expression on his face so broken. My heart lurched painfully in my chest.

Then suddenly, he turned his unbearably broken expression onto me.

"You knew," he whispered so quietly I barely heard it. And that's when my heart tore in two. Yes, Embrosine and Shar had lied to him, but me—I had betrayed him the most. And he was looking at me as if I was a stranger now.

"Mid, he told me not to tell you." I instinctively reached out for him, wanting to comfort him.

"Don't touch me," he spat, pushing my hand off of him.

And just like that, the brief paradisiacal moment we'd shared together in the treehouse was gone.

Mid glanced at Embrosine and Shar one last time with that hurt, broken expression. And before anything more could be said, he turned around and started back down the hallway, not looking back.

PART TWO

THIRTY

SUNN

The sails in the distance appeared like white billowing clouds—arching and dancing against the wind. The salty tang that touched everything made me lick my lips. I was thirsty. But now was not the time to be distracted.

I tugged the soot-colored hat further down on my brow and weaved through the group of sailors on the dock. The shoes I wore were too big for me, and they clapped loudly against the planks. Luckily the pounding of my boots was barely noticeable amongst the other sounds of the harbor; the slap of braided rope against the rotting wood of the dock, the grunts of men hauling cargo from the ships, the slide, and shuffle of crates scraping against the boat ramps, and the fizzle of sea foam that seemed to cover everything.

I kept my head down, lifting the collar of my tawny sea jacket around my neck. It, like my shoes, was also too big for me. But that's what I got for stealing.

I spotted the Trenador, knowing with perfect recollection

the flag with the palm leaf and the one dark blue sail interrupting the celestial white of the other boats. I knew getting onto it wouldn't be difficult. But the trouble I'd get into if my father found out sent a surge of adrenaline through my veins that I craved. Instead of being afraid I'd get caught, I felt light, my chest expanded, and I could finally breathe. The danger was what made me feel alive.

I kept my head down the best I could as I fell into line with a couple other crew members. I used them to blend in as I climbed the ramp onto the ship. Ducking beneath the shrouds, I weaved through the chaos of scrambling deck men and pools of sloshing ocean water all the way to the quarter-deck.

I vaulted the sides of the ship and settled onto the wooden ledge straddling it to stay balanced.

Things were always a little chaotic on ships. The sails and main stay had to be put into position, and all the crewmates moved rapidly around to their posts. As the boat began to push away from the dock, I couldn't help but smile as the briny sea wind began to blow across my face. I glanced back at the shore, feeling the excitement that I always felt when I got to leave home for a while.

My father, Ashelor, didn't like when I left the island. I got a severe scolding every time he found out about one of my escapades. But it was the only way I found relief being trapped on that tiny little bit of sand with palm trees. It was much too small a landmass for me to roam.

I knew it was to keep me safe. I don't think I'd ever be able to forget the real reason I'd been isolated to the Isles of Arradale. Because of a curse that was on our race, my parents had thought it best for me to go live with my father's family for a while. To stay away from everything that might hurt me. My father was prince of the Saphirene Tribe. It was basically a kingdom that lived on an island with an epic set of trained sailors with the most extensive fleet in the entire realm. I had gone back and forth between Ethydon and the Isles my entire life. My father spent most of his time out at sea while I'd been in Ethydon with my mother, but we'd travel to the Isles for important events every once in a while. So it wasn't completely foreign to me. But I'd never been on the Isles for such a long period. And after a year, it was starting to make me feel a little insane.

So until the curse was defeated, I was stuck on the Isles of Arradale. And I planned to take as many secret expeditions on the ocean to maintain my sanity as possible.

"Is that who I think it is?" A husky voice spoke from beside me, the twangy accent unmistakable.

I turned to see a burly man with thick blonde hair and bushy beard. His blue eyes were bright in greeting. He was dressed in cotton canvas doublet and breeches. He had a knitted Monmouth cap and a red scarf tied around his neck. Down to the stockings and his black boots, he was wearing a classic sailor's outfit.

"Hello, Rissen," I greeted, saluting him. He was the captain of the Trenador, one of my father's ships. I liked the Trenador the most because of its captain, who let me work on the ship, and because it was the biggest ship and was an absolute beauty on the water.

"Lovely seein you, Salt." Salt was the crew name Rissen had given me a while back. One day I'd commented about how salty his famous whitefish stew was, and ever since, I'd been called Salt. "Ur daddy isn't going to be too happy when he be findin out you snuck off onto my ship again," he scolded, but his snaggle-toothed smile told me he wasn't about to send me back.

"Oh, don't worry about him." I waved my hand dismissively. "Now tell me, how can I help?" I jumped off the ledge, shifting my feet deeper into my boots so they'd stay on my feet better. "You know I'll earn my keep,"

He gestured to the bow of the ship. "Why don't you get to helpin Joon clean the deck up at the bow. He wasn't handling that mop very well."

"Aye, Aye captain," I saluted again and scurried off to the bow of the ship.

I found Joon fairly quickly. He wasn't Stone-Hearted yet, like me. And he had ahead of feather-thin brown hair and blemishes across his bright red cheeks. When he spotted me, his mud-brown eyes lit up, and he gestured to the mess at his feet. Presented before him were a bucket and a mop and absolutely no progress with the water on the deck.

"Thank goodness yur here," he said, wiping his brow.

"Give me that," I said, smiling good-naturedly. I snatched the mop from his hands and helped show him the correct way to collect the water, and he sighed in relief.

"Thanks, Salt."

Joon was one of the only crew members on the ship that knew I was a girl. Because I was still a year away from becoming Stone-Hearted, I could pass easily as a scrawny teenage boy when I put my hair into a hat. The freckles and blemishes helped too. I did it because if anyone found out how close I was to the royal family, there would be talk, and the more buzz that ensued, the more likely my father would find out, and I would be dragged back home.

Also, being on a ship with a bunch of men was only fun when they treated you like one of the guys. I knew the dynamic would change if they found out. Joon only knew the truth by accident when the wind blew my hat off one day, and my hair was let loose. The shock on his face was priceless. I thought for sure he'd sell me out or that it would be weird having someone know who I was, but instead, it created an unexpected bond between us. And, of course, the Captain knew. But we had an agreement, I helped out on the ship, and he was satisfied with keeping my little secret.

Joon and I worked on the deck for a while, but once we finished up, things became quieter. Soon the island was lost amongst the horizon mists, and all that surrounded us were flat aqua waters. I returned to my perch and watched the ship push through the waves, admiring the way the ocean swelled and bubbled around the edges of the hull. Joon joined me. Taking an orange from his pocket, he started peeling it beside me as we both just enjoyed the windy whooshing song the ocean provided.

I reached up and fiddled with the edge of my necklace, twisting it around my finger out of habit. My mother had given me the necklace. It had a small gold sun pendant that dangled from the thin chain. She'd given it to me when I was a little girl. It was what connected me to her now that she was so far away. I got letters from her every once in a while. But I wished so badly I could actually see her. Sometimes when I snuck aboard the Trenador, I could pretend that I was traveling to see her, that once we reached the docks, I'd run down the ship ramp and into her arms. And it was almost enough. Almost.

Much of my time on the ship was spent like this. Overlooking the water, sitting next to Joon and thinking. It may have seemed dull to most people, but it wasn't to me. The journey was half the fun, and knowing I was breaking the rules made it that much more exciting. And when we reached whatever destination we were headed to, I usually spotted different animals and creatures on the smaller islands we passed. I would even get in the water and swim if the ship stopped for a time. It wasn't much to do on the boat, but it was something different from the monotonous life on the island.

As the day dragged on, night eventually came. Most of the crew that wasn't on night watch ambled down to the lower decks. I stayed awake with Joon, and together we watched the aquamarine sea turn to midnight. The moon's pearlescent glow greeted us, and we basked in its peaceful glow until the quiet of the night faded and the sun rose again.

THIRTY-ONE

SABEARA

Sun & Smoke

I think about the way you looked that day
So long ago
When I saved you
And how
You didn't even know how much you'd saved me too.
Sometimes I don't know who I am
Or what I'm doing
but when your eyes find mine
It becomes so clear to me—
I am falling deeper every day
For a girl who outshines the sun

I think sometimes we get caught up in the rainfall—
We get lost in the clouded darkness and the way things
So often aren't just easy for us

But through the storms and the fires
I still reach for you
And through each blaze
I do not know what will be left scanning

I only know that I love you

And I hope, so deeply,
That you will be there
when the smoke clears.

I reread the poem for what felt like the hundredth time since opening it. Mid had given it to me in the treehouse and told me not to read it until I was alone. I'd read it in the dim light of my room that fateful night of my birthday, tears dripping onto the pages as I realized I'd pretty much ruined everything.

The silent treatment. That was my punishment for my abetting of Shar's lies. Mid hadn't spoken to me since that night. We'd left for the ship a couple days after the mess that had been created, and the entire journey Mid hadn't spoken one word to me.

We ended up in Seaporte. The same small sea town I'd taken Sunn when transporting her to the Isles. It was barren now, the little bungalows ransacked and not a soul in sight. But the docks were still in good shape and available for anchoring ships.

I stood on the dock now, arms folded across my chest. It was a beautiful day. The sun was shining, seagulls mewing above us as they flapped circles in the sky. The waves made a soothing whooshing noise as they ascended onto the sands. I was watching Shar and Dusane haul the last of the cargo into the ship, trying not to feel the utter heartache I now felt.

"Ready to go?" Rouix came up beside me. Her small form was adorned in one of her black jumpsuits. The tattoo across her nose somehow making her silver eyes look sharper that day.

"I don't know, Rouix. Do you really think taking this many people is a good idea?" I bit my lip, looking out at the dock.

"Shar seemed to think so. And plus, there is plenty of room for us all." She looked out at the ship docked in front of us. It was a giant, and I had to admit it was rather impressive. It was one of the Isles ships, and it had huge letters embossed on the side reading *"Diagon."* The sails were massive, and the wood though not in the greatest shape, still looked sturdy. There was even a flag flickering off the ship's main pole, and it was bright red, emblazoned with black stars on it.

Joining us on this journey to find the compass was King Knadian and Embrosine. Embrosine refused to be left home, and Kind Knadian was our only chance at getting down to the compass once we reached it. He could control water, and Mid and Shar seemed to think it was our best chance at recovering the token. Oli and Jasper had stayed home with Ruby, but everyone else was tagging along for the ride. It was a bittersweet goodbye leaving home again. But I couldn't help the eagerness I felt to get this all over with.

"I really hope we can get the compass," I said, and Rouix nodded in agreement.

"Me too," she said quietly.

Just then, Shar came clomping down the boat ramp gesturing to Rouix and me.

"Time to go, you two," he said, and I tried my best not to glare at him. So I was mad at Shar. Mad that he hadn't informed Mid about his little secret and had caused this tension between Mid and me. *But what was new?*

I took one last glance at the trees behind us where several Knadiel guards were setting up camp further up the beach. They would be waiting for us to return, keeping watch over our animals as we sailed the sea. I caught sight of Diablo's black wings and felt a nervousness seep into my body. I wished so badly he could come with me.

I faced forwards, trying to ignore the uneasiness I felt, and boarded the ship alongside Rouix. I stayed near her, hoping to avoid all confrontations with any grumpy males that morning.

"I've never been on a ship before," I told Rouix. I eyed the poles and ropes, more than a little confused about how all the pulleys worked and what everything did.

"That's what you've got me for!" Embrosine came up beside me, and I immediately tensed. I wanted to be mad at Embrosine, wondering why she'd never tell her brother about what happened between her and Shar. But something told me she probably wasn't the one in the wrong in this situation. I forced myself to remain calm and be civil.

"Do you know how all this stuff works?" Rouix asked, also looking around at all the foreign objects perplexed.

"I do, actually. I've been sailing on my father's ships since I was a child. He taught me everything I know." She smiled, her big brown eyes bright that morning. This expedition seemed to make her happy as if this was precisely where she wanted to be.

"Well, you'll have to teach us what to do," I said, forcing a kind smile onto my face. Embrosine threaded her arm through mine, gratitude in her eyes.

"I'd love to."

~

Embrosine guided us around the ship, showing us the ropes of how we were to manage the sails. None of the guards that had journeyed with us were joining us on the trip. We were the crew. And we were going to be operating the ship on our journey.

So I was a little surprised when we returned from Embrosine, showing us the ship's hull to find a new person was talking with King Knadian and Shar at the helm.

"Who's that?" I asked. He hadn't traveled with us, and I hadn't seen him when we'd been preparing the ship.

"Oh did I forget to mention, That's Captain Whitemane," Embrosine said.

The young man speaking with Knadian and Shar had a head of honey blonde hair and a handsome beard. As we got closer, I noticed he had a silvery heart, and his eyes were a light, nearly white blue. He smiled at us when we climbed the steps to get to them.

"Well, well, well, I didn't know you were bringing the ladies along for the ride." The blonde Captain sauntered over to us, a swagger to his steps. He reached out for Embrosine's hand and kissed it. Then he kissed mine, then Rouix's, who looked more than a little uncomfortable when the brightly spirited pirate brushed his lips across her knuckles.

"It's lovely to meet you, I'm Captain Whitemane, but you can call me Thane."

My brow furrowed, but I couldn't help but smile back at him. He was contagious.

"This is my friend. He'll be helping us cross the waters to the compass. I've been out of practice sailing for a time, so I thought he could help us navigate the waters," King Knadian explained.

I nodded, finally understanding. "Thank you for helping us," I said.

Thane winked at me. "It's my pleasure, love."

"We're going to start tightening the sails and get moving soon." Mid came up the steps, his brow slicked with sweat. He didn't even look at me as he approached his father and Captain Whitemane. Something in my chest felt tight seeing him there. Playing back the memories of that dreadful night only a couple days before, I couldn't help but inwardly beg. *Please, look at me.*

"Sounds terrific. Why don't I join you?" Captain Whitemane said to Mid, and to my disappointment, the two disappeared in the direction of the lower deck.

"Can we help with anything, Father?" Embrosine asked. The king gripped the pegs on the helm, gazing out at the water we had yet to start moving on. He looked as if he belonged there.

"Oh, we're just settling in. Why don't you girls go ahead and pick your sleeping quarters? We can handle this."

Embrosine frowned but nodded, gesturing for us to follow her down to the sleeping quarters.

I was surprised by how many rooms there were beneath the deck. One of them was dedicated to storage, holding all our food and water supplies for the days we'd be away. Then the rest were bedrooms. We each were allowed our own room that had a small cot inside. We spent the rest of the afternoon throwing sheets on our beds and putting our belongings away. Then because we had time, we did up the rest of the rooms down the hallway, quiet conversation passing between us as we went.

As we worked, I'd never felt so. . . domesticated. The men

working on the ship above and us girls fixing up the beds below.

"Anyone else feel as if we've been downgraded to domestic maidservants?"

Embrosine giggled, and Rouix gave me an exasperated expression.

"We will be allowed in on the action soon enough," Embrosine assured us.

"Oh yeah? And when will that be?" I grumbled. Making the beds didn't feel like curse defeating work.

"Soon. Trust me."

Rouix sat down on one of the cots we'd finished making, leaning casually against the wall.

"So Embrosine," I began, taking a seat beside Rouix. "How's Sunn doing?"

"Oh, she's doing well. I finally got a letter back from her father. She's safe and healthy. The Isles, I think, have been good for her." There was a saddened look in her eyes.

"Did she ever hear about. . . what happened?" I asked.

"Her father thought it best not to tell her. He held out hope I'd be found. And I guess he was right not to worry her." She looked down at her hands.

"But he knows you're safe now?" I asked.

"Yes, Ashelor was very relieved."

"You must miss your daughter," I said gently, remembering the bright red-headed teenager I'd met what felt like ages ago.

"I do, very much," she sighed, and just as she looked about to say something, a knock sounded on the door.

"Sorry to interrupt, but we're setting up dinner in the Captain's quarters." Dusane was standing in the door frame, and his cerulean eyes locked on me.

"We're moving? I didn't even notice!" Embrosine exclaimed.

"We took off about an hour ago," Dusane said.

Embrosine's eyes widened, and Rouix and I both stood up to follow her as she hurried out the door.

Dusane stopped me as I passed by him. I turned to look at his tan hand resting on my shoulder.

"You alright?" he asked quietly. Embrosine and Rouix kept walking toward the stairs leaving Dusane and me alone.

"I'm fine," I looked down at the ground, unable to meet his gaze.

"What happened?" he asked calmly.

"He's just mad at me. . ." I said, my voice almost a whisper. But I didn't elaborate. I didn't know how to tell him about the night of my birthday. I'd kissed Mid. . . I thought I knew what I wanted. But now, things were so complicated again, and I felt like my emotions had taken ten steps back.

"Why?" His brow furrowed.

"I didn't tell him about Shar and Embrosine," I sighed.

"What about Shar and Embrosine?"

"They're sort of . . . um . . . in love with each other," I said awkwardly, and Dusane looked astonished.

"That's unexpected. . ." he said slowly, and I nodded.

"Yeah, and now he's mad at me for keeping it from him," I sighed, putting a hand to my forehead.

"Hey, it's not your fault," he said gently. Reaching out, he grabbed my wrist, the one that had the bracelet he'd given me. He touched the amethyst stone dangling from one of the golden pendants. "He'll forgive you. I know he will,"

"I don't know Dusane, he seemed pretty hurt." I was unsure why he was reassuring me about the man that owned the other half of my heart. It seemed unfair to be talking to him about it all. But at the same time, I couldn't help but consider maybe all of this was happening for a reason. Perhaps this was the Spirit's way of telling me I'd made a wrong move the other night kissing Mid.

"No one can stay mad at you," he whispered softly, and I blushed immediately at his words. "I mean, I know I couldn't." He leaned down, pressing a gentle kiss to my cheek, then gestured toward the stairs leading up to the deck. "Come on, I'm sure they're waiting for us."

THIRTY-TWO

SUNN

"Spirits, it's hot outin here," Joon complained, wiping his forehead with a handkerchief.

It was blistering out on the waters the next day. I was sweating enough that salty perspiration was falling into my eyes. I sipped at the canteen at my side, wishing the water was colder and squinting to get the salty burn to stop stinging my irises.

"The sun will go down soon, Joon. Then we can rest." I hoped to encourage him, but even my tone lacked enthusiasm. I was tired.

Late afternoon we shifted the sails and started heading northeast. I didn't know where Rissen was headed. The journey would take a day or two. Or it could take weeks. I never knew how long I might be gone for, but I liked it that way.

"I see a ship in the distance, Capin!" one of the crewmates called out.

Joon and I looked at each other.

"Is it Saphirene?" I asked Joon, but he just shook his head, unsure.

"I don't know," he squinted to see what the other cremate was yelling about. But I could see it, a tiny black speck, interrupting the exquisite ocean view in the distance.

"Positions! Man your stations," the captain ordered.

Something cold flooded through my blood, and I could feel fear clench in my core. Suddenly the view didn't seem as beautiful and carefree. Something ominous was prickling the edges of the situation, making everything suddenly very serious.

I gritted my teeth, forcing myself not to panic as I hurried across the ship to where Captain Rissen stood at the helm.

"Captain, is it an enemy ship?" I asked.

Rissen's eyes remained locked on the ocean and the boat coming toward us.

"They haven't come this close in months," he murmured more to himself than to me.

"What does this mean?"

"Nothin good. I'm afraid you should've stayed home this time, Sunn."

I felt my stomach turn at his words, and my breathing quickened. I looked out at the ship where the men were taking up defensive positions.

"What do we do?"

"I want you to go down to my quarters, lock yourself inside, and take Joon with you. Push as many things as you can in front of the door." His voice was eerily calm as he spoke. He didn't sound panicked, but his calm collectiveness somehow made it worse than if he had been panicking.

"But. . ."

"Sunn, that's Captain's orders." He looked at me, and that's when I saw it. The fear in his eyes, barely hovering beneath the surface of his pacified expression.

I didn't hesitate then. I ran to find Joon, who was scrambling to help some of the other men raise another sail. I tugged fiercely on his arm, nearly causing him to fall over.

"Follow me," I demanded.

He didn't protest. He stumbled after me as we made our way to the ship's hull where Rissen's quarters were located.

I slammed the creaky wooden door behind us when we got inside and fumbled with the brassy lock and key. I cursed as my fingers shook, and it took me twice as long. When I finally locked us in, I turned around. I found the Captain's desk and other assorted furniture he collected cluttering the tiny room. There were bookshelves stacked with volumes of big books, a table with chairs, and a couple of empty Lush Fire bottles sitting out. Crates of ropes and other ship materials lay hoarded in the corners of the room. I cursed again and began doing my best to push whatever furniture I could in front of the door.

"Joon, help me with this table, "I said, trying my best to keep the quiver out of my voice.

He obeyed, and together we managed to push the table and the chairs in front of the door. Huffing and puffing, we moved to the crates next and then a couple other random things we'd managed to find— a barrel, a big box of candlesticks, a sack of oranges.

When we had moved all we could, I looked over at Joon and felt the severity of the situation settle in.

"The ship is going to be attacked," I said, and my voice didn't sound like myself.

Joon reached out and squeezed my shoulder.

"I'm sure we will be alright," he said, but he didn't sound confident.

What had my father told me? *Don't go out on those ships alone. You could get attacked,* he said. *It could be raided,* he said. *If someone found out who you were, you'd become leverage in this war.*

Joon took a seat on the floor while I paced, unable to sit.

Spirits, I thought. *Spirits, spirits, spirits. Why was I so stupid?* I directed a series of negative bywords at myself for the next several minutes.

"I promise I will listen to you from now on," I spoke aloud to my father even though he wasn't there, and I might never see him again.

Then we heard the crash. A wood splintering crack echoed through the ship and caused the entire hull to tremble dramatically. I pitched to the floor, unable to handle the momentum. Our pyramid of random furniture blocking the door came tumbling down as everything was roughly jolted.

After the quake settled, I pushed myself up off my hands and knees, where I could feel the bruises already forming. Oranges that had come free from the sack rolled helplessly around me.

"What was that?" Joon asked, pushing off boxes that had fallen on top of him.

"I think they crashed into our ship," I said, and I felt a similar fear as the day the Ethydon castle had been raided. I remember the adrenaline fueling my veins, sharpening my senses. And most of all, the dread. The same feeling came over me, and it was an unwelcome reminder of what it was like to truly be afraid.

The ship began to sink, and we could feel it as everything tilted slightly to the left.

"If we stay down here, we'll die," I said to Joon, and just then, water began to leak beneath the door and into the Captain's chambers.

Shouts sounded through the layers of wood above us and the muffled thunder of people running. Cries and yells erupted as if a fight were breaking out, and I forced myself to breathe deeply. I stood up the best I could amidst the disarray and began trying to make my way to the door.

"If we go out there, we will die too," Joon said, his eyes wide.

The two of us were the smallest and weakest links on the entire boat. Joon had only been working on the ship for a couple months, and he didn't have any skills other than carrying a bucket around and tightening a few ropes. And me. . . well, I was basically useless too, and because the both of us weren't Stone-Hearted, we had nothing in our favor.

I tried to conjure an ounce of courage, to not give up hope that we would be all right. But then something pounded on the door. My heart rattled in my chest. My breath caught in my throat.

The door handle jangled too, and I squeaked in fear.

"Someone is trying to get in!" I reached for Joon as he reached for me, and we clung to each other, waiting for whatever might come barging in.

More banging assaulted the door, followed by inaudible shouts and yells.

Then the door handle fell loose, and the door came swinging open. And that was the very moment everything in my life changed forever.

THIRTY-THREE

SABEARA

I followed Dusane up to the deck, and when we reached the top, the wind immediately ruffled my hair, a pleasant scent of salt and brine filling the air.

I walked over to the edge for a moment in my distraction and gazed out in wonder at how fast we seemed to be moving. The sails were holding the wind, sending the ship cutting through the vast blue waves. I gazed out at the horizon and could barely see the speck of land we'd departed from in the distance.

I sighed and turned back to Dusane, who was waiting patiently for me, and together, we walked to the captain's quarters where dinner was being held.

When we stepped inside, laughter and chatter immediately surrounded us.

It was a pretty cramped space, but somehow someone managed to get a large table in the quarters. Food was set out, a mixture of breads, cheeses, and meats. I took a seat by Captain Whitemane, and Dusane sat on my other side. I realized my mistake all too quickly and looked up to find Mid right across from me.

I quickly averted my gaze from his penetrating emerald-scarlet eyes and started putting food on my plate. It looked as if everyone had already started eating.

"Glad you could join us! Tell me again, what is your name, young lady?" Captain Whitemane beside me was clutching a goblet in one hand while resting his leg over the armrest. He looked laid back—casual. He seemed to be drunk too.

"I'm Ehren," I told him while scooping some potatoes onto my plate.

"Well, it's nice to have you onboard," he winked at me, his beautiful white blue eyes shimmering.

"This is a fabulous dinner," Embrosine commented, "Who prepared it?"

"Myself and this lad here." Captain Whitemane reached out and clapped Mid on the shoulder. Mid smiled, but it looked forced.

"Well, it's lovely," Embrosine said.

"Wanted to celebrate the occasion. It's not every day I get to sail on the seas again with one of my greatest friends." Whitemane raised his glass to King Knadian on the other end of the table. The king chuckled and raised his glass in response.

"To all the adventures we had together." King Knadian made a toast, and we all reached out to clink glasses.

Captain Whitemane started telling stories then of being on Knadian's ship when he was just a teenager and how he had taught him everything he knew. I wondered why Knadian had brought him on board the vessel if he'd been the one to teach the Captain and if it really was because he needed help to sail the Diagon. But somehow, I highly doubted that. I couldn't help but wonder if there was another reason that the boisterous Captain was aboard with us.

"So, Captain Whitemane, how long have you been a sea captain?" I asked.

"Please, call me Thane," he said while leaning toward me a tad and flashing a dazzling smile in my direction.

I gave him an incredulous expression and shook my head. "Okay, *Thane*, how long have you been a sea captain?"

"Going on ten years, little lady. And I'm the best in the Saphirene Seas." He sat up a little straighter, and I chuckled at the arrogance coming off him.

"Is that so?" I took a bite of bread, unable to stop smiling.

"Indeed it is. My power gives me heightened senses. I can navigate the ocean better than anyone else because of it. I can sense a storm before it hits—hear the flap of a ship's sails miles away." He winked, and I found myself impressed by such an unusual power. Every Stone-Hearted, when granted, was given a small level of heightened senses, but Whitemane's must have been unparalleled. "So tell me, how long have you been part of the Peace Tribe?" He reached out, clasping my hand lightly in his. He turned my arm over, revealing the tattoo on the underside of my arm. I blushed.

"Not long," I said, unsure exactly how to respond.

"It's rare for me to encounter a group of Envorydians." His eyes gleamed with interest, and I carefully pulled my arm away from him.

"Well," I warned. "I wouldn't be too excited if I were you." I took a bite of my meat, chewing carefully as I watched the young captain.

"Oh really? Why is that?" The amused twinkle in his eye seemed to sparkle even brighter.

"Because we eat pirates for breakfast."

The captain threw his head back, letting out a hearty chuckle. "Well, I guess I better watch myself around you."

I gave a friendly laugh, letting off the anxiousness that had overtaken me when he'd revealed my tattoo. Somehow it felt intimate, personal—the symbol on my arm. The way Thane had examined it felt as if he were seeing a private part of me. I tried my best to seem unfazed.

"So, Captain, how long do you think it will take us to reach the compass?" Shar asked, thankfully grabbing Thane's attention away from me.

"Well, according to Mid, who was the last to find the sunken ship, it will take us about a week to get there, retrieve the token, and return," he explained.

"Where exactly is this sunken ship? And how do we know it's the right one?" I asked. I remembered Mid talking about his expedition when we'd come home from Obscurum. He'd said they'd found a sunken ship where they assumed the compass could be hidden.

"It's just on the edge of the South Territory," Mid spoke up. "And the reason we think it's Linsulong's ship is because in the Ethirical, it talks about him being a great sea captain and him owning a compass that allowed him to never get lost."

"I don't recall a story about his ship crashing," I said, and irritation appeared in Mid's eyes.

"That's because there's not. We spoke to townsfolk rumored to know more about the ancient king. They told us this story, or rather a tale about beautiful women with fins taking down the ship of a mighty king. And that's when I considered maybe it wasn't just a tale."

"Beautiful women with fins? You mean mermaids?" I asked, and Mid nodded.

"So when we found the ship, we swam down near it, and we spotted something inside, something glowing, similar to a heart." He pointed to my glowing gold chest. "But we couldn't stay down long enough to get inside and find out."

It explained why Knadian was with us now. We needed him to manipulate the water to get the compass. I could only hope the glowing object they'd seen was indeed the token and that this talk of mermaids was a myth. The last thing we needed was more enemies. I let out a breath, inwardly praying we were on the right track and that this wouldn't be a huge waste of effort.

"No worries, we will get that compass! I have a great feeling about this expedition!" Captain Whitemane exclaimed.

Well, I thought. *I'm glad one of us does.*

~

That night after dinner, I decided not to sleep right away, and I took a stroll out on the deck. I found a quiet place and watched the moonlight glistening off of the water. Most everyone had gone to bed, except for Captain Whitemane, who was taking turns with King Knadian as helmsman from what I'd heard him call it. Luckily, the ship was large, and I could be by myself at the other end of the boat.

The white noise of the ship's sails flapping and the waves crashing against the side of the vessel was soothing. I sighed, leaning against the railing, wondering how I'd managed to end up here. On a ship, in the middle of the ocean, searching for a magical compass.

"You should really get to bed." Rouix's musical voice startled me from my pensive thoughts, and I turned around to see her walking towards me.

"Couldn't sleep," I said, and she joined me at the railing.

"I got seasick, so I couldn't sleep either," she replied.

"I'm sorry," I frowned.

She waved her hand dismissively. "It's nothing I can't handle."

Silence stretched between us, and I realized it had been a long time since Rouix and I had been alone together, talking like this. The last time I could recall was back in Obscurum when we'd camped together on the way to raid the castle.

"Rouix, can I ask you something?"

She turned her silver gaze on me and nodded, curiosity in her eyes. "Sure"

"It's about Dusane. Do you have . . . feelings for him?" I managed to spit out the last part, regretting it almost as soon as I'd said it.

Her eyes widened, and she seemed taken aback by the question. It took her a moment to respond.

"Yes, I do," she finally admitted. My gut twisted with guilt for some reason. "But that doesn't mean that he feels the same way about me," she smiled sadly.

"Are you upset. . .that we. . ." I stumbled on my words.

"No, E, Of course I'm not upset." She sighed. "I was a little jealous at first. But then I realized how stupid that was and got over it."

"Were you ever. . ."

She seemed to know what I was going to ask again as I trailed off awkwardly.

"Once. We tried, but he just could never fully view me that way. He sees me more like a sister than as any sort of lover." She laughed, and it was just as sad as her smile. "I'm glad he's found someone he truly loves. Dusane hasn't felt that way for anyone since I've known him." She turned to look me directly in the eye. "You're a lucky girl."

I felt my heart constrict as the word "love" settled over me. *He loved me? How did she know that?* He'd never said the word aloud to me. Now my heart was even more confused. I thought my heart had made its decision the other night when I'd been in the treehouse with Mid, and we'd kissed. But after what happened, and now hearing Rouix say Dusane loved me. . .

"I'm sorry, Rouix," I whispered, unsure what to say.

"Don't be," she said gently. "Just promise me something," she said, reaching out to lay a dainty hand on my shoulder. "Figure out what your heart wants. It's killing me to see him this way."

She gave me one last melancholy smile and turned to walk away before I could assure her of keeping the promise she'd told me to keep. I heard her quiet footfalls slowly disappear behind me, and I sighed as I leaned against the railing again.

I had tried to make a decision, but it hadn't really turned out well. And now I was questioning ever making the decision in the first place. And what made it all so much worse was everyone could see what was happening. And I was hurting both Dusane and Mid with all the back and forth.

I put my head in my hands, letting out a small groan.

My heart was conflicted. Split in two. After Rouix had said the word love, I couldn't help but feel that I did love them both. They'd stood by me when I'd mourned the death of my father, when I'd become an Envorydian, and when I asked them to wait for me. But even after all of that, I didn't know my heart well enough to tell who I loved most. It felt as if they'd both been with me in separate parts of my life. Mid knew one side of me.

And Dusane the other. And now that those two sides were colliding, I was extremely conflicted.

But Rouix was right. I needed to figure it out. Because eventually, the curse would end. And I'd have to decide what kind of life I wanted to live if it did. And most of all, with who.

My mind drifted to Mid, who was currently mad at me. And I felt a painful twinge in my chest thinking about how angry he'd been with me the night of my birthday. I couldn't very well make this sort of decision if I didn't know where he stood.

I needed to know if he'd ever forgive me for the secret I'd kept.

THIRTY-FOUR

SUNN

Big men in black cloaks seized Joon and me from the Captain's quarters, ignoring our cries of reluctance. I tried my best to fight the man's hold that had me, but he was much stronger than me.

Dragged through what was now several feet of ocean water filling the hull, my shoes that were too big for me came loose, getting lost amongst the rest of the debris that was floating around us.

When we reached the top deck, I could see the chaos that had been unleashed on the Trenador. Obscurum men were everywhere, subduing our crewmates. I spotted Captain Rissen, he had a giant wound on his head, and blood dripped down his forehead onto his cheek. Two Obscurum soldiers held him and forced him across a wooden platform that led onto another ship.

A big black ship much larger than the Trenador was the culprit of the raid and looked to be unscathed after it had inflicted an irreparable wound to the side of the Trenador. The

Obscurum soldiers transported our crew onto their ship, leaving the Trenador to sink to the bottom of the aqua sea.

I tried to bite the man holding me, but he simply increased the intensity of his clasp on my arms, and I whimpered beneath the pressure.

"Hold still, you little scoundrel," the Obscurum soldier muttered to me.

My hat was still firmly on my head, and I could only pray my identity would continue to be concealed.

Joon and I were the last ones to be pushed onto the enemy ship, and we were forced to join the rest of our crew. They'd tied up our crew members to several barrels and poles. The man holding me securely fastened my wrists and ankles with rope to a large barrel, and I could do nothing but struggle futilely against the restraints.

All of the crew looked beat up. Some were bleeding profusely and appeared to be badly injured after the fight that had taken place on the deck. They'd tried to defend the ship, and it hadn't been enough. And all Joon and I had been able to do was hide.

A man came walking down from the helm, dressed in black like the others. His hair was pure ebony and reached clear past his shoulders. He walked with a sure gate, his chin held high. He was flanked by two heavily armed crewmen. He stopped and looked down at us with eyes so black I couldn't even see his pupils.

"Where's the Captain?" The black-eyed man ordered. One of his soldiers gestured to Rissen. Rissen sat sprawled on the ground with his hands and feet tied behind him.

The terrifying man walked up to Captain Rissen and bent down, so he was closer to him.

"You're the leader of this ship?" The man asked. His voice was deep and husky but held an unmistakable sharpness.

Rissen didn't move, not answering him.

Unexpectedly the black-haired man's hand shot forward and smacked Rissen across the face. I gasped in surprise and watched in horror as blood spattered onto the ship floor, only to be swept quickly away by a wave of sloshing deck water.

"I asked if you were the leader of this ship?" he growled. Rissen reluctantly nodded, his cheek already turning purple and his eye starting to swell.

"Can you tell me where the Diagon ship is?"

"The Diagon?" Rissen's brow furrowed.

"You see, I need to find a ship, and I thought your ship was that ship. But it turns out it's not, and now you've set me back on my search. So I'd appreciate it if you'd answer the question unless you'd prefer a matching purple cheek," the black-eyed man threatened.

"I haven't heard of the Diagon leaving our ports. If it has, it was without my knowledge. I don't know where it is," Rissen managed to say through bloodied teeth.

The man let out another angry growl, then straightened, and as if unable to contain his rage, he kicked Rissen in the side with his thick black boots. Rissen moaned and curled into a ball. I was sick to my stomach watching Rissen be kicked around much like a wounded animal and had to look away. Whoever this man was, he was awful.

"Throw them overboard," the man demanded.

"They may be of some help to us, Obsidian," The soldier beside him spoke again. He was a younger Stone-Hearted from the looks of his. He had bright childlike blue eyes and dark brown hair. He seemed to be the terrifying captain's right-hand man.

"Then only keep those that will benefit me, James, and do it quickly," the man named Obsidian said, dismissing his comrade and walking back toward the helm.

The young soldier appeared to be distressed by this demand, and he came to address the group of us, tied and at their mercy.

"We require men that can navigate these parts of the Saphirene Seas," he looked at Rissen. "You. Do you agree to help us navigate this ship in exchange for your life?"

Rissen looked about to object, then he hung his head and said quietly. "Yes."

James went around to the rest of the crew, and those unwilling to serve them were taken from the pack and lined up at the ship's edge. I was too weak to swim to any sort of safety, and I'd probably be eaten by some creature even if I tried. I knew I had no choice but to fight for my life and pray to the spirits I'd find a way off the boat.

I was the last to be asked to stay on the ship.

"Will you stay and help operate the ship?" I was asked. My tongue stuck in my throat. Fear and anxiety overwhelmed me. "Speak up, boy," James pressed.

"Yes," I managed to whisper. Joon beside me sighed in relief. We would both stay. But I doubted we'd be able to stick around if we didn't prove we could help this Obsidian man get the boat he was attempting to find.

"Your sleeping quarters will be below deck, shared amongst all of you. We have minimal blankets and pillows. Some of you may be sleeping without. If you cause any commotion, you will be thrown overboard, and if you attempt to start an uprising, you will be dealt with in a more brutal manner than death. So I suggest you follow orders," James warned, but oddly enough, he didn't seem as if he wanted to be telling us all these things. He seemed softer than his master. Trying to keep us from being injured by the man above him.

James walked over to those unwilling to serve on the boat. There were about ten men, which left only seven of us left on the enemy ship.

"All of you will be thrown to the sea. This is your last chance to decide to stay."

"Wait," Rissen suddenly spoke up.

He struggled to get to his feet with the rope wrapped around his wrist and ankles. When he finally got to a standing position, he lifted his chin high, facing James. "I want to go with them. A captain goes down with his ship,"

"No," I whispered and instinctively pulled at the rope binding me.

But despite my quiet plea, Rissen joined his men.

Black cloaked soldiers guided those I'd considered my crew-mates to stand on the ledge of the ship and pushed them roughly into the awaiting ocean. I had to look away, unable to witness those I considered my friends being cast out to sea.

I heard splash after splash, and as I clenched my eyes closed, I couldn't do anything other than let hot silent tears stream down my cheeks.

THIRTY-FIVE

SABEARA

The following day I woke up earlier than the rest of the crew. Which wasn't uncommon for me. I was an early riser. It allowed me time to think on my own. The quiet of the morning was a precious time. Peaceful and serene. It was something I needed more of.

As I got up on deck, the sun was barely peeking over the horizon. In every direction, it was glassy blue, the ocean the only view. I walked the deck and breathed in the moist salty air, allowing the chilly morning temperature to wake up my tired bones.

I spotted Thane at the helm and waved to him as I passed. I then headed to the ship's bow and, to my surprise, found Shar already there.

He stood in a battle stance, his eyes were closed, and he seemed to be concentrating, meditating. I slowed my pace, not wanting to disturb him as I watched him move methodically through the motions of several common combat stances.

"I know you're there, Ehren," Shar said, eyes still closed.

"I didn't mean to disturb you," I said sheepishly. Now that I was discovered, I walked over to him, not bothering to keep my footsteps light.

"It's a little late for that." Shar returned to a normal standing position, and his eyes opened. His green irises were calm and serious as he apprised me. "You're still mad at me, I see," he observed.

I sighed, crossing my arms over my chest. "I sort of have a reason to be."

"You can't stay mad at me forever." He took a seat on an empty wood crate and motioned for me to sit beside him. I hesitantly took a seat next to him.

"Why didn't you just tell Mid?" I asked. "None of this would be happening if you'd just told him earlier."

Shar sighed heavily. "I couldn't. Embrosine married Ashelor, and if anyone found out about her feelings for me, it would have severely tainted her reputation and the alliance with the Isles."

"Mid wouldn't have told anyone," I argued.

"He was young. Too young to comprehend or understand what was going on between us at the time. And by the time he was old enough to tell, I didn't think it was wise to dredge up the past." His jaw clenched.

"Well, from what I saw the night of my birthday, it's definitely not over." I gave him a pointed look, remembering all too clearly the way I'd caught them kissing each other in that hallway. "Are you going to tell Ashelor? You can't keep going on like this."

"Embrosine plans to send word to him. She wants to speak with him in person. You're right that things can't keep going on like this." He looked back up, his eyes pleading. "I messed up, Ehren. But please, don't be angry with me."

"Mid won't speak to me," I said, a lump forming in my throat.

"He'll forgive you," he said. "As for me, well, I'm not so sure." It was rare to see Shar so torn up. He was usually so cold and grumpy. Now he just looked. . . sad.

I couldn't help but think back to when I'd kept Mid and our relationship a secret. I'd felt it was necessary at one time, even if it had been foolish. I couldn't stay mad at Shar for something I had done once.

"I know you didn't mean to hurt anyone," I whispered. "Just promise me no more secrets, please." I looked up, and the relief was evident in his expression.

"I'm sorry about not telling Mid. And most of all, I'm sorry for not telling you about your father right away." He reached out to grab my hand. "I consider you my friend. And as your friend, I shouldn't have done that."

"I accept your apology." I leaned over to press a quick kiss to his cheek. He shoved me away lightly, and I chuckled.

"Okay old man, are you going to let me train with you now?" I stood up, smirking at him and his eyes widened in feigned shock.

"Train with me? You couldn't keep up."

"Oh, I think I can." I raised my fists in a fight position, and he slowly stood to match me.

"You may think I'm an old man, but let's get one thing straight. This old man always wins."

"We'll see about that."

It felt good not to be angry with Shar anymore. I was tired of being angry and tired of people being mad at me. I just wished that everyone could get along. But maybe that was asking for too much...

We trained together on the front deck for an hour or so, hand-to-hand combat, and I forgot how nice it was to train with a partner. I'd been doing exercises on my own when I'd been in Knadiel, and it just wasn't the same.

The sun rose higher, causing me to sweat more as it burned away the chilly morning air. With the sun up, the others began to wake. Soon Shar and I weren't alone anymore.

"You're dropping your right shoulder," Dusane said behind me. I jumped a little when I felt his hand fall gently onto my shoulder. "I taught you better, Envorydian," he scolded teasingly.

"I'll keep my right shoulder up when you stop leading with your left foot, *Captain*." I turned around and gave him a teasing smirk. I was in a good mood. Having one less person to hold a grudge against that morning was lifting my spirits. Now if I could just get Mid to forgive me...

Shar stifled a laugh, but it was too late. Dusane shot him a glare.

"Oh, I see how it is." Dusane's eyes narrowed on me, but I could see the flirtation twinkling there. "Why don't we settle this right now." He raised an eyebrow and gestured toward the open space where Shar and I had been training.

"Not so fast, you two," Embrosine appeared around one of the flapping white sails. She wore an adorable sailor's coat with a red scarf tied around her neck. Her auburn red hair glistened even more red in the sun, and I had to admit once again how stunning she looked. She could pull off anything. "Breakfast is ready."

Her eyes landed on Shar, and I watched them look at each other for a moment. Obviously, they still needed to work things out with one another because the tension increased as we all stood there, and I quickly took the chance to escape the uncomfortable situation.

"Sounds great!" I grabbed Dusane's hand and hurried away from Embrosine and Shar, leaving them alone.

"What was that about?" Dusane whispered as we made our way to the captain's quarters.

"Embrosine. Shar. In love with each other secretly, remember?"

"Oh right," Dusane pursed his lips together, fighting a smile. "Is it just me, or does it seem bizarre that Shar is actually in love with someone?"

"Trust me, it's not just you."

~

I planned to talk to Mid after breakfast. I was determined to figure things out between us. But Thane was particularly chatty that morning, and the two walked away together before I could even approach Mid. It was apparent he was still avoiding me, and it was driving me crazy.

I stifled my disappointment and followed Rouix and Embrosine back out onto the deck. We all were needed that morning to help, and Embrosine once again walked us through all the things she'd previously shown us the day before. She knew the ship well, and soon we were moving the sails and adjusting the pulleys without help. It was calming being on the boat, fun even. I was beginning to understand the appeal it held.

All afternoon and into the evening, we worked on the ship. We even cleaned the deck and got rid of the extra water floating around. I was sweating and exhausted by the time dinner rolled around. I tried to catch Mid's eye throughout the day, but he always managed to be on the opposite end of the ship as far away from me as possible.

Then to my further disappointment, Mid wasn't at dinner. I tried knocking on his door that evening, but he wouldn't open it, and I gave up after a couple minutes of trying. Feeling defeated, I slept that night wondering if I'd ever get the chance to fix things.

THIRTY-SIX

SUNN

The hull of the ship was as bad as I imagined it to be. Hot, sweaty, and reeking of bodily odors. The lack of hygiene was appalling. I had to squeeze my eyes shut at some point when Joon warned me of men undressing.

"On yur left," Joon whispered as one of the Obscurum men began to disrobe in front of everyone.

"Joon, we have to get out of here," I said desperately, my eyes still closed.

Our crew merged with the rest of the Obscurum soldiers, and I could immediately feel the defeat from everyone on our side. We were tossed into the hull with not an ounce of welcome. All the beds were taken and what remained was a cold, wet floor and a couple of blankets.

"How'r we gonna do that?" Joon asked.

We managed to find one small blanket amongst the scarce amount of bedding and curled up together in the farthest end of the room.

Joon was shivering, and so was I. When it became dark out at sea, it would get quite chilly, but the additional wetness from the water made everything miserable.

"I don't know yet, but I'll find a way," I said.

The door to the hull opened unexpectedly, and James came through the door.

"Lights out, men," he ordered, and the soldiers did as commanded, blowing out lanterns and candles around the room until it was pitch black. I could hear Joon's nervous breathing beside me as he laid down to sleep.

I tried to close my eyes and shut out the nightmare I'd stepped into, but sounds of men turning over, grunting, and snoring kept me awake. So to keep out the panic that threatened to smother me and to keep the fear from consuming me, I reached up and clutched the necklace around my neck and hummed a song. The lullaby Mid wrote for me as a child. And that's when it happened. Staring into the blackness, humming the quiet harmonic tune to myself that soothed my terrified soul, a plan to escape began to form in my head.

~

The next morning we were woken at the crack of dawn. I shuffled out onto the main deck, the light causing me to squint against the brightness.

"To your stations. New crewmates, find a place to fill in." James was already giving orders. Oddly enough, I didn't feel the same malicious intent coming from James as I did from Obsidian. He seemed to be doing the Captain's bidding, and almost reluctantly. His bright blue eyes were too kind, too innocent to be part of something so vicious. That's when I decided he was as much a slave as we were. And hopefully, I could use that to my advantage.

Joon and I quietly found a place to stand station and help raise sails with the other men. One of the cremates from the Trenador named Vilet, who I'd known in passing, was assigned to take over leading the crew. Not many of the Obscurum soldiers knew how to run anything. Most of my day was spent trying to fix stupid mistakes made by the men in black cloaks. I don't know how they'd made it this far on the water, but I was starting to theorize why Obsidian had attacked the Trenador in the first place. Maybe it wasn't because he mistook the ship for the Diagon. Perhaps it was because he didn't know what he was doing, and he needed help running the ship.

We worked quietly, the morning reasonably calm. That was until the captain woke up.

He came up from his quarters and checked in with James first. Then he walked up to the helm and gazed out at the ship and his crew with his soulless black eyes. I stole glances up at him when I could, trying to get a read on him. I hoped my plan would work to get Joon and me off the ship.

I was still shaken up about what happened to Rissen and the others, but the angry fire inside me fueled my need for escape. All night it had been building. And I couldn't allow Joon and I or any of the other remaining crewmen that I knew to end up with the rest of them out at sea. I wouldn't, couldn't, let this cruel bastard get away with it.

I was surprised to find that the anger inside me that had been a quiet kindling all night was now a full-blown fire. I had a little bit of an anger problem at times. And a swearing problem, according to my father. I don't know where it came from, but I had a short fuse. I could light quickly, and I burned fast, destroying everything in my path. But I forced myself not to get carried away right away, I needed to be strategic, so I couldn't let my emotions get away from me.

I blew out a heavy breath and decided it was now or never if I would instigate this plan.

"I'll be back, Joon," I told him, and before he could protest, I left my station and walked over to James, who was diligently making sure every person manned their station.

I tapped on his shoulder, and he turned around. I was pretty short, so it took him a moment to look down and notice me.

"Why are you off your station, boy?" he asked me, and that's when I saw it. A flicker of panic in his eyes, but not for himself, for me. He cared. He was making sure we manned our stations because he knew the repercussions evil Black Eyes could inflict and didn't want any of us getting killed.

"I need to speak with the captain," I said boldly.

"You need to get back to your station. No one demands to speak to the captain," he turned me around, shoving me back toward where I'd come from.

I fought with reluctance and twisted around, doing my best to find traction with my socks on the slippery deck.

"It's important, please. I need to speak with him."

"Are you trying to get yourself killed?" James asked beneath his breath in a warning tone that I probably should've listened to.

"What's going on here?" The sound of the Captain's voice caused both of us to still.

James cursed then turned around to face Obsidian. I was partly hidden behind him.

"Nothing, Captain, just redirecting this crewmate back to his station."

"Actually, I need to talk to you." I pushed past James and heard him curse again beneath his breath.

Obsidian raised an eyebrow as I went to stand in front of him. He was at least a foot and a half taller than me, and I had to tilt my head back a lot to look up at him.

"I have some information you need," I stated boldly.

"Is that so?" he asked, and I did my best not to shiver looking into his black irises. They were even creepier up close.

"I have information on the Diagon's location." It was a lie. I had no idea where this stupid ship was that he was looking for. But he didn't know that, and I figured my best bet on survival was to pretend to have what he needed. The supplies on the ship were waning. The longer we stayed, the more chances there were of us getting thrown off the ship. I needed to be invaluable. I needed him to trust me.

"Really?" His eyes narrowed, and he leaned down so we were level with each other. "And where is the Diagon, boy?"

"It went en route to the South Territory. They were carrying cargo." The lie came out smoothly enough.

The captain flashed an unconvinced smile, then he straightened and gestured for James to come to him.

James hurried over to his side, and then Obsidian gestured to the mast in the center of the ship.

"Tie him up. Don't give him food or drink."

James's eyes widened, but he nodded.

"What?" I asked, my heart sinking into my stomach. "I told you the location!" My voice rose as James took me by the arm and began leading me toward the mast.

"You see, unfortunately for you child, I know the Diagon ship isn't carrying cargo. The Diagon is searching for something. Something I need. So I know you're lying to me."

I fought futilely against James as he tied my wrists and feet with thick braided rope to the mast pole. All the crewmen stopped and watched as I struggled. James stepped away after securing my limbs, an apologetic look on his face.

"I tried to warn you," he said quietly before returning to the captain's side.

"Let this be a testament to all of you that if you lie to me, you will suffer the repercussions," Obsidian said, addressing the wide-eyed group of crewmates.

"I'm not lying," I cried out desperately.

Obsidian took several methodical steps toward me and bent down, so we were face to face again.

"It would be merciful for me to throw you overboard. So instead, your pain will be made an example to the others. Each lie from your mouth is another day on this pole."

I glared at him, wanting to spit in his face. But I refrained. He was a monster, but taking out a monster like him wasn't going to be accomplished by getting angry. I needed to bide my time. He'd get desperate. He'd ask for my help because I will have been the only one brave enough to offer. I just had to be patient.

THIRTY-SEVEN

SABEARA

On the third day of our journey, we found the sunken ship.

The morning was much the same, helping out on the deck, adjusting the sails, and doing as Thane and Knadian instructed us. Then the afternoon came, the sun was high in the sky, my skin was hot and slick with sweat. I had conjured thoughts of taking a rest, drinking some water in the shade, but then Thane called out from the helm. His voice caused all of us to jump to attention.

"I see the ship!" he yelled.

We all hurried to the edge of the ship to see for ourselves. And sure enough, in the distance, a long mast pole stuck out of the water, a torn black flag flickering in the sea winds. As we neared, I could see the distorted image of broken ship parts in the water. We hurried to anchor, dropping the sails so we could slow down.

"Drop the mainsail!" Thane Shouted. "Anchor down, come on, lads!"

Soon the ship was anchored, the sails slackened, and we came to a standstill on the water. Everything was suddenly quieter without the sails moving in the wind and the waves pushing against the ship.

"That was fast," I said aloud as we all leaned over the railing, admiring the eerie image of the shattered wood sunk deep below the surface. If the sun hadn't been shining, we wouldn't have even been able to see much of it. The deep blue waters were this ship's gravesite—the lone mast the headstone.

"What's the plan?" Dusane asked, peering down into the water beside me.

"I'll push the water out of the way, and someone will have to climb down to get the compass," Knadian said.

"I'll get a rope ladder," Embrosine said.

"And I'll go down to get the compass," Mid said. "I've swam down there before. I'll be the most likely to locate it."

I turned at the sound of his voice and was surprised at the longing that overwhelmed me. His hair was shaggier than usual, unruly and unkempt from the salty winds. The curls fell in disarray around his face, and my heartbeat quickened. I needed to talk to him.

"I'll go with you," I blurted.

His emerald-scarlet eyes snapped up to meet mine, and I could see he wasn't happy with my invitation.

"I don't need you to come with me," he said. The first sentence he'd spoken to me since that night. *Great.*

"You shouldn't go by yourself," Embrosine interjected as she returned with a long braided rope ladder. It was apparent

Embrosine was trying to get us alone, so I could speak with her brother.

Mid turned to glare at his sister. "Fine. But we don't know what's down there. She could get hurt."

"She can take care of herself," Dusane interjected.

I was surprised at Dusane's comment. I don't know why he was helping me speak with Mid. Maybe he knew I needed to smooth things out with him before anything else could move forward with either of them.

"Dusane's right. I am more than capable of taking care of myself, thank you."

Things were put into action then. Embrosine and Shar helped throw the rope ladder off the side of the ship. While Rouix returned with two canteens of freshwater for Mid and me to take with us. Thane and Knadian discussed ways to manipulate the ocean, planning the best path for execution.

A couple minutes later, I was standing on the edge of the ship, Mid beside me.

"My powers are weaker due to the curse, so I don't know how long I can hold the water. So hurry," Knadian said.

"Want to give us an estimate of how much time you think we have?" Mid asked, his jaw rigged.

"Maximum thirty minutes," Knadian didn't look so confident.

Mid and I vaulted ourselves onto the ship's ledge and waited.

The king closed his eyes, seeming to be concentrating. Then the water began to move. A loud whooshing sound reverberated as the waters parted. I watched in awe as the waves were pushed to the side, creating two walls of solid water on either side of the sunken ship. Free of its watery grave, it could be seen that the boat was much larger than I'd imagined. Though decaying from being in the depths of the sea, a sparkling golden figurehead sculpted into a mermaid could be seen still attached to the ship. Matching gold plating and other decorative materials also adorned the broken remains, shimmering brightly. It must have been beautiful in its former glory.

Knadian had almost wholly dried the ship now as the last bits of water dripped free of the cracked and splintered parts. It was magnificent how the king held the water in place as if there were glass walls surrounding the ship. The water swirled and glimmered, and I could even see little fish and other sea creatures swimming around.

Mid gestured to the rope ladder tied securely to the Diagon's railing.

"Ladies first," he said indignantly.

I ignored his grumpy tone and swung tentatively over the side, the soles of my boots meeting the first rung of braided rope. Then I descended down to the sunken remains below.

THIRTY-EIGHT

SUNN

I could feel I was dying. Two days had passed, and my body was desperate for food and water. During the day, the hot sun would beat down on me. The only relief was when one of the sails offered me a bit of shade. My wrists and ankles hurt so much I was no longer standing on my own. I was a loose rag doll, everything aching.

The waves would pick up at night, and my feet would get so cold I feared they might actually fall off. Ocean spray covered me, and by morning I was soaked to the bone.

By day three, I knew I wouldn't last much longer.

Joon would look at me while he worked, pity in his eyes, but I always shook my head at him. I knew Joon wanted to help, but it would be worse for the both of us if he tried to free me.

The captain did nothing but watch. Every morning he'd come from his quarters, stand at the helm directing the wheel on the ship a tad to one direction or another. Then he'd just stand there, black eyes brooding—assessing everything as the evil dictator he was. He was awful, and each day confirmed my suspicions that he didn't even know how to run a ship. He didn't seem like the sailing type at all. *So what was he doing here?* He said he was trying to find something, *but what?*

It was a mystery. And one I didn't get any closer to solving by being tied up.

The third night came, and that's when things started to look very bleak. My mind was fuzzy, my lips blue and quivering. I could feel my heart beating slower and knew it would give out soon. My stomach stopped aching on day one. Now I was just slowly decaying away, it seemed.

Something shuffled on the deck that was now empty. The only company I had were the stars twinkling above me. I hadn't had visitors before this night.

A dark figure came up to me and removed the black hood from their head. It was James.

"What are you. . . doing here?" I croaked. My throat was so dry it felt like sandpaper.

"Eat this," he said, and then something cold was put up to my lips. I tasted a little bit of it and knew it was a piece of fruit. I felt tears prick the corners of my eyes when I bit into the piece of apple. It was a shock to my taste buds, and I felt a zing when the sourness filled my mouth. The water came next, and he carefully poured some into my mouth. Nothing was said as he fed me tiny pieces of apple and sips of water.

I looked into his kind blue eyes, wondering once again how he ended up here.

"Why are you saving me?" I asked.

He sighed, running a hand through his dark brown hair. "I guess you could say I'm not keen on seeing people die,"

"You work for an Obscurum captain," I deadpanned.

"Not by choice," he admitted.

So I was right, I thought. He didn't want to be malicious. He was just a puppet.

"What is the Captain looking for?" I asked, feeling the tiniest bit of energy come back into my body.

James pursed his lips. "He's looking for an artifact."

"Like for the curse?"

"Something like that."

Knowing now that it was a token that Obsidian was looking for, it all made sense.

"He's looking for a ship with an artifact on it?"

"Well, you see, others are looking for this artifact. He thinks they have it and are on the Diagon. So he's trying to find the ship so he can steal the artifact."

Everything came together, clicking into place. I gasped aloud when I figured it out.

"The compass," I said quietly. Over the last year, my father had received many letters from my family back on the mainland. Most of the time, he wouldn't allow me to read them. But I had gotten ahold of a few. Apparently, early last year after the war, they'd moved to a hidden location in the mountains known as Knadiel. My father was informed that they would be sending some of their people, including my uncle Mid, to search for a compass that would help defeat the curse. But I remember another letter coming a couple months later saying they hadn't found it. So either Obsidian was searching in vain, or Mid and the others had set sail again to try and find it. This would mean that if Obsidian was looking for them, he had to be someone dangerous.

"Who is he?" I asked.

"Obsidian?" James asked, brow furrowing.

"Yes, who is he?"

"He's the prince of Obscurum."

"Spirits in the tree, you have to be kidding me!" I cursed.

"Do you really know where the Diagon is, or were you lying?"

I had lied. I had told Obsidian a made-up location where the ship was headed. But now, it was no longer a lie. I'd read those letters. I knew where they'd attempted to look the first time. The South Territory. And I bet they were headed to the same place again. So the made-up location actually was the actual location. I really did know where they were going, and my fib was no longer a fib. If they had indeed set sail again to find the compass, then I was the only one on the ship that knew where.

"Spirits, spirits, spirits," I cursed.

"You've got quite a mouth on you, don't you," James observed.

"I was lying before James. But I'm not anymore." I groaned, and James looked even more confused.

"So the Diagon is headed to the South Territory?" he asked.

I nodded. "Yes, but your captain doesn't believe me." A surge of hope swelled inside me. Maybe he wouldn't believe me, and I wouldn't have to give away the token's location.

James sighed. "Well, he might have no other choice soon. He's getting frustrated. We have been out searching for weeks now."

I felt more tears come to my eyes. There was a chance my plan could work then. Obsidian could trust me to lead him to the South Seas. I had wanted more time to find a way off the ship, but now. . . now, if I stuck to that plan, I would be leading him to my family, to the compass.

"Please don't cry, boy. I'm sure he will let you off the ropes tomorrow," James said assuringly. But I just shook my head.

"That's not why I'm crying," I said. I tried thinking of a way out of telling Obsidian where the compass really was, but I'd already told him the South Territory. If I changed the location now, he'd really think I wasn't telling the truth, and I'd probably be killed. I had to stick to the plan. I had to hope that when Obsidian asked for my help, I could stall enough on the way there that he wouldn't reach them in time. Or if we did find them, they'd be strong enough to defeat Obsidian.

THIRTY-NINE

SABEARA

The braided rope ended, and my feet met with the deck of the ship. Tilted and off-centered due to its odd position halfway buried in the sand, I did my best to stand up straight. Mid jumped down beside me, landing with a heavy thud.

The deck was a mess. Ripped sails entangled with frayed rope. Only one mast was still standing. The others had fallen and were decaying away, blending in with the mess of fish bones and seaweed. Mid motioned to a small cracked hole in the deck, leading down into the ship's hull.

We hurried over to it, and Mid jumped down feet first. I heard him land with a grunt somewhere below, then he called up to me.

"Jump, Ehren. It's a short fall," he assured me.

Taking a deep breath and recalling the time I'd told myself I'd never jump down into a dark hole again, I forced myself to be courageous and shimmy my way into the darkness.

I landed a little clumsily on my feet, and Mid helped steady me. Once I was balanced, I didn't miss the way he released me, as if I was hot to the touch. Like if he held me too long, I might actually burn him.

Now beneath the ship's deck, the first thing I noticed was how much stuff there was.

Chest after chest of assorted objects filled the room. Gems, jewelry, necklaces, statues, and even weapons. It was scattered about, covered in sand and seaweed, and smelling like rotten fish and salt. Some of the items were tarnishing, rotting away. Chipped, and broken most of it was useless. It was a sad sight to see. I walked around curiously, wondering where the compass could be in a mess like this. The afternoon sun shined through cracks and holes in the wood, giving us a tiny bit of light every couple of feet.

"You said the compass was glowing?" I asked.

"I said I saw *something* glowing. I don't know if it was the compass." Mid ignored the hordes of once lavish objects covering the room, and he ventured deeper.

I followed after him, and together we made our way over fallen pieces of wood and cracks in the ship's frame. The vessel had definitely been attacked or caught in a bad storm. With the broken pieces and parts, I thought that it must have sunk rather quickly and couldn't help but wonder if anyone survived.

"Do you know where you're going?" I asked him, remembering what Knadian said about time and starting to feel the anxiety kick in.

"Yes, I know where I am going," he said, his tone clipped.

"I don't want you to be mad at me anymore, Mid," I said abruptly, and he stalled in his tracks. He turned on me, his eyes bright with a scorned fire.

"You agreed to come down here to help me find the compass. No one said anything about talking."

I glared at him, crossing my arms over my chest. "I'm sick of you ignoring me. We need to talk."

"Well, I don't want to talk." He turned back around and continued walking, his pace picking up as if he were trying to distance himself from me as much as possible.

"That's not fair, Mid. You know that the only reason I didn't tell you was because Shar asked me—"

"When Shar didn't tell you about your father, did it make it any better when he said he was doing it to protect you?" Mid asked, his hand clenching at his side.

I tried to respond to his question, but it was impossible to refute.

"It took you months to forgive Shar for what he hid from you. What makes you think I don't need just as much time?" he asked bitterly.

"No one died, Mid," I whispered. "They love each other. Shouldn't you be happy about this?"

He was silent for many moments, and then he faced me once again. It seemed to pain him to even have to look at me.

"Happy? Just like you were happy about Jasper and Oli?"

Okay, so I was a hypocrite. A big hypocrite, and maybe I was finally getting a taste of my own medicine, but he didn't have to be so rude.

"Mid. . ."

"Embrosine is *married,* Ehren. *Married.* She has a child with Ashelor. How can I not be upset that my sister and my closest friend are adulterers?"

"That's a pretty strong word, Mid," I said slowly, hoping to calm the situation.

"Think of what this would do to Sunn. Finding out that her mother never even really loved her father? That their entire marriage was a lie?"

"You need to talk to Shar and Embrosine. Get the full story—"

"I don't need the whole story. I already know the pain this will cause my niece when she finds out. And I think I'm allowed to be a little upset over the consequences of the mess they've made."

He had a point. I know I would've been upset, finding out that one of my parents actually loved someone else. My parents had loved each other immensely. It would be hard to swallow as a kid if they'd told me that was a lie. Mid wasn't just mad that Shar hadn't told him. But he was upset about the consequences this would have on their entire family and his niece. My heart pounded painfully in my chest. I hadn't stopped to think about Sunn.

"Mid, I'm sorry. . ."

"We don't have time for this. Are you going to help me find this compass or not?" He dismissed my apology, and it felt like a wall of ice had suddenly been erected between us.

I gritted my teeth but forced myself to nod. Mid turned around and continued our obstacle course. As we walked, I wished so badly I could take back the idea of coming down here with him.

Several minutes later, we shimmied through an opening in one wall, and we emerged on the other side to find an open room. It was clear of the clutter, and the only thing inside it was a statue. A giant open hole in the deck allowed a beam of sunlight to shine angelically down onto the mermaid-like some divine experience. It was made of milky white stone, and seaweed was vining up its length, overtaking the fin and body of the statue. The mermaid statue was beautiful, her face obviously sculpted after someone with exquisite features. A crown adorned her head, and she was frozen in a position where her hands were cupped together with something between her palms. And it was glowing.

"Do you think that's it?" I whispered, but Mid didn't say anything. He simply stepped closer to the mermaid, eyeing the piece of art with wide eyes and the purple glowing object in its grasp.

I came up beside him, entranced by the violet hue. We couldn't really see the object because it was being suffocated by seaweed. So I reached into my boot, pulling out the dagger Shar had gotten me for my birthday.

I used the tip of the golden blade to cut the object free of the slimy green vines. The seaweed fell to the floor and revealed underneath was a compass.

"That must be it," I whispered, not believing we'd actually found it. It was a tiny little thing, inlaid with gold, and inside the glass face was an intricate fixed needle.

Unable to stop myself, I reached out to the object and tried to pull it from the mermaid statue's grasp.

But something happened when I touched the compass. When my fingers brushed the golden rim, a zing of pain erupted through my finger, up to my arm, and passed through my entire body. It was sharp and froze me in my tracks. I tried to open my mouth to say something, but before I could, my vision became blurry, and everything went black.

FORTY

SUNN

James had been right. The next morning I was let off the ropes. Obsidian had James untie me and allowed him to give me some food and water. Then he dropped a pair of boots onto the deck and helped me lace them around my cold, numb feet.

Everyone on the ship that morning was watching, and I caught Joon's muddy brown eyes. He looked scared by himself amongst the crew, even though several of the crewmen from the old ship remained. I wanted to get back to my friend so he wouldn't be preyed on by the others. Joon didn't do well on his own.

"The captain wants to speak to you in his quarters," James said quietly to me as he released the final rope. I stood up with wobbly legs in my new boots and attempted to rub away the pain in my wrists. They were red and raw from the rope.

"Why?" I asked him.

"He wants to talk to you about the Diagon," James said, his features tight.

So he'd been right. Obsidian was desperate. *Well, that didn't take long,* I thought.

"Has Obsidian even been on a ship before?" I asked James as he helped me limp toward the Captain's quarters.

"Not that I know of," James said, sighing.

I laughed aloud, but it was more of a shocked, sarcastic laugh. "So this prince just got on a ship with no sailing knowledge and what? Thought he could find the Diagon?"

"Pretty much," James deadpanned. One of my feet gave out a little, and James had to help catch me. I was still extremely weak from being on the pole, and I gave him a wry smile.

"He sounds stupid to me," I said, and James shook his head.

"Well, don't say that to him."

"I mean, come on, what guy in his right mind goes out on a ship with no sailing knowledge?"

"A desperate one," James said.

We arrived at the door, and James knocked. A muffled "Come in." sounded through the wood.

James pushed open the door and helped me inside.

Gazing around the room, I almost laughed aloud but managed to swallow it down.

Unlike Captain Rissen's quarters which were a little cluttered with ship supplies and a big beat-up desk and a bunch of empty Lush Fire bottles, this was. . . luxurious.

A big bed sat in the middle of the room with silky red sheets adorning it. The frame was made of black rod iron, twirling and twisting into beautiful complexities. Ebony black curtains hung on the windows that overlooked the ocean waves when drawn, while a velvet burgundy sofa rested against one wall. Food was splayed out on a foot table with various fruits, cheeses, and even meats on silver platters. And the room smelled of amber and spice, tantalizing my senses.

Obsidian was leaning casually on the velvet sofa, his bare feet up. His long black hair was sprawled across the cushions, and he had a glass of bubbling orange liquid in his hand. His cloak was off his shoulders, thrown haphazardly over the arm of the sofa, and he wore a white shirt, open at the neck. Through the thin fabric, I could see a pulsing golden light coming from his stone heart.

"Good, you're here," Obsidian said in a lazy, bored tone.

"You've got to be—"

James pinched my arm so hard I was unable to finish my sentence.

I should be afraid of this guy. *Spirits,* I *was* afraid of this guy. He'd raided our ship, and gotten many of my friends thrown overboard, and tied me up for nearly three days with no food or water. But the longer I survived, and the more I went through on this ship, the more I began to realize he was pretty pathetic. He could bark commands, and throw people overboard, and continue to try and instill fear with his dark black eyes, but I was starting to see right through him.

He was a spoiled, arrogant prince. Probably with many family problems that were making him lash out and become the devil of his own story. Well, I had news for him. The next chapter featured me—an angry spitfire with a swearing problem and a whole lot of spunk.

"Please take a seat." Obsidian waved to two oversized plush chairs opposite the sofa, and James helped guide me to one. I sat down, and instant relief was felt on my aching body.

James didn't take a seat instead, he went to stand by the door like a loyal soldier.

"So tell me, what is your name, boy?" Obsidian asked casually.

I told him my crew name Rissen had given me.

"Salt," I said. He gave me a skeptical expression but thankfully didn't question the name thing further.

"Well, Salt. The things you said the other day about knowing where the Diagon is? I've decided to believe you."

"Cause you're desperate?" I said before I could stop myself.

Obsidian's hand stilled on the Lush Fire bottle he was about to pour. His black eyes narrowed at me, and for a second, my heart skipped a beat. *Was he going to kill me? Awe, why couldn't I just keep my mouth shut.*

"Maybe I am a little desperate," he said, his black eyes somehow looking even darker now. "But that's not the point. The point is I've decided to let you help me. In exchange for your life,"

"So, in other words, if I don't help you, you'll kill me?" I asked.

"That's right," he replied.

"Throw me overboard?"

"If I feel like it," he said, taking a sip of his freshly poured drink.

"What about tying me to mast again? Are you planning on doing that?" I questioned, unsure why I was pestering the situation.

"It may very well come to that if you are non-compliant." His eyes narrowed, obviously not liking whatever word game I was playing. But I had this problem. I wasn't very good at stopping. I enjoyed pushing the limits. And Obsidian was just the next clam I planned to crack.

"Well, then I don't know if I want to help,"

I heard James make a noise by the door like he was choking.

Obsidian's head tilted to the side, like an animal assessing its prey. He could try to eat me, but I wouldn't taste very good. I pictured myself as a cute little porcupine and him as a big black panther. One step too close, and I'd shoot him with quills. I would get under his skin and fester.

"I don't think you're in any position to negotiate," he growled.

"Actually, I think I am," I said boldly. And I saw the slightest widening of his eyes. The surprise was there for a mere second before he quickly concealed it and regained control again. "You see, I'm the only person on this ship that knows where the Diagon is. So if you kill me, you'll be stuck out on these waters for who knows how long."

I was finally right where I wanted to be—the one with the advantage. I could only hope he'd take the bait.

"I could torture it out of you," he threatened while taking another sip of Lush Fire. He was still splayed out on the couch like he didn't have a care in the world. But I could see a slight tick in his jaw. He cared.

"Fine, do it. I won't talk," I said.

He raised an eyebrow. "You haven't been tortured by someone like me," he said arrogantly. I couldn't help it. I rolled my eyes.

"Why waste the time? I mean, seriously. Aren't you on a time constraint here?" I heard another strangled noise from James. "It will be much easier if you just give me what I want in return for helping you."

He didn't say anything for a moment. Then he sat up from the cushions and leaned across the table, causing his long black hair to fall into his eyes. He rested his elbows on his knees and clasped his fingers in front of him. The smell of amber became more potent, and I realized it was coming from him. The perfume was even more intoxicating when up close. "And what is it you want?" he asked, his voice suddenly low and husky. I felt chills erupt down my spine, but I did my best to keep my face calm.

"Two things," I started. "First, keep your hands off Joon."

"Who's Joon?" Obsidian's brow furrowed, and he looked at James for assistance.

"He's one of the crewmates that came with him, Captain," James answered loyally.

Obsidian sighed. "Okay, fine."

"And second. Joon and I don't want to sleep in the hull anymore."

I was getting tired of shielding my eyes from man parts, and the longer I stayed in that hull, the more at risk I was of someone figuring out I was a girl.

"You want your own room for you and your friend?" he asked, his face devoid of emotion.

"Yes," I stated, keeping my chin high and my eyes locked with his. After several long minutes of silence, Obsidian finally nodded.

"Fine, you can have your own room—" relief filled me until he continued. "—but only you, not your friend."

"Why?" I immediately asked.

"I shouldn't have to answer you," he said darkly, his eyes still glowing with that fierce fire. "But if you must know, I want to keep an eye on you. And I don't want you making secret plans at night with this *friend* of yours. So you'll stay with me."

My eyes widened. I should've stuck with one thing. He wasn't going to be easily manipulated, even in his desperation. *Spirits,* I thought. Once again, I'd pushed my luck too far. *One day I'd learn,* I thought wryly to myself.

"What do you mean by *stay* with you?" I whispered, trying to contain the fear that was now seeping into my bloodstream like ice. I glanced at the bed with silky red sheets for a moment and couldn't help but feel my gut twist nervously.

Obsidian gestured toward a door across the room. "You'll be staying in the room next to me," he said.

Instant relief overcame me. Of course, he didn't mean *to stay* with him in his room. I was a scrawny teen boy to him. *Breathe,* I told myself.

"Now that we've settled this, I've got to attend to the crew, if you'll excuse me," he flashed a wicked smirk in my direction before standing and retrieving his cloak from the armrest.

With the Captain gone, I looked over at James, and he gave me an exasperated sigh. "You've got to stop egging him on."

"Where's the fun in that?"

FORTY-ONE

SABEARA

I squinted against the blinding sun, taking in the shimmering image before me. Blue waters cascading over sparkling sands, palm trees, and jungle ferns—a castle made of shells, and white stone spires

I took a step closer, my bare feet sinking deeper into the sand. Another wave rushed in to meet the island, crashing into the back of my legs. I stumbled, trying to regain my footing.

I continued to gaze at the beautiful grandeur of the castle, feeling the urgent need to reach it. Someone came walking out of the treeline then, but before I could witness who it might be, a blur overcame my vision, a sharp pain sweeping through me, and I woke up.

My eyes flew open, and I gasped for air. The first thing I registered once catching my breath was that I was surrounded.

"Ehren, are you alright?" Mid and Dusane were kneeling beside me. My back was against the deck, and I could see I was no longer down in the sunken ship. The sails to the Diagon flapped overhead, and everyone was looking down at me with worried expressions on their faces.

"What happened?" I groaned, feeling the stiffness throughout my limbs like every bone in my body had been lightly bruised.

Dusane began to help me sit up.

"You passed out when you touched the compass," he explained, his expression grave.

"Did we get it?" I struggled to a sitting position, and Embrosine passed a canteen of water into my hand.

"Here, drink," she ordered, and I gratefully took a sip.

"I couldn't hold the water, so Midennen had to bring you back on board. We didn't get the compass." Knadian was standing beside Thane.

"Why didn't you grab it?" I turned to Mid, and he gave me an incredulous look.

"Yeah, cause the both of us passed out would've been a real help," Mid's words dripped with sarcasm.

"Why did it hurt me when I touched it?" I asked, ignoring Mid's comment.

"I think it might be enchanted," Thane spoke. He didn't look chipper anymore and seemed serious for the first time since I'd met him.

"Enchanted?" I asked, laughing in disbelief. "You're joking, right?"

"Ehren, did you see anything when you passed out? Dream anything?" Thane asked.

Vague images of an island and a castle filled my head. But they were so blurry I could barely form the pictures in my mind. The harder I tried to remember them, the faster they seemed to slip away.

"I saw an island. . . a castle," I put a hand to my head, feeling a headache coming on. "But that's all I remember."

"Then it's just as I suspected," Thane said, his icy blue eyes seemed to darken. "It's been enchanted by the people of Tetheria."

"Tetheria?" Mid asked, brow furrowed, and everyone looked to Thane, seemingly just as confused.

"You're not thinking. . ." Knadian didn't finish his sentence.

"It's exactly what I'm thinking. The people of the sea. Mermaids."

~

We all reconvened back in the captain's quarters. Slowly my body recovered from whatever happened after touching the statue. It took more time than expected to feel back to normal, and I couldn't help but feel nervous that it was the curse. Each time I got injured, it was starting to take longer and longer to heal.

I sat in one of the cushioned chairs spread throughout the room. The fatigue in my body was a painful reminder of everything that had happened.

"So, what do we do?" Shar asked. He was standing, pacing the old rug on the floor. Everyone else had taken either a seat at the table or in one of the other chairs around the room.

"If the mermaids enchant it, the only way to get it undone is to find one of their people and convince her or him to undo it," Thane explained. He propped his leg over the arm of his chair and grabbed a bottle of Lush Fire, and began to pour himself a drink.

"I thought mermaids were a myth," Rouix chimed in.

"They want everyone to think they're just a myth. It keeps them protected, so people won't go looking for them," Thane explained.

"Have you ever actually seen one or met one?" Mid asked. His brow was scrunched in concentration.

"No, but I've been on the sea long enough to hear plenty of stories," Thane assured him.

"So, how do we find them?" I asked.

"Well, I've never actually gone searching for Tetheria. But I have a pretty good idea where we'd start if I were going to," Thane said.

"You don't seriously think this is a good idea?" Mid asked me, and I narrowed my eyes at him.

"We don't have much of a choice, do we? If it's mermaids that enchanted it, then we need to find them and get them to undo it," I argued.

"If anything, the enchantment just confirms that this is indeed the compass from Linsulong. In the stories, the people of Tetheria are known for preserving the history of the sea. It would make sense they would protect this. Keep it from getting into the wrong hands," Knadian said.

"I agree with Ehren. I say we go find them," Embrosine spoke up.

"Alright, but we only packed supplies for several days," Mid argued.

"We brought extra supplies just in case something like this happened," Shar said, though he looked grim. He obviously didn't like the idea either.

"It's settled then. Let's change the course and head for Tetheria," Dusane spoke for the first time, and I turned to look at him, his cerulean eyes meeting mine.

"What happens if we find Tetheria, and they refuse to help us?" I posed the question, and the room was silent for many moments.

Thane sighed, taking a sip of the Lush Fire bottle in his hand. "We will just have to hope it doesn't come to that."

FORTY-TWO

SUNN

I found Joon as soon as I could after speaking with Obsidian. I returned to the menial tasks of working the ship and made sure to face away from Obsidian's scrutinizing gaze as I relayed what happened in the captain's quarters to Joon.

"Yur really going to help him?" Joon asked, worry lacing his tone.

"Joon, I don't have a choice. But the good news is you're safe."

"You'll be stayin in his quarters then?" he asked, his eyes flickering to Obsidian up by the helm.

"I tried to get him to let you stay in there too. I'm sorry," I whispered.

"It's okay, imma be fine in the hull. Just glad ur safe," he said, squeezing my shoulder.

We'd changed course about an hour after I'd made the deal with Obsidian. We were officially headed toward the south seas.

I didn't know if I'd be able to get myself and the rest of my old crewmates off the ship. But I had to try.

When nightfall came, and everyone started heading to the hull for the night, I found Vilet and stopped him before he disappeared. He was one of the crewmates from the previous ship that had been helping lead the crew since we arrived.

"Vilet, can I talk to you?" I hadn't been super close to the other crew members on the ship. Mostly just Joon and Captain Rissen. But I'd conversed with many of them in passing.

"What's up, Salt?" he asked, his eyes looking around to make sure no one was near us.

"I need you to keep an eye on Joon," I said, biting my lip.

"Joon? Why would I help you after you sold your soul to that devil." His eyes narrowed, and I was surprised at the sudden hostility.

"What do you mean?" I asked, my cheeks reddening with the accusation.

"We heard about your little stunt. Telling the captain you know where the Diagon is." He glared at me with dark purple eyes. "You saved yourself. Why would you even care about Joon?"

"I'm not saving myself. I'm trying to help us get off this ship," I hissed, angry he was accusing me of such selfishness. Yes, I wanted to survive. My father and my mother would be devastated if they thought I'd died out at sea. But I wasn't just looking out for myself. I wanted to help Joon and the rest of the crewmates.

"Nice try. But I'm not buying it."

"Please," I begged as he turned away from me. I reached out, clutching the edge of his coat sleeve so he'd turn back.

He shook off my hold and glared. "Fine, I'll look out for Joon. But not for you," he spat.

Vilet walked away toward the hull where the rest of the crew had started to disappear for the night.

I cursed under my breath and made my way to the captain's quarters, where I was now ordered to stay so Obsidian could keep an eye on me.

James was already waiting at the door for me, and he opened it without a word. The only way into my new quarters was through Obsidians. We stepped inside, and the captain was sitting on the sofa, examining a map spread out across the foot table. James led me past him, and he didn't so much as glance in our direction.

We came to the other door, and James retrieved a key from his pocket.

The door opened to reveal a small quaint room. Decorated not nearly as fancy as the captain's but still quite lavishly. A small bed with a fluffy blue quilt was on one wall, while an armoire sat in the corner. A long bookshelf lined one wall with a small desk and a stack of candles. On the nightstand was a silver tray of food. Not the luxurious spread Obsidian probably ate every day, but it had some bread and fruit and a glass of water. It was better than anything the hull had to offer. I was filled with guilt realizing I was going to be staying here. I felt terrible that Joon was in the hull, and I'd managed to label myself as the person who'd sold her soul to the captain.

You tried to convince him to let Joon come with you, I reasoned with myself. *And you're trying to help the others.*

My inner reasoning did little to stifle the guilt.

"You'll need to be up at dawn with the rest of the crew," James said, and I nodded. My duties on the ship weren't suspended despite my new promotional prison, and I sighed when James shut the door.

I walked over to the bed and sat on the soft comforter. I ran my hand over the quilted stitches and felt a sense of sadness overwhelm me. *What if I couldn't do this? What if I couldn't get home?* I forced those negative thoughts out of my mind and instead walked over to the mirror next to the armoire. I stared at my reflection and noticed immediately how haggard I looked and felt.

My wrists were still bright red and raw from being tied to the mast. My lips and cheeks were dry from the salty air, and my clothes were filthy. I'd stolen them from another sailor that must not have washed them, maybe ever, and my time on the ship these last several days was only adding to the collection of dirt and grime. I looked at my green eyes in the mirror and the freckles that dotted my nose. I wasn't well endowed in the chest department, so that had never been a problem trying to hide, and with my hair up in my hat, I truly looked like a scrawny teenage boy.

I sighed, wishing I could take down my hair for just a moment and comb through it. But I didn't want to risk it with Obsidian over in the next room. So I walked over to the bed, kicked off my boots, and climbed into the sheets. When I laid my head on my pillow, I fell asleep rather quickly.

And I felt guilty about that too.

~

The next morning I woke up to the sound of boots stomping above deck. The crew was moving to their stations, and I groggily started to get out of bed. My hat had fallen off in my sleep, so I had to hurry and pile the wild red curls atop my head and yank my hat down over them again. I checked the mirror, making sure I'd managed to hide each and every strand.

I opened the door to my room then to get to the deck on time and forgot that it was connected to Obsidian's quarters.

My eyes instantly landed on his tall, lanky form standing by the window. He was pulling a shirt over his head, and I caught a glimpse of his pale-skinned chest and abdomen. He wasn't bulky by any means, but he definitely had muscle. His body was defined, sharp angles lining his stomach leading down to the V in his hips. I blushed, having caught him dressing, and I quickly headed toward the door.

"I'm sorry, "I muttered.

"Salt, actually take a seat. I need your help with something."

I paused with my hand on the doorknob and turned around slowly.

He sat down on the sofa and gestured to the plush chair across from him. I moved hesitantly over to him and sat down. The map I'd seen him eyeing last night was laid out. He was looking intently at the lines on the paper, his chin resting in his hand.

"We've started heading this direction," he pointed to an area on the map that I assumed was the South Territory. "But this area is prone to storms." He pointed to another spot on the map a couple of miles west. "We encountered one on the way here, and I'm not keen on experiencing it again."

"You could go around," I suggested pointing to a route that would take at least a couple of days longer but would avoid the storm trap. The area he was referring to was called the

Monsoon Current. I'd never been near it, but my father had mentioned it once or twice.

"That will take us several extra days," Obsidian said, his brow furrowing.

A longer route meant more time for me to figure out a way home and off the boat. And would hopefully give more time to my uncle and his crew if they were searching for the compass.

"I think it's the best way," I told him, trying to sound convincing.

Obsidian grunted. "Unfortunately, I think you're right."

Just then, a knock at the door sounded, and James poked his head through the door.

"Captain, there's been a problem."

Obsidian groaned and stood up, following after James onto the main deck. I scurried after them wanting to know what had happened.

The sun was bright as we exited, and I squinted against the sun. After adjusting to the morning light, I spotted a group of men down on the deck near the edge of the ship. They were grouped together, all looking over the edge down at the ocean water below.

"What happened?" Obsidian demanded as we came upon the group.

"They're gone, sir." One of the Obscurum soldiers said, his voice shaky.

"Who?" I asked, pushing through the group and looking over the edge. Nothing was in the water that I could see, just waves slapping against the side of the ship.

"The other crewmates from the Trenador. One of the men named Vilet managed to take the escape boat last night, and they disappeared," James filled in.

My eyes widened, and I turned around to face Obsidian. His jaw was clenched angrily.

"You had an escape boat?" I asked, unsure how I'd missed something so important while wandering around the ship for several days.

"It was hidden in the base of the ship," Obsidian said. I looked around the group, desperately searching for Joon, but he wasn't there.

"They must have found it somehow," James said, worry in his eyes.

"Well, that's just wonderful," I said, throwing my hands into the air while letting out a panicked, slightly hysterical laugh. "This entire ship is being run by a bunch of helpless soldiers that don't know a thing about running a boat. I mean, how many of you actually know anything about sailing?" I asked, my voice rising.

One Obscurum soldier raised his hand.

"Great, one of you!" I was losing it.

Obsidian eyed me, his eyes getting darker in that creepy way they always did when he wasn't happy.

"I mean, you've basically been floating around for several weeks. I'm surprised you've made it this far! But getting to the South Territory isn't going to be easy. So how do you expect we're going to do that now?" I asked, the rhetorical question spitting from my lips.

"With you," Obsidian said abruptly.

Silence stretched on for several long seconds.

And that's when it hit me. I was the last person on this ship that could even get us to the South Territory. I knew the bare minimum of running a ship, and even then, I wasn't confident in those minor abilities. But Obsidian's crew were just plain old soldiers. They needed me. And my entire crew had left me, taking Joon with them. They'd thought I'd betrayed them and abandoned the ship. And now they might die out on the water trying to reach home. But I was too stubborn to go down this way. I would find a chance to escape. And maybe that made me selfish. I don't know, but I had a will to survive.

FORTY-THREE

SABEARA

We shifted our course according to Captain Whitmane's instructions. He was the only one with any idea where to begin. He claimed to have heard stories from other sailors, and those stories guided him on which direction we should take.

I tried not to worry too much about it, but anxiety still wore through me despite my attempt. Two days passed, and nothing new. The water was seemingly endless, and the longer we remained on the water, the more the blue waves surrounding us started to feel sort of like an aquamarine prison.

To keep myself distracted, I trained with Shar in the morning on the deck. It was good practice and a great way to burn off some steam. I'd never trained with anyone but Dusane before, and it was enlightening to get some tips from another Envorydian. Shar was a skilled fighter. *Very* skilled, actually, and I started to understand why everyone looked at him as a legend. I had yet to come close to getting the upper hand with him.

"I think that's enough for one day," Shar said, stepping down from his fighting stance. I allowed my body to relax and could feel the fire in my muscles from the workout we'd just completed.

"Do you think we'll ever find this Tetheria place," I said, reaching down for my canteen of water and taking several long sips.

"I don't know, to be honest with you." He ran a hand through his hair, he'd let it out of its usual ponytail, and it fell in long strands to his shoulders.

"It's disappointing how close we were," I said, remembering the beautiful violet hue of the compass clutched in the statue's hands.

Shar looked about to respond, but then footsteps were heard coming across the deck, and both of us turned to see Mid coming toward us. My heart sped up at the sight of him, and the familiar tightness settled into my chest. He didn't even glance in my direction. But I couldn't help but glance in his. He looked handsome that morning—wearing a fresh white tunic and black trousers. His untamed curly locks were slicked back from his face, and I could clearly see his brooding emerald-scarlet eyes.

"Whitemane wants to see you," Mid said to Shar. He could barely meet his guardian's gaze. He was mad at the both of us. I wished so badly I could take away the obvious tension now surrounding everything. This wasn't the way it was supposed to be.

Shar nodded, then gave me an apologetic smile. "Duty calls," he said, and then he started to gather his things to leave.

"I'll come with you," I said. With training done, I didn't have anywhere else to be.

"He didn't ask for you," Mid said abruptly, his jaw clenched. He was looking at me now, and his gaze was piercing.

I stopped in my tracks. "I'm sure Thane will be fine if I come along."

"Mid. . ." Shar cautioned.

"He wants to speak privately to Shar. He didn't say anything about you," Mid said. The sharpness in his voice cut through me like a knife.

"What's your problem?" I asked, folding my arms angrily across my chest. "Haven't you punished me enough already?"

"Punished you? I'm not punishing you," Mid scoffed.

"Oh, so ignoring me and making rude remarks isn't punishing me for me lying to you about Shar? Cause it sure seems that way to me." I could feel my skin heating, the fire in me flickering to a dangerous level.

"Look, I didn't come down here to fight. I'm just the messenger." His face was frustratingly passive as he said this. He turned to walk away, but something in me just couldn't let it go.

"Well, you may not be looking for a fight, but I am."

I don't know what came over me. But a very similar feeling to the day I'd fought those men on the mountain came crashing into me again. A sort of angry frenzy started to flood my veins, and I felt my sight narrow in on Mid like he was my prey. The livid emotions that had bubbled inside me were now boiling over. I was tired of this. If he wanted to fight, we would fight. But not with words. I was sick of the silent treatment and bitter comments. If he was angry, he could get it out of his system. Because I was so done tiptoeing around each other.

I lunged for him, jumping lithely onto his back as if I were some agile leopard. I wrapped my legs around his waist and my arms around his throat, securing myself there.

He stumbled, making a sound of surprised protest.

"Ehren!" Shar yelled, but his voice had faded to the background. It was just Mid and me now.

Mid's hands reached up to grab me, and his fighter response seemed to kick in.

Flipping me over his shoulder with a surprising amount of skill, suddenly I was falling, and I quickly twisted my torso, landing gracefully on my feet.

We were face to face, and he raised his arms into a combat stance. I did the same, and then we ran at each other.

Fists swinging, we started into a combat fight. I used every trick up my sleeve, landing several satisfying jabs to his stomach and chest. He seemed to be holding back, and that made me even angrier that he was taking it easy on me.

"Come on, Mid, take a hit," I taunted. His only response was an angry growl, and then he swung out to kick my feet out from underneath me. I quickly jumped aside, avoiding the attempt easily.

"Stop this, you two," Shar said from the side. He sounded like he was chiding little children.

Neither of us listened, and I continued to put up a fight. The rhythm felt good as I swung fist after fist. The more I swung, the lighter the tightness in my chest became.

Mid grunted when I landed another hit to his shoulder, and his emerald-scarlet eyes flashed with a rage I'd never seen. I knew he could fight. He'd kept up well so far. But I also knew there was more in him. Trained to fight by Shar, there had to be something hidden deep inside him. And I wanted to pull it out of him. If anyone needed to let off a little steam, it was Mid.

Just then, another angry growl came from Mid, and he feigned a left step. Taking advantage of my momentary lapse in concentration, he quickly kicked my feet from beneath me, and I wasn't quick enough to avoid it. My knees buckled, and I started to fall to my back.

Mid's hand wrapped around my neck, the other around my waist, and he came down with me, trying to slow my fall.

I landed on my back, cushioned by his arms, and was even more furious that he had tried to ease the blow.

I looked up at him, and our eyes locked on one another. His body was pressed flush against mine, and I could feel all of him. His chest, his arms, his legs entangled with mine. Suddenly all my anger evaporated, and I felt a surge of desperate longing overcome me. He was breathing heavily, his chest heaving. He stared into my eyes, looking to be feeling the exact same thing I was.

"I'm not ready to forgive you," he whispered.

He stood up then, and the pressure of him was released off of me. He wiped the sweat from his brow, then he brushed past Shar, returning the way he'd come.

FORTY-FOUR

SUNN

All night I contemplated strategies to get off the ship. The crew had left me, including Joon. It stung, and though I didn't want to feel weak, I cried for some time in my room. I was scared and alone. I hoped Joon hadn't had a choice in the matter. I imagined he'd tried to stand up for me and that Vilet hadn't given him the chance. That was the only way I found to cope.

But despite being left behind, I couldn't wallow. Now that Obsidian was desperate, and I was his only hope, I had to figure out how to use that to my advantage. I didn't want to lead him to my family, but I also didn't want him to kill me because I didn't. So all through the night, I stared at the ceiling, feeling the rhythmic rocking of the boat as I considered my options.

I could search for another escape boat, try and travel to safety by myself. But it was unlikely I would survive.

Or I could continue to lead Obsidian to the South Territory and stall as long as possible along the way, hoping that with that time, I could start an uprising amongst the crew. Which would allow me to get Obsidian off the ship, and I could sail home.

And the last option was I could lead us to the South Territory and hope that we would come into contact with Mid and his crew so that they could defeat Obsidian and rescue me off his ship.

All the options seemed risky—all of them difficult. I didn't want to put Mid and the token in danger. But I also didn't know if I could successfully cause an uprising.

In the end, I decided that I would continue to stall and try my best to turn Obsidian's crew against him. It didn't feel right to lead Obsidian to the compass. So I figured if it didn't work getting in with the crew and starting an uprising, I would go to the next plan, hoping that we found Mid's ship and they would rescue me.

The sun came up quicker than I wanted. My eyes were tired. My body felt heavy and sluggish. I forced myself out of bed and started for the deck.

When I opened the door, I noticed that Obsidian wasn't in his quarters. I curiously walked out into the morning light, the salty air immediately greeting me. I looked over the ship of crew members already starting to take up their duties and noticed Obsidian standing with James.

I headed toward one of the sails eyeing the two of them the entire time. They seemed to be in deep conversation about something.

I joined one of the Obscurum soldiers struggling with the ropes and helped him untangle them. He blushed but nodded in thanks as I moved on to the next crewmate that needed assistance.

I was definitely out of my element trying to help run the

ship, but no one else knew what they were doing. I did my best to assist the men and made sure the ship stayed the course, knowing we needed to be headed south.

As I reached the helm and began helping the soldier manning the steer, I heard the shouting.

I'd taken my eyes off of James and Obsidian, but now they weren't alone. One of the crew members was now with them, on the ground, clutching his chest. I don't know what had happened or what he had said to cause such a response from Obsidian, but it was probably unwarranted. I started toward them without thinking.

As I got closer, I could hear Obsidian speaking angrily to the soldier.

"If you ever question me again, "he threatened, and that's when I saw the light in the soldier's chest.

Where he clutched his chest, the light in his Stone-Hearted heart was fading away. And it looked like Obsidian was pulling the light from him.

My eyes widened as I watched Obsidian drain the life from the man, and when I reached them, I grabbed Obsidian's arm pulling him back from the fallen soldier.

"Stop! You're killing him!" I screamed, fear and desperation consuming me. The poor soldier looked to be gasping for air, mouth moving like a fish but not receiving any breath.

Obsidian shoved me off of him, turning on me within seconds.

"Get your hands off me, boy!" Obsidian growled.

The soldier gasped for air as he was released from Obsidian's power, and I was grateful he wasn't dead.

I was on the ground then, unable to catch myself after Obsidian shoved me. My knees scraped across the splintered wood floor, ripping my trousers, and I felt my hands pierce with several slivers as they slid across the aged deck.

I groaned and tried my best to stand up, but then he had a hold of me.

He yanked me up from the deck and grabbed me by the collar of my shirt. He held me up, so my feet dangled off the ground.

"Do not interfere again, do you hear me?" he said so close his lips brushed against my ear.

The back of his hand struck the side of my cheek, and my head fell to the side with the impact. I let out a whimper, unable to say anything in my terror. The skin stung where he slapped me, and I knew it was going to swell.

He dropped me then, and I slumped to the ground.

He was a cruel monster, and it was yet another reminder. As I lay on the wood, my clothes getting soaked from the deck water, my cheek throbbing, I gazed at the scars on my wrists from when he'd tied me to the mast, and a more profound hatred for the captain consumed me.

I heard Obsidian's boots as he stormed away and then the resonating slam of his door as he left into his quarters. I felt a hand on my arm, soft and gentle, begin to help me up from the floor.

"Are you alright?" James asked me, his wide blue eyes filled with worry. I nodded silently, and the sympathy on his face was evident. "Let's get you cleaned up."

James helped me over to a barrel where I could sit, and it looked like the other man Obsidian had injured was already there next to me. He had long blonde hair and a bushy beard with dark brown eyes. He looked to be slowly recovering, still pressing his hand over his blue heart as its color slowly began to pulse back to life.

"Thank you," The soldier said to me. I could merely nod.

James left to get something then returned a moment later with some supplies. He had a fish wrapped in a towel, and he had me press it to my cheek. The cold helped keep down the swelling as he dabbed at my scraped knees and removed the splinters from my palms.

It was a long process, and I could feel the eyes of all the crewmen as James helped me.

I forced myself not to cry, knowing that these men would see me as weak if I did. Hopefully, saving their friend would earn me some points, and I could successfully begin getting them to trust me. But I was too subdued to revel in my victory of saving the soldier.

"James, what was that he was doing to that soldier?" I whispered.

James's jaw clenched. "He has the power to drain life from a Stone-Hearted."

"That's horrible," I said, my voice quivering slightly.

"It only works on Stone-Hearted. You're safe." James said softly, taking a seat next to me. "You're a brave boy."

"I'm not brave," I whispered.

"You are. I've never seen anyone stand up to him like that."

"James, why don't you stand up to him?"

His blue eyes were sad when he spoke again. "I guess I'm afraid he'll kill me."

"I want to get off this ship, James," I said, my voice still a whisper. "Help me," I pleaded.

He sighed. "You and I aren't strong enough to take him, I'm afraid,"

"Then let's get all of the men to rebel against him." I reasoned, gesturing to the crew working around the ship.

"He has instilled a fear in them so deep, Salt, I doubt anything could sway them."

"What about you? Is the fear in you too deep?"

He seemed to think about my question for a moment. "After a time, it becomes a part of you. And you start to believe it's the only way. And you learn to live with the circumstances. "

"It doesn't have to be this way, James."

He looked up at me again, and our eyes met. I swore I saw hope in the reflection of his blue depths. "I wish I could believe you."

I knew then that Obsidian had broken these men. He'd bruised their souls, weakened their minds, and drained their hearts. His power was lethal. A heart-crushing monster with no soul and no empathy. He was going to be difficult to deal with. But I had to believe in what my mother had always told me. I was spirited. And that spirit wasn't going to be broken. And I had to find a way to mend the same spirit in this crew to stop the captain.

FORTY-FIVE

SABEARA

I was lying on my cot after the fight with Mid, staring up at the ceiling while trying to let the rocking of the boat soothe me. I know word had spread about the fight. I could practically hear the whispers through the walls.

So I shouldn't have attacked him.

I didn't know how to explain what had come over me. But every excuse I tried to bring up into my head sounded just as weak as the last.

I reached for the little scroll of paper on the table by my cot. I unrolled its tattered edges to find the poem he'd written me the night of my birthday. Tears filled my eyes, and the words blurred on the page.

A knock at my door sounded, and I quickly tossed the piece of paper back onto the side table, forcing myself to blink back the tears as I called to whoever it was to come in.

Dusane's dark head peeked around the door, and I sat up leaning against the wall.

"Can I come in?" he asked.

I nodded, and he walked over to sit on the edge of my bed. Nothing was said for many moments.

"I have to admit. I'm not completely upset with you," he admitted, and I glared at him, shocked at the joking in his tone. Dusane rarely joked.

"I didn't mean to hurt him or anything. . . something just came over me."

Duane pursed his lips. "I think I know what's going on."

"Please, tell me. Because I don't," I gave him an exasperated look.

"You're experiencing what I like to call the Rage."

"The Rage?"

"It's something newly trained Envorydians sometimes experience. It happens to those who go through a traumatic event after learning the Envoy techniques. Basically, you're using fighting to control the emotional aspects of your life."

"Every time I fight, I feel almost. . . eager. It's like I *want* to fight."

"It happened to me too. It will pass. You just have to get back to your core training. And work through the emotional traumas that are harming you."

I sighed and felt tears bubble up in the corners of my vision again. The last thing I wanted to do was cry in front of Dusane.

"Will you help me?" I whispered, feeling as if I might be unraveling.

Dusane reached to cup my face, wiping away a lone tear that had cascaded down my cheek.

"Why do you think I came down here?"

I let out a weak laugh. "I don't know, to scold me for losing the fight to Mid."

"You lost?" His eyebrows rose as if he hadn't heard that part yet.

"Dismantled me, then cushioned my fall," I gave him a derisive look.

"Don't beat yourself up too much. Shar trained him from his youth."

"Still." I pouted, and Dusane laughed, actually laughed. His husky chuckle was comforting.

"I think maybe you're more upset you lost than the fact you initiated the fight in the first place," Dusane challenged.

I sniffled but couldn't help but smile a little. "Maybe."

"Get some sleep. We will train as soon as we get back to Knadiel. Then we can work through the Rage together," he assured me.

"Thank you," I said.

He nodded, then pressed a gentle kiss to my tear-stained cheek before leaving the room.

~

I finally found the courage to leave my room later that evening, it was my turn for the night shift, and I wasn't about to let someone else shoulder the burden for me just because I was pouting.

I pulled my cloak tighter around my shoulders as I stepped onto the deck. The night was cold. The wind bounced off the sleek black waves and caused everything to quiver. The sails flapped wildly, and my hair whipped around my face. I could smell salt and fish wafting in the air. Despite the discomfort of the cold, I found the chilly scene before me to be oddly beautiful.

I glanced up at the helm and found King Knadian. He gave me a slight nod of his head as I passed by and walked further down the deck to the bow of the ship. I found Rouix there with Embrosine, the two working the sails.

"Ehren, you made it," Embrosine beamed at me, and I gave her a tentative smile.

"Sorry I've been. . . absent all day."

"Don't even worry. You're here now." Embrosine wrapped a friendly arm around my shoulder and gave me a little squeeze.

"How can I help?" I asked.

Rouix pointed to the shrouds beside her. "Wanna help me lengthen these?"

I quickly got to work then, helping with the ropes and sails as Embrosine instructed. A comfortable silence stretched between us as we worked and I was grateful none of them asked questions about the fight that had happened between Mid and me. Everyone else was asleep, so for several hours, we crewed all the stations. It helped get other things off my mind.

Sometime during the night, Knadian called out to us and worried something might be wrong, we hurried over to him.

"Father, what is it?" Embrosine asked, running up to his side. Knadian pointed to the dark horizon. It was nothing but the night heavens illuminating the waves.

"I think I see land ahead," he said, his green eyes bright with excitement.

"Tetheria?"

"I don't know, but I sure hope so. One of you go wake Captain Whitemane."

Rouix took off to wake the other captain before I could even volunteer. She returned moments later with Thane at her side.

His blonde hair was a disgruntled mess, and he groaned,

running a hand over his beard. His eyes were tired, and he appeared to be in a pretty bad mood.

"This better be good, Knadian, I was dreaming about a five-course meal, and you interrupted." Thane glared at his friend, and Knadian quickly urged him to look out at the water.

"Do you see that? That's land."

Thane squinted, and after several moments his ice blue eyes widened.

"Spirits in the tree. You're right, my friend! Land ho! Land ho!" He punched Knadian's shoulder good-naturedly, then ran down the steps toward the bow of the ship to get a better look.

We all followed him, and soon, our excitement had everyone awake and looking out at the small piece of the island in the distance. I could barely make out anything, but I could see trees and a sliver of something white.

"I think we've found 'em," Thane said boisterously. "The boys back home aren't going to believe this."

"Let's not get too excited. We still don't know for sure if it's the island of Tetheria," Shar cautioned.

Always the beloved realist, I thought sarcastically.

"Shar's right, let's not get our hopes up until we know for sure," Mid added. I looked over at him, and our eyes met. I wished I could say something. But nothing came out. We continued to stare at each other. Like some spell had taken over our bodies. I was unable to look away.

"Do you see that?" I heard Rouix say. "In the water. Is there something glowing?"

I tore my eyes away from Mid, Rouix's words, bringing me back to reality.

"I don't see anything," Embrosine said.

"Right there, I saw it again." Rouix's voice was pitched with curiosity.

Just then, a vibration passed through the entire ship, causing all of us to stumble. It only took several seconds as we regained our footing to realize that something had hit our ship.

FORTY-SIX

SUNN

Over the next two days, I did my best to speak to the crewmates. I thought the interference I'd made standing up for that crewmate would help me, but it would seem they trusted me even less.

I instructed the men on their posts and critiqued their work, but they would ignore me if I even tried to speak to them about something other than the task at hand. James was right. These men were fearful of Obsidian, so fearful even associating with me, a "boy" with a rebellious nature, was risking them getting in trouble.

The only one that even humored me was the one I had kept Obsidian from killing. His name was Elon. He must've taken pity on me after several days of watching me fail to speak to any of them.

"I appreciate what you did for me," Elon said, his eyes locked on the task ahead and speaking in hushed tones. Obsidian was at the helm, and he could spot us at any moment. "But unfortunately, we can all see what you're trying to do."

"And what is that?" I asked, reaching out to pretend to help him right one of the ropes.

"You want us to rise against him," Elon said easily.

"We could, you know. Rise against him," I insisted.

"Not without a couple of us getting killed in the process," he gestured to my chest. "And most likely, it wouldn't be you."

He was talking about my heart. I'd confirmed that Obsidian couldn't crush hearts that weren't Stone-Hearted. But that didn't make him any less dangerous.

"He could easily kill me with a weapon," I reasoned.

Elon clucked his tongue. "You are in over your head, boy, let it be. We were all like you in the beginning. We wanted to believe we could stop him. But we can't."

Elon walked over to the next station, and I sighed. They were all insistent on staying loyal to him—worried for their lives. And rightly so, but now they were starting to appear like a bunch of cowards, and it was making me angry.

He was just one man! One arrogant, spoiled, mean, and slightly dangerous man. But he was still just one person! There were at least twenty of us. Yes, some might get hurt, but wasn't it worth the risk? I would rather die than remain forever in Obsidian's servitude.

I huffed beneath my breath and decided I'd just have to do more to get them to trust me. An uprising was the best option. I had to believe it was still possible.

That night when I went to sleep, it was another restless night—tossing and turning as I contemplated my options. I sighed, turning on my side while tucking my hand beneath my cheek. I wanted so badly to go home. I could only imagine how worried my father was. He'd probably sent a letter to my mother, and the thought of her worrying about me made my stomach even sicker.

I was facing the door when a lantern light came on, shining beneath the crack in the door. I sat up a little, curious why Obsidian would be awake at such an hour.

Then I heard yelling.

Worried Obsidian might be hurting another crewmate, I drew back the covers and hurriedly pulled on my sea jacket and boots. Grabbing a lantern, I shuffled toward the door and opened it carefully, only to find the room to be empty. But the door leading out to the deck was left wide open—cold wind blowing into Obsidian's quarters.

I tentatively stepped over the threshold and outside into the salty night air.

The captain's quarters were elevated, a set of stairs leading up to it. So on the balcony, I could see the night crew below, huddled together with handheld lanterns, below the main mast. There seemed to be some sort of commotion, but Obsidian wasn't harming anyone.

I held my lantern up a little higher and squinted through the darkness, trying to see the squabble.

"What's going on?" I called down to them. The wind at night was brutal, and as the sea tossed more fervently, the flame in my lantern flickered dangerously. I clung to the railing, trying not to fall over.

When I called out to them, James was the only one that turned at the sound of my voice. When he saw me, he started toward me at a near run. His boots clomped on the stairs as he made his way up the steps.

"Salt, get back inside," James ordered.

"What's going on?" I asked, worry filling my tone.

"Miles was in the crow's nest, and he spotted something in the water."

There was always one man up in the nest at all times, looking out over the water for anything dangerous.

"What did he see?" I asked, confusion coloring my tone.

"We don't know. But it's something big." James said. His blue eyes were wide. He looked pale.

"It's probably just a school of fish," I said weakly, not even believing my own words.

I looked out at the sea then, blacker than the night sky. The moonlight reflected off the sleek glass surface, and it was hauntingly eerie. It was then I felt something pulling at my memory. We were traveling to the South Territory. Halfway we would be passing through Monsoon Current, but because we were going around, we'd be passing through. . . Trojan waters.

I gasped.

"What's the matter, Salt?" James asked.

I was frozen, realizing my mistake, and the fear that coursed through me was so real I began to shake.

"Trojan waters," I whispered.

James's brow furrowed even more.

"In Trojan waters, there is this legend or a myth," I stumbled on my words, unsure if it was true or not but having a gut-wrenching feeling that it wasn't a myth at all.

"What myth?" James asked.

"There are these creatures people talk about living in the Trojan waters. They are called Oculor. They are sort of like a poisonous octopus, but they're a lot larger, and they have a skeletal structure." My voice quivered as I continued. "I've heard stories of them climbing onto ships and killing entire crews. Their ink is poisonous."

"What? You knew about this and didn't tell us?" James nearly yelled, eyes wide.

"I forgot about it until now! And I always thought it was just a scary story!" I tried to defend myself.

"Maybe we are fine then, maybe it's just legend, and it's fi. . ." James's reasoning was cut short when the boat shook. . .*hard.*

Something hit the side of the ship, and it tossed, heaving all of us to the left. I crashed to the floor alongside James, barely holding my lantern as we rolled into each other. I groaned.

A spray of ocean water came up over the side of the ship with the impact peppering our faces with salt water, and I squinted through the burning sensation to look to the side of the ship that was hit.

A series of sucking noises were heard, and gradually the chorus of suction began to get louder and louder. And that's when I saw it. I spotted bright white suckers as a black tentacle came probing over the edge of the ship, and I lost my breath.

More tentacles appeared, the bow now overflowing with them. There were dozens. They indeed weren't a myth.

I couldn't scream and couldn't do anything but remain frozen as they surged over the edge, crawling atop one another like spindly spiders trying to get onto the ship. They were pure black, glossed with slime, their heads large and their eyes bright white like the underside of their tentacles. They shimmered much like the black waters they came from. But there was something odd about them that I'd never seen before with any creature. Their hearts glowed like a Stone-Hearted heart. Colors radiated from beneath their black flesh, indeed alive with power. They moved quickly, their tentacles twirling and writhing in an attempt to reach us.

I heard several crewmen scream, and when the ship righted itself, chaos erupted.

I ran toward James and helped him stand from the ground where he'd fallen.

He stood with a grunt and handed me a knife from his belt.

"Here, take this," he said. "Now, how do we kill them?"

"I don't know," I said breathlessly as we both stood on the balcony and watched them start toward the stairs.

As the first Oculor reached us, James let out a battle cry and jumped down to attack it. He swung and cut off two of the tentacles with his sword. The Oculor shrieked, making a shrill noise as black blood squirted onto the wood from the blunt tentacles James had cut. The tentacle was still moving despite the amputation.

The attack only seemed to make the creature angrier. In a desperate attempt to help, I stretched out the knife James had given me awkwardly and tried to poke the beast from where I stood. The blade of the knife sunk into the skin of the Ocular, and more black blood seeped from its slimy flesh. I managed not to heave, but only barely.

James tried again, aiming for its eye and managing to slice right through its head. The creature squealed again, tentacles waving frantically as it tumbled down the steps. Its large, slimy body fell with a thud to the deck and a pool of inky black liquid spilled out from its body where it lay. I realized that the liquid was probably poisonous ink.

It didn't take long for more Oculor to swarm over their fallen comrade up the steps toward us, and just when we were about to continue the fight, the boat shook again.

I fell, my knees banging into the wood, and this time I dropped the lantern.

I heard the glass of the lantern shatter on the steps below, and I looked over the edge at the damage it had done.

I gasped at what I saw.

Shrill shrieks from the Oculor came in a chorus as I saw that the flame in my lantern had actually lit the black ink on the stairs and the ground below it. The black liquid appeared to be flammable, eating up the trail of ink, including the Oculor. Soon, the dozens coming up the steps were surrounded by bright orange flame, the blaze reflecting off the ocean surface. The Oculor became burned corpses, and the smell of smoked fish permeated the air.

James got to his feet, and his eyes were wide as he took in the scene.

"The ink is flammable," I said, gasping as I managed to get to my feet too. The heat from the flame caressed my skin, and I tried to shield my eyes from the intense smoldering light.

"Maybe we can use it to our advantage," James said.

Just then, something louder than even the Oculor let out a shrieking cry, and we turned to see what had rocked the ship for a second time.

A big black head came out of the ocean beside the ship, water sliding off its body in waterfalls. Its white eyes were like two large moons, its round ebony head and sleek tentacles a hundred times larger than the creatures we'd just encountered.

It was then I realized we hadn't been fighting the Oculor. *This* was the Ocular.

It, too, had a glowing heart, a bright golden color, and attached to its body like barnacles on a ship were the tiny creatures we just encountered. Whether they were Oculor babies or something else, the curses that left my mouth at the sight of this thing were anything but virtuous.

"Spirits in the tree, please help us," I said to myself.

"What is that?" James asked.

"*That* is the Oculor," I said gravely.

We looked down at the crew below, who were still fighting the remaining Oculor creatures. Obsidian was amongst them. He was managing six or seven at a time, and the Ocular babies seemed keen on him. That's when I noticed he was draining their hearts. Because they were Stone-Hearted, he could kill them almost instantly. Over and over, I watched as he drained the Ocular of life, their slimy tentacle bodies falling to the ground instantly upon feeling the wrath of his power.

They were gravitating toward him now. The remaining Ocular babies focused on him.

I watched in awe as he stood like some sort of sea god, black hair whipping in time with the baby Oculor tentacles. His shirt was in shreds from baby Oculor grabbing at the seams, and his golden heart was visible, muscles clenching with effort as he drained the creatures of light. They swarmed him, a myriad of black tentacles coming within inches of him. It was a storm, and he was the eye.

The big Oculor seemed to notice Obsidian killing its babies, and it let out another loud curdling shriek as one of its tentacles stretched out, reaching for Obsidian.

"Captain!" James yelled. But it was too late.

The tentacles curled around Obsidian, lifting him into the air and away from the corpses of smaller Oculor.

The creature lifted Obsidian toward him, and I watched as he struggled against its grasp.

"We have to kill it," I said to James.

"How?" he asked, and I gestured to the fire on the stairs that was gradually starting to die down.

"Let's take the corpses. They are covered in the oil. We can light them and throw them at the Oculor,"

"You think that will work?" James asked.

"We have to try,"

James didn't protest then, and we started down the steps toward the other crewmates on the lower deck. Together we stomped out little fires as we descended the steps. Luckily, the ocean waters helped us, sending a spray that helped subdue the flames every once in a while.

"Wait," I reached out to his arm. "Don't touch the ink. It's poisonous and will cause you to hallucinate."

James paused for a moment before taking off his jacket and covering his hands with the fabric. I took off mine too and did the same.

We did our best to avoid puddles of black ink as we went.

Some crewmates had already suffered death by the baby Oculor. The adrenaline coursing through me was the only thing helping me not to break down at the sight. I did my best to avoid looking at those that had died in the arms of black tentacles and focused on those still alive.

Out of the few who remained, half seemed to be hallucinating, having come into contact with the ink.

I reached Elon, who was one of the remaining soldiers who hadn't been injured, and gestured toward the men who needed help. "Take these men to the hull. They can't be out here in this state,"

Some were crying, others wandering around aimlessly.

Elon nodded and quickly began taking those he could down to the hull to safety.

Those still in their right mind that remained, I started instructing them to take off some of their layers to bandage their hands to keep from touching the ink on the bodies of the dead Oculor.

"We need to light the limbs and throw them at that thing." I gestured toward the big Oculor still in the water. The giant Oculor was still fighting Obsidian. It was shrieking again, and I wondered if Obsidian was trying to drain its heart. If so, it was happening slowly, and I guessed because it was larger, it was harder to kill.

"Do any of you have powers that can help us in this situation?" I asked, breathing heavily.

One of the soldiers raised his hand.

"I can understand animals,"

I gave the boy a confused expression. "You can do what?"

The soldier sighed and then pointed at the giant Oculor in the water.

"It's very angry and upset," he explained.

I stared at the soldier incredulously. "Thank you, but I think I figured that one out on my own."

The soldier shrugged.

"Anyone else?" I asked, desperate for help.

They all shook their heads.

"None of us have physical powers," one of the men spoke.

I looked at James, and he shook his head. "I have perfect recall, that's it."

I sighed but nodded.

"Alright, start grabbing limbs and lighting them with lanterns."

The soldiers didn't waste time, thankfully listening to my command without question. Together we got to work on gathering the pieces of slimy tentacles to throw at the Oculor. I tried my best to ignore the feel of the flesh and sliminess beneath my cloth-covered hands, forcing myself to remain focused.

Together, the remaining crew and I came to the boat's edge and began lighting severed tentacles with the lanterns on the deck. The smell was awful, like smoky fish, blood, and a hint of some wet pungent smell.

"Alright on the count of three," I yelled. "One, two, three,"

A chorus of shouts sounded as we all heaved fish limbs encased in fire at the creature in the water. Some didn't hit the Oculor, and splashed into the waves, but the ones that did, elicited a shriek from the Ocular when it hit its slimy flesh.

"We need to get the fire inside it somehow," James said to me.

"If it opened its mouth, we could get it that way," I suggested.

Just then, the creature gave another hideous shriek, and its mouth opened. White razor-sharp teeth flashed in the moonlight, a sudden stark contrast against the darkness. It angled the tentacle holding Obsidian toward its cavernous mouth, and I realized then that it was going to eat him.

I stared in horror up at the creature and felt almost frozen watching the scene before me.

But then James shook my shoulder and gestured to the gaping mouth of the creature.

"We need to throw the fire in now!" he yelled.

I nodded, snapping back to reality as I began lighting more

ink-covered Oculor limbs with fire. Once the crew had secured enough, we all lined up at the edge again.

"On the count of three. One, two, three!" I screamed at the men again, and together we threw the limbs in the direction of the beast's mouth.

The blaze that ensued was a fiery inferno. Immediately the creature whipped its tentacles angrily, shrieking so loudly I had to cover my ear. Burning fish smell filled the air. The creature writhed and contorted in the water as the fire consumed its flesh, and soon the blaze was so bright it was like the sun had risen. We watched as it ate away at the black flesh of the beast until it fell beneath the waves leaving only a few fiery remains licking at the oil on the choppy surface of the waves.

Everything was silent then except for the crackling of fire and the waves hitting the side of the ship. We all stared out at the blackness, eyes wide. My heart was beating so fast as I searched the ocean for Obsidian. But after five minutes, a new hope began to settle in.

"Is he gone?" I whispered to James.

"I think so," he replied. He seemed to be in as much shock as I was.

I looked over at him, and our eyes met. "You know what this means, right?" I asked, trying not to feel too much joy after the chaos that had just ensued. But unable to not feel relief that maybe the captain was gone. If he were gone, I wouldn't have to cause an uprising against him. Perhaps the beast had defeated him for me.

"Let's worry about that later. Why won't we go down to the hull and help the men that are injured?"

I nodded.

Together we started toward the hull, and I had a feeling as we walked it was going to be a long night of helping the wounded and getting rid of the remaining Ocular and those that had died. And the cleanup of the poisonous ink everywhere was going to be tricky.

Just then, a sound hit the deck, and we all turned around again. My heart leaped into my throat, worrying it was another baby Ocular attacking.

A pale white hand gripped the edge of the ship. Then a grunt sounded as someone heaved their way over the side of the boat. A body clothed in ebony hit the deck with a heavy flop, and my heart stopped.

Obsidian. He was alive.

FORTY-SEVEN

SABEARA

I clung to the edge of the ship as I looked over to see what was causing the commotion. I saw something reflected in the sunlight. Something bright and colorful. My eyes widened when I realized it was a fin.

"They're trying to sink the ship!" I screamed. We'd found the mermaids. But they obviously weren't happy we had found them.

I stumbled over to Embrosine and Shar, who were desperately trying to lift the ropes that hung over the side of the ship that the mermaids had hold of and were using as extra leverage to pull us under.

The boat shifted roughly again, and I grunted, trying to keep myself upright.

"What do we do?" Dusane yelled.

"We have to fight back," Mid had disappeared into the hull but had now returned with his bow and arrows.

"Do not shoot them, Mid, or they surely won't help us," Thane ordered.

"So, what's the plan? Just let them sink our ship?" Rouix asked, her high-pitched voice raising even more with anxiety.

"No, we get them to listen," Knadian said, and he took position on the edge of the boat.

"How?" I heard Mid ask his father, then Knadian began to manipulate the waves, using his power. The waters made a loud whooshing sound as they started to part, moving the mermaids away from the ship on the swell he created. Knadian grunted with frustration.

I couldn't see how many mermaids there were, but if there were many, Knadian was surely going to be using a lot of power to push them back.

His power seemed to do the trick, though, and soon, the violent rocking of the ship ceased. We loosened our hold on the ropes hanging off the side of the vessel. They were no longer taut with tension.

I watched in awe as the tails of the mermaids flickered in the water in an attempt to avoid Knadian's waves. The shiny scales on their fins were similar to a Crykon's—colorful and scintillating.

Knadian released some of the waves as if testing to see if they would back off. Everything was quiet for many minutes as we watched the waters calm to a quiet lull. As the giant waves died, the atmosphere became nearly silent. All that could be heard were our ragged breaths and a couple of seagulls overhead. No more scales were seen in the water for a lengthy amount of time.

"Did they leave?" I heard Embrosine whisper.

Just then, something shot out of the water. A sparkling blur passed through the air and descended toward the deck. The boat shook when it landed.

We all turned, wide-eyed, to find a woman standing before us. She glistened with droplets of water still clinging to her dark skin. She had long black hair reaching clear to her waist and eyes so green they reminded me of sea moss. A crown of seashells and jewels adorned her head, and a pulsing blue light thrummed beneath her skin. She wore barely anything—her physique draped in sheer cobalt fabric. In her right hand was a long golden spear, the tip sharp and white as if made of bone. She pointed the weapon towards us, her face contorted with anger.

"This is the land of Tetheria. Why do you trespass on our turf?"

I was confused. Not sure if this was one of the mermaids. She stood on two legs.

"We do not mean to cause trouble—" Knadian raised his hands in surrender and slowly walked toward the woman.

She jabbed her spear out further, threatening Knadian if he stepped any closer. The King stilled.

"Your ship in my waters is a threat to my people. Leave now before I have to kill you."

"We come seeking your help to undo the enchantment on the compass," Mid stepped forward, pushing past his father. He spoke with confidence. Not a glimpse of fear in his eyes.

The woman didn't say anything for a moment as she looked at Mid. Then slowly, she lowered her spear and tilted her head to one side in contemplation.

"And who are you?"

"I'm Midennen Knadian, Prince of Ethydon," he said

formally. It rolled off his tongue so naturally as if he'd practiced those words a thousand times.

The woman's eyebrows lifted, and she took several careful steps towards him.

"Well, Prince of Ethydon. How do you know about the King's Compass?"

"We learned of its existence from the Ethirical. We are trying to stop the curse."

"Do you seek the compass for personal gain?" she asked, eyes narrowing.

Mid quickly shook his head. "The opposite, I assure you."

She seemed to be taking in his answer. Then suddenly, her face broke into a kind smile.

"Well then. It seems I must formally introduce myself. My name is Emiress. I'm the Queen of Tetheria."

~

With the mermaid queen's alabaster spear no longer raised, everyone seemed to relax.

"I'm sorry our introduction was so . . . violent," she said. Amusement sparkled in her dark green eyes.

"No need for an apology. I understand. We are protective of our lands as well," Knadian said politely.

"How are you standing on two legs?" The question tumbled out of my mouth before I could stop it. I was confused by what I'd seen in the waters and what I was seeing before me now. I berated myself for prying.

"I am only in need of a fin when I'm in the water. And I am in control of which form I take," she said, looking me up and down. She seemed to be noticing me for the first time. She eyed me with poised scrutiny. And she didn't seem impressed. My cheeks reddened at her careful assessment.

"I've only heard stories of your kind. It is well to know you truly exist," Thane said, gazing in awe at the mermaid.

"You must come to my castle. Dine with me. We can talk about the enchantment on the compass there." She gestured toward the island. I vaguely remembered the dream I'd had. Faint images of the palm trees and a white castle filled my head.

"We don't wish to trouble you. . ." Knadian started to say

"It is no trouble. Please, I insist. I want to hear about your journey." She smiled. Her teeth were bright white and dazzling.

Her eyes shifted to Mid again.

"Prince of Ethydon, would you escort me to the side of the ship? I will journey by water to inform my people of your arrival." She held out her hand, and Mid's eyes widened in surprise. He took her hand and gingerly placed it over his arm, dutifully walking her across the deck to the bow of the ship.

We watched from a distance as she mounted the side of the ship and gracefully dove back into the water.

"Are we really going to her castle?" I asked everyone.

"We don't have a choice. I doubt she'll give us any help without a formal meeting," Thane said.

"I think she wants something in return." Knadian had his fingers pressed to his lips, his brow furrowed in concentration.

"So this invitation to her castle has nothing to do with wanting to get to know us?" Embrosine asked, her tone unimpressed.

"I'm afraid not," Knadian said.

Worry and apprehension flooded my veins. "We will just have to do everything in our power to convince her to help us." I bit my lip.

"That we will," Shar agreed, his sharp green eyes gazing out at the waters where the queen had disappeared.

As the Diagon moved across the waters, closer and closer to the island of Tetheria the apprehension became almost unbearable. I couldn't help but fear that Queen Emiress wouldn't agree to help us. But the only way to find out would be to meet with her as she requested. But it suddenly felt as if we were no longer in control.

At the mercy of this woman, I couldn't help but fear the outcome.

What side was she on?

FORTY-EIGHT

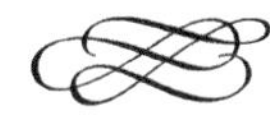

SUNN

The Captain was covered in ink, and he was already in a state of hallucination when he heaved himself onto the deck.

I wanted to throw him back overboard. Let him drown in the depths of the sea in ink-induced madness. It was a perfect time. He didn't know what was happening to him. He couldn't even really fight back.

But James said no.

"Are you serious? Now is our chance to defeat him!" I was yelling at James now. The entire night and its subsequent events were making me feel crazy. *Maybe I'd touched the ink after all...*

We were the only ones on the deck now. The others had gone to the hull to help the rest of the crewmates. Moaning and groaning, Obsidian was at our feet, and our argument had been going on for several minutes now.

"What if we encounter more Oculor. We will need him," James argued.

"We aren't going to get attacked by more Oculor," I said, but I wasn't exactly sure about that.

"How do you know? We aren't even close to being out of Trojan waters yet."

"He's a monster, James."

"I know you want him gone so you can return home. And I promise to help you get home if you keep him around just a little longer. The only reason we survived tonight was because he killed most of the Oculor."

I growled under my breath, letting out a few curses.

"I hate this. Why would I save him? He wouldn't save any of us!" I gestured toward him.

"Please, Salt."

I looked down at Obsidian. He was on his back, staring up at the sky. He was shaking with what appeared to be the effects of the fever and mumbling incoherencies to himself. I knew that it would pass. From what I heard of the myth, the poison wasn't deadly unless ingested. The fever and hallucinations would pass with time.

"Fine, but you promise to help me?"

"I promise," James said, holding out his hand.

I shook it hesitantly. But maybe having James on my side meant something. Maybe if the crew didn't trust me, they would trust James. My new bond that had been born amidst this crisis with him would hopefully tether us together. At least he was officially on my side now. And he was right. We needed Obsidian just a little longer.

It's just until you get out of Trojan waters, I told myself. *Then you can get rid of him.*

I bit my lip. It seemed risky though, Obsidian was weakened in a state of hallucination, but if we attacked him while he was sobered, he would have full control of his powers. People would die during an uprising against him.

Men had already died tonight. . .

In the darkness, I could see several fallen bodies, still wrapped in the merciless tentacles of the Oculor.

To avoid breaking down right then and there, I forced myself not to dwell on the casualties and focus on Obsidian.

We had to strip him of his clothes and carry him into his quarters. It took some time, he was dead weight, and we both struggled to get him inside. We settled for the floor as we helped wash Obsidian's body of the ink, being careful not to get it on ourselves in the process. I did my best to keep my eyes away from the parts of him that made him a man. But it was impossible not to at least look at some parts of him. Like his pale-skinned chest, taught with muscle. And every time my hand happened to brush up against his skin, accidentally, I couldn't help but notice how soft it was. It gave me an unsettling feeling that I was having trouble not admiring him. I was grateful when James found him a new pair of trousers, and he was clothed from the wait up again.

After cleaning him, we used our last remaining strength to lay him on the red silk sheets of the bed.

He shivered, his forehead slick with sweat.

"Do you know how to treat it?" James asked, worry wrinkling his brow as he stared at Obsidian.

"All I've heard is that it takes several days to pass. Let's just keep giving him fluids and hope it leaves him quickly."

James nodded then gestured toward the door. "I'm going to check on the others,"

"James," I called out to him before he could leave.

"Yes?"

"Is this all my fault?" My lower lip trembled a little, thinking about those men who had died fighting the Oculor.

"You couldn't have known they were real, Salt. Don't blame yourself."

I nodded, not so sure I could completely shed the guilt. "I'll stay here with him."

James looked about to say more but then stopped himself. When the door shut behind him, it was quiet, and I sighed, taking a seat on the other side of the bed.

He hadn't stopped shaking, his dark black eyes still staring blankly at the ceiling as he trembled. His skin was already so pale when he wasn't sick, but now he looked like a ghost. The incoherent mumbling continued.

For several hours I nursed him back to health. I would lift his head to help give him water, and most of it would dribble out onto his chin. At one point, I went into my room and changed, careful not to let any of the ink splattered on my clothes touch me. I put them into a pile in the corner of my room, knowing I'd have to burn them the next day.

When I was in a fresh shirt and trousers, I returned to Obsidian's room. For another several hours, I kept him hydrated as I sat beside him.

"I should've let you die out there," I said to him. I knew he couldn't hear me, but I needed to talk to someone or something, even if it was an incoherent hallucinating monster.

"You've tied me up for three days with no food or water, threw my friends from my old crew overboard, and you've been nothing but cruel to me." I got choked up thinking about Captain Rissen. "It's villains like you that keep these wars alive."

I leaned my head back against the headboard. I was exhausted and drained from the nightmarish events. Thinking

I'd try and get some sleep, I closed my eyes and tried to clear my head.

"Mother?" Obsidian suddenly spoke, and I jumped in surprise. He hadn't said anything coherent since he'd been under the fever.

"What did you say?" I asked.

"Mother, what are you doing here?" Obsidian's dark black eyes stared at me now as if he were seeing a ghost. He reached a clammy white hand toward me, and I was too stunned to move when his fingers wrapped limply around mine. "You're alive," he whispered.

"I'm not. . . your mother," I said, my voice reduced to a whisper.

"I tried to come and rescue you when they took you to that prison, I tried," he said desperately. I was shocked when tears filled his eyes, becoming glassy black orbs. "But they wouldn't release you."

“Obsidian . . .” I tried to explain again, but he cut me off when he clenched my hand tighter and pulled it to his chest.

"They knew you were trapped in that prison. And they lied to father and me." He moved to lay his head on my lap while still grasping my hand like a lifeline. Then his shoulders suddenly shook with sobs.

I was frozen, unsure what to do with him in this state of emotion.

"Who lied to you?" I whispered, too curious not to play along.

"Sabeara and Jasper," he said, another sob wracking his body. "You were in that prison, and they knew. And they didn't tell me."

"What happened after you found out where I was?" I asked, realization dawning slowly the more he spoke.

"Father did the only thing he could do, mother. He killed her to avenge you."

"Killed who?" I asked, barely able to speak the words.

"Ehren."

FORTY-NINE

SABEARA

The island of Tetheria was just as I'd dreamed. When I'd touched the compass, it must have been a vision. Because it was exactly as I'd seen it in my mind, only it was much clearer now—the island even more breathtaking in real life.

The island was lush with foliage, the sands nearly white as snow. The water was so blue you could see everything when you gazed into it. We anchored the ship, and together, we lowered a ramp onto the sand. As my feet met the beach, I couldn't help but feel relief. It had been days since I'd felt the security of solid ground.

As we walked up the beach, the trees shook with movement, and several sentries emerged from the tree-line. They were dressed in armor made of what looked to be shells and jungle foliage, holding similar spears as the mermaid queens, the men, and women before us wore no expressions on their faces. One gestured with her hand to follow, and we trailed after them into the jungle.

As we walked, Dusane was on my right, with Rouix on my left. We stole glances at each other, all of us seemingly uncomfortable. I wanted to trust this mermaid queen. But something was holding me back. And maybe it was my Envoy training telling me not to trust anyone, but I was hesitant. *What did she want from us? Couldn't she have just agreed to help us with the compass on the boat? Then take us to the compass and then undo the enchantment? What was with all this presumptive stuff?*

A path was cleared through the trees that we were led down. Small creatures admired us as we passed. An assortment of tropical birds and curious monkeys flitted through the vines. Shrill caws and monkey shrieks echoed through the trees, and I stayed close to the middle of the path, wanting to avoid any species that might be confrontational.

It took us about an hour to make the trek to the castle. When it finally appeared before us my eyes widened. I'd never seen anything like it.

The pearl white architecture of the castle walls was a beautiful contrast to the trees surrounding it. Tall spires and round clay-colored turrets gave the architecture a royal appearance, the wide double front doors a magnificent entrance. A long set of stairs led up to them, and together we climbed to meet the queen who was waiting for us.

She'd changed from the scanty attire she'd been in previously. Now she wore a stunning green gown that gave the illusion she had a fin. The dress was tight against her body, hugging every curve until trumpeting out at the base into frilly convolutions. The jewels adorned in the fabric sparkled much the way her fin would in the water.

"Thank you for joining me." Emiress gestured to the foyer. "Please, come this way to the meal I've prepared."

The inside of the castle was just as stunning as the outside. The floors were a dark turquoise green stone, and rolled out across them were long white rugs. Stunning vases and art pieces adorned the walls and side tables. It seemed that everything in sight was embellished with pebbles, shells, or jewels. After a while, the endless finery and regalia seemed to blend together. I found the display of treasures to be overwhelming.

We were led to a large banquet room where a large table was set out. An assortment of clams, crabs, and other seafare covered the table, along with tropical fruits and seaweed-covered delectables.

I sat down between Rouix and Dusane. Embrosine sat with her father and Thane at the other end of the table. While Shar and Midennen sat closest to Queen Emiress.

"Thank you for having us at your table, Queen Emiress. It is very kind of you to invite us," Knadian started into the conversation.

"It is my pleasure," the queen said, smiling. "We do not have guests often, so this is delightful for me."

Several servants walked around the table, pouring us glasses of Lush Fire and dishing portions of the delicacies in front of us onto our porcelain plates. I tentatively scooped up a forkful of fish and tried not to moan when it melted on my tongue. It was the most fantastic fish I'd ever tasted.

"So, Emiress, how long have you been ruler of this island?" Embrosine questioned. Her diplomatic demeanor was immediately brought to life, and once again, I admired the way she carried herself. She was a natural at this sort of thing.

"Ever since I was Stone-Hearted. You see, for a long time, our kind was taken advantage of. We used to live in the kingdoms, but we were unfairly treated."

I frowned, not liking the sound of that.

"How are your kind Stone-Hearted? And how does that work being a mermaid?"

"Believe it or not, every creature in this realm can be Stone-Hearted. You don't just have to be human," Emiress explained. "I was Stone-Hearted just as you all were when I turned eighteen. And I received Sonar ability. I can measure the water's depth by emitting sound pulses and detect objects in the water as the sound is reflected."

I immediately thought back to the snake with the glowing heart. Animals, mermaids, humans. We could all be Stone-Hearted. It made me wonder what other species existed in our realm.

"So you found people like yourself and left the confines of the kingdoms?" King Knadian asked, jaw clenching.

"Yes, but don't take it personally, King Knadian. We left long before your kingdom was even established. And I'm sure you're not the type of ruler to take advantage of people like me." Her eyebrow raised, and I think I heard a challenge in her voice.

"I assure you, we would never use mermaids to our advantage," King Knadian said.

"That is good. But we will continue to remain on this island until the kingdoms find peace again. Accepting all creatures and all colors of hearts," she said boldly. The determination in her voice was unmistakable.

"Are there other kingdoms like yours?" I suddenly asked. "Hiding?"

"We are the only mermaid clan I am aware of that still exists. But long ago, there were more of us. Greater Aveladon used to be filled with wonders you can't even begin to imagine." The queen's viridian eyes seemed to glow as she spoke and the intensity in her voice took my breath away.

"Queen Emiress, I hate to be the first to ask, but would you mind if we talked about the compass?" Mid asked. He sat tall in his chair, and despite his slightly disheveled appearance from being on the ship for days, he still managed to look regal and handsome.

"I don't mind at all. You all must be eager to have it in your possession," Emiress presumed.

"We are worried about it getting into the wrong hands," Dusane chimed in beside me.

"I assure you, I won't let that happen." The queen let out a biting laugh.

"Would you be willing to undo the enchantment? To help us defeat the curse?" Mid pressed, and Emiress sighed, taking a sip from the opal goblet she held between her delicate fingers.

"Undoing an ancient mermaid enchantment on an object like the compass can only be done by someone that knows the spirit's ancient tongue."

"And do you know the ancient tongue?" Mid asked, not backing down.

The mermaid queen looked at Mid, a curious smile tugging at the corners of her lips. "You're persistent, aren't you?"

"Most people find that a charming quality." Mid flashed Emiress a playful smile. "But the question is, Queen, do you find it redeemable?"

"Quite," she purred, and I felt my mouth drop open a little.

Were they . . . flirting?

"If you're so insistent on getting my help, I only require one thing." Her eyes remained locked on Mid. "You and your friends must join me for a night of festivities at the castle. I'm hosting our annual Tetherian Gala tomorrow."

"You are agreeing to help us on terms that we accept *your* hospitality? Hardly seems fair," Mid questioned, but his eyes were bright and playful still.

"Well, you see, as I said, I don't have guests often. You'll be helping a lonely queen such as myself have a memorable night. That is if you accept one other condition, and that is that you come as my date." The queen smiled at Mid, a sultry innuendo in her eyes.

"It would be my honor to accompany you." Mid reached his hand out from under the table and revealed a single red rose in his hand. It glistened with morning dew, the illusioned flower more beautiful than what it could have been in reality.

"What's this?" The queen's eyes widened in surprise at the gesture. "You are an illusionist?" She took the rose from his fingertips, admiring it for a moment before looking back up at him. "I'm afraid I'm the type of person looking for something real, Prince Midennen. But the gesture is . . . endearing."

"I assure you I'm *very* real, Your Majesty," Mid nearly purred.

Something dark started to swirl inside of me. I could suddenly taste something bitter on my tongue.

I'm not jealous. I practically shouted at myself internally. *He's just trying to convince her to help with the compass,* I assured myself. But the malicious feeling continued to spread throughout my body, and I knew I was tainted with some form of envious rage.

"Well then, I'm looking forward to having you accompany me to tomorrow's gala." Emiress turned back to the table. "You'll all join me, I hope."

"We would love to come to your celebration," King Knadian assured her, giving her a polite smile.

"Wonderful. Now, if you'll excuse me, I'm going to head to my chambers. I fear I have some things to attend to before tomorrow's gala. Selon will escort you to your rooms."

Queen Emiress stood from her seat, and several guards were beside her almost instantly. She left the dining hall, the click of her heels echoing off the tall ceilings as she departed. Just then, a man moved from his position by the wall, dressed in shimmering green robes. He strode out of the shadows and over to the table. His long brown hair was tied back in a bun at the nape of his neck, and his dark eyes were serious.

"If you'd please, follow me," he said formally.

We all stood from the table and followed after Selon. His robes swished across the floor as we were guided through the halls and up to several flights of stairs. We each received our own rooms, and I didn't even get the chance to say goodbye to the others.

Suddenly the door closed behind me, and I found myself in a giant room with the most breathtaking floor to cleaning windows I'd ever witnessed. Except as I looked closer, I realized there was no glass in the frames. Warm island winds breezed freely into the room, ruffling the white canopy on the four-poster bed.

The colors and decor were much like the rest of the palace. Sparkling trinkets and trays dazzled each table and cabinet in the room. I couldn't help but wonder where all the peculiar treasures camc from. Pale opal statues, paintings, tiaras on pedestals, and elegant swords. Greens and golds hued each blanket, curtain, and rug. The colors were the palette of the ocean. They resembled the likes of pebbles you might find buried in the sand.

I found a clean nightgown in the closet and changed out of

my rumpled sea attire. I tossed the dirty garments into a pile on the floor, too exhausted to find a laundering basket. Then I crawled into the soft sheets, grateful that there was no rocking movement when I laid down my head—only a soft, firm mattress.

I fell asleep that night dreaming of Queen Emiress, dressed in her trumped gown, her skin turning to crimson roses.

FIFTY

SUNN

Obsidian fell back into his voiceless delirium soon after his confessions. I'd wanted to find James that very second and ask him about everything I'd heard. Still, Obsidian was wrapped around me like one of the Ocular, and no matter how hard I tried, he wouldn't budge. I had to wait until he rolled back over and released me from his vice-like grip. By the time I managed to free myself, the sun was streaming into the room, and I went to find James as fast as I could.

My mind was reeling. The information Obsidian had spilled during the hallucination was almost too much for my mind to handle. *Jasper and Sabeara?* Sabeara had been the one to take me to the docks when the Ethydon war happened. If Obsidian was speaking truthfully despite his madness, it sounded like he was involved with the Aigoviel family. Something I'd had yet to be made aware of.

I found James in the hull, assisting a mumbling soldier.

"James, I need to talk to you,"

"Salt, I'm a little busy," he said irritably. He didn't look to have slept at all the night before. Hair disheveled and bags beneath his eyes. Then again, I hadn't done much sleeping either.

"It's important. Now," I ordered, and I was surprised at the demand in my tone.

He paused what he was doing, also seemingly surprised by my tone, and he followed me out onto the deck.

"What's going on, Salt," James asked, concern taking over the agitation in his blue eyes.

"How does Obsidian know Sabeara and Jasper Aigoviel?" I asked, and his eyes widened immediately.

"How did you hear about that?"

"He told me. He was hallucinating and started talking about them and something about his mother being in prison."

James's face paled. "He told you about his mother?"

"James, do you know what he's talking about?" I could nearly taste the secrets I was about to pull out of him. They were on the tip of his tongue, and I was so curious for him to spill them it was painful.

"He's related to the Aigoviel family." James averted his gaze as if ashamed at himself for telling me the secret.

"How is Obsidian related to the Aigoviels?"

"I shouldn't be telling you this, Salt."

"Spirits, James. Just tell me, please," I begged.

"Okay." He ran a hand through his hair. "But you have to promise not to tell anyone." James pulled me around to an even more private part of the deck. He crouched behind a barrel and gestured for me to take a seat beside him.

"Obsidian's father, Elysian Reyes, was the brother of Ehren Reyes."

"So Sabeara's mother is Obsidian's aunt?"

"Yes,"

"So what happened to Obsidian's mother?"

"His mother Mirella was cast into prison by King Casimir when he allegedly accused her of treason."

"Treason?".

"She was thrown into the castle prisons for her crimes, and she died there. King Elysian blamed Casimir for his wife's death and killed Ehren for revenge,"

"He killed his own sister to get revenge?" I put a hand over my heart, feeling the ache there at the thought of something so barbaric.

"Casimir took his wife, so Elysian did the same to him,"

"Obsidian said something about Jasper and Sabeara that they knew about his mother?"

"From what I've gathered, Obsidian and his cousins were very close as children. He feels betrayed because he thinks Jasper and Sabeara were knowledgeable of his mother's imprisonment and subsequent death by the hands of King Casimir."

"So he thinks not only that his uncle betrayed him but his cousins? How does Obsidian know that his mother wasn't guilty of the crime? And why was she charged with treason?"

"That I still don't know. And would you believe it if someone told you your mother committed treason?"

I thought about it and realized I wouldn't. I would assume they were lying if someone told me my mother had committed such a crime.

"What a mess," I whispered.

"Yes, what a mess is right. A mess that has caused a curse and a war." James sighed.

"Obsidian thinks he's on the good side of this," I said, more to myself than to James.

"Haven't you ever heard the saying, every villain is the hero of his own story?"

I pursed my lips, thinking about all the things he'd told me.

"Salt, how do you know so much about the royal family in Aveladon?" James asked.

"I guess I just learned a lot in history," I lied to him.

He eyed me suspiciously. "You're taking this a little more personally than someone who is interested in a little history lesson,"

"Don't you have somewhere to be?" I reminded him, and he glared at me. It was hard for James to look menacing. He had boyish features, and his baby blue eyes, even when in a glare, were hardly intimidating.

"I'm not done with this conversation," he said, exasperated.

As he disappeared back to help the other injured men, I hurried back to the Captain's quarters, the new information about Obsidian and his family a whirlwind in my head.

FIFTY-ONE

SABEARA

The next morning I woke to the sound of something shuffling beside my bed. When I groggily opened my eyes, a pair of cerulean eyes met mine, and I jolted upright—my hand covering my mouth to subdue the scream that elicited through me.

"What are you doing in here?" I shrieked, my heartbeat thundering in my ears. Dusane was lounging casually in a teal blue chair, several feet from the bed. My pile of dirty laundry that had been in the corner beside it was gone, and I had a good idea who'd moved it.

"Our balconies are connected," Dusane said simply. I narrowed my eyes at him while glancing to the balcony that was letting air flow freely through the glassless windows.

"You could've knocked," I glared at him. "You scared me."

"Sorry," Dusane said, emotionless as usual. He was already clean and dressed for the day. His long black hair fell into his eyes, and he ran a hand through it only to have it fall back into place seconds later. "You gotta come see this," he said. Getting up from the chair, he walked out onto the balcony and gestured to the view.

I sighed, rubbed my eyes, and forced myself to get out of the warmth and comfort of the sheets. A little embarrassed, I was in nothing but a nightgown. I crossed my arms over my chest as I went over to stand by him.

"This better be good. . ." I trailed off when I saw the scene before me.

The ocean surrounding the lush island was an endless turquoise horizon. The morning sun was making the sky all different shades of pinks and purples, winking off the surface of the waves in magnificent coruscation.

"It's beautiful," I whispered.

Dusane smiled, "I thought you'd like it."

I turned to him after a moment of admiring the view and raised my eyebrows questioningly at him. "As grateful as I am for this view, mind telling me what you're doing waking me at such an hour?"

"Don't shoot," he said teasingly, "I'm only the messenger."

My eyebrows remained raised.

"I was told to inform you about a package you'll be receiving this morning."

"Package?"

"You guess is as good as mine," he said, turning away from the balcony and walking back into the shade of the room.

"Why would I be receiving a package. . ."

Just then, a knock at the door sounded. Dusane and I looked at one another.

"I'll get it," Dusane opened the door and revealed on the other side were several of the queen's ladies maids. Dusane opened the door wider for them to enter, and all three of them rushed in. One was holding a big white box in her hands, and she quickly placed it on the sofa.

Dusane shut the door behind them with a kick of his foot.

I stared at the package and the glittering bow wrapped around it.

"What is this?" I asked, hesitant.

"It is for you, miss," one of the ladies' maids said.

"Just open it," Dusane said, and it sounded like an order. I shot him a glare but proceeded to move toward the box. Slowly I untied the bow.

As I unraveled the ribbon, I found a note attached, and I opened the small card to read the inscription on the paper.

From Queen Emiress

I removed the lid after reading the note and revealed inside were layers and layers of atrocious dark green fabric. I lifted the dress and found it to be the plainest, most unadorned gown I had ever seen. Not a bead or jewel was sewn into the bodice, and the neckline was so high I was sure it would choke me. It even had long sleeves, which would be utterly stifling in a climate like this.

I was speechless looking at the dress I'd been gifted, and for a moment, I couldn't do anything except stare in utter disbelief.

"I think she wants you to wear this tonight," Dusane mused, reaching out to touch some of the silk fabric tentatively.

"You think?" I looked over at him, feeling slightly rattled.

I remembered how she'd flirted with Mid at the dinner the night before, and that bitter taste returned to my mouth.

I didn't know who this queen thought she was, but something wasn't quite right about the way she was inviting us to her gala. We'd trespassed on her land, she almost *sunk* our ship, and then when we asked for her help unenchanting the compass, all she asked for in return was that we join her at her gala? And now there was this. Gifting me a dress that was so blatantly horrendous. She obviously wanted to be the most beautiful person in the room that night. The dress was a clear message. *You are plain compared to me.*

I was really starting to dislike this mermaid queen.

"If she thinks I'm going to wear this, she's mad." I pulled the green gown out of the box and handed it to one of the maids. The girl's eyes were wide in what looked to be fear as she clutched it to her chest. "Grab your scissors and sewing kits. We're going to change the dress." I told the girls.

Dusane looked at me, puzzlement and maybe even a little amusement in his eyes as the girls scrambled around the room. But thankfully, he didn't question me.

"Mark my words Dusane, something is not right about that woman. She's up to something."

Dusane remained quiet for a moment as if thinking on my words.

"You may be right," he said, considering it. "But the safest thing to do right now is to play along."

I could see the reason in his blue depths, but I was numb to reciprocating his logic because of everything I was feeling toward the queen.

The queen was playing some sort of game. And the way she'd acted around Mid last night was proof of that. And maybe the rest of them were okay with playing. Mid seemed more than happy to participate, and even Dusane seemed to think it was necessary.

But I wasn't going to be as easily manipulated.

~

It wasn't until I was inside the ballroom that night that I started to contemplate that I'd overreacted. But it was too late to back down now that I was there, dressed in the gown I altered, in front of an entire audience.

The maids had done a fantastic job of altering the gown. They'd removed the sleeves and stifling neckline, then they'd beaded the bodice and tightened the waistline. They'd curled and pinned my hair atop my head and put dangling seashell earrings on my ears. And the amulet that usually hid beneath my shirt was in full display on my neck, resting in the perfect crevice of my cleavage. I was revealing more skin than I was used to showing. But I'd also never felt so daring and vibrant.

Everyone's eyes fell on me as I entered the room, and I seemed to be one of the last to arrive. Which had been intentional, of course. But now, as wide-eyed looks were sent like daggers in my direction, I was starting to question my boldness.

I spotted Shar standing next to Embrosine in the crowd and quickly made a beeline for them. As if they were my safe haven, I squeezed in beside them, letting out a breath I was holding.

"Everyone is staring at me," I whispered, my cheeks hot with embarrassment.

"Well, of course they're staring at you! You look stunning, Ehren," Embrosine gushed and reached out to touch one of the beads on my bodice.

"People are going to stare if you give them something to stare at," Shar said, his expression completely serious. I didn't miss the way his eyes glanced at the plunging V neckline of the dress and then raised his eyebrow at me.

"You're a real jerk sometimes," I said to him in a hissed whisper.

"It comes naturally," was his only response.

I ignored him then and turned back to Embrosine.

"You don't think it's too much?" I asked nervously.

"Not at all. I think it's perfect. Mid is going to literally die when he sees you in that dress."

Shar chuckled derisively.

My cheeks flushed. I hadn't really done it for Mid. Mainly I wanted to do it to prove to Queen Emriess that she couldn't force me to wear her hideous gown to her party. But something nagged at my insides deep within me, feeling almost happy at Embrosine's words. *Would he notice me?*

I forced that thought from my mind and proceeded to tell myself I was doing this to spite the queen. Not to get anyone's attention.

Just then, Dusane and Rouix came through the crowd joining our little group. Rouix wore a beautiful red gown, showcasing her delicate form. Her silvery hair fell around her shoulders, and a string of seashells was tied into her hair.

Dusane beside her was dressed in the finest attire I think I'd ever seen him in. Looking much like a prince would. He wore a white dress shirt and black trousers. His hair was slicked back from his face unlike I'd ever seen before, revealing the sharp angles of his cheekbones and his cerulean eyes.

When he spotted me, his eyes widened slightly.

"Ehren, you look. . ." he started to say.

"She looks amazing, doesn't she?" Embrosine interrupted, slipping her arm through mine.

"Amazing would suffice," Dusane agreed, smiling a little.

I blushed again and couldn't help but glance nervously around the room. There were Tetheria civilians everywhere. Hearts glowing and reflecting off the castle's treasures adorning the ballroom. People were dancing and laughing and eating to their heart's content.

But I was too paranoid to enjoy the scenery. We still had yet to get the queen's help with the compass. I wondered if she would stay true to her word, that if we went to this party of hers, she'd really help us. The skepticism was running deep in my blood. That bitter taste in my mouth had moved to the very marrow in my bones. I didn't trust her.

My gaze found Knadian and Thane standing, talking to several strangers. Then my gaze moved a little farther down the room, and that's when I spotted Mid.

He sat at a table with the queen.

And it felt for a moment that someone had punched me in the gut.

He was laughing at something Emiress was saying, captivated by the story she was telling. All his attention was directed at her, his body language open and inviting. His hair was cut short, his emerald-scarlet eyes twinkling like the treasures around the room. He was wearing a fancy tunic embellished with green and blue beads. He even had a seashell crown adorning his head.

Everything else in the room seemed to fade into the background as I watched them. A familiar feeling spread through me that I had unconsciously wished never to feel again.

I remembered a moment, long ago, when he'd looked the same way when courting my sister. Someone also refined, beautiful, and on the very pinnacle of perfection. Just like Jasper, this woman was a picturesque image of what royalty should be. She emanated strength, prowess, and beauty.

I sucked in a sharp breath, shoving back down the memory of that time in my life.

I looked over at Dusane, and somehow, I could breathe again.

The only person that can ever make you feel worthy is you. The words echoed in my mind.

I stepped away from Embrosine and over to Dusane. "Want to dance?" I asked, needing to get entirely out of sight of that table as quickly as possible.

I didn't give him a chance to deny my wishes and simply dragged him onto the dance floor.

"I really don't danc. . ." Dusane started to argue.

"Oh, can you please just humor me?" I begged, placing my arms around his neck and forcing us into a waltz.

Thankfully he picked up on my rhythm, and he moved his feet. He seemed perfectly capable as we started to twirl around the dance floor.

"You really do look stunning tonight," Dusane said. "That dress is much better than the one the queen gave you."

"She wanted to make me look bad," I grumbled. Looking at the other gowns in the room and knowing if I'd worn what the queen gave me, I'd have stood out, and not in a good way.

"Are you sure she meant to. . ."

"I'm sure, Dusane," I glared at him, and he immediately closed his mouth, not finishing his sentence.

Maybe the queen wasn't targeting me. I mean, she barely knew me. But it sure felt like it with that dress she'd given me. At that moment, I dared to think that maybe I was being too sensitive to the queen's gestures.

I sighed. "I'm sorry. I know I'm being snappy."

"Nothing I can't handle," he assured me, impassive. "I've taken down dozens of men in brawls before. I'm hardly affected by the likes of your sharp tongue."

I narrowed my eyes, but his gaze didn't falter.

"We'll get the compass," he said, his voice softening.

"I hope so," I said, and I started biting my lip, the anxiety throughout my body in full bloom.

"Stop worrying so much. Can't you just enjoy yourself?" he asked. Obvious judgment was in his tone, speaking to me like my captain again.

"I'll enjoy myself when you enjoy yourself," I challenged, and he actually smiled.

"Fair enough."

We danced together for several more minutes, the orchestra's music leading us into several dances before someone interrupted us.

"May I cut in?"

I turned, not expecting the voice that broke the moment of our peaceful twirling.

Mid stood, waiting expectantly for our attention.

We came to a stop, and I found no words as I looked at him.

"As long as I can come back and have the last dance," Dusane bargained, his eyes flitting meaningfully to me, then back to Mid.

"Of course. Granted, she doesn't desire to stay out here on the dance floor with me," Mid said to him. The two looked at each other, the tension so thick I could almost see it.

"Go, I'll come get you after," I said to Dusane, wanting to get the two as far away from each other as possible. The last thing I needed was a fight breaking out in the middle of the ballroom.

Dusane gave Mid one last look before leaving the floor.

I stood with my hands limp at my sides, not knowing what to do. He hadn't approached me like this in days.

"May I?" he gestured towards my hand. I could barely nod my head.

He reached for me then, intertwining one hand with mine then resting the other on my waist. He was careful not to touch the bare skin on my back, and it was blatantly obvious. I gritted my teeth.

"Are you enjoying the party?" he asked me, and I wanted to yell, scream. Anything but do this game of small talk with him. But I couldn't deny that I was grateful he was even talking to me. So I shoved down the anger in my chest and played along.

"It's quite the setup," I admitted.

"Emiress outdid herself," Mid agreed.

"Has she said anything? About the compass?" I asked him.

"Tomorrow morning, she plans on helping us break the enchantment," Mid said. His emerald-scarlet eyes stayed on me, and I had to look away for a moment, not wanting to get lost in them.

"Are you sure she's to be trusted?" I asked.

"To be honest, I don't know. But it's our only chance at the moment," he sighed.

"You two seemed to be having an awful lot of fun together." I couldn't hold back the bitterness in my voice.

"You have to know I'm only entertaining her to get the compass," Mid said seriously.

"Do I?" I forced myself to meet his gaze again, and disbelief filled his expression.

"I'm tired of this," he suddenly blurted.

"Tired of what?" I glared at him, hating that he sounded so defeated. I was the one that should be defeated.

"This," he gestured between the two of us. "Fighting. I just want to stop lying to each other," he said. "I want to stop hurting each other."

"Well, maybe you should just be with someone like queen Emiress then. She seems like the type to never lie to you." My voice dripped with sarcasm.

His eyes flashed with a pained emotion as the words hit him. "Is that really what you want? For me to be with someone else? It seems that no matter what I do, you're always pushing me away."

"You pushed yourself away!"

"When I found out you were lying to me!" He sighed in frustration. "You kept Shar and Embrosines' relationship a secret. You'd have reacted the same way if you were me." He reached up to run a hand through his hair as if it were a habit with his long hair, but he stopped himself. His hand returned to my waist. "Just because I said I wasn't ready to forgive you doesn't mean I won't."

"How long is it going to take for you to trust me again?"

"I don't know," Mid sighed, slowing our movement. "But I know I will. I've always trusted you up until this point. So don't worry about me. You should really be asking yourself the same question. When are you going to trust *me*?"

"You think I don't trust you?"

"I think you're afraid of trusting your heart. Trusting that you can tell me anything. That you can be anything and anyone with me. And trusting that I'm not going to stop loving you." He gestured to the table where Queen Emiress sat. "And trust that I'm never going to want anyone else."

"It's kinda hard to believe you'll always love me when you're distancing yourself like this."

"Sometimes people fight and need time apart, but then they make up. It doesn't mean I don't love you anymore." His brow furrowed. "And did you ever stop to think that maybe I'm doing this more for you than for me?"

"Why would you be doing this for me?" I scoffed.

"You need to figure out what you want, Sabeara."

"I was figuring it out Mid, I was ready to. . ."

"You were ready to what? Swear yourself to me? To give up on Dusane and love me wholeheartedly?" He pulled me closer to him, so close his breath caressed my cheek. His hand moved from the safe place on the fabric of my dress to the bare skin of my back. With the close proximity, I could do nothing but stare into his emerald-scarlet eyes, his pine scent like a drug as I breathed him in. "You were ready to let go? To finally allow yourself to believe that what we have is stronger than what you have with him? Because that is what I'm asking for here."

His forehead fell against mine as if he were exhausted. We slowed to a stop. The couples continued to move around us on the dance floor. We were the stillness amidst the chaos. The hush amidst the noise.

"I want you to believe, Little Bear," he said, his voice choked with emotion. "Believe in us."

"I do believe," I whispered, a wave of emotion sweeping over me and crashing against my heart.

"Not enough," he said sadly.

He released me then. All the heat and strength of his body—suddenly gone. He disappeared into the masses, and I could but stand there, staring after him.

FIFTY-TWO

SUNN

Obsidian was still with a fever the following night. I heard the news that a couple of the other crewmates had awoken, so I had hopes he'd wake soon too. I sat on the edge of the bed, with nothing but my thoughts, waiting for something to change.

I offered to switch some of the other crewmates who were taking care of the dead and cleaning the deck of the poison ink, but they insisted they were fine. I think the crewmates were still scared of him and probably didn't want the job of babysitting. It was pretty boring. With no one to talk to, I felt like my thoughts might literally drown me.

After everything James had told me, a new light had been shed on what I knew about the Aigoviels. I had only met them briefly. I barely knew anything about them. But now, I felt like I may know even more about their family than they did.

I looked down, and Obsidian's dark black eyes were open,

staring at the ceiling. His hair was slick with sweat, and I grabbed another washcloth on the nightstand to dab at his face.

I found that after James had told me about Obsidian, a sort of unwanted sympathy had come over me. Yes, he was a monster. A very cruel man indeed, but now that I knew he was doing all this because he thought his mother was imprisoned unjustly, well. . . I couldn't help but imagine what it would feel like. I would do just about anything for my family, especially my mother.

And from what James had told me, he had just been a child when these events had taken place. It's a question I think every hero asks in their story, how did the villain become the way he is? I guess he could just be malicious. But something told me he wasn't always that way.

"Mother?" Obsidian mumbled, coming awake slightly from his statuesque state.

"It's me, Salt," I said quietly.

His ebony eyes searched my face, confusion on his brow. "I never got to say goodbye to you," he whispered, the husk in his voice deeper from lack of speaking and the emotion in his tone.

I decided not to fight him. He was too deep in the fever to listen to me when I told him I was Salt. And something inside me broke a little seeing him this way. I wasn't his mother, but maybe I could offer him some peace of mind for a moment.

"I'm here now," I whispered.

He started to move then, slowly trying to sit up in bed. I hurried to help him as he struggled to get to a sitting position.

"Obsidian, maybe you should take it easy," I said cautiously, but he ignored me.

"I have to tell you something." He grunted as he sat up fully then and turned to face me. I had a hand on his arm for precaution, worried he might fall over.

He had drooping, tired eyes and a sweat-stained face. He looked sickly pale, and a shiver would wrack his body every couple of seconds.

He looked at me then, and a small, sad smile broke out across his lips.

My heart thumped wildly. *What is happening to me?* It felt like a herd of seagulls were suddenly released inside me, wings beating furiously against my chest cavity.

"I love you," he said, and as he said this, tears wobbled in the edges of his vision and dribbled out onto his cheeks.

I'd never seen Obsidian smile. Not like that. Not like in such an innocent, childlike way, his eyes wide and raw with pure emotion. He didn't have any walls up in this state, no illusion of superior strength or domination. He wasn't the Captain of the Obscurum army, the feared enemy searching to kill and drain hearts. He was just Obsidian. A man that grew up thinking his mother died in prison at the hands of his family.

Oh dear, spirits no. I inwardly begged as he continued to smile so sadly and tenderly at me. *Stop it, stop whatever it is you're doing,* I demanded my heart. Because something was changing inside me for him. And it was the most dangerous thing I'd ever felt in my entire life.

"I love you too," I whispered back, trying to remember as fiercely as I could that he thought he was speaking to his mother.

"I can say goodbye now," he whispered, then as if he used all his energy to say those words, he slowly fell back down to the covers. I helped him to his lying position and watched as his eyes fluttered closed.

"Goodbye," I whispered.

FIFTY-THREE

SABEARA

I left the party early, unable to force myself to stay any longer after the conversation Mid and I had. I returned to my room, desperate to get out of the dress I wore. I tugged recklessly at the ties at my back until they came loose, and then with an angry grunt, threw the beautiful gown across the room. It floated to the floor into a pile of sparkling silk. I felt the tears coming, blurring the edges of my vision.

I grasped blindly for a shirt and pair of pants in the closet and clumsily pulled them on. I walked over to the open balcony once I finished dressing and leaned against the marble rail. The view was just as painstakingly beautiful at night as in the day. The moon glinting off the glassy ocean surface, the palms and jungle trees rustling in the warm tropical breeze.

My lip trembled as the weight of the situation fell over me, and I allowed myself to just cry for a moment.

Everything was such a mess. And I'd been the one to create the mess.

I was really starting to believe that night in the treehouse that I could be with Mid. I thought I'd chosen him.

But the last week was proof that Mid had more than enough potential to rattle my emotions. And despite wanting to be able to trust that he would always love me, that he would always be there for me—it was moments like this last week that made me realize how painful it would be if I did trust him, and something changed his mind. He could shatter me.

Admitting it in my mind made the tears fall harder.

"You could shatter me," I whispered to the night, tasting the salt from my tears.

I crossed my arms over my stomach. It felt like a hole had formed inside me. I wanted to love Mid. I did love Mid. But after everything and everyone I'd already lost—losing him too would surely undo me completely.

He was the cliff's edge, the rushing river. And I'd always known this. Which had been the reason I'd stayed away. And it was there, standing on the balcony overlooking Tetheria, that I realized he was the sun.

But get too close to the sun, and you could burn.

I glanced at the moon. Its light was pale and beautiful, even peaceful on a night like this. The moon was safe.

And I made the decision then—right there on that balcony. To do what was best for my heart. I closed off a section of my heart, forcing away the feelings for Mid. I somehow managed to smother them to the darkest, most hidden compartment of my soul. It was painful, agonizing even, and my heart protested as I worked to subdue the intense emotions.

After several minutes of this, trying to reign in the chaos consuming my heart and mind, I finally managed to somewhat minimize my emotions to a quiet ache.

The tears slowly subsided as I closed myself off. And I stared at the moon for many minutes after. I loved the moon too. And the moon would never hurt me.

I tore my gaze from the sky and looked over at the open balcony next door to the room where Dusane stayed. I slowly made my way across my balcony over to his and hesitantly stepped into his room.

It was much the same as mine. Only everything was mirrored. I carefully sat on one of the cushioned chairs in the room, and I waited. For how long, I don't know. But eventually, the door opened, and Dusane stepped inside.

He halted in his tracks when he spotted me.

"Ehren, what are you doing here?"

I slowly stood from the chair, not answering right away.

He closed the door after taking a quick peek outside to check if anyone was in the hallway. Then he turned to face me again, his cerulean eyes locking with mine.

"Ehren, why did you leave. . ."

"Kiss me," I said, interrupting him.

"What?" he asked, his eyes widening.

I walked up to him, reaching out to take his hand. I placed it on my cheek.

"I said, kiss me."

His cerulean eyes searched my face, and to my disappointment, he pulled his hand away in hesitation. "Ehren, you're not thinking straight."

"Dusane, I'm *begging* you to kiss me," I pleaded.

He froze, all the muscles in his body going rigid. Everything went still. The whistle of the winds coming through the open windows was all that was heard for several long moments. Then his eyes darkened, and his eyes flitted down to my lips.

"Please," I whispered. It was the last remnant of desperation I could conjure.

And it was all he needed, it seemed, because he finally reached for me, crushing his lips to mine.

His hands gripped my waist, and he lifted me in one swift movement as my legs wrapped around him. He took several steps across the room, pinning me against the wall.

It wasn't a soft kiss. It was hungry. Ravenous.

His lips ground against mine, and we were a mess of gasping breaths and desperate caresses. The soft growls in his throat were causing little fireworks to go off in my brain, and I tugged him closer to me even though he couldn't seem to get any closer.

His hands found the band of bare skin where my shirt met my trousers. The heat of his hand there, on the skin of my waist, made my insides erupt with butterflies.

I fisted his shirt in my hand, a sigh escaping me.

The way his lips moved against mine was distracting me from the pain and hurt that was coursing through me. It was a glorious numbness, and the longer he kissed me, the more it spread through my body like a healing wildfire. The heat consumed all my grief, cauterizing the wounds in my heart back together. And I knew he'd never hurt me. I was safe here with him.

Dusane pulled away abruptly, and he spoke between haggard breaths.

"Hold on, does this mean. . ." he didn't finish the sentence. But his eyes were hopeful.

I ran my hands into his hair and leaned my forehead against his. "I choose you, Dusane."

My words seemed to freeze him in place for a moment. Then

after several seconds of processing what I'd said, he smiled. It was the rawest, most beautiful smile I'd ever seen from him before.

He leaned in to press the softest of kisses to my lips. "I choose you too, Envorydian."

FIFTY-FOUR

SUNN

I woke up the next day beside Obsidian. I must've fallen asleep sometime during my watch. I rubbed my eyes and turned to check that he was still alive. I found him still breathing, and to my surprise, he looked to be improving. His skin had some color to it, and his brow wasn't sleek with sweat.

Deciding he'd be fine on his own for a moment, I left to check on the crew. Most of the men could handle their stations without help now, and things were running smoothly that morning. The deck was near spotless, and I was surprised to see all the ink had been scrubbed away. The bodies of those who had suffered casualties by the Oculor were also gone. A pang of sadness squeezed my heart as I thought about the men we'd lost that night. I still couldn't shake the feeling that it was my fault. I'd been the one to lead us into those waters.

You couldn't have known the Oculor were real. I tried to reason with myself. It did little to assuage the guilt.

It was early morning, the sun barely starting to peek over the horizon. A couple morning crewmen were wandering about. Everything had almost returned to normal again.

The ship wasn't moving, and I guessed we'd anchored. We'd been traveling for a couple days now, and we seemed to be clear of the Trojan waters.

"Why are we anchored?" I asked one of the men.

"A little maintenance needed to be done on the hull," a man I knew as Willis said to me.

I nodded in understanding and continued on down the deck. We hadn't been attacked a second time by the Oculor for which I was grateful. I walked across the clean wood planks and to the bow of the ship. The wind was blowing a little that morning, and I wished so badly to feel it rustling through my hair. It was the best feeling in the world when the ocean breeze ruffled my hair.

Clutching my necklace in my hand and fiddling with the sun pendant, I stared down at the open water and admired its dark blue color. It was calm that morning, the waves small and perfect for swimming.

Feeling the sudden desire to get in the water, I decided with only a couple crewmates out and about, I'd get clean while we were anchored.

Seeing that they were all preoccupied, I quickly grabbed one of the hefty braided ropes and threw it over the side of the ship. I'd use it to climb back up later. Then I kicked off my boots and mounted the side of the vessel. Not thinking twice, I took the leap off the ledge and felt my stomach twist and curl as I dived toward the water.

When the cool waves encased me, it was a sharp awakening. Every cell in my body was shocked by the cold, and I felt suddenly wide awake. The weight of the ocean pushed against me with every stroke, and it felt heavenly the way the water brushed away the dirt and grime on my clothes and skin.

I came up for air, and as I did, pulled my hair free of my hat and then plunged back down into the water again. I ran a hand through my red tendrils that floated like mermaid hair in the water. I let out some air, and a stream of bubbles rose in the water.

Arms and legs moving in slow motion, it seemed I went deeper and deeper until I allowed myself to close my eyes for a moment and just relax. I let the water hold me, cradle me in its embrace. I was good at holding my breath, so it didn't bother me that I'd been down for a couple minutes.

I contemplated many things in the muted quiet the ocean provided. Obsidian attacking our ship, the crewmates I'd lost. The things Obsidian had told me in his delirium. His past hadn't been what I'd expected. And I feared the things I'd learned had changed my view of him. I didn't want to sympathize with a monster. But things were definitely different now that I'd learned more about his side of the story.

I was brought from my thoughtful state when I heard a splash above me. My eyes popped open in surprise. I stared curiously up at the flickering surface. The sun was now up fully, beaming down at me. Causing shafts of light to arc through the water. I spotted a dark figure swimming toward me, and my eyes widened. I started to panic, looking left then right to where I could swim away. But it was too late, the individual reached me quickly, and a hand clasped around my wrist, pulling me up to the surface.

The dark-cloaked individual lifted me from the surface, and I squealed when I sucked in a lungful of air, trying to kick and push against the person that had grabbed me. My hair was wet and in my eyes, so I couldn't see. And with my arms clasped in a vice-like grip, I was unable to push it from my eyes to see who was the culprit.

A grunt sounded from the person who'd dragged me from the water, but their hold was strong.

I heard the sound of rope hitting the side of the boat, and soon I could feel the sensation of swaying as we climbed back up to the ship. Not long later, I was heaved over the side and pushed onto my back against the deck, my hands pinned by my head.

"Let go of me!" I shrieked, and when the hands finally released me, I desperately pushed the hair out of my face to see who had interrupted my morning swim.

Black eyes stared into mine.

Obsidian was crouched over me, shirtless and wet.

"What were you thinking!" he growled, "I thought I told you you weren't allowed to throw yourself overboard."

"I wasn't trying to run away! I was taking a swim!" I snarled.

That was when everything stopped. Obsidian's gaze moved from my face to my long red hair sprawled out on the deck.

"You're a . . . girl."

A million curses fired off in my brain.

"Spirits in the tree."

FIFTY-FIVE

SABEARA

The next morning it took me a moment to realize where I was.

My tired eyes took in the white canopy fluttering in the breeze, a stream of morning sunlight illuminating the room and causing dust to dance in the shaft of light. My cheek was pressed against something hard and warm.

Gradually my surroundings began to register. My eyes widened when I realized the warm hard thing I was lying against was a body. Memories of the night before rushed back to me. The gala, Mid asking me to believe in us, my decision to protect my heart . . . kissing Dusane and telling him I chose him. . .

I had been sleeping on Dusane's bare chest. We had fallen asleep next to each other the night before. We had been talking when I'd drifted off, and Dusane must have taken off his shirt sometime during the night because I hadn't remembered it being absent when I'd drifted.

We also hadn't been this entwined when we'd fallen asleep either.

I slowly and ever so carefully untangled myself from his arms, not wanting to wake him. When I was free, I reached up to touch my hair and cringed. I could only imagine what I must look like.

Suddenly worried he might wake and see me like this, I carefully padded across the rug to the mirror on the wall. I rubbed my eyes awake and pinched my cheeks to return some color into them. Then I continued to try and untangle my hair. The masterpiece the ladies' maids had twisted my long dark locks into for the gala was now a lopsided mess on top of my head. I was trying my best to undo the pins when I heard a rustling behind me in the sheets.

I froze, pin between my teeth, and slowly turned around to see a pair of cerulean eyes staring right at me.

"Well, good morning," Dusane drawled. He was leaning against the headboard, his arms crossed over his chest. The amusement in his hint of a smile was unmistakable. I knew him well enough to know that barely visible expression meant he was laughing at me.

I pulled the pin from my teeth and gave him a pointed expression."Are you laughing at me, Captain?"

He tried to stifle the chuckle that escaped him, but it was futile. "Not at all."

I reached for one of the throw pillows on the chair nearest to me and threw it at his head. He caught it easily, more quiet laughter ensuing.

His delight was too contagious. He was already forgiven. I rolled my eyes good-naturedly and went to sit on the edge of the bed.

"You could help me, you know?" I suggested, gesturing to the mess atop my head.

"Here, turn around," he said, still fighting back a smile.

I obeyed, and soon, his fingers found their way into my hair, pulling out pins methodically. It was a comfortable silence between us as he helped me untangle my hair.

"There," he said. "All fixed." I reached up to feel my hair, and sure enough, all the pins were gone. It was still slightly tangled but no longer confined.

I turned around to thank him. Only to be unexpectedly given a kiss.

His soft lips pressed against mine, and I made a small surprised noise.

"How did you sleep?" he murmured against my mouth.

He broke the kiss, and leaned back against the headboard again, and I couldn't help when my gaze drifted to his solid tan chest. An attractive silver ring pierced his left nipple that I'd only witnessed once before, and his hair was slightly disheveled, the black locks falling into his eyes the way I liked. His expression toward me was anything but innocent. He looked like he might kiss me again, and I suddenly remembered the intense moment we'd had the night before. Without the heat of the moment hanging over us, I was suddenly embarrassed. I'd *begged* him to kiss me.

"Good," I said, feeling suddenly nervous. I'd never fallen asleep next to a man before. I mean, I'd slept between him and Mid almost naked in a tent once. But for some reason, this felt significantly different. We had been on the verge of freezing to death the last time. And now we were alone, in a room together, just the two of us. It felt a lot different. I'd never been in this situation with a man before, *ever*.

Everything had changed last night. I'd made a decision about being with him, and a weight had been lifted from my shoulders. I was glad I'd made the decision. Glad I didn't have to fight with my heart anymore. . . I mean, there was still a pain in my chest when I thought about Mid and how we'd left our conversation at the gala. But I knew eventually that feeling would fade.

And Dusane. Well, he seemed to have adjusted quickly. I'd never seen him so relaxed. . . so happy.

So why was I so *not* relaxed?

Unable to sit any longer, I went back over to stand by the mirror again. I grabbed a brush off the vanity and began work through my hair now that it was free of pins.

"I should probably head back over to my room," I said, trying to keep my voice even.

"Why the rush?" Dusane asked, his husky voice sent tingles down my spine. I caught his gaze in the mirror, and suddenly I was remembering the way he'd kissed that Rosie girl in the pub back in Severesi. I couldn't help but think this was probably not Dusane's first time waking up next to a girl. *How many women had he been with in the past?* Dusane seemed much more experienced than me in this area of things. What if he had been expecting. . . more?

Stop overthinking, I berated myself.

"I'm not in a rush," I said, a slight tremble making its way into my voice. "Just need to change." I tried to give him a confident smile.

Dusane raised an eyebrow.

Spirits. I thought. *He can see right through me.*

"What's wrong," he asked.

"I just want to be careful, you know. Someone could walk in and find us here together. And think. . ."

"And think what?" he asked, his brow furrowed.

"You know," I said, looking away from his penetrating gaze. My cheeks were hot. And my reflection proved they were as red as they felt.

"No, I don't think I do know," he said.

I turned around and saw the unmistakable humor in his expression. He was teasing me.

"You're laughing at me again," I said.

"Can you even say it?" he asked, challenging me.

"I can say it," I scoffed, but my inexperienced mind was definitely panicking.

He got out of bed and walked over to me. Every step he took closed the distance between us and caused my heart to beat faster.

When he reached me, he brushed the back of his knuckles across my heated cheek. "Sex," he said.

My innocent mind processed the word by making my cheeks burn even hotter.

"You're worried someone will come in and think we had sex," he clarified.

"Um. . .uh. . ." I stuttered, unable to form a coherent sentence. "Maybe. . ."

"Ehren, trust me. No one would think that." He pressed a kiss to my forehead and then stepped away, walking toward the closet. He grabbed a shirt off the top shelf and pulled it over his head.

"How can you be so sure?" I crossed my arms over my chest defiantly.

"Because, if we'd had sex—" he finished tying his weapons belt to his waist before coming to stand in front of me again. "—someone would have definitely heard us." He looked up, and his eyes were glittering with humor. "And since both of us were sleeping soundly. . . and quietly. I assure you, no one is thinking that."

My cheeks were so hot now I worried I might actually melt where I stood.

He pursed his lips, fighting a smile, then he nodded toward the balcony leading to my room.

"Go get changed, my little Envorydian." He said. "I'll meet you in the hall."

I was about to say more on the subject, not wanting him to think I was a complete fool about the relations between a man and a woman, but he was already walking towards the door.

"I'll see you in a minute," I replied pathetically.

When the door shut behind him, I groaned aloud, putting my head in my hands.

"Nice, Ehren," I said to my reflection. "Might as well tattoo *virgin* across your forehead."

~

When I stepped outside my door, Dusane was leaning up against the wall. His arms crossed over his chest casually.

"Ready to go?" he asked me, holding out his hand.

"Where are we going?" I found the courage to reach out and grasp his hand, and our fingers intertwined. A warm and foreign feeling spread throughout my body, and I felt like a young girl with a massive crush.

"Shar told me at the gala last night that Emiress promised to break the enchantment this morning."

We started down the hallway, our hands swinging a little with our movements.

"It all seems so odd, don't you think? Attending her gala in return for breaking the enchantment?"

"Or maybe it's just that easy," Dusane mused.

"Nothing is ever that easy," I said stubbornly. "Not when it comes to the tokens."

"I guess we'll see."

Just then, Shar came around the corner up ahead and spotted us.

"There you guys are." he let out a frustrated breath. "I've been looking for you."

"Is something wrong?" I asked, and without thinking, I pulled my hand from Dusane's. Dusane raised a questioning eyebrow at me, but I pretended not to see it.

I knew that I'd have to break the news to everybody at some point and tell them that I'd chosen Dusane. But I just needed some time to think of a way to let Mid down easy. The last thing I needed was Shar finding out and then telling Mid in the most unsympathetic way possible. Shar wasn't the warmest, most fuzzy person. I'd rather be the one to tell Mid.

"Not exactly. The queen is going to break the enchantment," Shar said, and he gestured for us to follow him. We picked up our pace to match his.

"How is she going to do it?" I asked.

"We don't know yet, but we want everyone to be there. Just in case." Shar sounded on edge. Like he, too, was worried about what this mermaid queen was up to. Were we walking right into a trap?"

"Is she lying to us, Shar?" I asked. His power was to know if someone was lying or not.

"It's hard to say. No one ever tells the whole truth all the time. But from what I've gathered so far, she's been fairly truthful about everything." He didn't seem very confident.

"Why do you seem so worried then?"

"Because she's been so truthful, it almost makes me more suspicious of her."

We walked through the castle for a while until finally, Shar came to a stop. We ended up in front of a small round door. A mermaid-shaped knocker adorned it. But he didn't bother to announce our presence; instead, Shar reached for the knob and pushed the door open.

The room was pretty small. There were no windows, and bookshelves covered every inch of the walls. In the center of the room stood a pedestal with an open book. Surrounding the Pedestal were Queen Emiress, Knadian, Mid, and Embrosine.

"Where are Rouix and Thane?" I whispered to Shar.

"They are preparing the ship?"

That sent a chill down my spine. *Why the rush?* It seemed almost like Shar was expecting us to have to flee after this encounter. I hoped we wouldn't be fighting our way out of here.

We went to stand by the others, and just then, the door opened again, and two men walked in.

I recognized the first man. He had escorted us from the dining hall previously. He wore long green robes and had his dark hair pulled back into a bun at the nape of his neck. I noticed now the faint sight of wrinkles on his face. I remembered his name was Selon.

The other man beside him was young and dressed in soldier attire, much like what Oli used to wear as my guard. He had a green heart and short black hair.

They both went to stand on either side of Queen Emiress.

"Thank you for joining me here today and for accepting my invitation to my annual Tetherian Gala last night." The queen smiled at us all. "As promised, I will undo the enchantment on the compass for you."

We all were grouped together, waiting to see what the queen and these two men would do. *Did she lead us all into this room to capture us?* My eyes flitted to Dusane, and I could see the distrust in his eyes. His hand was at his side, clutching the hilt of the sword.

He obviously felt as uncertain of this situation now as I did.

"If you would all please stay against the walls while we undo the enchantment," the queen ordered.

All of us took several steps back, giving Emiress and her two emissaries some more space.

They formed a small circle around the stand and started to whisper amongst each other.

I began to feel more nervous as the time passed.

Suddenly they stopped talking to one another. And Selon stepped up to the book on the podium. He flipped the pages with careful hands and then stopped on one of the pages. Then he backed away, letting the young soldier step forward. I hadn't expected Selon to only flip pages in a book, but maybe that was really all he needed to do.

"Allard, you may now place the shell," Emiress said to the young man. Allard reached into his pocket and pulled out a small conch shell from the depths of his pocket. He placed it on the book and then stepped away. Then the queen stepped up to the podium.

I thought maybe Emiress would break out into a series of chants or something but, instead, she just looked up, and her eyes landed on Mid.

"Would you like to do the honors, Prince Midennen?" She asked.

Mid looked surprised at the suggestion. He hesitated, but only for a moment before going to stand by the queen.

"I don't know what to do," he said nervously. "And I thought only someone who knows the ancient tongue could undo the enchantment."

"Don't worry, I will help you." The queen smiled softly at him and directed him to take off the crown he wore. He was still sporting the seashell wreath he'd been wearing the night before, and I wondered if the queen had told him to wear it. She asked him to remove the crown, then place it on the book so that the small conch shell rested in the center.

I watched carefully, curiosity coursing through my veins.

The crown began to glow, and Mid took a small step back. The queen reassured him with a small pat on the shoulder, and the two remained, watching as the shells glistened pale colors of aqua and cobalt on top of the book. The colors filled the room for several minutes until finally, they dimmed, and the crown returned to its normal state.

"Now read the inscription on the inside of the band," the queen said to Mid.

With shaking hands, Mid reached for the seashell crown and lifted it from off the book.

He peered at the inside of the crown. I couldn't see what he was looking at from far away, but there was obviously something there because he started to read the words aloud.

"The light is Enn, and the life is en."

After Mid spoke the inscription aloud, the crown began to change again. Deep green leaves sprouted from the seashells, growing at an alarming rate right before our eyes. What looked to be seaweed twisted and grew from the shells and swirled together in the air. A hook-like design took shape and the seaweed made soft brushing sounds as the leaves moved against each other to create a symbol. When the symbol was complete, the seaweed stopped growing, and I became transfixed. It was beautiful and complex. The hook was made up of twisting lines and angles. What it meant was a complete mystery to me.

Then it suddenly shot forward. Wrapping around Mid's body, the vines began to encase him.

We all watched in horror as the seaweed moved at an uncanny speed, slithering around Mid's body like a snake taking over every inch of him until he was covered in the deep green leaves.

Panic filled the room, and Knadian, along with Shar, lunged toward Mid. Selon stopped Knadian while Allard blocked Shar. Knadian withdrew his sword, ready to take down the emissary. Shar took out Wesoltinces's hammer, an intensity in his eyes I'd never before seen.

"What are you doing to him! Stop this now!" Knadian growled.

"Release him, or so help me Spirits, I will kill you right now," Shar threatened.

"He is fine. No need to panic," Emiress said. She stood calmly next to Mid as he became swathed in the weeds. Mid looked to be struggling against the growth. Small muffled grunts sounded as he fought against the restraints.

I stepped forward too, but Allard shot me a warning glance. I froze, my heart racing, my breath coming out in short, rapid breaths. The seaweed completely shrouded Mid for several agonizing seconds, and then he stopped struggling.

I worried he might not be able to breathe in the cocoon of sea vines.

Then the seaweed abruptly wilted.

The leaves fell to the floor, creating a mess of green foliage at Mid's feet. All of us stared wide-eyed, unsure what we'd just witnessed. Emiress looked to be completely unsurprised. She glanced down at the seaweed on the den's rug then turned to give us all an unnervingly triumphant smile.

"It is done."

We were all looking at Mid. He was standing in the same place and thankfully appeared to be unharmed. He still held the crown, and he was gazing with wide eyes at it, breathing heavily.

Instant relief overcame me, and it almost made my knees buckle.

But then I saw it. The light in Mid's chest and my eyes widened. He wasn't exactly himself. Something was different. His silver heart no longer pulsated inside his chest.

The ritual has changed him.

His heart was now glowing gold.

FIFTY-SIX

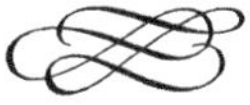

SUNN

He was still crouched over me, face contorted into a look of utter confusion.

"You lied to me?" The anger flashed in his ebony eyes, hot and bright like coals.

"I had to. . ." I didn't get to finish my argument before he lifted me from the deck, gripping me by the front of my tunic, and he shoved me up against one of the ship poles.

I grunted when a loose nail in the wood dug into my spine. Gritting my teeth, I glared at him with as much hatred as I could muster.

"I thought you knew my tolerance for lying was limited," he said, leaning in close so I could feel the heat of his breath on my cheek. "*Very*, limited," he repeated.

"You're overreacting," I said, flashing him a smirk. I couldn't help it. He was just so dramatic.

"I'm not overreacting," he spat. "Women don't belong on ships." Taking a fistful of my curly red locks, he tugged me away from the pole and then proceeded to drag me to the edge of the ship again. I dug my bare feet in the best I could, trying to get traction on the slippery deck while ignoring the pain on my scalp as he led me by my hair.

I berated myself for *ever* thinking sympathetic thoughts towards him. Every nicety I'd managed to feel while babysitting him over the last several days was vanquished almost instantly.

I could feel the eyes of the other sailors and knew that the commotion must've started to draw a crowd.

"You're hurting me," I whined. Just when his hold on my hair was no longer felt, he hefted me up so I was now leaning dangerously over the side of the ship.

"Give me one good reason I shouldn't throw you in the water right now, and leave you behind?" The fury in his voice sent shivers down my spine. But instead of reacting submissively to his domineering attitude, like I probably should have, it only fueled my own fire. I was frustrated now and angry at myself for managing to think something remotely good about him. *What a waste of sympathy,* I thought.

"I saved you," I yelled. The muscles in my back started to ache as I tried to keep myself from falling over the ledge. He feigned a shove, and I squealed as I almost went tumbling into the water.

"You saved me? More like you came on this ship and gave me a headache," he growled.

"You know what, fine. Punish me for not telling you I'm a girl. But you won't make it to the South Territory without me."

"I think we can manage just fine," he chuckled darkly.

"You know, you're pathetic, really. Threatened by a small little girl like me. I thought you were supposed to be the Captain of Obscurum, not a pansy in a black cloak."

Suddenly I was off the ledge. He could move and throw me

around like a rag doll. I gasped as he abruptly placed me in front of him again. He gripped my upper arms, holding me firmly in place. Our eyes met, and I could see into his dark eyes again, witnessing every furious emotion in them as we stared at each other.

"I'm not threatened by you. I just don't like being lied to." The muscle in his jaw ticked. "The presence of a girl on my ship could cause some problems." He gestured to the group of men staring with wide eyes at the tantrum happening before them. "What do I do when one of them takes advantage of you? Gets distracted because they can't focus?"

I rolled my eyes again. At this point, if he kept talking, my eyes were going to roll out of my head.

"Look at me," I stated, gesturing to my soaked clothes and hair. "You thought I was a boy for weeks now. Can you honestly say I'm going to be distracting?"

He looked me up and down, and my cheeks burned as he assessed me.

"Maybe you're right." I couldn't ignore the sting that elicited. "But let me make this very clear." He began to release his vice-like hold on me. "If you cause any of my men, and I mean any of my men, to misbehave, you'll be the first to go."

I wanted to spit on him so badly and slap him too.

Now I could add to his list of ever so redeemable qualities, misogynistic pig. But I shouldn't have expected less. *So it was my problem if the men misbehaved? And it was immediately my problem if they became distracted by my what? My voluminous chest and long legs?* I didn't think so. *Or how about my fizzy orange curls that washed out my freckled skinned face?* He had nothing to worry about, and it made me angry that he was making it my fault if any of them did react to those things.

"You sicken me," I spat, unable to hold back now.

"Good," he said, dark eyes still simmering with anger. "Now get back to work,"

He walked away then, snatching up his shirt and boots he'd donned on the deck on the way back to his quarters.

I stared after him, fuming with anger while cursing myself for not ridding the ship of him when I could have.

~

"So, you've been pretending to be a boy this whole time?" James looked at me with wide blue eyes. The shock on his face was almost endearing.

"Are you mad?" I asked. We were on the night shift. We sat together on one of the barrels looking out at the sea. We had lifted the anchor hours ago and had continued our route to the South Territory.

"No, I'm just a little surprised I didn't notice." He reached up to scratch his head. "I have to admit I didn't even suspect."

"Well, thank you, I guess?" I chuckled.

He laughed too, and some of the tension was released from the awkwardness surrounding us.

"I'm sorry he reacted the way he did," James said, sobering.

"It's not your fault," I said, remembering the way Obsidian had almost thrown me overboard after discovering I was a girl. Just thinking about it caused the hatred inside me to start burning all over again.

"Maybe you were right. Maybe we should have thrown Obsidian off the ship when we had the chance," James said guiltily.

I sighed. "Maybe, but we can't take it back now."

"I guess you're right." A long moment of silence stretched between us. "So, what do we do now?" James asked quietly.

"Are you still open to helping me?" I asked, and he nodded.

"We need to convince the other crew members to rise against him. Before we reach the Diagon."

"Can I ask you something, Salt?" His brow furrowed. "If that's even your name."

"Of course it's not my name," I laughed. "It's my crew name."

"What is your real name?" He asked quietly.

I pursued my lips. "I don't think I can tell you that."

His brow furrowed.

"James, what were you going to ask me?" I rerouted the conversation again.

He sighed but let go of the name thing. "I understand your desire for escape. But why are you so insistent on him not reaching the Diagon?"

"Is it not enough that I don't want him to attack any more people?" I asked.

"No, I guess that's reason enough, but I have a feeling there's more to it. Do you know someone on the Diagon?"

I sighed. "Yes, I do. Someone close to me."

"Salt, I know who's on that ship too. So if it's someone close to you. . ."

"My name is Sunn." I blurted. "My uncle Midennen Knadian is on that ship probably with others I know and care about."

"If your uncle is Midennen Knadian, that would make you Embrosine's daughter." His face went pale, and he blew out a shaky breath.

"James, what's wrong," I laid a hand on his arm. "What's the matter?"

"You can't let him know who you really are, Sunn." He was

suddenly speaking in a fast whispered voice. "He'll kill you. Or worse, use you as leverage."

"You don't think I know that?" I asked. "If he's after my uncle and finds out I'm related, he'd definitely use me to his advantage."

"Not only that but because of what happened. "

"What do you mean what happened?" My brow furrowed.

James went quiet for a moment, staring at me with his scared blue eyes. I didn't think he could look anymore shocked.

"You don't know?" he whispered as if realization dawned on him.

"Know what?" I asked, brow furrowing.

"Nothing," he said, shaking his head. "It's not important right now. Let's just focus on getting Obsidian off this ship so we can get you home and avoid Obsidian finding the Diagon."

My eyes narrowed. Not liking that he was keeping something from me. Everything in me wanted to scream at him to tell me, but instead, I just nodded. I was grateful he was on my side. James was a good man, and I knew he had it in him to fight back. But I didn't want to push him too hard. He seemed to have a part of him that still wanted to be loyal to the Captain. Maybe that was because of years of living in fear, or perhaps it was something else. I didn't know exactly, but I was just grateful he was helping me now.

"I was thinking of a plan to get the other crewmates to rebel with us," I said.

"What is it?" he asked, the eagerness in his eyes evident.

"How do you feel about throwing a party?"

FIFTY-SEVEN

SABEARA

"I'm fine, really," Mid said for the thousandth time.

The seaweed monster had attacked Mid, and now his heart was a different color.

Knadian was livid with the queen for endangering his son and got quite the earful from himself and Shar. Embrosine was hovering around Mid like an overprotective mama bear, asking him over and over if he was okay.

"Mid, are you sure you are all right?" she asked again.

"Yes, I'm fine," he sighed.

"He'll be okay, Embrosine. We will have him see a healer immediately when we get home," Shar said. His arms were crossed over his chest. He was glaring at Emiress as he said this. I'd been on the other end of that glare, and I knew its intensity.

I was still trying to process the events. I don't know what the book did or how it made all the stuff with the seaweed and the weird symbol. These were definitely foreign concepts. Until today I had no idea such rituals even existed. I wondered if I'd ever know the truth about everything in our world. But something told me this was just the beginning.

Dusane laid a hand on my arm, and I jumped a little, having gotten lost in thought.

"What do you think that was?" he asked quietly. I guessed he was referring to the weird seaweed ritual we'd just witnessed.

"I don't know, but something is definitely not right about all this," I whispered. I could feel a wave of anxiousness creating a hole in my gut.

"You got what you wanted. The compass is unenchanted, I did exactly what you asked." The queen was facing off against Knadian, still acting unaffected by the situation.

"She's telling the truth," Shar said, obviously not happy about that fact.

"I still don't trust her. So I'm not risking leaving here, not knowing if she actually undid the enchantment," Knadian said fiercely. It was sort of terrifying seeing this side of him.

"I'll come with you to retrieve the compass if that will ease your fears," Emiress said calmly.

"It would," Shar stepped in. "Now, may I escort you to the ship, Queen Emiress?" It wasn't exactly a friendly gesture. More like he wanted to escort her to make sure he had hold of her so she wouldn't run or something.

The two emissaries beside her took several protective steps in front of her, but she ordered them to stand by.

"Don't worry, he won't hurt me," she said to them, and they both reluctantly eased off.

She smiled ruefully and took Shar's arm. They started out the door of the den, the queen's emissaries at their heels.

Knadian gestured for the rest of us to follow, and on the way out the door, I stopped awkwardly beside Mid.

"You good?" I asked.

He nodded. "I don't feel any different." He tried to smile reassuringly, but I could see the emotional hurt in his eyes. The same hurt I saw last night. And it matched the pain in my heart. *How was I going to tell him?*

Embrosine forced Mid to put his arm around her shoulder.

"I said I'm fine, Embrosine, I don't need help walking," Mid grumbled as his sister forced him to lean on him for support as they walked out the door.

"Just lean on me, Midennen. Please, for the love of all the spirits in the tree, cooperate with me for once, or I'll zap you," she threatened.

More protests ensued, but they became muffled as they went into the hallway.

I turned around to face Dusane, who was patiently waiting for me.

"I guess we're leaving then," I said, feeling suddenly exhausted.

"Party's over," Dusane joked, but it was half-hearted. He held out his hand, and I hesitated for a moment before reaching out and clasping it.

~

We departed from the castle, and it was as abrupt as it felt. And even though it wasn't a dramatic fight to escape the clutches of the queen's mermaid army, it felt as serious. Almost like at any moment, a fight might break out. The queen obviously couldn't be trusted. And whatever she'd done to Mid, well, we didn't exactly know what she'd done to Mid. I hoped bringing her on the ship was a good idea.

Dusane and I hadn't brought much with us, so we didn't even go to our rooms before leaving. We left and immediately went to the ship. When we boarded Thane and Rouix had already readied the boat to set sail. They were the only two out on the deck, so I assumed Embrosine had forced Mid to rest in his quarters and that Knadian and Shar were with Emiress and her two emissaries in the Captain's quarters, probably keeping an eye on them.

Dusane left my side to talk to Thane, so I went over to Rouix, letting out a sigh when I came up beside her.

"What happened?" she asked. "It looked like Midennen was hurt."

"The Queen did some weird seaweed thing to break the enchantment, and it turned Mid's heart gold."

Rouix's crimson eyes widened. "Is he alright?"

"He seems to be, but we don't really know yet."

"Is that why Shar was guiding Queen Emiress like a prisoner onto the ship?" Rouix asked.

"Something like that," I sighed. "Knadian doesn't trust her. And he wants to make sure she really undid the enchantment on the compass. So he's taking her with us."

Silence passed between us, and soon Thane called out to leave the beach. We unanchored and started to push away from the shores of Tetheria. I gazed out at the beautiful white castle and its clay-colored spires. I wondered if I'd ever get to see it again or if this would be the last time I witnessed the mermaid kingdom.

"I saw you and Dusane holding hands," Rouix blurted, and heat immediately flooded my cheeks.

"Oh . ." was the only pathetic reply I could manage.

"What happened?" she asked, and I sighed, somehow

managing to look my friend in the eyes. My friend had always held a place in her heart for the man I was with now.

"I made a decision," I said, and Rouix just looked at me. No reaction in her face for several long moments. My palms began to sweat, fearful of her reaction.

Then abruptly, she smiled and hugged me.

Rouix never hugged. Ever.

I wrapped my arms around her tentatively, shocked by the gesture.

"Thank you," she said, her twinkling voice thick with emotion. When she pulled away, I could only stare at her in confusion. "He deserves to be happy," she said, and I could've sworn I saw a tear leak onto her cheek.

Then, she looked away, tending to one of the rope lines, and I realized the moment was over.

I awkwardly slipped away then, wondering if she needed a moment to herself. Everything on the deck appeared to be under control, so I slipped away to my room beneath the deck.

As I walked down the hall, I passed by Embrosine's room, and sure enough, Mid and her were arguing. I caught the tail end of their conversation as I neared.

"I'm going to get you some food. I'll be right back," Embrosine said.

"I don't need to be babied. Please Embrosine, just go."

"I know you're still mad at me for what happened with Shar, but I don't think I deserve to be treated this way for trying to help you," Embrosine said stubbornly.

"This has nothing to do with what happened with Shar." He sighed, and just then, I passed by the open door. I hoped neither of them would see me and I would be able to just slip into my room, but I didn't have much luck. Embrosine immediately spotted me and called me into the room.

"Ehren! Thank goodness. Will you sit with Mid while I go get him some food?"

I halted in my tracks, and my eyes flitted from Embrosine's pleading face to Mid's horrified expression.

"I don't need a babysitter!" Mid growled.

"Please?" Embrosine ignored Mid and started to walk past me and out the door. "I'll only be a couple minutes," she said.

And then she was gone.

My mouth was slightly agape watching Embrosine disappear down the hallway, and I turned my confused expression onto Mid.

"Sorry about her. She's just freaked out." He put his head in his hands. "You don't have to stay."

"I don't mind." I walked into the room and tentatively took a seat on the bed beside him.

An awkward silence stretched between us.

"That was quite the scare back there," I admitted. "I didn't know what was going to happen."

"I have to admit I was scared too. I mean, I could breathe the whole time. I just couldn't fight against the seaweed. And then everything was so dark and my heart, it started to feel like it was burning. . ." He put a hand to his heart that was now giving off a beautiful golden hue. "Then once the burning stopped, the seaweed wilted."

"Have you tested out your powers?" I asked, and he shook his head.

"Not yet, but maybe I should." His hand gave off a gold flash of light, and then in his hand was a red rose.

Questions swirled in my mind as he handed the crimson

flower to me. I held it tentatively between my fingertips. The stem felt so real, and the floral scent coming off the supple petals even smelled just like a rose.

"Your hands, they didn't glow when you gave Emiress the rose. And when you created the fake amulet in front of Elysian, I didn't see the flash of yellow light either."

"You're observant," Mid smiled. "It's a side effect, the light from my hands. If I concentrate really hard, I can keep it hidden. But when I'm with you, I'm not trying to hide anything," he explained.

I looked at the rose, contemplating his words and at the same time feeling my heart sink heavily as I thought about the night before and how he'd given Emiress a rose as well.

"Do you give every girl roses?" I asked, and he didn't miss the indignation behind my tone.

"They're just my specialty," he said, smiling. Then his hand lit up again. "But I can do daisies." A beautiful pink daisy appeared in his hand. "Tulips." A white tulip materialized. "Daffodils." A purple daffodil was the next flower to jump into existence. "Or something not even real." A flower I'd never seen before came to life. The petals were long and pointed and colored the shade of vibrant sapphire—the petals glowing. The stem was an intense ebony, along with its center. "I'll name it after you—Little Bear."

I stared at the gorgeous creation and tentatively took the bouquet of flowers as he handed them to me.

"I'd learn to create worlds for you, Ehren. If you'd let me," he said gently, and something inside me broke at his words.

"But they wouldn't be real," I whispered, trying to subdue the emotion in my voice and failing.

"Then let me be part of this world—with you," he said, and he reached out to clasp my hand where it rested atop the comforter. I averted my gaze, and in the minimal light from the porthole beneath the water, I looked at the bracelet Dusane had given me. I pulled my hand away and placed it in my lap.

"Mid. . . I have to tell you something . . ."

Just then, Embrosine came into the doorway, a tray of food in her arms.

"I've got one of everything! Some cheese, apples, fish, chocolate sweets I found in Whitemane's hidden stash."

I was forced to scoot out of the way so Embroinse could set the tray on the bed between us.

The moment was broken. The chance to tell him I was with Dusane abruptly lost.

Embrosine went on to explain all the food she'd gathered for him, and he gave me an exhausted expression as she started to fuss again. Knowing she wouldn't be stopping anytime soon, I stood quietly from the bed and gave Mid one last glance before quietly leaving.

Bouquet in hand, I walked down the hall toward my room. I placed the flowers on the bedside table next to the poem he'd given me. I knew the flowers would probably disappear soon. How long the illusion would hold, I didn't know. I stared at the beautiful bouquet, hoping to cherish its existence a little longer.

These flowers were much like Mid in a way. Beautiful, impossible—unreal.

Something that was never meant to last.

FIFTY-EIGHT

SUNN

"Do you really think this is such a good idea?" James asked nervously as we entered the hull.

Obsidian was asleep. The perfect time to set my plan into action.

"It's a great idea. I've been on many ships and seen many crew parties. Believe me, this will make them trust us more."

James sighed as we started through the hordes of men. I could feel the pressure of curious glances as we walked by, but I refused to seem intimidated. I held my head high and smiled as we passed to the row of tables set up.

Men were already mingling about as we took our seats.

"Who's ready to get beaten?" I asked, and no one said anything for a moment. Then one guy chuckled, taking a seat across from me. He had dark eyes and bright blonde hair.

"I think you're in the wrong league, little lady."

Fox Luck. A game of betting, lying, and luck. I'd watched Rissen's crew play many times. I played every so often but only when I had the money to spare. It was a high-stakes game. You could lose coins fast. But you could also win them too. It was a common ship game, played in the night in the hull of the ship. Lush Fire intoxicated chatter intermixed with crude jokes. It was its own pastime out at sea. But these men weren't sailors, and it was time they learned what it was like to have a little fun. Something I doubted they'd had the chance to experience since Obsidian had made them his puppets. And so, I thought it would be a good way to earn their trust. Maybe it was far-fetched, believing I could show them a good time and they'd trust me. But also, maybe it really was as simple as that. I wanted to show them that I was one of them.

James beside me looked nervous, sweating a little on his brow.

"Never played Fox Luck?" I asked him.

"I've played."

"Then what are you so worried about?" I asked him as one man began to deal out a stack of cards.

"Do you know how upset he'd be if he found out about this?"

"James, you worry too much." I tried to assuage his fears, but little did he know how fearful I was too. This was my last attempt. We were running out of time to convince the crew to help us rise up against Obsidian.

"He's still recovering from the incident with the Oculor," James said. "I feel like he's not in his right mind completely."

"Was he ever?" I snorted. "What did he say to you? Does he even remember what happened?"

"He had me tell him everything again because it's all fuzzy for him."

"Great, so he doesn't even remember the fact that we saved his life."

"Even if he did, he wouldn't think of thanking us."

I took my cards in hand. Taking a look at the numbers in the corners and the symbols on the face. I had a good hand, good enough that I could probably land a solid first win.

"Ladies first," one of the men cooed, and a chorus of snickers passed around the room.

I grinned at the men around the table, fluttering my lashes a little. So I'd dressed up a bit. Or at least cleaned up. I had found a fresh tunic in my room, and I'd brushed through my hair and put a little bit of water on them, so the curls weren't so fuzzy, and I'd even put charcoal on my eyelids. After the fit Obsidian had thrown, his fear of me being a distraction to his soldiers. Well, I guess it sort of gave me an idea. If he was so confident I could cause a stir, maybe that's precisely what I would do. To spite him firstly, and secondly to possibly get the crew to like me so much, they abandoned their old captain.

I'd already been leading them for a while now. Since the other crew left, I'd been the only person on the ship with common shipping knowledge. I had proved to them already I could lead them. Now I had to do what Obsidian could never do. Make them like me. And if being a woman helped, so be it. Obsidian sure believed I could cause a stir.

Thank you, captain. You've made me realize my potential, I snickered internally.

I made the first move, and turns were passed around the table. Cards were laid, and when I splayed out my hand of cards, a couple surprised gasps were heard throughout the hull.

"You Vixen," someone in the crowd accused. The blonde man across from me smiled approvingly.

"Good play," he said, and I winked at him.

"Beginners luck," another man shouted.

"Someone pass me some Lush Fire?" I asked. A wooden cup sloshing with liquid was passed into my hand. I tilted my head back, letting the liquid dribble down my chin, then I slammed the cup onto the table, feeling the warm buzz consume my mind. I wiped my mouth with my sleeve.

James's eyes widened, and he put his head in his hands. "Spirits help me," he said to himself.

"Another round?" I proposed, and the men cheered.

We played for hours. The more Lush Fire I consumed, the more giddy and lighthearted I became. This was what I loved about hull parties, about Fox Luck amongst men adrift the intoxication of bubbling Lush Fire. It was nothing but fun. I could barely remember my name, let alone the problems that existed on deck. I forgot I was a prisoner to a lethal Obscurum captain. I forgot about my parents, who were probably worried sick about me. I forgot about the war the kingdoms were fighting and the curse that was causing all the hearts in the room to dim slowly. Here it was, just the games and the laughter.

I lost a couple plays, but I always won back my money in the following round. People switched places, and a new set of men challenged me each game. I could tell they were starting to be impressed. Then one of the men suggested we up the stakes.

"This is too easy. Let's make this more fun." It was the blonde soldier with dark eyes. Throughout the night, I'd learned his name was Vincent.

"What do you suggest?" I asked, my words slurring together a little.

"Each loss, someone has to take off an article of clothing to keep playing." He was leaning across the table, palms laid flat on the wood. His smile was contagious, and I couldn't help it. I stood up and matched his stance.

"Fine." I flipped my cards face up, and he laid out his. I'd lost the round. The men in the room shook with laughter, but I wasn't disappointed. This was the thrill I lived for. After all, *what did I have to lose?*

With a sly smile, I reached for my jacket and shrugged out of it. I had lots of layers to go, so I wasn't concerned. But it still caused the men to whistle and hoot.

"Sunn, I think it's time we stop. You've made your point. They've had a good time, and we can hope they'll side with us over these next couple days but. . ."

"But nothing, James. I'm all in," I said, swooning slightly into him as I lost balance with the rocking of the boat.

He helped me right myself, disapproval in his eyes. "Please, if the Captain finds you like this—"

"Let him find me. I'm not scared of him," I said, and James sighed heavily.

I turned back to the table and kept playing. Soon, many shirtless soldiers surrounded me as my luck outshined them. In the end, a couple of men were in nothing but their underwear. It was a good old time. As for me, I only lost twice.

After my jacket, I shook off my boots. Then, to evoke a stronger response, I took off my tunic. I still had a slim tank top beneath it, but it seemed to do the trick for all the drunken men in the room. I giggled, knowing it was harmless. I was the only woman on the ship, I wasn't anything special to look at either, but they didn't seem to care. And it still felt flattering when intoxicated.

James reached for my tunic on the ground and shoved it back at me.

"Okay, that's enough. It's early in the morning now. The captain will be up soon."

"Oh James, what's he gonna do?" I slurred, taking the tunic from him. I didn't put it back on. Instead, I threw it into the middle of the table. "Throw a tantrum?" I stretched my arms wide, inviting everyone in the room into the conversation.

"What's it, he says all the time? 'Give me one good reason I shouldn't throw you overboard right now!" The men laughed as I tried my best to imitate the captain's husky demanding voice. "'I could torture it out of you,'" I added, and more laughter ensued.

"Why should we be scared of him?" I asked the men loudly. Taking the liberty while I had their attention, I climbed a chair to stand up on the table. "All he does is stand at the helm and look down at everybody with his brooding expressions." I imitated, crossing my arms over my chest, and glared at them all.

"He can threaten us all he wants. But there are way more of us than there are of him!" I shouted, and the men cheered in agreement. "I say we kick him off this ship. He's ruining all the fun."

James looked mortified, watching me on the table.

"Get down from there," James ordered. Coming over to me, he stretched his hand out, but I refused to take it.

"Come on, James, you know I'm right. All he needs is scales and sharp fangs, and he'd be a snake on the outside too."

"That's enough," a dark voice bellowed, and everyone in the hull went silent.

I turned, and a pair of dark black eyes met mine.

FIFTY-NINE

SABEARA

When I woke up, the first thing I saw was the flowers on my bedside. The array of colors in the bouquet were startling and unexpected to my tired eyes. I sat up. Studying the flowers with a furrowed brow.

How are they still here?

I reached out and touched the tulip. It was wilting slightly along with the other flowers because I hadn't put them in water due to the fact I thought they'd have vanished by now.

A knock at my door sounded, and my head whipped around toward the door.

"One second!" I called and hurried to stuff the flowers beneath my pillow. I hurried over to the door and swung it open. Dusane was standing on the other side.

"Good Morning," he said, leaning up against the door frame, he smiled at me, and my heart did a couple flips. He was wearing black pants and a tight black shirt that morning which did well to show off the toned muscles in his arms. His wet hair was slicked back from his face, and his ear-piercing twinkled.

"Good morning," I said, a little breathless. I hoped I'd stuffed the flowers far enough beneath the pillow and took one step to the left to block his view just in case I hadn't.

"We've reached the compass. I was told to come and get you," he said while reaching out to cup my cheek in his hand.

Because we were so close in height, I could see all too clearly the suddenly hungry look in his eyes.

"Oh really? Well, we should probably get up there. . ." I started to try to move past him, but his other hand reached out, landing on my waist and hindering my escape.

"Not so fast," he pulled me to him, and I was soon pressed up against him. He leaned in, so his nose brushed against mine. "I didn't see you at dinner last night." His eyes glanced down to my lips, then back up to my eyes again. "I missed you," he said.

"I fell asleep pretty early," I lied. After the talk with Mid, I'd been pretty conflicted. I'd skipped dinner and tried to sleep. I didn't have much luck and ended up staring up at the ceiling most of the night. I didn't know how to tell Mid I'd chosen Dusane. And didn't want to risk him seeing something between Dusane and me without telling him first.

"If I didn't know better, I'd think you were avoiding me," he murmured while leaning down to press several soft kisses against my neck. A shiver coursed through my body, and I reached out to grasp the fabric of his shirt. *Spirits that felt good.*

"I'm not avoiding you," I said breathlessly.

"You haven't told him, have you?" he murmured against my neck, his voice husky. He spoke the words more like a caress than a rebuke.

"Please don't be mad," I pleaded. "I'll tell him. I'm just trying to find the right moment."

"I understand," he said, lifting his head. His expression was completely free of concern.

My brow furrowed. "You do?"

"Of course. If you'd chosen him, I'd have wanted you to consider my feelings when breaking the news to me," he said, and I felt even more guilty for not thinking he'd understand.

"Thank you," I whispered, getting a little emotional.

He leaned in again, this time kissing me on the lips. It was a heart-stopping kiss. His lips moved against mine with an expertise that was hard not to appreciate.

When we broke apart, he gave me an intent look. "Just tell him soon, please?"

"Yes, Captain," I said teasingly, and he smiled.

"Good, now let's go get this compass."

When we got up onto the deck, Dusane didn't grab my hand or anything. He went to stand by Shar, and I went over by Rouix. I was grateful he was giving me space until I could tell Mid everything.

Everyone was standing by the edge of the ship, preparing to go down and get the compass.

"I'll move the waters, and you'll have a couple minutes to reach the compass and bring it back," Knadian explained.

"You'll be coming with us, just in case," Shar said, glaring at Emiress with open dislike now after the incident with Mid.

"If that is what you wish." Emiress smiled, her two emissaries still standing next to her like loyal guardians.

"Dusane, Ehren, will you come too?" Mid asked. I was a little surprised by the invitation, But I glanced at Dusane, and we both nodded.

"Just in case you try anything," Shar hissed as he grabbed the queen's arm and started to push her toward the ledge. Her guards looked upset by Shar's manhandling but didn't fight him.

Embrosine stayed aboard with Rouix, Knadian, and Thane. The rest of us were going down to get the compass and ensure the queen wasn't double-crossing us.

The rope was let down over the edge and made a slapping noise when it hit the water. Then Knadian closed his eyes and began pushing the water away from the ship with his power.

Just like the first time, a great whooshing began to sound, and the waves pushed apart so that the boat beneath the waters could be unveiled. I watched the queen, and she looked to be admiring Knadian's power with curious fascination.

Soon the sunken ship was revealed, and walls of water surrounded it on all sides, waiting to collapse back to its natural position.

We all hurried down the ladder. Shar first with the queen and her emissaries, then Mid, and lastly Dusane and me. As I descended and my feet hit the deck, I couldn't help feeling uncertain about what would happen next.

Why did it feel like we were walking into a trap?

SIXTY

SUNN

It didn't take long for me to realize the fuse had been lit, and a full-blown explosion had ignited. I wasn't shocked when Obsidian dragged me up to the top deck, gripping me by the collar. I didn't even try to fight. My mind was still a little fuzzy, and my body was numb. Everything was spinning slightly too. I actually giggled as he pushed me up the steps, unable to contain my laughter at the moment that somehow seemed hilarious.

Obsidian turned me around and gripped me by the shoulders.

The morning light was barely breaking the horizon, and I could see a couple of morning crewmen doing their duties.

"What were you thinking?" Obsidian growled.

I looked up at him, and it appeared there were two of him.

"You're always so angry," I feigned a pout. His black eyes flashed again with annoyance, and he shook me a little.

"I come down and find you taking your clothes off in front of my men. What did I tell you. . ."

"You told me not to be a distraction and that if any of your men misbehaved because of m—"

"So you do remember?" he fumed, cutting me off. "Then explain this!" He hooked his finger beneath the thin strap on my tank-top, and his nostrils flared.

I shoved his hand away, smirking.

"What does it look like? We were just having a little fun," I said, and he released me then, jaw clenching. It was like he couldn't bear to touch me any longer. But his eyes, I could've sworn I saw traces of desire in their black depths.

"Ever since you've got on this ship, you've caused me nothing but trouble," he said, and he began to pace the deck then. I meandered over to an empty crate and took a seat, leaning back casually. I was suddenly very tired.

"When was the last time any of your men were allowed to have a good time?"

"They aren't here to have a good time! They are here to do what I tell them, and you'd do well to do the same." He stopped in his tracks, and his long black locks were wild and disheveled from sleep, falling into his face. Why did he suddenly look so. . . beautiful?

The morning light broke over the water, and a stream of gold hit the boat. The light hit his face, and his black eyes glistened. He wore a white tunic, the ties at the neck left open. I could see his pale white skin beneath it. For a man full of darkness, inside and out, he looked awfully good in the sun. Then again, maybe I was just lushed.

"Are you done now?" I asked, and I realized at that moment that I sort of enjoyed pushing the limits with him. Something about the danger of seeing what was going to happen next was thrilling. But it was also neurotic. I was masochistic when it came to a good rush.

Obsidian stomped over to me again, boots clipping against the wood. I spotted James behind him, watching the entire thing with a look of hopelessness on his face. James had warned me after all.

Obsidian tugged me up from the crate I was sitting on so he could bring our faces within mere inches of each other. My feet dangled as he fisted the front of my collar, and I gritted my teeth, glaring at him.

"I am done. *Done* with you." He kept hold of me but turned slightly toward James. "James, throw her overboard."

"But, Captain," James started to argue.

"Now," he dropped me then, and I stumbled, trying to catch my footing.

He stormed away, back toward his cabin, but just as he was climbing the stairs, a creaking sound came from the bow of the ship, and the group of sailors working that morning could be heard shouting at one another.

"Hurry, the jib sail is falling!" One of them yelled.

I turned just in time to see one of the long white sails rip down the center, and the pole made a loud creaking noise as it began to fall. The group of men hurried to reach it, but it was too late. The thick wood pole smacked into the deck, causing a rattling reverberation to pass through the boat.

The world seemed to stop for a moment.

The men looked over to James and me, horror on their faces. Then James and I turned to Obsidian. He had one foot on the bottom step, and he turned to meet my gaze.

"I suppose you're going to know how to fix that then when

I'm gone?" I asked, gesturing to the broken sail. And I couldn't help it. I smirked.

~

"Leo and Wesley are in," James whispered to me. We stood together at the edge of the ship, watching the sun fall over the water. I'd remained on the boat after all. Saved by the broken jib sail. I'd barely escaped Obsidian's wrath.

"So, how many does that make?" I asked.

"We have nine men willing to help us."

"But that still leaves five. We need to sway at least two more." My eyes flitted to the Captain's cabin door. He'd retired for the night already. But I was still careful of him overhearing. I'd managed to convince him to keep me on the boat a little longer, but I had a feeling one more mistake and his already thin patience would snap completely.

"I'll work on it." James sighed, and he started to walk away.

"Hey, are you alright?" I asked him. His blue eyes held apprehension.

"I'm fine. I just hope you know what you're doing, Sunn."

"James, trust me." I reached out and laid a hand on his arm. He relaxed a little.

Ever since our little party, things had begun to change. I think it had the effect I had planned on the crewmates. A sense of excitement to free themselves from Obsidian had started to take hold. And I used every opportunity during our daily work to talk with them, get them to trust me. And so far, nine men had sworn allegiance to James about overthrowing Obsidian. I tried not to think about the chances of them going back on their word. I had to believe this would work. From my calculations, we were close to the South Territory, or maybe we'd already reached it. Which gave me only a day, maybe two, to complete this.

"I'm trying to trust you," he admitted. "I just never imagined we'd ever be doing this,"

"What? Rising against him?"

"Yeah. . ." He looked down. "You may think me a coward for not thinking the way you do, Sunn, but you have to know I've just been trying to survive."

"I know, James. I don't think you're a coward." I moved my hand from his arm down to his hand, and I gave it a squeeze. "I'm just grateful you're deciding now to help me."

He smiled a little and looked down at our hands. I blushed, realizing I'd been hanging on to it a little longer than was normal, and quickly released him.

"I consider you my friend, Sunn."

"Thanks, James. I consider you my friend too."

"You'll get home, I promise." He gave me a nod of his head then left to check on the rest of the crewmates who would be taking the night shift.

I sighed, turned back to stare out at the water, and tried not to worry about time running out.

SIXTY-ONE

SABEARA

The ship was just as I remembered. Cluttered and filled with rusted trinkets and useless broken ship parts. It was quiet as we walked through the hull, a wariness settling like a thick cloud around our group. The compass was essential to stopping the curse, the suspense of the moment's importance making my heart race.

Together we emerged into the room with the statue. We all surrounded the mermaid figure. Her hands were still holding the glowing compass.

"What are you waiting for?" Shar gave the queen a nudge towards the compass. "Get the compass for us."

"The token is unenchanted. Any one of you could retrieve it now." Emiress gave Shar a rueful smile.

"I don't think so. Not after what it did the first time." Shar gestured sharply towards the compass again. "Get it for me."

The queen raised an eyebrow at Shar's demands but did as he said. She sauntered over to the mermaid statue and pulled the token from its alabaster fingers. Nothing happened to her. She didn't cry out in pain or fall into a deep sleep. Relief flooded through me, confident now we hadn't been deceived, and she'd actually stuck to her word and undone the enchantment.

Emiress walked back over to Shar but paused before handing it to him.

"Are you aware of what the compass is capable of?" she asked.

"No offense, Queen Emiress, but that is sort of the least of our concerns right now," Mid spoke up, and her eyes flitted over to him. She smiled warmly, that same fascination in her eyes that had been present when she'd first met him.

"You wish to have a token from the Kings? But you do not wish to know its power?"

The edge in Emiress's voice was barely noticeable, but it was enough to make the hair rise on the back of my neck.

Time was starting to run out, and the longer we remained down in this ship, the longer Knadian had to hold back the water.

"King Knadian is holding the waves. We don't have much time. Can we discuss this once we get back on deck?" I tried not to sound desperate, but impatience bled into my tone.

The queen's head snapped back to me, and she openly glared at me. The expression was so unexpected I took a step back.

"You want this compass to save the Stone-Hearted. But have not considered what it was truly meant for." Her gaze was piercing, and I felt paralyzed as she continued to glare at me.

Shar stepped towards her then, and I could feel the tension in the room escalate.

"Emiress. Hand. Me. The compass," Shar ordered.

Her gaze left mine and snapped back to Shar. She made no

moves to give it to him. Instead, she took a couple steps back toward Selon and Allard flanking her.

Emiress laughed wickedly and instead handed the compass to Allard on her left. He took the compass and wrapped his fingers around it slowly as if savoring getting to finally touch it.

"The compass is part of the sea. And its power was made to exalt the Tetherian people." Emiress said, her smile just as iniquitous as her laugh. "With it, we change the course of our kind."

Shar lunged for Allard, but it was too late. He dove into the walls of water Knadian was still managing to hold and changed forms. His bright glittering fin could be seen swimming through the waves, exiting the scene. Selon and Queen Emiress were the only two left, and a fight immediately erupted.

Dusane drew a knife at his side, and I pulled my dagger from its sheath. Shar withdrew Wesoltinece's hammer and swung it into the ship's wood flooring.

A violent earthquake shook the boat causing the wood boards to splinter and sending all of us stumbling. I gripped one of the mast poles within reach and managed to cling to it, staying upright. Once I could realign myself, I turned to find Emiress struggling to stand. A smile still remained on her face as she wiped the blood from her arm where she'd been hit with debris. Selon, who was still loyally beside her, also regained his footing.

Dusane and I made our way towards Emiress while Shar and Mid headed for Selon.

Emiress pulled a small bone spear from somewhere beneath the skirts of her gown, resembling what looked to be a giant shark tooth. She let out a mighty battle cry and tried to stab me. I evaded her first strike, but she was quick and obviously skilled. She came back with another rapid strike and then turned to block Dusane's blow. She took both of us on, matching our fervor with a grace that was obviously refined.

The familiar fighting frenzy overcame me, the feeling blooming inside me, the one that Dusane called the Rage. It started to take over. It honed my attention, made my senses sharper. It pushed away the worries that Knadian wasn't going to be able to hold the water much longer. It silenced the fear that the compass was now lost again. It narrowed my attention on the queen, and I was headed for the kill.

I gave a guttural cry and leaned harder into my steps, giving more power to my strikes. Soon Emiress faltered, she lunged for the wall of water, trying to make an escape like her young emissary, but before she could, I landed a fatal blow to her right side.

She stumbled, crimson liquid gushing through the tresses of her gown. Dusane took the opportunity to seize her, grasping her hands behind her and pulling her to him so she wouldn't struggle.

I lifted my dagger again, seeing red in the corners of my vision. I wanted to finish her. I needed to know I had erased the threat.

"Ehren, no!" Dusane frantically yelled, his voice barely penetrating my heightened senses. "Put down the dagger."

I barely heard him. The words registered as if spoken in slow motion. My heartbeat was pounding in my ears, thrumming like a drum. My ragged breathing matched the fervid tempo of my heart, and it took me several long seconds to finally take in the scene before me. Emiress was hunched over, clutching her side. She let out an agonizing moan.

"Heal her," Dusane ordered.

"What?" I asked, shocked by his request.

"I said heal her, Ehren. We aren't murderers."

"She wants the compass for herself. She doesn't want to save the Stone-Hearted."

"Ehren, I have her detained. We will take her back with us to the Knadiel." Dusane reached for his weapons belt and pulled out the device Nixie had made for us. The one we were supposed to use on Obsidian. He latched it onto Emiress's wrist, inhibiting her power.

"What are you doing? That's for Obsidian," I argued.

"Doesn't mean we can't make use of it until we find him," Dusane said.

I still had my dagger raised, my body strung for a fight.

"You let me kill those men in Severesi," I said, my chest still aching with rage. "Let me just finish her."

"Those *Rouges* were going to kill us if we hadn't. And I knew they were monsters."

"And she isn't?" I gestured angrily toward Emiress again.

"We don't know all that she's done. And until we do, we aren't going to sentence her to death."

I lowered my dagger, still breathing raggedly. I had almost killed her unjustly. *When had life become so minimal to me?*

I felt my heart twist painfully, almost sending me to my knees. The guilt washed over me so heavily. My emotions must have crossed over my face because Dusane's gaze softened.

"Hold it together, Envorydian. Come help me," he urged.

I walked over numbly and helped grab hold of Emiress's other arm, my chest burned as my healing power encased her, and she sucked in a thick lungful of air when the wound stitched back together. She raised her head to look at me as she found her strength.

"My power, it's gone." The confidence in Emiress's eyes

immediately vanished. She looked at me with a wide, frightened expression

"It's over, Emiress," I said.

She looked panicked, but then her gaze hardened again. Determination glowing in her eyes. "You'll never find it," she smiled, the crevices of her teeth bloody from one of the hits I'd landed on her.

I ignored her, turned my attention to Mid and Shar, and discovered they successfully defeated Selon. They had the old man detained, and he was struggling futilely against them.

"We have to go," Mid said, jaw clenched as he struggled to hold Selon.

Together we led Emiress and Selon back towards the Diagon.

We hurried as fast as we could back to the ship, but it took us some time with two struggling captives. I tried to remain calm and not think about the compass, but images of Allard and his glistening tail swimming away filled my mind, making my heart sink. We had been so close.

We finally emerged from the sunken ship and started for the rope ladder. Dusane went first, still holding Emiress captive in his grasp. I followed behind, and as my feet hit the first rung, the water started coming down.

"I can't hold it any longer!" We heard Knadian yell from above us.

"Hurry! Climb!" Dusane called down at us.

I helped force the queen upwards, but it was hard for her to climb with bound hands. As the walls of water began to break, waterfalls of salty sea poured around us, slowly starting to fill back up the vacancy that had been created. Fear scorched hot in my veins as the precious seconds slipped away faster and faster.

Dusane and I made it over the side of the ship, still keeping a tight hold on the queen. Shar dragging Selon behind him soon followed, and Mid, who had been the last person to emerge, barely heaved himself over the side of the ship as the water came crashing back down, completely overtaking the sunken ship once again.

We all looked down at the water that now sloshed and splashed against the side of the ship. We easily could have been smothered by its wake. We all seemed to be in shock staring at the water until an anxious cry pulled our attention away from the waves.

"Father, please, wake up!"

Knadian was no longer standing on the edge of the ship. He was now prostrated on the ground, unconscious. Embrosine was kneeling at his side, shaking him.

Mid hurried over to his father's side while Shar continued to keep hold of Selon.

I wanted to help but instead stayed close to queen Emiress. I looked around for Thane and Rouix as they were nowhere in sight.

"Where's Rouix?" I asked Dusane. "And Thane?"

Just as I finished the sentence, I spotted them.

Further down the deck, some sort of scuffle had broken out. Thane and Rouix were fighting someone.

"Dusane, look," I yelled, pointing to the commotion.

It was then I realized who was struggling against them. Allard, the emissary that had taken the compass.

SIXTY-TWO

SUNN

I had a hard time sleeping that night. I was Tossing and turning constantly throughout the night. The restlessness was almost unbearable. My mind wouldn't quiet down.

I ended up staring up at the ceiling. The rocking of the boat wasn't soothing at the moment and instead was only making my insomnia worse. It was so dark that if I put my hand in front of my face, I couldn't even see it. I felt lost in the darkness, with only my fears and thoughts.

Startling my quiet anxiety, a sound came from the other room. At first, I thought maybe it was just the boat creaking, but then I heard it again. Someone groaned as if in pain, and I sat upright in bed.

"No, stay away from her!" The shout from the other side of the door was so abrupt I shot to my feet, adrenaline pumping through my veins.

It was Obsidian. He was yelling at someone. Confused and

worried something was wrong, I hurried to the door and ran into his quarters without thinking.

It was so dark that all I could manage to make out was an erratic movement of the sheets on the bed.

"Let go of me!" I heard him say, anguish in his voice.

Rushing to the nightstand, I fumbled around for a lantern. When I finally got it lit, I could see Obsidian tossing and turning in the dim shadows. His eyes were closed. His brow furrowed as his arms and legs were tangled with the crimson fabric.

"Please, don't, please!" he moaned, and it was then I realized he was having a nightmare.

I hesitantly went to his side and, doing my best to avoid getting hit by a writhing limb, laid a hand on his bare shoulder. He wasn't wearing a shirt, and I could see all the lines and crevices of his sweat-slicked chest and abdomen.

"Obsidian, wake up. It's just a dream," I said, but his eyes remained closed.

"Let go, let go," he mumbled, and I shook him again, trying to rouse him from whatever nightmare he was trapped within.

"Wake up, it's not real," I said louder, and that's when his eyes flew open. Black orbs, vast and unsettled—filled with the intent to kill.

I tried to jump back, but it wasn't fast enough, and he grabbed me. Gripping me by the upper arms, he managed to flip me so quickly I ended up with my back against the sheets, him above me. He caged me in with his arms and legs, clutching me so hard by the arms I knew I'd have bruises in the morning.

He was panting. And I could do nothing but stare up at him in shock, unsure what had just happened.

"It's just a dream," I whispered.

His wide black eyes, that had been filled with dark intent,

finally dimmed. He seemed to realize he was awake, and he slowly sat back on his heels.

I stayed where I was, my heart hammering in my chest.

"I'm sorry," he mumbled. As if still processing what just happened, he ran a hand through his long black hair.

"It's okay," I said, a little shocked by the apology. My limbs slowly became unfrozen with the fear that had elicited through me from his attack, and I sat up.

"You were having a nightmare," I managed to say.

He looked around the room, gathering his bearings. Then when his eyes landed on me again, he seemed to finally notice he was on top of me, and he stiffened, quickly climbing off of me.

"You should get back to sleep. You'll be needed early in the morning for your shift." Whatever vulnerable state he'd been in a moment ago suddenly vanished. And soon, he was just the captain again. Angry and cold.

"Of course," I managed to say. Awkwardly scooting off his bed, I started back toward my room.

When I shut the door behind me, my heart was still beating furiously in my chest. I climbed in the sheets, and I knew going to sleep would be impossible.

With my head on my pillow, I watched the lantern light beneath the crack in the door, and it didn't go out the rest of the night. Separated by just that thin piece of wood, it was like I could feel him.

Neither of us slept that night.

Passing from my room to the deck the next day was awkward. I wished my room wasn't connected to his. It would have been a lot easier to avoid confrontation.

I kept my eyes down the best I could as I passed him. He sat in his chair, the maps set out on the table in front of him. It was what he did every morning. But today, instead of ignoring me as usual, I could feel his gaze like daggers on me as I made my way to the door.

"Salt," he said.

I halted in my tracks. Then slowly turned around.

"Yes, Captain?" I did my best to keep the disdain from my voice, but I think we both still heard it.

"About last night, I don't need the rest of the crew knowing about—"

"My lips are sealed." I gestured toward the door, "Can I go now?" I hadn't planned on telling any cremates about last night's. . . events. It had already kept me awake the rest of the night, thinking about the things he'd said in his sleep and that look in his eyes when he attacked me. I couldn't deny I was curious to know what he'd been dreaming about.

Obsidian narrowed his eyes at me, but he nodded, and I slipped out the door as quickly as possible.

I took in a big lungful of salty air when I descended the steps and found James among a group of sailors standing near the bow. They were in a circle staring down at something, talking amongst one another.

I squeezed through them and found lying on the ground a bunch of empty crates.

"What's going on here?" I asked.

"The food, we're out," James said, his face grim.

"Completely?" I asked, my voice rising slightly.

James nodded solemnly. "Completely."

I groaned and put a hand to my forehead. "Spirits. I guess we'll have to fish then."

The crew looked at me, confusion on their faces.

"Oh, don't look at me like that, grab the nets in the hull, we gotta get started if we're going to eat tonight,"

They dispersed then, searching for the fishing gear. I went over to James while the others were busing themselves. I lowered my voice so none of them would hear me.

"We're in the South Seas. Any day now, we could come into contact with the Diagon. It's only a matter of time," I whispered.

"So, what are you saying?" James asked.

"I'm saying we need to attack. Today. And we should do it while we're fishing,"

"Today? I don't think that's such a good idea," James's eyes widened in protest.

"It's the perfect time. We can use the nets to subdue him. . ."

"He's not an animal, Salt. He's going to see that coming. And we need to make sure the others know the plan. A last-minute attack could get sloppy."

"Well, do you have a better idea?" I asked, crossing my arms over my chest.

"Tonight, I'll talk to the men, lay out the plan for the attack, so we're all on the same page."

"Okay, and what exactly *is* the plan?"

"It's your turn to trust me," he said, blue eyes serious.

I blew out a breath, vibrating my lips. "Okay, if you say so. But we have to do it tomorrow. We're running out of time,"

"We will, I promise. Don't worry."

~

Fishing off the side of the ship was significantly harder than having a small fishing boat to take out. But since the other men had taken that small fishing boat, we were left to deal with what we had.

The men worked quickly to get the nets up on deck, and then I explained to them the best way to catch the fish. I'd only seen Rissen fish a couple times, but I was the one with the most experience, so I just did my best to explain. It seemed pretty straightforward. Put the net on the back of the ship, stretch it out wide, and catch fish in the net as we sailed. So we got to work.

My mind was working quickly, trying to conjure scenarios of tomorrow's attack. It was hard not to stress about taking the Captain on. I worried about people getting injured and worried we wouldn't be able to accomplish the task of ridding ourselves of him. But I had to try. The anxiety was getting more intense the longer we remained in the South Seas. I knew that if Mid was on a ship, we'd have to come into contact soon. The South Seas were large but not large enough to keep us from running into one another eventually.

"What's going on here?" Obsidian came walking over to us. I was in the process of helping a couple Obscurum soldiers haul the heavy net over the back of the boat.

"We are fishing," I told him.

"We're out of food, Captain," James explained.

I heard Obsidian sigh. "That's just great." He started to mumble something under his breath but ignored him as we continued to heave the net over the side.

It finally cleared the back of the ship, and it fell to the water hitting the waves with a splash as it sank deep into the depths of the ocean.

I leaned over the edge, satisfied with the results. "Alright, now we will have to pick up speed and hope we catch some fish in the net."

I looked at Obsidian, and he raised an eyebrow at my pointed expression.

I gestured to the helm of the ship. "Would you like to do the honors?" I asked, and he didn't say anything. He simply walked over to the helm, taking his place behind it. He titled our angel a little, and the sails caught the wind, causing the ship to pick up some speed.

We tied the net off, and I stood watching it swish through the water. We sailed for about an hour, and that's when I called for Obsidian to put some slack on the sails again. We slowed for a moment as we moved away from the wind, and I gestured for the other men to come over by me.

"Now we gotta check it, see if it's working at all,"

Together we started gathering the net. The rope, when wet, was a lot heavier, and with fish inside, it was a hefty process. I grunted as I started pulling up the ropes. We'd definitely caught fish.

"I think we got some," I grunted, trying my best to make my puny arms pull the rope.

I could hear the other men grunting as well.

I leaned over the side to grab another section of rope, stubborn on getting the stupid thing to come up. As I bent over, my long red curls got into my eyes, and I brushed them back from my face in frustration. Then I felt one of my boots slip on the deck, and I let out a squeak as I started to fall over the side.

A hand grabbed the back of my shirt, quick as lightning, and tugged me back from my almost epic fall.

The momentum caused me to stumble heavily against my rescuer, and I looked up to see Obsidian holding me against him. His chest was hard, his arms secure. His long black locks brushed against my cheek, and my heart stuttered like a scared rabbit.

"Now we're even," he said, not a glimpse of teasing in his tone.

He still hadn't released me, and I knew the other crewman must be staring at us. But his black eyes held me captive, orbs of fiendish onyx. *Why did I find their vile potential oddly beautiful?*

"Saving me from falling into the water is hardly equal to me saving your life," I said. And to my disappointment, I sounded a little breathless.

"You don't make the rules," he said, and his husky voice held a purr to it that made my toes curl.

"Well, maybe I should," I shoved him away then, more forcibly than I thought possible. He stepped back, and I felt as if I could finally breathe again. *Tomorrow,* I told myself. *Tomorrow he'll be gone.*

I looked around at the crewmen, who weren't even pretending to be occupied. "What are you staring at? Get back to work," I ordered.

All hands returned to the net. With heaving breaths and grunts, we eventually got the net onboard, a couple dozen fish trapped inside. Giant, glistening silverfish that would hopefully keep us fed for a time.

We threw in the net a couple more times. And the entire morning of our fishing escapade, I could feel Obsidian's gaze on me. I did my best to ignore him, but it was hard. For some reason, I could still feel the way his arms felt when they'd wrapped around me. That bothered me. Who gets trapped in the claws of an angry lion and daydreams of recurrence? *A masochist,* I thought to myself.

I sighed, hauling in the last net of the day. As I did this, I noticed that the clouds had turned from pale white to a dusky grey. My brow furrowed.

"It looks like a storm is coming in," I said aloud.

James appeared at my side and looked up where I was gazing. "Let's hurry and get this fish packed away, and we can prepare the ship."

I hated getting caught in storms out at sea. It was dangerous and terrifying. I tried my best not to feel worried as we started to haul the fish away.

It took us another hour to get the fish stored, and at that point, the sky was nearly black. We worked as quickly as possible, getting the sails in a safe position for winds and putting anything that could get toppled over by the wind safely in the hull. The rain started to fall not long later. Big fat droplets splattered onto the deck, and it sounded like a million pebbles were being dropped onto the wood. A moist earthy smell filled the air, and as I breathed it in, I thought ironically that such a beautiful smell would only inflict chaos.

I stayed out on the deck with James and a couple other men. While the rest of them took shelter in the hull. Obsidian stayed out, too to my surprise, manning the helm.

The winds started up soon after the rain, and I clung to one of the ropes, my knuckles turning white as I was pushed by a big gust of wind. The rain started to pelt my face, and I narrowed my eyes so I could see through the downpour.

Waiting out a storm wasn't easy. It required each man on

deck to remain at his station, keeping the sails where they should be and simply riding out the waves until things calmed. One never knew how long or hard a storm would hit out on the water.

The waves increased, getting bigger and bigger with each minute. We tossed for a time, the boat rocking dangerously from left to right as we rode over waves five times the size of the ones we'd been used to sailing across.

I could barely see through the sheet of rain James on the other side of the boat, clinging to one of the masts trying to stay steady. I glanced to the helm as well and could see Obsidian's dark form still standing strong at the wheel, his black cloak whipping wildly in the wind.

I began to shiver, the rain becoming cold as ice. I pushed back my wet hair that clung to my cheeks and neck in chunks and forced myself to grit my teeth and endure how uncomfortable I was.

The first thirty minutes were bearable, but it only got worse as the hour mark approached, and the dark, booming storm clouds covered the entire sky. I knew it wasn't going to let up anytime soon.

A streak of lightning illuminated the clouds, followed by a loud thunderous rumble. I whimpered as I could nearly feel the electric static as the bolt of bright white light penetrated the waves nearby. It was close, too close.

"Is there a lightning rod on the ship?" I screamed out to whoever could hear me. But the wind drowned out my voice.

On Rissen's ship, there was a lighting rod in case of storms like these. It would strike the rode instead of the rest of the vessel. The rain stung my eyes as I searched for a rod. Everything was blurry, and I grunted in frustration.

"Salt, are you okay?" James was beside me then, and I reached out to grab him by the arm.

"Is there a lightning rod on the ship? The strikes are close. We could get hit any moment, "I yelled over the commotion.

"I don't think there is!" he yelled back.

I cursed many times beneath my breath. "Go back to your station. We are just going to have to wait it out and hope we don't get hit."

James nodded, his hair and clothes soaked to extremes by the rain. He stumbled back over to the other sails, disappearing amongst the grey mist that seemed to consume everything.

I growled in frustration and started for the main mast hoping that James was wrong and the lightning rod did exist. It took me some time to cross the deck. The water sloshing all over the deck mixed with the heavy winds made it nearly impossible to move around. I fell multiple times and could barely see a thing.

Finally, I made it to the main mast, and I looked around, searching for a metal pole. I knew I was searching in vain. I'd been on the ship for weeks. I would have noticed a lighting rod. *Maybe I had missed it,* I tried to tell myself. But I was giving myself false hope.

Another flash of lightning lit up the bleak sky, and a loud boom of thunder cracked so loudly it hurt my ears. The light struck so close to me if I had reached out my hand, I would've touched it.

I realized we'd been hit when the ship whined in protest, and I looked up to see the main mast smoking. A singed black line ran down the entire length of it, and I gasped in horror. It was the same pole that had fallen the other day. I'd done my best to secure it when it had fallen the first time, but I was helpless to stop a lightning bolt.

The pole began to fall, dragging down the sails with it, and I hurried to dive out of the way.

But with the rocking of the boat and the rain making everything so slick, I couldn't manage to get away fast enough.

Everything moved in slow motion then.

Someone appeared through the downpour, a black-cloaked figure. Hands pushed me to the side, and I crashed to the deck, my palms slamming against the wet wood.

The sound of the pole hitting the deck was like another boom of thunder. A groan sounded, and with wide eyes, I saw the pole now on the ground, crushing the black-cloaked figure beneath it.

SIXTY-THREE

SABEARA

I left Queen Emiress in Dusane's hands and ran to Rouix and Thane.

"What happened?" I asked, still in shock that Allard was now lying on the deck.

Rouix continued to pin him down with one hand while holding the glowing compass in the other.

"I saw him leave through the water, and so I jumped in after him," she said. "He couldn't see me coming, so that helped."

I looked to Thane, my eyes wide with shock. He was holding down the young emissary's legs while looking at Rouix with a pleasing smile.

"I thought I was imaginin things when she'd turned invisible," he chuckled.

"Thank you, Rouix" I walked over to her side, and she passed me the compass.

I held the glowing gold object in my hands, feeling the

weight of it and relief pushing away all the fear and anxiety I felt.

We had the compass.

Cries of happiness came from the front of the deck, and we all turned to see that Knadian had finally regained consciousness. Embrosine hugged her father while Mid helped him to stand.

"Let's get this fellow up to my quarters," Thane said, and Rouix helped drag Allard to his feet.

"That compass belongs to us," the young soldier growled.

"This compass *belongs* to Greater Aveladon," I said, narrowing my eyes at him.

The soldier spit at me, but he missed. I glared back at him with disgust.

Thane shoved the soldier forward, "Try disrespecting the lady again, and see where that gets you," he warned.

I put the compass in my pocket and left them to return to help Dusane.

"Is that what I think it is?" Dusane asked, gesturing to my pocket.

I nodded, retaking hold of Emiress's arm.

"You said we'd never find it," I said to her, and a look of fear had filled her expression. "You were wrong."

~

"You promised to help us get the compass. You broke the deal," Shar said to Emiress.

We were all in the Captain's Quarters. The interrogation had begun a while ago. The queen and her two emissaries were secured and sitting in chairs on one end of the room.

"Must we discuss these things in such a manner?" Knadian asked, obviously uncomfortable with the three individuals tied up before us as if we'd kidnapped them.

"They gave us no choice," Shar said to Knadian. "She did something to Mid, who knows what. And then double-crossed us. Until we know whose side they are on, we can't let them leave."

"We are all out for something, Captain. I did what was necessary," Emiress said, eyes narrowed on Shar.

"Emiress, without the compass, we can't stop the curse. A curse that, if not defeated, could eradicate our race. Is that what you want?" There was a slight edge of desperation in my tone.

The queen didn't answer.

"If the tokens get into the wrong hands, a very horrible man could get enough power to rule everything," I added.

"We only want the compass to free our people," Selon spoke up for the first time.

"Are your people not free?" Dusane asked.

"We've been hiding. Because in the kingdoms, we aren't viewed as individuals. But as creatures."

"Our ancestors were used for their abilities," Allard added.

"If we promised to give you your freedom with us in our kingdom, would you stop trying to take the compass?" Knadian asked.

"How do we know over time you wouldn't become like the old kings? Using us and sacrificing us to fight wars for you?" the queen asked Knadian.

"My question is, what power does the compass have that

makes you believe you can use it to free yourselves?" Mid interrupted.

"It's a summoner," Emiress said quietly.

"A what?" Rouix asked.

"It can call the creatures of the sea," Selon elaborated.

"They want to use the sea creatures to stand against those of us on the land," Thane said. He looked grave, a look I had yet to see on him. This summoning must be serious.

"If we controlled the waters, we would never have to bend to those on the land again," Selon said.

"Hold up, you mean the compass can control sea creatures?" I asked, shocked at the power that was now sitting in my pocket.

"Whoever has the compass becomes ruler of the sea. The animals and fish within it will worship you."

The room was quiet for a moment as everyone took in this information.

"Queen Emiress, please. We don't want another enemy. I promise that you will have all the freedoms of any other Stone-Hearted living in our kingdom," Knandian was pleading with the queen now.

She looked at Knadian, as if wanting to believe him.

"It's in my blood not to trust you, King Knadian. I'm sorry," she said,

I put my head in my hands, rubbing my temples.

"I need some air," I said. Leaving the Captain's quarters, I stepped out onto the deck. The night sky had taken over. Dotted with tiny white stars and the opal light of the moon. I walked down the stairs and ambled towards the bow of the ship.

I wanted to feel relief over finally having the compass in our possession. But I couldn't when we had Emiress and Selon as our prisoners. *Why couldn't she just see our side? Why did she insist on becoming our enemy?*

I looked out at the dark waters, leaning against the side of the boat. I tried to imagine what life would have been like for Emiress's ancestors. Because they were mermaids, Stone-Hearted man had taken advantage of them. Run them out of the kingdoms as she made it sound. I couldn't blame Emiress for her skepticism towards Knadian and his offer.

I thought about the little island of Tetheria and the clay castle that rested on it. It was a beautiful place to be, but I was well aware of beautiful places becoming prisons.

"You alright?"

I turned around to see Dusane walking toward me. He had his hand shoved into his pockets, looking uncertain if he should approach me.

"Not really. This whole thing is a mess," I admitted.

He pursed his lips while nodding. "Emiress has definitely put a strain on things," he said.

I sighed and put my head in my hands. "I just want this whole thing to be over."

"I know, me too." Dusane reached out to touch my arm. "We will get through this."

"How? We still have to find two more tokens." I looked up at him, and his cerulean eyes were a mix of emotions. "And what are we supposed to do about Emiress wanting to summon the entire ocean to attack the land? She isn't listening to reason."

"We will find them the same way we have the others. And as for Emiress, I'm sure she'll come around." He reached out and gently caressed the golden light in my chest with the back of his hand. "But it's not going to happen overnight."

He gave me a lopsided smile, an unusual expression for him.

"You think I'm impatient," I took the bait, narrowing my eyes at him, and he chuckled.

"I know you're impatient," he bantered. Moving his hand from my heart to my waist, he tugged me closer to him. He was evaporating the seriousness of the moment, alleviating my anxiety with his sweet talk.

Our faces were very close now, and his breath mingling with mine was causing me to lose my train of thought.

"Dusane," I trailed off. Not knowing exactly what I was protesting. *We were together now.*

I didn't get to finish my thought before he closed the gap and kissed me. It was tentative at first, almost hesitant as he tasted me. Then he backed me up against the ship's railing, taking away any space that was between us. I reached up, tangling my fingers into his hair.

It was a wonderful kiss. Blazing with need and full of desire. But as the seconds passed, something changed. The hands on my hips, and the feeling of his lips, it somehow started to feel different. The way he kissed me changed. The *feel* of him changed. And a fire began to burn inside me that was different from the fire Dusane usually ignited.

The slow burning spread throughout my body and gradually gained momentum. Becoming a wildfire, rapid, and untamed. It held a passion reserved for a side of myself I had vowed to lock away. Because it was impulsive and risked sweeping me away to a place where control ceased to exist.

I stilled, recognizing the feeling.

I knew those hands.

Those lips.

That unquenchable fire.

It was Mid.

My eyes flew open, and I was suddenly staring into emerald-scarlet eyes.

SIXTY-FOUR

SUNN

I hurried to my feet, grunting when I could feel my body protest.

I ignored the sting of the rain as I stumbled over to the fallen figure. I could see his long black hair sprawled across the deck and knew it was him.

"Obsidian!" I screamed. He wasn't moving. I felt a brief moment of panic and reached for the pole, trying desperately to get it off him. But I was too weak, and my attempt was in vain.

It was then I heard another grunt, and then suddenly he moved. My hands stilled on the fallen mast, and I watched in awe as he began to lift it off himself. He used his arms to get to a kneeling position, then shoved the heavy piece of wood off his back. The pole crashed back down to the deck again, rolling a couple feet away.

"Get in the cabin!" he yelled to me. His black hair was soaked, slicked down his face—dark as his eyes.

"But the boat!" I yelled.

"I said get to the cabin!" he roared.

Soaked and shivering, I didn't protest. I followed him towards the captain's quarters.

With the boat rocking so viciously, we both slipped a couple times, but eventually, we made it to the door of his quarters. It was wide open. The wind had pushed it open. Water rushed inside, and it took some effort to close the door behind us.

"James is out there with the others. I need to help them!" I said, panting, my hands pressed against the door holding it in place. The wood rattled beneath my fingertips, the wind beating against it threatening to push it open again.

My wet hair caused drops of water to fall down my face. I could taste salt on my lips.

"I'm injured. I need you to check the wound." He grunted in pain, and I could see he was hunched over a little, his hand pressed against his lower back. He winced, trying to remove the black cloak from his shoulders.

"Why would I help you?" I couldn't help it. The venom in my voice was thick. I was worried and anxious about James out on the deck with the others. But my mind was also racing with the events that had transpired minutes before. He'd pushed me out of the way. He'd saved me, again.

"I'm not asking," he said. He finally ripped free the soaked ebony fabric from his neck and threw it over the back of the sofa in frustration. His jaw was clenched, and I could see he was in a great measure of pain. He breathed what appeared to be a painful breath as he made his way over to the bed and sat down.

Something pricked my chest as I watched him. It felt like someone was twisting my heart. Plucking my heartstrings like a fiddle playing a sad song. *Spirits,* I thought. *He's horrible, don't feel sorry for him.*

"You're mad if you think just because you pushed me out of the way back there that I'm going to help you. Nurse yourself back to health," I grabbed the knob on the door, trying to ignore the unwanted sensation of empathy in my chest.

"Salt, get over here and help me," he growled.

I cursed again. I wanted to go back out on the deck. But I also knew we could probably do nothing to help the ship at this point. The storm was too wild. We'd just get tossed around. Maybe even struck by lighting. At this point, with the way the boat was rocking, we might even capsize. If James was smart, he'd probably taken shelter with the others in the hull by now.

I mentally berated myself for what I was about to do.

Leaning my forehead against the wood, I looked down and could see rivulets of water seeping beneath the door.

I turned around slowly and faced Obsidian.

"I'm so going to regret this."

~

I walked over to the bed where Obsidian struggled to get his shirt off.

"Let me help you," I ordered. Patience wasn't a virtue I possessed.

He stopped his attempt, and I reached for the hem of his shirt, pulling it up and over him. He sucked in a painful breath, but he didn't say anything.

I tossed the shirt to the floor and tried my best to ignore the fact he was half-naked now.

"The pole hit my back," he winced and turned to the side a little, allowing me more access to his injury.

"For a man that is supposed to be super powerful, you get hurt an awful lot," I commented.

Just then, the boat rocked hard. And I stumbled, falling into him. His pale skin was hot and surprisingly smooth. I recoiled as quickly as I could, cursing the stupid sea gods and their timing.

"Sorry," I muttered, reorienting myself.

"You'll need to grab a cloth from the drawer over there, clean it out—"

"I know what to do," I snapped, cutting him off.

Cheeks flaming from falling into him still, I walked over and grabbed a cloth from the dresser that was now several feet from its usual location and a canister of clean water that was rolling around on the floor. The tossing of the boat had made everything in the room shift. A lamp had fallen over in one corner, the maps on the foot table were in a soggy mess on the floor, and even a Lush Fire bottle had broken, leaving a trail of glass shards across the room. But I didn't have time to worry about the state of the cabin.

I sat on the bed, thinking it was safer than standing at the moment.

Grabbing the clean canister of water, I popped the top and drenched the cloth. Pushing back the hair from my face again, I looked carefully at the wound on his back and could see that it wasn't just a bruise. His entire lower back was starting to turn purple, and there was also a long gash reaching from one end of his back to the other. It was bleeding pretty heavily, and my stomach twisted at the sight.

"How did this happen?"

I pressed the cloth to the wound, and he jumped, making a sound of protest.

"There was something attached to the mast, a nail or a hook."

He said, his voice sounded strained as if trying to control the pain.

I continued to clean the gash and did my best to stay steady as the boat rocked.

"You shouldn't have jumped in the way," I said.

"Yeah, and let my only chance at finding the Diagon get killed," he scoffed.

"I thought you said you didn't need me."

"I say a lot of things I don't mean when I'm angry."

"I'll say."

Several minutes passed by then. The silence stretching between us. My cloth got completely soaked with blood, so I had to grab another one. The wound was big enough to need stitches, so Obsidian directed me to a kit in the drawer, telling me to sew up the wound.

"I've never stitched anyone up before," I said nervously.

"You'll be fine. Even if you stitch poorly, there won't be signs of scarring. I'll heal fairly quickly."

"Right," I muttered, knowing that Stone-Hearted healed much faster and better than humans.

"It will just make it easier if the tissues are closed off," he explained.

I sighed and started to sew up the wound, knowing I wouldn't be able to convince him otherwise. I had taken many needlepoint lessons, so I tried to remain calm and just pretend he was a cushion I was sewing a flower onto. Then again, every time I'd done needlepoint, no one could really tell what I'd been trying to make in the first place, but I didn't tell him that.

It took me some time to sew the entire wound together. I was not used to poking human skin, and it made me nervous. Also, with the boat rocking, it made it extremely difficult to stay steady. Obsidian, to my surprise, didn't say anything during the process. He simply sat patiently, waiting for me to finish.

The storm began to die down finally after a while, and the whooshing of the wind became a quiet whistling. The rain reduced to a gentle pattering, and I began to relax a little.

When I finished, I found a cloth bandage and helped wrap it around his stomach.

I secured the bandage and stepped away to examine my work.

"There, all finished," I said, surprised at my own handiwork.

He turned around and touched the bandage with his fingers lightly. He didn't say anything, and I didn't hold my breath for a thank you.

Just as expected, he didn't look at me or say anything. Instead, he slouched against the headboard and reached for the canteen on the bedside table, and took a swig of water.

While he did this, I noticed dried blood adorned his chest.

"You've got another scratch," I said.

He looked down, confused for a moment, then let out an exasperated sigh.

"I didn't see that one," he muttered, reaching for the rag in my hand.

"Here, let me do it," I pulled my hand away before he could grab it.

I sat back down on the bed and reached out to press the cloth to his chest.

He let out a small hiss as I touched the wound.

"Sorry," I said again. But I don't lift the cloth.

"This is unnecessary. This one is just a little scratch. I'll heal," Obsidian got a deep-set scowl on his face, but I knew that the annoyed emotion now covering his features was his attempt to cloud the pain. But I could see it in his eyes no matter what emotion he tried to display. Somehow I could always read his eyes.

I paused, and my hand stilled on his chest. He looked up to meet my gaze as if he was surprised I was actually listening.

"Why do you do that?" I asked.

"Do what?" The deep black of his eyes went wide with honest confusion.

"Put on a mask," I blurted out. But it was a mistake.

Rule number one. Never point out weakness to a wounded monster.

"It's time for you to leave now," his eyes hardened. And his hand snapped to clasp my wrist that I still had pressed to the cloth on his chest.

When is he going to learn that his intimidating expression doesn't work on me?

"You're afraid of me," I said boldly.

His eyes narrowed, and instead of snapping immediately, ordering me to leave his chambers again, he sat up straighter, his hand still clasped around mine. My heart lurched, and my breath caught in my throat, not expecting this reaction. I waited in nervous suspense as he straightened into a sitting position.

We were so close. So close that the hair falling around his shoulders brushed across the skin of my arm.

I forced myself to keep my eyes locked with his.

"Afraid of you?" he whispered, and I felt every muscle in my body tense.

I wondered if I should leave. Run and escape for the door. I gulped and forced myself to remain calm.

Obsidian pulled my hand from the cloth, and I let it go, my fingers going limp. The cloth fell to the comforter, and then I was touching his bare chest, the spot right above his heart. He was hot, burning up. I could feel the steady beating of his heart as it pulsed beneath my fingertips.

"I'm not afraid of you." His whisper turned husky as if he was struggling to say the words. "I'm *terrified* of you."

I gasped, unsure if I heard him correctly.

His other hand reached up, hovering a mere inch from my face like he wanted to touch me but couldn't.

"Leave. Now," he demanded. And it wasn't a threat. It was a warning.

And I knew at that moment some sort of self-control he was maintaining was about to shatter if I didn't get away. But I didn't move.

"No," I said, surprised at how strong my voice sounded.

"Salt," A shiver passed through my spine. The agony in his voice was unmistakable.

I didn't think before doing what I did next. But after he had said my name, with such constraint lingering behind his tone. It was too much. And I was suddenly furious.

"Don't you dare," I growled. "Don't you dare say my name like that." I pulled my hand from beneath his and did what I had wanted to do for so long.

I slapped him.

A perfect thwack filled the air and his head whipped to the side with the impact.

I didn't move. Even though I knew the repercussions would be absolutely lethal.

He reached up to touch his cheek, stunned.

But I wasn't even close to done.

"Don't say my name like you're suffering even having to speak it aloud." I reached out again, knowing that I may appear to have gone insane but not even caring. I grasped a fistful of his hair in my hands, and the silky black strands slid between my fingertips before I yanked *hard* and forced his head to tilt up towards me. His jaw clenched. "And most of all, don't you dare say my name like you wish you were something other than a monster."

I released him and stood abruptly, heading for my room. I was so angry I was shaking.

"But I do wish I was something different," he said, and I could hear him stand from the bed.

I halted in my tracks. Two feet away from my door.

"I know I'm a monster. I know that." His voice sounded haggard as if he were exhausted. "And I deserve that. Not to mention so much more."

I slowly turned back around.

"Then why don't you change?" I asked, my jaw set determinedly.

"Because I can't," he said, throwing up his hands a little. "And you and I both know. . ."

"Both know what? What are you even saying right now?" My emotions were all over the place. Unsaid words and emotions were passing between us. Neither of us was admitting something. . . something that I didn't even have a name for. My heart was burning, my emotions twisting and changing like the ocean waves. Except I didn't know if I could weather this storm. I was angry, frustrated. . . heartbroken. *Over what? I* felt as if I needed to gasp for breath. *What was happening?*

"I'm saying," he took a step toward me, and I took a matching step back. "That I know what you're feeling." he took one more step, and I took my last available one, trapping myself against the door.

I reached for the door handle. Just as I did this, Obsidian closed the gap between us, reaching out to place his hand over mine, stopping me from turning the knob.

"And what am I feeling?" I whispered, all too aware of the way his hand suddenly felt wrapped around mine.

"This," he whispered. He tilted my chin up toward him and grasped my lips with his.

Something exploded inside me when he kissed me, and conflict raged—a war declared. One side fighting for righteousness. The other for the unexplainable euphoria that bled throughout my body. I heard something like a whimper or maybe a groan, and it took a second to realize it had come from me.

His lips were soft and sweet. The opposite of every other trait that possessed him. My hands, on their own accord, found their way into his hair, the hair I had just seconds ago yanked in frustration. The long strands mingled around my fingers, and the guilt wasn't enough to stop me from enjoying the silky feeling.

He moved his hands to grab my waist and pulled me tighter against him. He was so much taller than me he had to bend down quite a ways to reach me. The kiss deepened, and as my lips trembled, I realized this was the biggest rush I'd ever felt before. No journey, or swimming expedition, or high jump off a boat ledge could compare to the adrenaline coursing through me now.

But it was so wrong.

Everything about it was wrong, and we both knew that.

"Stop, stop," he gasped, forcing me suddenly away from him.

I stumbled as he pushed us apart, my heartbeat pounding in my ears.

I put my fingers to my bruised lips, shocked at what we'd just done.

He'd kissed me. And I'd kissed him back.

He didn't say anything, and when I looked at him again, I could see his dark eyes were. . .pained. His chest moved up and down with his ragged breaths, and he ran a hand through his tousled hair.

"I'm sorry," he whispered.

He brushed past me then, moving quickly as he rushed out the door, leaving me in the cabin alone.

SIXTY-FIVE

SABEARA

Realization dawned, and I backed away as if burned by a flame.

"Mid?" It was all I could manage to say in my shock.

"So you are with him?" he said, and then the anger settled in that he'd tricked me.

"What was that! Pretending to be Dusane? Are you crazy?" I glared at him, stumbling to find the right words for reprimand. But my cheeks were hot and burning with shame. He knew.

"When were you going to tell me? Or were you just going to keep me in the dark forever?" he asked, bitterness coating his tone.

"I was going to tell you!" I nearly shrieked, and he scoffed. Anger boiled in my blood, and I felt ready to fight him again. My fingers itched for my blade.

"So that's it? You've picked him, and it's over. Just like that," he threw his hands up.

"I made a decision because I can't keep doing this!" I gestured to the two of us. "I was sick of fighting, and I didn't want to hurt either of you any longer. So I made a decision."

I could see the hurt and the pain in his eyes as I said the words. It reminded me of the day I'd said goodbye to him before he went to the altar. That same, foreboding gaze that seemed to beg me to stay. But I couldn't find it in me to console him. He'd pretended to be Dusane and violated the small thread of trust between us that had managed to remain. It was gone now, a useless whisp of string in the wind. I didn't know if that trust would ever be seen again.

"I know you haven't chosen him," he said, his expression hardening. I could see the reluctance, the familiar unruly reaction whenever something didn't go his way.

"I have," I said firmly, needing him to understand that the decision had been made.

"You still love me, Sabeara." The use of my real name poked at open wounds, and I gritted my teeth.

"I've chosen Dusane. It's over Mid." I said, and tears filled my eyes unwillingly. Now that I'd said the words aloud, it was real.

He began to pace the deck, running a hand through his wind tousled hair.

"What's going on out here?" Dusane's voice penetrated the tempestuous air making my blood run cold.

"Dusane, go back to the cabin," I pleaded, but he was already heading towards us. And as he neared, he noticed the tears on my cheeks.

"What did you do to her?" Duane growled at Mid, and the absolute lethal expression in his cerulean eyes was unlike anything I'd ever seen. Now that we were together, he must not have felt the need to tiptoe around any longer. Because the protectiveness in his expression was almost animalistic.

"She doesn't know what she wants," was Mid's immediate response.

I reached out to halt Dusane, pressing my hands against his chest.

"Please just go," I begged. But his eyes were locked on Mid.

"She made her decision." Dusane's arm wrapped around me possessively, and Mid's eyes locked onto where his hand gripped my waist.

"Whatever choice you think she's made, it's temporary," Mid said, and the confidence in his voice sent my heart trembling.

"Both of you, please, stop." More tears came, and I saw both of them look at me, jaws clenched. Thankfully both of them stayed quiet. "I'm sorry, Mid. I was going to tell you. But there's nothing I can do about that now. It's over. I'm with Dusane. So can we please just leave it be?"

Mid didn't respond, and he didn't get the chance to because I looked out at the water past him, and a dark shadow was coming towards us over the horizon. The sun was just beginning to rise, tinting the sky with a sweet violet hue. At first, I thought I was imagining things because it was still quite dark. But then I saw movement again and knew I wasn't wrong. A boat was heading towards us.

"Is that a ship?" I whispered, and both of them seemed confused at my sudden change of attention. Then they both turned to look out at the water, and they saw it too.

"I'll get Whitemane," Mid immediately said, heading back towards the cabin.

Soon Thane was out on the deck with us. He didn't need a

spyglass because of his power, so he looked out, examining the dark waters to the east and the ship floating towards us.

"It's not Sapherine," Thane said, the emotion undetectable in his voice.

"What ship is it?" I pressed.

"It's Obscurum."

SIXTY-SIX

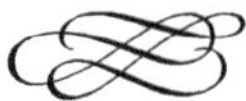

SUNN

I was unable to move for many minutes. The kiss was playing on a loop inside my head, and it wouldn't stop. I leaned against the door for support, sliding down to the floor because my legs were shaky.

I put my head in my hands, trying to calm myself down.

He'd kissed me. . . I kissed him back. . . I mentally cursed, trying to understand why I'd do something so stupid. He was an Obscurum prince. He was the enemy. And I'd willingly allowed myself to trespass over a line I should never have crossed. The guilt and shame consumed my chest. But the warmth and tingling sensation he'd ignited still wouldn't leave my skin. I was ridden with mixed emotions. Unable to comprehend.

I blew out a breath, trying to calm my racing heart.

And then I heard shouting.

The storm had died down, but the chaos on the deck was still in need of attention. James immediately popped into my mind. I pushed aside all the other emotional chaos coursing through my body and hurried out onto the deck to see what remained.

It was early morning, the sky barely starting to lighten, and I could just make out several men huddled together beside the fallen poles that had collapsed during the storm. I meandered through an obstacle of buckets and barrels, across slippery wood, and over toppled sails and poles to where the group stood conversing.

James was there, and relief flooded my body at the sight of him. He saw me and came over to pull me into a quick hug.

"I'm glad you're alright," he said, and I hugged him back, grateful for the unexpected comfort.

"What's going on?" I asked, and as James pulled away, I could see even in the darkness that he was pale.

"We've found the Diagon," he said, and my heart may have literally stopped in my chest.

I looked down the deck as if in a dream and spotted Obsidian with a couple of the crewmen staring out at the water. There was an object in the distance, a mere shadow from this far. But there was no doubt something headed for us.

"It's too late," I whispered, my insides constricting with fear.

"I'm sorry, Sunn, I tried." James looked down remorsefully as if unable to meet my gaze, and my mind raced for a solution. But there were none.

Obsidian turned around, and I already knew what he would say before he even said it.

"Men, to your stations. We've found the Diagon."

SIXTY-SEVEN

SABEARA

I didn't know if it was Obsidian. But something deep in my gut told me it couldn't be anyone else. He'd found us.

We all moved on instinct, gathering our weapons and securing the front deck. We worked like a well-oiled machine. Each of us had a station and quickly manned our positions. I headed for the Captain's cabin, knowing I needed to get the device from Emiress.

Dusane was on my tail, and as we entered the room, we found Emiress and her emissaries exactly as we'd left them.

"What's going on?" Emiress asked, probably having heard the commotion outside.

"We're being attacked," Dusane said cooley, kneeling down next to the chair the queen was tightly secured to. He reached for her wrist and quickly undid the band that rested there.

"By who?" Emiress's eyes widened.

"It's an Obscurum ship," I said flatly, and the fear that crossed the queen's face matched the carefully controlled fear that was flooding quietly in my blood.

We didn't waste time explaining things to them. We left the cabin and got back outside as quickly as we could. The sky had swirls of orange in it now, brightening with each passing minute. Soon it would be daylight.

I gripped the device in my hand, my gaze locked on the ship that was now so much closer than it was before.

"What if he has an entire ship full of men?" I said to Dusane.

"I thought we talked about hypotheticals," he said, and I looked at him, eyes pleading. He sighed and reached out to squeeze my shoulder.

"Even if they have an army on that boat, would it stop us from fighting?" he asked, and I knew the answer. No. It wouldn't. Because my greatest desire was to stop Obsidian. To keep him from hurting anyone else. I'd fight multiple armies if I had to.

We hurried back to the front of the deck. Mid had his bow ready. Knadian stood at the edge, already manipulating the water, swirling it around as if testing the waters. Thane stood next to Knadian, his posture sure as stone.

Embrosine was with Rouix, her fingertips kindling with blue sparks. And Rouix had both of her knives drawn, firmly gripping them in her hands.

The boat got closer and closer, and soon I began to see men on the deck, black cloaks huddled between the billowing white sails. My heart beat faster as the anticipation grew.

Just as the ship came within a hundred yards was when I heard the creaking of the deck boards behind us.

I turned around, just in time to see Emiress and her emissaries coming towards us.

I started to run towards her, panic rising in my chest at the sight of them. Somehow they had escaped their confines in the Captain's quarters.

But before I could go even a couple feet, she opened her mouth, and that's when the world shattered.

The sonar waves that spilled from her lips froze me in my tracks, it immobilized my limbs, and I groaned as I fell to my knees. The others fell too, and I heard my friends pitch forwards onto the floor. The ringing sound was an incessant shrill—piercing the air with an acute soprano making my brain feel like it was on fire.

I reached up to cup my ears, trying to keep out the noise, but it was impossible to escape. My body succumbed to the feverish pitch, and I became a statue, clenching every muscle in my body in an attempt to fight off the noise.

I could only watch, stilled in my agony, as the three of them jumped the side of the ship, disappearing into the water.

The minute they escaped into the sea, the noise ceased, and we were all released from Emiress's power.

I gasped for air, then groaned when I felt the aftermath of her sonar abilities. My head ached and throbbed as I sat up. I clutched my head and fumbled for the compass in my pocket, so overwhelmed with relief that she hadn't tried to take it in her escape.

We all slowly got to our feet, Dusane rushed to my side, but I quickly assured him I was alright.

We didn't have time to follow Emiress. I didn't even have a second to process what had even happened because the Obscurum ship was so close now, and I could see him standing at the bow. His black cloak whipping in the wind, his ebony hair a midnight flutter in the now blazing sun.

SIXTY-EIGHT

SUNN

I ran to him, needing him not to do this. To turn the ship around and abandon this fight. But before I could even get the words out, his black eyes zeroed in on me. A mix of emotions crossed over his features, and then he was walking swiftly towards me.

"Obsidian," I started to say, but he ignored me. He gripped me by the arm and started leading me back towards his quarters. "Obsidian, don't do this," I begged.

"You need to stay in the cabin, Salt, don't come out until I come get you."

He dragged me up the steps, and I tried to resist, digging my heels into the wood.

"I'm not going to cower away in your room," I snarled. He tugged on me harder until my feet gave way, and he was able to drag me the rest of the way inside.

"You don't have a choice," he said, shoving me into the cabin.

"I'm not staying here!" I yelled, struggling roughly against his hold.

He glanced from me, then to the chair where his maps rested.

"Fine, I'll make you then."

My eyes widened, unsure if I heard him correctly. But before I could even process the words, he had me slung off his shoulder. He strode across the room, then planted me in the cushioned chair across from the map table. He pulled a sleek string from his cloak pocket and began to fasten me to the chair.

"Obsidian, you can't tie me up!" I growled.

"Oh yes, I can." His dark black eyes were wild. I could see something in them I'd never seen before. It was a sort of mad expression. A frenzy. I knew Mid must be on that ship, and the panic swelled so heavily in my chest, tears pricked the corners of my eyes.

"Please, don't do this," I begged again, my voice reduced to a whisper. I was unable to compose myself.

He finished tying my wrists to the chair then reached out to cup my cheek, wiping away the tear that escaped.

My heart betrayed me. Fluttering at his touch.

"I'm sorry," he whispered, and it was the same thing he'd said when he kissed me. "I wouldn't be able to forgive myself if you got hurt."

I was shocked. Unsure if I heard him correctly. *He was protecting me?*

The prince of Obscurum was protecting me? From my own family? From a fight where he might very well end up killing someone I loved. . .

It was all wrong. All twisted and awry. I didn't need to be

protected from the people on that ship. I needed to be protected from him. He was the enemy.

Before I could even find the coherent words to respond, he leaned in and pressed a kiss to my forehead, and strode out of the room.

It was then the most blasphemous thought of all passed through my mind—that maybe the people on the boat coming towards us weren't the only people that I loved.

SIXTY-NINE

SABEARA

Black cloaks swarmed onto our ship, and I watched almost instantly as Embrosine immobilized two Obscurum soldiers with her electric blue light. I flew past her, my attention fixated on Obsidian. His gaze was on me too, the murderous expression in his those black orbs exactly as I recalled.

An arrow flew past my shoulder, hitting a man that was sneaking up on me. I knew it was Mid.

I managed to amble through the chaos, the rage boiling in my blood. I clung to the dagger in my hand and took comfort in the tokens I had with me and the device in my pocket. I could do this.

He didn't waste any time. He jumped over the ledge of his ship onto the deck of the Diagon. He didn't need weapons. He was one.

Before I could take another step, he tapped my heart with his power. It was just a small stroke, but it made me stumble. I clutched my chest and glared at him.

"Is this really how you want to play?" I asked, my voice strained as I tried to speak through the pain. Chaos continued to advance around us, the buzz of disarray a familiar sound.

Obsidian smiled wickedly. "This is the only way I play, Cousin."

His eyes narrowed, and the clutching sensation on my heart intensified. I gasped and fell to one knee. Unable to stand fully.

I should've thought this out better, I thought. But I hadn't expected to find him again like this. In the middle of the seas, on a boat. I had thought our next encounter would be much different. *I would've been more prepared.* I mentally berated myself for being so stupid and not considering the possibility of a run-in on the waters.

Slowly he drained the life from me, but my healing ability wouldn't allow me to ultimately succumb. So it was a painful torture. Endless and agonizing.

Then I watched something shoot up from beneath Obsidian's feet. Splintering the wooden deck and wrapping around his black boots. Seaweed curled through the floorboards and up around him, encasing him in the green foliage. Obsidian's eyes widened in surprise, and the momentary lapse in his concentration allowed me a brief moment of reprieve.

Mid came up beside me, his hands glowing like the sun as he conjured the plant to surround Obsidian.

I watched from my kneeling position on the deck as he attempted to subdue him.

A loud growl reverberated from Obsidian as he kicked in annoyance at the seaweed now circling his legs.

"James!" Obsidian yelled, and almost instantly, a young man came running over to him.

I headed for the soldier, not keen on this moment being interrupted. I swung my dagger at the boy, and his sword met mine with a loud ring. The soldier grunted but managed to fight off my blow. And then I saw his eyes.

Blue as the ocean— innocent and tender. That innocence brought back memories I hadn't known I'd been harboring.

"James," I whispered, and he paused. Our daggers came apart, and the boy could but stare at me in awe.

"Princess," he said, but we didn't have time to elaborate because Mid cried out, and soon he was on the ground, clutching his chest.

Obsidian kicked away the seaweed like it was nothing, and I ran to Mid's side. I fell to my knees, flashbacks of Conland sending fear through my veins like cold ice.

Then the ground shook, and everyone stumbled. I fell to my side, hitting my head on the deck unintentionally. I groaned, wishing Shar would start to give us some sort of warning when he did that. I winced when I felt the pounding in my head and then looked up to see Shar walking towards Obsidian, hammer in hand.

Mid was released from the confines of Obsidian's power, and I was just grateful to see he was alive. Then just as I was helping him to his feet, a war cry sounded from behind us, and I turned to see a soldier barreling our way. His facc was contorted with rage, his eyes blank of humanity. I took a swift strike at the man, landing a satisfying blow to his chest, and he crumpled to the ground.

I looked around, grateful that the rest of our crew had managed to keep off the other Obscurum soldiers.

Obsidian regained his footing, brushing the long ebony locks from his forehead. He smiled at Shar as he came his way.

"Surrender," Shar ordered.

Obsidian smirked. "I don't surrender to anyone," he growled, and he held out his hand as if preparing to drain the life from him.

SEVENTY

SUNN

I struggled against the ropes, wincing as I could feel raw red sores begin to form. Ignoring the pain, I pressed through until one hand came free. I sighed in relief and quickly worked on getting my other hand untied.

*I can't believe he'd try and keep me her*e. I was livid. This was my only chance to get off this ship. My family could be on that other boat, and I wasn't going to spend another minute here.

I told myself that was why I was working so frantically to escape the cabin. But I knew deep down there were other reasons for the fear that pulsated through my veins.

My family could get hurt. James could get hurt. Obsidian could get hurt.

I forced myself not to linger on that last thought. Knowing I shouldn't be worried about his well-being.

I finally freed my other hand and didn't waste time heading for the door. I fumbled with the handle, then finally, with shaking hands, I opened it and ran outside to see the commotion.

It was a swell of people, black cloaks mixed in with faces I knew so well my heart stopped.

Mid and Sabeara were down below on the other ship I expected was the Diagon. Next to them, I saw Obsidian and Shar.

Then my eyes flitted to the others. I saw two men and a woman I didn't recognize fighting off the other Obscurum soliders. Then I saw my grandfather and my mother.

I gasped, unable to comprehend that she was actually here. The blue flames that she could form on her fingertips were her weapon as she fought Obsidian's men. She didn't seem to be in imminent danger, but panic still constricted my muscles.

My feet moved as if I were in a dream then. I ran as fast as I could with my panic-stricken muscles, down the steps, heading for Obsidian so he would stop this.

My eyes remained on my family, the target I vowed to reach. Then I spotted Shar. He fell like the soldier Obsidian had almost killed that day when he'd done some unfathomable thing to anger him. It was that gasping expression that told me he was killing Shar.

He pitched to the floor, a golden hammer falling from his grasp.

"No!" I screamed, pumping my legs faster. "Stop!"

I leaped in between them and turned around to face Obsidian.

"Please, you're killing him!" My hair whipped in the ocean wind like a fire, and I brushed it away from my eyes, begging him to see the agony this would cause me.

Obsidian's gaze found mine, and the surprise on his face

lasted a split second. Then his eyes flitted to something else behind me, and the surprise turned to horror.

He reached for me, pulling me to his chest as he shielded me from some threat I couldn't see. I was enveloped in his arms when I felt his body stiffen.

Everything seemed to stand still.

He faltered, and I fell to my knees with him.

"Obsidian," I whispered in shock, and I could see pain bloom in his black eyes. I was uncertain for a second what had happened until I saw the arrow in his side.

SEVENTY-ONE

SABEARA

It all happened so fast. One moment I was kneeling by Mid's side, watching as Shar tried to resist Obsidians' power, thinking it was all over, that the device we'd retrieved in Severesi had all been in vain, that Shar was about to be killed. Then I found Dusane among the chaos. Somehow he'd managed to grab Mid's bow and arrow on the deck. He aimed for Obsidian and let the silver-tipped arrow fly.

I watched it arc towards Obsidian's chest, holding my breath, hoping maybe we could hinder him long enough to get the device onto his wrist. But then a streak of crimson interrupted the scene. Stepping in front of the arrow was a girl.

The wild red curls cascading around her shoulders were such a familiar sight that it took my breath away. I knew this girl. Those wild green eyes and freckled cheeks. Only she was older now, on the verge of what I'd call a woman.

Obsidian's arms wrapped around her, shielding her from the arrow, now headed straight for her.

The arrow embedded into Obsidian's side, and together, they fell to the ground.

I gasped, and the whispered name fell from my lips.

"Sunn."

EPILOGUE

The gold from Mid's palms illuminated the darkness, casting long, shapeless shadows onto the walls.

He watched with wide, almost crazed eyes at the tree he sprouted in the center of the room. It came to life, beautiful branches and evergreen leaves taking form. Soon fruit blossomed, and weighing down the limbs were bright purple plumbs.

Mid's palms stopped glowing, and his shoulders slumped. Sweat trickled down his brow. Ever since they'd returned to Knadiel, it felt like he'd been using his power. And with the curse slowly siphoning that power, he could feel the toll it was taking on his body to expend this much effort.

The door to his room creaked open, and Shar stepped inside. His guardian didn't say anything for a long moment.

"What happened in here?" Shar asked.

Mid looked up at what Shar was seeing, and his mouth quirked into a smirk. He felt like he may have lost his mind.

The entire room was covered in plants—pines, aspens, oaks, fruit trees. The room was a forest. Branches and tree limbs overtook his dresser and bed frame. But not only was the room covered in foliage; rabbits scurried across the carpet, birds sang from the branches near the ceiling, and a deer was eating a shrubbery on the veranda.

Mid sat amongst his illusions, hunched in a sitting position. He looked back down at his hands that were the source of his creations.

"It's all real," Mid said, his voice sounded foreign to even himself.

"What do you mean it's all real?" Shar slowly walked over to Mid and knelt at his side, placing a hand on his shoulder.

"Everything I create," Mid said, his voice gravelly from lack of sleep. "It's no longer just an illusion."

Mid met Shar's shocked green eyes.

"Everything I create comes alive."

PRONUNCATION GUIDE

Emiress: Eh-mihr-ehs

Joon: June

Rissen: Reese-ehn

Nixie: Nihx-ee

Niafell: Nigh-uh-fell

Iradence: Ear-uh-dense

Saerus: Sair-us

Saphirene: Sah-fuh-reene

Diagon: Die-gone

Tetheria: Teh-theer-ee-uh

Oculor- Ahk-you-lore

Selon: See-lawn

Massauka: Mah-sawk-uh

ACKNOWLEDGMENTS

Publishing Beloved has been bittersweet for me. It feels like everything is coming to an end when at the same time, it feels like I've just begun. It wasn't that long ago I was struggling over Granted and pouring my blood, sweat, and tears into that first book.

Beloved is a book I never imagined I'd get to. I thought I'd be stuck forever trying to finish book one. But here I am, and I have so many people to thank for helping me get this far.

I want to thank my readers who have stuck by me and made me feel like this story is worth something. Without you, I wouldn't have the motivation to finish this series.

I must thank Vick because Obsidian and Sunn would never have existed without you. You helped me create them, and you helped me fall in love with them.

I would like to thank my friend Kelly Bertzyk for writing Sun & Smoke. You saved me from the torture of having to write my own poem. You are far more talented in the poetry department, and I am honored to have your work in my book.

I want to thank my husband and my family for supporting me in this journey and helping me stay sane. Especially you, Dad, who made these beautiful Envoy symbols. Your artistic talent continues to amaze me.

I want to thank Kolarp Em for creating such beautiful character art of Obsidian and Sunn. You brought them to life, and that means so much to me.

Lastly, I want to thank my editor Marnie Meredith for helping me get this book done and agreeing to do this project.

It takes a village to get a book published, and I have the most loving, supportive, and caring village out there. So, for those reading this, thank you for taking the time to read the Granted Series and helping me make my dreams a reality.

ABOUT THE AUTHOR

Kendra Thomas is from Mapleton Utah, a small town pressed against the beautiful Rocky Mountains. Kendra has been an aspiring author since she was in sixth grade. She has a passion for fairy tales and fiction books. Along with songwriting, horse riding, and playing the guitar.

Kendra Thomas is a Dental Hygienist by day and a writer by night. She earned her bachelor's degree at the Utah College of Dental Hygiene at the young age of nineteen years old. She is also happily married to her best friend, Cade Thomas, who is always pushing her to be ambitious and creative.

Her most wanted dream is for others to love her stories and characters as much as she cherishes them. She hopes to inspire other young authors to pursue their dreams, and to write about the worlds inside their heads as she was once inspired to do as a young girl.

She hopes that the Granted Series might be a place of sanctuary for those seeking a whimsical getaway and a thrilling adventure.

www.ingramcontent.com/pod-product-compliance
Lightning Source LLC
Chambersburg PA
CBHW070838020826
48982CB00021B/1434/J

* 9 7 8 1 7 3 5 0 1 5 3 9 2 *